Li

The goat was f

Verity kicked and squirmed in his arms while he cursed and groped for a purchase on her body.

"By God! You don't weigh more than a half-grown cat, but you're twice as hard to get a grip on."

There was no answer except a muffled grunt and a hard, tiny fist jamming into his Adam's apple silencing him as effectively as a muzzle. Then a knee in his upper leg, sharp enough and near enough to vital organs to make him take a step back. His arms around her waist slipped and rode high up the ribcage, and he let go as suddenly as if he'd grabbed hold of any angry rattlesnake. They both went sprawling.

"You're not a boy," he said, stupidly, and watched her crawl after her hat and jam it down firmly on her head, mud and all. She glared at him from a dirty face, still on her hands and knees. The goat now stood quietly watching them, having righted itself under its own power. The rope dangled loose.

Trey struggled to his feet and offered a hand to help her. With a hostile stare she ignored the outstretched palm, picked up the trailing rope and crabbed her way up to the trail, bent nearly double into the hillside.

"Well, I'll be damned!" Trey stood open-mouthed in astonishment.

She whirled. "You probably will, but not in front of me." The man had a mouth like a barnyard.

Trey spread his hands wide and grinned. "I don't know what in hell's got your dander up, but—

"*Sir!*"

"What, no thanks for all my trouble? No apology for almost maiming me for life?"

"My sorrow is that you won't be walking crooked for the next ten miles." Horrified, Verity clapped a hand over her mouth and closed her eyes. How could she have said such a thing? How could she even have thought it? She felt her face flushing hot.

Trey threw back his head and laughed.

What They Are Saying About
Like A River, My Love

Travel with Verity, Trey and the families under Clark's supervision, as they navigate the Ohio River to their new home (in the Illinois Country in 1778). Characters are well defined and invite readers to share quiet, and harrowing, moments in the long journey. There's not enough time for anyone to become bored, when pressed with the needs of survival. Join them on the flatboats for a close up look, or become part of the forests with eyes watching the weary travelers. Scenic descriptions provide marvelous backdrop for much of the action and will have you turning pages to see the characters work their way through hardships.

Marilyn Gardiner has done well in capturing the essence of the times, and the courage of people to find a new place to start new lives. As depicted by the title, the plot, suspense and romance, flow, not always steadily, but sometimes with a fierceness that dares readers to leave the story. Like A River, the tale's depth will hold you fast until you reach the end of the journey.

—Brenda
The Rite Lifestyle

Wings

Like A River, My Love

by

Marilyn Gardiner

A Wings ePress, Inc.

Historical Romance Novel

Wings ePress, Inc.

Edited by: Lorraine Stephens
Copy Edited by: Sara V. Olds
Senior Editor: Sara V. Olds
Managing Editor: Crystal Laver
Executive Editor: Lorraine Stephens
Cover Artist: Chrissie Poe

Wings ePress Books
http://www.wings-press.com

ISBN 1-59088-920-7

Published In the United States Of America

May 2002

Wings ePress Inc.
P. O. Box 38
Richmond, KY 40476-0038

Dedication

LIKE A RIVER, MY LOVE is for all those librarians and teachers who take the time to encourage young people to put their dreams on paper and imagine "What if..." My greatest admiration and gratitude, especially to those in Sparta IL, for a difficult job well done, with patience, day after day after day.

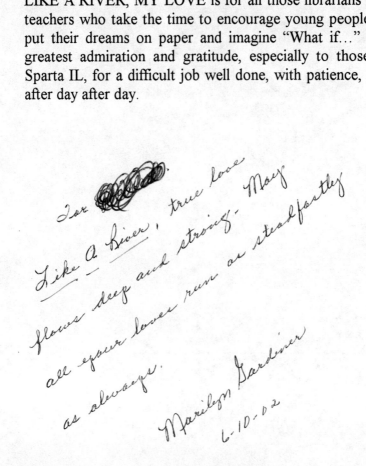

For [redacted].
Like A River, true love
flows deep and strong - May
all your loves run as steadfastly
as always.

Marilyn Gardiner
6-10-02

Prologue

Across the Blue Ridge
Virginia, 1768

Eight-year-old Verity shivered in spite of the heat of the forest and glanced over her shoulder at her brother. Joe's basket was almost full while only three lonesome buckberries rolled around the bottom of hers.

"Come on, Verity." Joe's voice urged her forward. "Ma promised a pie for supper after we picked enough for jam. You're eating all yours!"

Dutifully, Verity put a few berries in her basket. Usually she tried to do what Joe said. He was two years older and knew more. Or thought he did. But today she couldn't seem to keep her mind on berrying. She glanced around, uneasily. The hair on the back of her neck prickled. Maybe little Lissy had sneaked up and stood ready to leap giggling from behind a tree and scare them. But there was no one. The insects buzzed as usual, a gentle breeze sighed through the treetops and Joe carefully stripped one berry bush and moved on to the next. Verity picked another handful of the purple fruit. There was a queer itching between her shoulder blades. "How many does it take before we can go home?"

"More than we got. If we don't bring in enough this trip, you may have to come back this afternoon by yourself."

The threat was empty and Verity knew it. Mama would never send her into the forest alone, but just the possibility was scary and she started picking again. Joe would carry the noon meal to Papa and then work along side him with the haying until dusk. Verity would stay at the cabin to watch Lissy and help Mama with the jam making.

Verity's fingers moved among the berries. There was a strange feel to the woods today. She had the idea that if she turned her head quickly she'd see…something. But when she swung her eyes around there was only a long, golden shaft of sunlight filtering through the thick green shade of mid-summer trees. Not even the leaves moved in the heat.

Joe straightened and scratched the calf of one leg with the toe of the other foot. He was impatient. "What are you doing now? Looking for Indians?"

Verity shook her head and picked faster.

"'Cause if there were any, they'd be back at the cabin wolfing down Ma's bread and jam, not out here watching us scratch our poison itch."

Verity bent her head and felt for more berries. It was true. The only Indians they ever saw were peaceful people, traveling through the valley on their way somewhere else. Mama fed them, Papa let them water their horses and Verity stared with a mixture of fear and fascination. They poked their fingers in the stew on the hearth, in Lissy's mouth alongside her thumb and laughed at Verity's suspicious watchfulness. They also stole anything they could get their hands on.

Verity always thought of their valley like the story of Eden from the Bible—perfect. But she didn't like the forest today. The shadows seemed extra deep and she wasn't sure the trees weren't somehow moving closer together. Even the undergrowth where the fattest berries were to be found gave her the creepy-crawlies.

"Joe, I have lots of berries. Can we go home, now?"

Joe raised his head to look in her basket. "It ain't full, yet. You heard Ma say—"

"You'd better not let Mama hear you say 'ain't'." Mama's Pa had been a school teacher and she was strict about their grammar. Verity, Mama and Joe all spoke French as well as English and could cipher in both languages better than anyone in the valley. Verity set her jaw, ready to deliver a sermon about there being no excuse for ignorance like Mama always said, when a whiff of breeze bore a faint sound past them and beyond. Joe's eyes lifted toward the cabin. It came again. A shrill edge of sound that sent a shaft of fear plunging into Verity's stomach.

Joe dropped his basket and didn't even notice when all the berries bounced out in an uneven spill on the ground. He took a step toward the sound and then another. Blindly he groped for Verity's hand and began to run, dragging her along behind, willy-nilly among the thorns and brambles, her basket banging on her legs every step of the way.

"Joe—" she gasped. "What's—wha—? Joe?"

"Shut up," he grunted hoarsely. He sounded like he had something caught in his throat. "And don't make noise."

Grimly she pounded along behind him, trying to make her legs longer, trying to make them reach farther. She ran headlong into a tree and her basket was torn from her grasp. She bumped her head, hard, but was too afraid to cry. And all the while the sounds were getting louder. She could hear screaming, her mother's voice, Lissy's, the dogs snarling—then Papa's deep bass thundered in an outrage like she'd never heard, and the gun went off.

Verity and Joe clawed their way through the forest, toward the cabin. Verity fell, tripped up by shin-tangle, and Joe hauled her to her feet almost without breaking stride. She could hear his voice, sobbing as he labored to drag her behind him, and felt her own lungs burn with the effort of keeping up. When Joe stopped, she slammed into his back, nearly bringing them both to their knees. It was only then she was aware of the silence.

There was no sound at all. The dogs had stopped barking. Even the insects had stopped their incessant whirring. Verity started to step around Joe, but saw only the edge of the clearing before he whirled and shoved her face down on the ground.

"Shh!" he whispered fiercely.

He jammed her up tight against a rotting log and flung himself down on top of her. Wriggling backward he pulled them both into the sanctuary of a bushy overhang.

"Don't move," he commanded, his voice no more than a shudder on her ear.

Her nose was pressed into the forest floor. The familiar scent of pine, leaf mold and earth was mixed with another unpleasant odor and she wrinkled her nose in distaste. Bear grease. Indians! The word exploded in her head. She'd smelled them many times in her mother's clean kitchen, out by the shed where the creek narrowed, and now at the edge of the clearing with Joe's berry-stained hand clenched in a fist near her head. She could feel his trembling along the whole length of her body.

Cautiously Verity raised her eyes, peering between the leafy fronds. There were three Indians moving around, waving various items of clothing. Another walked directly toward them, lifted his loin cloth and made water on the body of a dead dog. He turned and stood watching the cabin, his dirty moccasined heel not six feet from the end of Verity's nose.

Her mother lay at the corner of the cabin, one arm outstretched toward Lissy who was crumpled in a little heap against the bottom logs. Her father sprawled across the wood pile, a hatchet buried in his head. The gun lay at his feet.

Verity's heart hammered against her ribs so loudly she was sure the Indian in front of her must hear. They were dead. They were all dead. A rage began to build in her, so strong she didn't even know what it was. If Joe's weight had not pinned her to the ground she would have flown at the Indian with teeth and nails and feet and all the strength in her hard little body.

And then, her mother groaned and turned on one side. She pulled at her skirts slowly, like it hurt to move, and pushed herself into a sitting position. Her hair, long and sable-brown just like Verity's own, had come loose from its neat bun and hung in straggles around her face. There was a scarlet smear of blood on one cheek. But, Mama was alive! Hope caught in Verity's throat so strong she almost coughed.

And then, the Indians began to leave. They ignored Mama and gathered an odd assortment of things. One wore Mama's petticoat draped around his shoulders, another carried the big cooking kettle still full of steaming, stewed berries, and Verity's own cornhusk doll that she'd named Patience for her grandmother, rode another bronze arm.

Verity's Indian, the one right in front of her, strode to her father and tugged on the hatchet handle. It came loose with a loud sucking sound, and in a neat circular motion he took Papa's scalp and let his head fall with a dull thud back on the wood pile.

A scream started in Verity's body from someplace deep inside. It was a wild, hurting, animal-like screech that seemed torn from her bowels. But before it could get past her lips Joe had his hand clamped over her mouth.

"Not now," he whispered. "Some day, I promise. But not now."

The Indians ambled away laughing among themselves and licking their fingers from the jam pot. Verity and Joe lay motionless until the Indians were lost to sight in the trees across the valley. They lay long enough that Verity's hatred solidified into a hard mass that seemed to encase her heart like wet leather, tightening and thickening and expanding like a live thing.

She would never forget. Never.

One

Little Canhawa River Valley,
1778

Twenty acres and a flop-eared mule. That's all he thought she was worth! Well, he could think again. She was not, was *not* going to marry Old Man Hargraves in exchange for twenty acres and the loan of a mule so Otis could plant more land. Step-father or not, he couldn't make her marry that filthy old man for any reason. He could do what he wanted, he couldn't force her.

Verity Philp dug one hand deeper into the pocket of her brother's greatcoat and hurried her footsteps along the mountain trail. She knew a desperate urgency to put as much ground behind her as possible before she was missed. The goat she dragged on a short lead gave a bleat of defiance and shook its head. Verity hauled on the rope and plodded onward. Maybe the movers she'd talked to the night before were early risers and maybe they weren't. She absolutely had to catch them before they crossed the river.

Below her, down a steeply slanted hillside, an icy March wind rattled the branches of a frozen forest. At a break in the trees she could see the Little Canhawa River meandering through the creases of the hills and on to the fir-trimmed ridges and the horizon. Somewhere out there her brother Joe scouted for George Rogers Clark's militia. There were things she needed to talk over with Joe.

And Edward. She mustn't forget Edward. He was out there, too, with Joe. Before the boys left she and Edward had pledged themselves to each other. He'd been like another brother ever since Mama married Otis and they'd settled in the valley.

Mama's marriage to Otis had been one of necessity, not uncommon on the frontier. Mama had been desperate for a roof over their heads and if the bargain had been a poor one, she didn't complain. Things weren't really unbearable, though, until Mama died and Otis married Lena. Joe had gotten the worst of it. Otis had been tough on him and, early on, Joe had a belly-full.

If only she knew where Joe and Edward were now. However badly she had needed them, though, the fact was that they weren't here and she'd been forced to make her own decision.

Not for the first time, Verity wished that she'd been born a boy. She wouldn't be in this fix, having to run away rather than bow to Otis's demands, if she were a boy. Men were free, could make their own decisions, not have to do what someone else said from the day they were born to the day they died. A man could take off with nothing but his gun and, like Joe, head for the wilderness.

News was infrequent and it wasn't often that she thought about the bloody clashes of war with England in Massachusetts and New York. She did, however, think about Joe and Clark's militia carrying on their own isolated piece of the same war far to the west.

Her thoughts were bitter. Joe had lit out in the middle of the night a year ago, tired unto death, he said, of Otis's mouth and his fists, and hadn't been back. He and Edward left together and they had promised to send for her, but beyond one short letter telling her they were under Clark's command and heading west for the winter toward Kaskaskia and the Illinois country, she'd heard nothing.

And now there was no more time. After last night, Verity knew her days of waiting for word of Joe and Edward were over.

She swiped a strand of long dark hair, damp with rain, from her eyes, anchored it behind one ear and tramped on, pulling the balking goat behind. The river seemed to beckon. A week, maybe two, of rough going along the Little Canhawa and then the Ohio. She could imagine what it would be like with great green bushes hanging low alongside the river, the water running smooth and fast, taking you farther and farther away. Taking you west. Could she do it? Would it really be possible for her to get to the river and then down it? She trembled in the face of the unknown, but after Otis's declaration at the supper table she had no choice.

He had leaned back in his chair with the assumed air of a man proud of himself. A sharp catch had pinched at Verity's breath.

He belched, pounded himself briefly on the chest and said, "Our Verity here's going to take herself a husband."

His words fell like a thunderclap. Lena's mouth closed with a soft plop, the three littlest children sat up straight with curious eyes and, after a horrified moment, Verity whispered a strangled, "Husband?"

Her mind raced over the possibilities. There wasn't an eligible man within fifty miles. Verity had considered the same thing, herself, if only to get away from the sharp cruelty of her step-father's temper and the meanness of Lena's tongue.

"Who?" she asked in a voice she hardly recognized as her own.

Otis smiled, making the most of the moment, drawing it out, stretching it to the fullest. "Hargraves," he said at last with a victorious flash of tobacco-stained teeth. "Mr. Elihue J. Hargraves, Esquire. That's who."

Verity sat stunned. All the juice in her body drained away. Her mouth went dry. The Hargraves farm was their nearest neighbor to the south. It was some of the best valley land in the Virginia territory and coveted by many men, including her step-father, who barely managed to eke out a living from his own rock-infested hillside farm. But—

"Old Man Hargraves?" There was hollow disbelief in her tone.

"Yep." Otis tilted his chair back on two legs and teetered importantly. "In return," his voice hardened and his eyes pierced hers, "I get twenty acres of bottom land and the use of his mule whenever I need it."

Twenty acres and the borrowed use of a mule. The words dropped into Verity's mind and lodged big as a mountain. She tried to speak and tried again.

"Oh, no. Not him."

"I drove a hard bargain for you, girl, and there ain't no use arguing."

"No." The word was an anguished avowal of disbelief.

Verity could see the red coming up in Otis's face and knew it would soon be purple. At purple his razor strap came off the wall.

"I'll take no sass off you, girl. You'll do as I say and you'll smile about it so's Hargraves don't renege on his word."

Verity was on her feet. "He doesn't want me. He wants a slave. He's already worked two wives to death. You said so yourself."

His chair scraped back from the table. "You're young and strong and there ain't no reason you can't work and still give him all the sons he wants."

Verity thought she might be sick. Mr. Hargraves bragged that the only time he'd ever been wet all over was the day he fell in the river and almost drowned at the age of nine. The gorge came up in her throat.

"I can't do it, Otis. Don't ask me. Mama wouldn't want—"

"Your ma's dead a long time and you're still putting your feet under my table." Otis was on his feet, too, leaning forward, the cords in his neck bulging. "You'll do what I say."

For a long moment they stared at one another and then he pulled his eyes away and stomped toward the door. A gust of cold, wet air blew in. "All you got to remember is that I said you're marrying him and that's what's going to happen." The door slammed.

Verity's mind seemed to accelerate, filtering ideas and thoughts in such rapid succession she couldn't keep them straight. She would not marry Old Man Hargraves. She'd sooner drown in the river although that wasn't much of a possibility since she swam, as Joe used to say, better than some fish. So, what then? She could no longer live with Otis.

Still standing at the table, she knew her choices were few. She would never find someone to hire her. By now Otis had likely told everyone he knew that he would soon be related by marriage to Old Man Hargraves. No one would risk alienating Mr. Hargraves by hiring her out from under him, so to speak.

Twenty acres and the loan of a mule. The words echoed in her head like a litany. Twen-ty-acres-and-a-flop-eared-mule. Twen-ty-acres-and-a-flop-eared—

Joe. Edward. Where were they? Her thoughts skittered frantically. The two of them had plans beyond the militia. Once you'd served your time in the militia the congress gave you two hundred acres of land. If only a letter had come sending for her. She'd have been gone in the flick of a rabbit's ear.

If only—if only she could do like Joe. Take off for the west, join Clark's army and be rid of Otis and Lena and the degrading need for a man to take care of her.

Why couldn't she follow Joe? Ever since she could remember she had been as good a shot as he and was almost as good at following a trail. She couldn't join the army, but she could find Joe somehow, in Kaskaskia, and Edward, and together they would plan for the future.

Her heart gave a leap. She could do it, she was sure of it. Hadn't she always done everything Joe did, and sometimes better? She could outrun Joe and out-climb him, and maybe a few other things, too. Ma had insisted she learn woods knowledge right along with Joe as well as reading and figuring. Ma had been a great one for learning things. Anything.

Verity hardened her resolve. She would not let this unexpected opportunity pass her by.

Placing her feet carefully on the rain-slick leaves carpeting the ridge and yanking the goat behind her, her eyes narrowed with satisfaction as she remembered how the solution to her problem had literally walked into view. She had left the cabin and climbed to a rocky ledge just off the trace where she often sat and contemplated the shadow-creased mountains to the west.

Within minutes, a short pack train of a broken down old horse and a mule-drawn, two-wheeled cart with several people trudging behind, came around a gray granite boulder jutting into the trace. There was a sick-looking woman in the cart with a baby. They both looked bad off. And two hollow-eyed children hung on to the sides of the cart.

They didn't waste words. They were in a hurry. While one man, short and stocky, stared wordlessly at Verity until she decided he was both ignorant and rude, another asked for directions to the Little Canhawa and for the use of the family cow.

Apparently, the woman's milk had dried up and neither she nor the baby looked to Verity to be capable of traveling another foot. Unfortunately, Otis did not have a cow and Verity sadly sent them on their weary way. The baby likely wouldn't make it across the river, she thought. The mother's fate was doubtful. The odd thing was that they were set on doing just what she herself had been dreaming about: going down river with Clark and his militia.

She had watched them off with a great lump of bitterness caught in her chest. If she were only a boy she wouldn't be saddled with the threat of Old Man Hargraves for the rest of her life. She could go with them. Going across the Wilderness Trail or down the Ohio on a flatboat couldn't possibly be worse than belonging to that smelly old goat of a man Otis had promised her to.

Goat! In a small pocket of thinking, an idea blossomed. And in that moment, she had known how to set her course. She just had to catch the movers and convince them to take her along.

Ha! Otis would think twenty acres and a flop-eared mule. And Old Man Hargraves. She leaned over and spat on the ground to get the very taste of the name out of her mouth. Hargraves! Maybe his mule could bear his sons.

Verity smiled as she stepped on down the mountain through the pouring rain. She was on her way. For better or worse, she was heading for the Ohio river and George Rogers Clark. She had stolen Otis's goat and, unwilling though it might be, the animal was her ticket. She'd consider the sin of thievery later.

Two

Trey Owens awakened at precisely the time for which he'd set his mind the night before. An hour before dawn. With his first breath he realized it was going to be a miserable morning. The chill cut through his soggy blanket with the slice of a cold knife and the mizzling rain that had been falling last night was still misting down.

He'd come a long way in the past ten days with little success to report and had a long way yet to go. With the threat of another Indian uprising, no one was willing to leave their own families and farms unprotected while they went off to fight other Indians in the west. Hell, he couldn't blame them. If he had anyone to worry about he'd think twice about leaving, too. But there was no one except his younger brother, and Billy was in Williamsburg finishing out the last of his apprenticeship with Thomas Stone the bookbinder.

Stone was a good man, honest and fair-minded, but Trey remembered his own seven-year apprenticeship to the man and felt anew the anxious, driving need to be free. He squinted impatiently at the overcast sky. Even a wretched and rainy morning in the forest was better than being warm and dry before another man's fire.

Trey rolled to his feet and checked the small clearing where he'd spent the night. No sign of anyone creeping around while he slept. He retrieved the remains of a turkey from the tree where he'd hung it out of the way of prowling animals and eyed it morosely. The bird had been tough and stringy and skinny, but he'd eaten from it yesterday afternoon late and it would have to do for breakfast. Within minutes he was on the trail, chewing on the dry and tasteless bird as he went.

No matter how you looked at it, he thought, even in the rain a man would be a fool to ask much more than traveling through forests that stretched to the limitless west, fording crystal clear streams revealing more fish than any one man could ever use and knowing that he scouted for George Rogers Clark. Just now he was recruiting men to flesh out the army, and only God and Clark knew how thinly that army was stretched.

He strode through the forest with long free strides, cradling the gun in a crook of his arm. Even after four years of freedom from the printing business he felt the need to stretch his arms wide every morning just to make sure he didn't butt into any walls. He felt incredibly lucky.

It was the possibility of exploring the western part of the continent, the tracking and mapping, that had rendered him so restless he couldn't sleep nights in his small room behind Stone's.

One wild spring night George Washington and his retinue had stopped overnight at the tavern beside Stone's. They had stayed up late talking about the wilderness, the Indians, the virgin lands yet to be explored and Trey had been spellbound. In his gut, he knew he had to see the land beyond the mountains. And after a week of wakeful nights and scarcely being able to eat for excitement and indecision, he knew that one way or another he would be a part of the westward push.

He simply walked out, two months short of the end of his indenture. He left a note for Billy and another for Thomas Stone, then put on his hat and walked out the front door. He tried to explain this incredible draw that he seemed powerless to set aside. He was twenty-six years old, had all his own teeth and a body honed to solid muscle. He was a happy man.

After he'd met George Rogers Clark, he was even happier. He was recruiting for the spring campaign against Lord Henry Hamilton, the English lieutenant governor and his Indians, and scouting new country. Life didn't get much better.

He followed a deer path around the shoulder of a hollow and skirted the base of a hill. The wet forest made little sucking sounds, live sounds.

At the river—he hoped it was the Little Canhawa, if it wasn't he was lost and he'd never hear the end of it if Clark found out—he washed his hands of the grease from the turkey in a small tidal pool of frigid water. His reflection stared back at him from the rippling surface. Dark hair, pulled back by a leather thong, dark eyes, set deep in a face much like the father he remembered vividly as vital and vigorous, and the cleft in his chin, another remembrance of his father, lost along with his mother to a sickness that swept the boat as they immigrated. He had been fourteen and Billy only ten. When they reached the shores of the New World upon which they'd all pinned so many hopes, both Trey and Billy were indentured to Thomas Stone. Trey hadn't quite made it; Billy would.

He stared at the water a moment longer and stood on the bank to shake the memories from his mind. The river would be like ice, but he had to get across. Resolutely he stripped down, rolled his buckskins and woolen capote tightly and waded into the river holding the bundle above his head. He swam on his side with one hand, gritting his teeth against the cold, while his eyes scanned the bank rising before him. Trey stepped out in the lee of a clump of thick bushes and immediately began to run, counting on his own body heat to dry him quickly. Dawn was beginning to pink the eastern sky, although the dark had not lifted yet. He wanted to be deep into the forest before daylight.

He ran upriver to make up for ground the current cost him and at the point he'd noted from the opposite bank he stopped to put on his clothes. With the shirt half over his head, he froze into immobility. Apparently he wasn't the only one in the forest this morning. The snuffling sounds he'd heard were those a man makes in his sleep. The issue was whether his company was friend or foe. White man or red.

Cautiously he crossed a creek bed clogged with rotting logs, tumbled boulders and moss-slick stones. In front of him was a screen of fallen trees canting crazily into the crotches of other trees, all overgrown with dried and brittle vines, tough as rawhide after the winter. He moved carefully around this debris of some long-ago storm and found himself nose to nose with a sheer rocky bluff. Water from a dozen hidden streams dribbled down the face of the cliff, half-frozen in the frosty morning and he knew he couldn't climb. Not wasting time on what couldn't be helped he moved to his right, around the bluff. The ground rose beneath his feet and as he neared the peak he shifted his gun into a handier position.

Stealthily he crept nearer the sound. The last five yards were covered on his belly and when he was safely concealed behind a fallen log, he raised his head slowly, an inch at a time.

One sweeping glance was all it took. Three white men, one woman, two children and a baby. One old mule and a near-broken down horse. Not much plunder, a half-wagon that was none too sturdy and, the proof of non-experienced travelers, a fire that had been allowed to go out.

Trey rose to his feet and watched in disdain as the three men awakened and struggled upright. One reached cautiously for his gun, leaning against the wagon wheel.

Openly Trey lowered the butt of his own gun to the ground. "No need for that, friend. I'm traveling, too. Peaceable."

The big man relaxed his hold on the gun and ran his hand down a straggly, yellow beard.

"You come up awful quiet. Where'd you spring from?"

Trey tilted his head toward the river without removing his eyes from the men. "Crossed downstream a way. Are you heading over?"

"North." The answer was short.

"You're nosing into some heavy country. Going far?"

The three men exchanged a look and seemed to make some sort of agreement for the bearded one said, "Goin' almost to Pittsburgh. To Redstone, to catch Clark and his party headin' down the Ohio."

He moved toward the fire and called over his shoulder. "Name's Clem Dawson. My brothers Bart and Abner. If you've a mind to, set a spell while I put on some coffee. Maybe you can tell us what we're headin' into."

Trey nodded, thinking why not? Maybe he could talk one of them into joining Clark's army. A moment later he changed his mind. Between the three of them they had trouble getting a fire going and not a one paid any attention to the forest around them. Clark needed fighters. This was a mover family. They'd fight, maybe, for their land, but they wouldn't make good soldiers. And while Clark was taking movers down river with him, Trey's commitment was to find men for the army.

However, he might as well be sociable and start their fire. He scooped up a handful of dry punk from inside the fallen log at his feet and took out his own striker and flint. Before they had the fire blazing he'd found out why they were traveling and where they were heading.

"Land's free out west, if you can hold it, and us Dawsons always been stubborn. Give us a thing that's our'n and nobody's goin' to take it away. We'll make out."

"There's plenty of land," Trey agreed. "Are there any men back where you come from that would be interested in pushing the Indians back far enough that we can get at it?"

Clem worried his beard and looked to his brothers before he answered. "Nary a one, that we know of. Ever'one's bent on stayin' home and protectin' what he's got. Maybe next year."

"Next year will be too late. Hamilton, Old Hairbuyer, is gathering the Indians for a big summer offensive. If we don't wipe them out before they get started, there might not be a next year for us. Clark is heading for Kaskaskia and he needs more men."

Clem stroked his beard. "What we know about fighting Indians would fit snug in a gnat's navel. Plantin' corn, we know. Plowin' straight furrows, we know. Hangin' on to what we got, we know. But we ain't your men for joinin' a militia."

"I hope there are a few between here and North Carolina who feel different."

"Not much point in your traipsin' all the way down there and back. Won't find nobody." This from the one they called Bart who Trey had almost decided was a mute. Nothing to him but beady, close-set, staring eyes and shoulders like a bull buffalo. Bart spat on the ground without lifting his gaze from Trey and went on. "But I reckon you're set on goin' anyway."

Trey held his eye. "I reckon," he said, wondering what it was about this one that he found disturbing. There was a darkness around Bart's eyes that made Trey wary. The others might be ignorant of what they were getting into, there was no shame in that, but this one had a mean cast to his gaze, somehow. He wasn't one to turn your back on.

One of the children made water noisily in the bushes and came to the side of the cart. It was a small girl with slumping shoulders and a thumb in her mouth. She just stood and looked at Trey with the first spark of friendliness he'd seen in the family.

"Hey," Trey said, smiling. "You're an early bird. Found your worm, yet?"

The thumb came out of her mouth. "What worm?"

"You know…the early bird is the one that gets the worm." And, at her open lack of understanding, he explained. "The one who gets up first to get the work done is the one who always has enough to ea—"

With no warning, Bart's hand smacked across the side of the child's head and she fell sideways, over the tongue of the cart. "Shut up and go get your brother. We're wasting daylight standin' here with our jaws flappin'. Oughten to be listenin' in on men's talk, anyways."

Trey took one instinctive step forward. The blow hadn't been vicious, just off-hand, like swatting a mosquito, but there had been no reason to hit the child. Trey's step toward her, however, seemed to be a signal for all three men to lay hands on their muskets.

He said, "It was my fault. I was talking to her."

Clem spoke so quietly that the yellow beard didn't even move. "She's mine and if'n my brother thinks she needs remindin' of her manners, he'll do it. Sally," he yelled. "Go fill the bucket in the river, and be quick about it."

The child hurried to the back of the cart and disappeared upriver, lugging the heavy bucket in both hands.

In deliberate slow motion, Trey relaxed his stance and picked up his gun. "Guess I'll pass on that coffee and be on my way." He nodded his head in a northerly direction and said, "If you catch up with Clark, tell him Trey Owens will find him one of these days."

He left the miserable little camp and went south into the forest. He couldn't forget the little girl's eyes. First, a dawning of delight in his statement about early birds and then, defeat and resignation at the unfair and unexpected blow from her uncle. He felt responsible, somehow.

Trey picked up the trail wondering what earthly business sorry folks like these had in thinking they'd make it in the wilderness. They could plant a field of corn, but they couldn't keep a campfire going. They could father children, but they hadn't the sense to know they might never raise them on the frontier. They probably prayed to the Almighty every night, but by day were as mean and small-minded as snakes.

Trey increased his pace on the plainly marked trail and thought that he wouldn't be George Rogers Clark for anything in the world, condemned to be responsible for getting movers, people like the Dawsons, out to the Illinois country to settle. Soldiers were one thing. Movers, something else. However, finding more soldiers was his job. Anything in pants would do, if he knew the business end of a gun and was willing to take orders. And giving orders was a thing Clark knew how to do. Finding men was what Trey knew how to do.

~ * ~

By dawn the rain had settled into a steady drenching drizzle. For three hours Verity had slogged through enough mire and muck to carpet Albemarle County. She was tired and wet and her defiant leave-taking no longer seemed noble, only necessary. The one thing that kept her moving was the appalling alternative waiting back home.

Actually, she'd planned on being farther down the trail by dawn, but the goat held her back. The stupid animal wanted to stop every ten feet and inspect the scenery. Verity was so disgusted she wished she could set her free, but without the goat the movers would have no need of Verity herself and she was counting on how badly the baby needed milk.

She yanked again on the rope and dragged the animal up a rocky grade. Otis would be up by now and missing both her and the goat. She wasn't worried about what he might do. If, by remote chance, he guessed she was heading west, he'd surely think she'd go overland and not risk the Ohio.

In any case, it wouldn't occur to him that she would make for Illinois. Illinois was peopled mostly with Tories and Frenchmen. There were few stations there who'd welcome American settlers.

She peered into the dull pearly lightness that was only slightly brighter than night and wondered, again, if she was the only one on the trail. The woods were quiet except for the relentless drip of rain from skeletal tree limbs. The sky seemed to clamp down on the earth like the lid on a kettle.

"Come on, goat," she muttered grimly, grabbing an ear and twisting. "We don't know how lazy these folks are. And, if we don't catch them before they cross the Little Canhawa, we can forget the Ohio."

Thankfully the goat seemed to have gotten the drift of her message, for it stepped out briskly and Verity had to trot to keep up.

Her heart pounded with exertion and excitement. She was on her way. Really on her way west. She tried to remember everything she knew about the river. High banks, treacherous hidden currents, unexpected waterfalls, spring floods. And inaccessible bluffs with watching hostile Indians. She wouldn't think of the murdering Indians yet, that would come soon enough, but how glad she was that she had learned to swim. It was one of the earliest battles she could remember.

"Girls don't swim," Joe had stated contemptuously.

"I will," she'd retorted.

"You'll drown," her mother said, wringing her hands.

"I won't!"

"You'll scream and cry and I'll have to jump in and fish you out," Joe predicted in disgust.

"I won't. You know I won't!"

"I forbid it," Mama had stated finally.

Verity had only glared in defiance until Joe turned to his mother. "I'd better teach her. She'll only jump in on her own and then, maybe, she will drown."

And so, Joe had taught her to swim. He disgustedly threw her in and yelled instructions from the bank while she floundered grim-faced and determined in water over her head, and Mama went back to the cabin, unable to watch. But Verity had learned to swim. Tight-lipped now, she pulled again on the tether and dragged the goat along behind her.

She hitched her blanket roll higher under her arm and took up another loop on the rope. She was traveling light. All she'd brought along were a change of clothes and, except for the one skirt rolled in her blanket they were Joe's clothes, and a couple handsful of pounded corn in a pouch hung at her waist. A second pouch contained a small knife, a horn comb, her mother's thimble and the most precious commodity of all: a needle. The coat she wore was Joe's, as was the wide-brimmed hat she pulled low over her eyes with her hair bundled up inside.

The goat trotted along, seeming to be committed at last to the trail. She wondered uncomfortably if taking the goat could really be labeled as stealing. When she'd first thought of how the goat could help her, she'd reasoned that Mama had always said God helped those who helped themselves, and He'd surely put the idea into her head to use the goat as a bargaining tool to get to the Ohio River. Just as surely, however, she knew that the decision had been hers. God hadn't knotted the rope around the goat's neck and dragged it unwillingly away from it's straw bed.

She might be fuzzy about whether or not she should feel guilty for taking the goat, but she knew for a certainty it couldn't be God's will for her to meekly submit to being Old Man Hargraves's wife. Hargraves was dirty and cruel and old! And a conviction deep within her said she was doing the right thing.

A small stone rolled beneath her foot, causing a minor rock-slide, and by the time she got her feet firmly beneath her the goat was on the downhill side, struggling on the end of the rope. She scolded the goat, the hillside, the sodden and dripping skies of a dawn that wasn't quite daybreak, and most of all herself for not setting out earlier. If she failed to catch the movers before they crossed the river… It didn't bear thinking about. She couldn't go back.

Nor could she seem to get the stupid goat on its feet and turned the right direction. She grunted and heaved on her end of the rope while the goat jerked convulsively on the other. One glance down the hillside was all she allowed. The pitch was near perpendicular, down sheer rocky slabs to a narrow gorge filled with an avalanche of boulders jutting from a rushing creek. She dug in with both heels.

"Stand still, you mangy, ignorant, good-for-nothing animal," she shouted. "You're making it worse." Desperately she fought for a handhold on the rope.

"You're the one making it worse." The voice came from somewhere over her shoulder and Verity swiveled a face red from exertion and anger to meet it.

He made his way carefully down the slope toward her. "Never did know a goat that spoke English," he said.

Verity gaped at him. His dark hair and almost black eyes were accompanied by a massive frown that creased his forehead in the same way the little indention marked his chin. Her mouth all but fell open.

He reached for the rope and elbowed her aside. “Don’t you know anything about animals, boy? Lord God, that goat’s damned near strangled.”

He had taken a half hitch around a young maple before his words penetrated Verity’s thinking. He thought she was a boy. He thought she was slow-witted. Not only that but he needed his mouth washed out with soap.

“I don’t remember asking for help.” She spaced the words out. “Don’t trouble yourself.” She reached for the rope.

He batted her hand away. “Just go and sit down someplace where you won’t be in the way and let me get this goat back to the trail before it hangs itself.”

He was trying to take the goat away from her! In a pig’s eye he was! In the space of a heartbeat she had jabbed a sharp elbow into his ribs and aimed a boot at his shins. He gasped and grabbed first his rib cage and then a knee. Verity reached for the rope.

“Damnation!” he gasped. “Are you daft?” He still had his hand on the rope.

Grinding her teeth together, Verity fought for the rope. Just as stubbornly, he held on to it. With a sudden yank Verity turned her back and stamped her heel down, hard, on his toes. She heard the sharp hiss as he sucked in air and then he grabbed her from behind.

The goat was forgotten. She kicked and squirmed in his arms while he cursed and groped for a purchase on her body.

“By God! You don’t weigh more than a half grown cat, but you’re twice as hard to get a grip on. What’s wrong with you? I’m trying to help!”

There was no answer except a muffled grunt and a hard, tiny fist jamming into his Adam’s apple, silencing him as effectively as a muzzle, and then a knee in his upper leg, sharp enough and near enough to vital organs to make him take a step back. His arms around the youngster's waist slipped and rode high up the ribcage, and he let go as suddenly as if he'd grabbed hold of an angry rattlesnake. They both went sprawling.

"Hell!" It was a frustrated expulsion of breath. He sat, tilting downhill with both hands braced behind him, wrist deep in mud, and stared. Heat seared through Verity's whole body. His hands had skimmed up and over her breasts!

"You're not a boy," he said, stupidly, and watched her crawl after her hat and jam it down firmly on her head, mud and all. She glared at him from a dirty face, still on her hands and knees. The goat now stood quietly watching them, having righted itself under its own power. The rope dangled loose.

He struggled to his feet and offered a hand to help her. With a hostile glare she ignored the outstretched palm, picked up the trailing rope and crabbed her way up to the trail, bent nearly double into the hillside.

"You will kindly…shut your blaspheming mouth…*sir*. I will not tolerate…such vile language."

"Well, I'll be damned!" Trey stood open-mouthed in astonishment.

She whirled. "You probably will, but not in front of me." She'd had to listen to Otis's disgusting talk, but she most certainly did not have to take such disrespect from a stranger. "If you can't speak decently, then hold your tongue!"

Trey spread his hands wide. "I don't know what in hell's got your dander up, but—"

"*Sir!*"

Trey followed her up the hillside in silence and then stood looking at her. He shrugged his shoulders. "Here I was, just moseying along, thinking I had the trail all to myself. Thought I was offering my help to a boy," and he grinned, an abrupt softening of his features that changed his entire appearance. He looked, and Verity hesitated, nice. Friendly.

His face was strong with a finely chiseled brow and a mass of curling black hair. And he was clean shaven. Most men wore beards and in spite of her anger Verity looked again. He had a marked indenture in the center of his chin. A cleft chin it was called, although she'd never before seen one. It was his eyes, however, that riveted her to the trail. Dark as bits of coal and flat, giving away nothing of what he was thinking, he gave the appearance of seeing everything. She pulled her thoughts away from a fascinating sort of softening. The man had a mouth like a barnyard.

His grin broadened. "Doesn't pay to let your attention wander in this country," he said cheerfully. "Might miss something you'd regret.

"You could also blunder into more than you could handle." Her tone was decidedly cool.

His eyes narrowed and the smile thinned. "More than I can handle?" he echoed. "I guess we could debate that, but it might be more fun to start over with me knowing all the rules this time."

"I'd sooner play games with the goat. Good day to you, sir."

She moved to step by him. He shifted his weight and blocked her path.

"What, no thanks for all my trouble? No apology for almost maiming me for life?"

"My sorrow is that you won't be walking crooked for the next ten miles." Horrified, Verity clapped a hand over her mouth and closed her eyes. How could she possibly have said such a thing? How could she even have thought it? She felt her face flushing hot.

He threw back his head and laughed. "Ah. I've found me a lady. A true dyed-in-the-wool bluestocking. One who doesn't condone the smallest swear word, but is honest enough to admit she meant me grievous harm."

She stuck out her jaw, determined not to be intimidated. "What do you want?"

His insolent grin grew wider. "Spunky as well as sassy," and the smile faded. He looked beyond her up the trail. "You aren't alone?" It was a question.

Verity ignored him. "I asked what you wanted."

"I make it a rule to always know who is traveling the same trail as me. It's healthier. And you, my friend, aren't listening. A lone woman isn't safe. Even those traveling with a sharp-shooting goat." He smiled again making the little dent in his chin more pronounced.

Verity didn't relax a muscle. "As you can see I'm fine. You're the only problem I have. Step aside, please."

The smile disappeared and his eyes were suddenly serious. "As soon as you tell me where you're going."

"To the river, if you must know."

"Why?"

"That's none of your business."

He considered this and then shook his head. "I'm making it my business. How do we know who might be lurking in the bushes and bent on mischief?"

In spite of herself Verity glanced into the shadow-filled forest and took a tighter grip on the rope. The tiny knife was tucked safely in the bag at her waist and, although he didn't appear to mean her harm, she wished it were handier.

"Let me by. I'm going to be late. I'll miss them."

"Ah. Now we're getting somewhere. Who will you miss?"

"My...friends. I'm meeting them at daybreak. We're crossing together." What was a small fib when she'd just broken the Eighth Commandment into smithereens by stealing a goat? Her chin lifted. "Let me pass."

He looked curiously from her to the goat, but didn't voice a question. "Fair enough. I guess more than that really is none of my business. Anyway, the river is only a mile farther. There's nothing but a little rock and a lot of rain between here and there. You're safe enough."

Verity frowned and put a hand on each hip. "Then please remove yourself from the middle of the trail so I can pass."

He only smiled.

Her voice lowered and she spoke carefully through gritted teeth. "Get out of my way."

His expression altered and he abruptly stopped baiting her. In an exaggeratedly courtly manner he moved obediently aside. "Can't fault a man for taking advantage of a little sunshine when he finds it." He lifted his voice as she hurried away. "I was serious. You aren't safe in the forest, alone. Don't make a habit of strolling around by yourself. You and your goat, that is."

The nerve of the man, giving her orders. She was finished with taking orders from a man. From any man.

"Maybe we'll meet again, down the trace somewhere," he called at her back.

"Not likely," she shouted without turning.

She spent the next few minutes planting her feet as if she were digging holes into the ground and wondering who he was and where he was going. He was infuriating. He was insufferably rude. She wished he'd taken another trail down country. And, yet, it would be just a little bit nice if they would meet again, as he said, somewhere. That funny dent in his chin—The hard, strong feel of his arms hoisting her around—And, the sudden sparkle in his eyes when he'd said the thing about finding sunshine.

It was galling, however, to have to admit he was right. Travel was safer in a group. She knew that. But if she was going to worry about her safety, she ought never to have left home. Mama had always said her first words were: "Me do myself." And she generally did. She would again. After all, the man had said the river was almost within reach.

A slight thinning of trees was the first indication she was nearing water. And then her nostrils picked up a whiff of smoke. In another few minutes she broke through the tree line and there they were, the two-wheeled cart, the three men and children, just breaking camp.

Verity's first thought was that they were incredibly unorganized and her second was that the woman was still in the cart, under a piece of oilskin, and probably hadn't moved since last evening.

One man, a short, balding runt of a man, was dousing the fire with water from the river. The second, a younger dark-haired man, the one who had stared at her yesterday, straightened from harnessing the mule to the cart. He turned and looked at Verity with sudden interest. The third, the yellow-bearded man who had done the talking last night, paused with an armload of kettles and pots half-gathered and watched silently as Verity plodded toward him through the rain.

The men straightened as she approached and moved shoulder to shoulder as if confronting a threat. The three of them waited until she spoke. A rivulet of water ran from the brim of Verity's hat and formed a puddle between her feet. The goat waited with its head hanging and bleated mournfully.

Verity squared her shoulders. She spoke to the bearded one. "I thought your wife and children could do with some goat's milk."

He eyed her suspiciously. "Maybe. What makes you so generous all of a sudden?"

Verity took a breath and looked him in the eye. “I want to go with you. Your wife is sick and you have a baby and two children to feed and care for. I’m strong and healthy and know how to work.”

There was silence while the men conferred with their eyes. Then, the bearded one, the leader, spoke. “No doubt about needin’ the goat, but we got no use for another mouth to feed. Me and my brothers here, can cook enough to get by.”

“I can cook better. And I’ll look after the children and your wife.”

The brothers exchanged another long look. “You won’t mind tellin’ us why you’re so all-fired anxious to leave this country, then?”

Verity hesitated and decided to tell a half-truth. “I’m pledged to a man in the Illinois country. He and my brother are scouting for Clark and I’m going west to meet them.”

“Your Pa, he’s agreeable to this? The goat and all?”

“Yes,” she lied in an even tone. They had to take her. They had to!

“Well, I don’t know. The goat, yes, but a single woman—”

Verity stood her ground. She said firmly, “The goat doesn’t go without me.”

The goat chose that moment to bleat, again. Her bag was swollen. She needed to be milked.

Verity held her breath while the men communicated with their eyes. The deciding voice came from the cart. “Clem.” It was the thin, tired voice of the woman. “Take her.”

Clem glanced at the cart, but the woman didn’t rise. Then he nodded. “You can come along, I reckon. But you got to pull your own weight. First off, you better milk that goat and see if the baby can keep some of it down, while we finish loadin’ up. And, if you got a skirt, put it on. You ain’t goin’ to travel with unmarried men, indecent like you are in britches. And hurry. The mornin's half gone while we stand here blatherin'."

Verity swallowed her retort that the morning had been half-gone when she arrived and if they'd been off at first light like most folks, she would have missed them altogether. However, the satisfaction wouldn't be worth it; she'd already won. The cost was a blatant out-and-out lie, another half-truth, stealing Otis's goat, and the way she couldn't forget the little dent in the chin of that man on the trail. A man who seemed to use vulgar language with every breath he drew.

She sighed. She'd have to deal with her squirming conscience sometime later, but for now—her throat caught a triumphant laugh before she could give it voice—for now, she was going west.

Three

Verity had never worked so hard in her life. Zelma and the children warmed to her before nightfall and by the third day "the boys," as Zelma called them, lost their self-consciousness and moved and spoke freely, too. Except Bart. He rarely spoke at all. He worked, however, with the dogged determination and sheer brute strength of a range-hardened buffalo and, Verity thought privately, had just about as much personality.

Abner was the eldest and the runty one. He had little to say. Bart came next with eyes that seemed to skewer Verity to the side of a hill every time he looked at her. He made her nervous. Clem, of the wash-tub-sized belly, made decisions when a mutual agreement could not be reached, but was becoming more and more distracted with the fear that his wife was dying. Verity refused to admit that she feared the same thing.

Because of Zelma, the cart was a necessity, but it was also the source of much of their frustration. The earth was soggy from spring rains and the unwieldy thing mired down a dozen times a day. By nightfall the mule was ready to drop in its tracks. Verity understood.

The cart had to be maneuvered around fallen trees, across gullies and streams, and around the lip of endless mountain trails. An occasional game path was a blessing because it meant the cart could pass without manhandling it through boulders and brush. Even the children had to help when the cart must be lightened.

Sally tired quickly and often needed to be carried. Occasionally she was permitted to ride in a corner of the cart. Gideon, the ten-year-old boy, appeared to have more energy and enthusiasm than any of them. He carried his own gun and he practiced his aim on every squirrel or rabbit in sight. Verity was relieved that, at least, they frequently had fresh meat to eat and all the milk they wanted to drink. The baby didn't begin to use all the milk the goat provided them.

"I'm not complaining," Verity said the fourth night out. "But why are we going at such a breakneck pace? Clark can't leave until after the spring floods, can he?"

Sally sat in Verity's lap noisily sucking a thumb and Gideon leaned against a blanket roll, trying not to fall asleep.

Clem lit his pipe before answering. He did everything slowly, thoughtfully. Especially talking. In fact, he often didn't answer Verity's questions at all. It was another of Verity's frustrations. Just now, however, he said, "Clark, he's set to take off from Redstone, that's just below Pittsburgh, the very minute the water'll let him. That could be early as mid-April. And we'uns got to be in place so's he knows he can count on us before then."

"Where is this Redstone? How long will it take us to get there?" Verity wanted to know.

He shrugged. "It's a good piece."

Bart spat into the fire with a hissing sizzle and made one of his rare comments. "Ain't no way we're agoing to catch Clark before he leaves."

Abner spoke. "Wouldn't of been no problem at all if we'd had a normal spring. But it rained ever' day solid for four weeks."

So, they'd gotten a later start than they'd planned and somewhere along the trail Zelma had given birth and was not getting over it the way she should. Verity worried the inside of her lip. Lena had always gone to bed at night and produced her babies before dawn with as little effort as a cat having kittens. Verity didn't know what to do about Zelma. How could they cope with a sickly woman in a frontier station?

"Where is this station Clark wants to start?" she asked, shifting Sally to a more comfortable position. "In Kentucky?"

"Nope. I hear they's a place closer to the river than the Kentucky stations. It'll be smack dab on the front lines, a sort of outlyin' settlement with stockades and ever'thin' for thirty or forty families. Clark'll drop us off and get us started, and then take the militia and go on down river to Illinois and wherever them Indians is nestin'. He's set on burning them out so's the country'll be safe for the rest of us."

It was a long speech for Clem and Verity was grateful. Now that she knew what Clark had in mind her plans would adapt perfectly. "You know all this for sure?" she asked.

All three men nodded. Clem answered. "We'd heard some of it down home, but we met up with a man that morning just before you come upon us at the river. He's a soldier with Clark."

Verity's interest quickened. The man in buckskins along the trail. It had to be. The man with the cleft chin. The one who had made her heart quicken. There hadn't been anyone else, it had to have been him. And, he was a soldier with Clark.

"Name of Trey Owens," Clem explained. "Left Harrodsburg with Clark back in October and came out this away to recruit men for the militia. Clark went on to Williamsburg to confer with Governor Henry. Picked up his signed orders the first part of December and lit out for Redstone next mornin'. This Trey, he said Clark's in a hurry and if'n we wanted to go, we'd best not be more'n two weeks gettin' there. They's already near' twenty families signed up."

"This man you met. He was a soldier with Clark."

Clem shrugged. "Recruitin'. I ain't surprised, he's got the bearin' for it. A man like that…he's one to tie to."

Twenty families. And Trey Owens, a soldier with Clark. Yes, hurrying made sense. If you had your heart set on going down the Ohio this summer, connecting up with Clark was the sensible thing to do.

But hurrying was hardly the word for it, Verity thought, in the days following. They forced their way through swamps and forests and up one side of the mountain and down the other, and waded streams until none of them remembered what it felt like to be dry and rested. They were all, without exception, ready to fall asleep on their feet if they paused for thirty seconds to reconnoiter their path. And Verity yearned, desperately, for an honest-to-goodness bath, with soap. She could hardly abide feeling dirty all the time.

The mountains rose higher and yet higher. The inclines seemed to sharpen. With the appearance of the sun the days became perceptibly warmer and it was with a glad heart that one morning Verity discovered a patch of snowy wake-robin beside the trail. A few days later delicate wands of dogwood burst into pink and white bloom.

There was no time, however, to rejoice in the birth of spring. The days and the hills and the camps seemed to meld into one. She could no longer remember which day it was when Gideon caught his foot in a crevice and wrenched his knee, or in which creek she'd washed the baby's soiled clothing.

There were nights when Verity did not even remember rolling into her blanket. She'd awaken to the sound of the ax and wonder where the night had gone. Then, there were nights when she laid, spent and weary, wondering how long it took a person to die when they'd given up the will to live. For Zelma faded a little with each day. When Verity joined them, Zelma had seemed to be holding her own. She was clear-eyed all the way into the evening, giving Verity instructions in a weak but firm tone.

"Gideon's a good boy. He'll be ten in July but can hoe corn beyond his years. Sally, now, has got dandelion fuzz in her head and you got to keep a close eye on her or she'll plain wander off. She ain't but six, I know, but... Just make sure she hangs onto the cart when we're moving."

Verity nodded and thought, herself, that Sally was old enough to be of more help. She was a sweet child and willing to help when asked, but slow moving and even slower thinking.

"Clem'll get you where you're going. He's stubborn, but you can count on him to bail was your boat sinking. The other boys are good, too. Bart has a temper sometimes and is dead set when he wants something to go his way, but you couldn't do no better than Abner, yourself—" her voice trailed off.

With a shock Verity realized Zelma was offering her Abner. "I'm promised," she said more sharply than she'd intended. "I told you. To a man in the Illinois country."

And the subject didn't come up again, although Verity felt a bit odd, knowing she'd been discussed as a possible wife for one of "the boys." Aware now of what they were thinking, she saw that Bart, especially, watched her constantly. Every time she raised her head, her eyes collided with his flat stare.

Being watched made her irritable, although she tried to ignore him. He never offered to help but, instead, seemed to be sizing her up, deciding whether or not she was equal to the task. However, there was an undercurrent of something more behind his eyes. While he rarely spoke, Verity was careful not to make the mistake of assuming he didn't think either. There was a lot going on behind Bart's eyes. She only wished, in moments when she had time to consider, that she knew what it was. His constant, unblinking attention made her vaguely uncomfortable.

She reminded herself, again and again, that she was working out her wages in a straight-forward business deal with Clem. She straightened her back and defied any of them to think differently.

One afternoon while skirting the base of a small hillock, a wheel on the cart caught a stone, flipped the cart and all the contents down an embankment and slid to a halt with one wheel spinning lazily in the spring sunshine. Zelma and the baby were unhurt, the plunder quickly gathered for repacking, but one wheel was broken into splinters.

They camped where they stopped, right on the trail. Even without the drawn look on the men's faces, Verity knew this was serious.

"If'n we had time, wouldn't take nothin' to make us a new wheel," Abner said, and it was plain he knew this suggestion was not workable.

"Yeah, and if buffalo had wings it'd be rainin' chips," Bart said uncharacteristically, proving the gravity of the situation.

Clem put his head in his hands. "Never catch Clark now. He'll be long gone before we get to the river."

Verity looked at the three of them. They were defeated. They sat around the fire dejected and stooped with failure. Well, they weren't going to quit. Verity wouldn't allow it. She stepped into the light. "We could make a pole cart, like the Indians."

No one answered. She began again, "I said we could—"

"I heard you," Clem muttered around the stem of his pipe, but didn't bother to glance up.

"We have to do something," she said, her back stiff with determination. "We can't just sit on our thumbs like a bunch of ninnies and wait for somebody to rescue us. There isn't anyone."

Clem almost snarled, "Shut your mouth and let a man think."

Verity ground her teeth together so hard her jaw ached. Because she wore skirts they thought her brain was the size of an acorn. She clenched her hands into fists at her side and forced herself to wait in silence. She refused to back away from the fire. After all, her future was in jeopardy also, but she did manage to keep her mouth shut.

As always, Clem smoked awhile before making any comment. Finally he sat up straighter and knocked out his pipe on a stone.

"This means we ain't agoin' to catch Clark at Redstone. What we could do is plan to catch him somewheres down river. Remember Clark's man that mornin' tellin' us about holin' up one whole winter just below Wheeling? He said there was a little river called Fat Meat Creek that fed into the Ohio right at a long string of islands. We could strike for that spot and hope for the best."

Silence.

Abner pulled his hat lower. He said, "Reckon one of us ought to ride on up to Redstone, so's Clark'll be expectin' us? If we was to just rise up on the banks of the river and hail him, Clark's liable not to stop, not knowin' who we was or anythin'. We could be robbers. He'd not stop."

No one answered him. The fire crackled and leaped in the wind.

Verity couldn't keep still any longer. "He's right. Somebody should take the horse and ride ahead so Clark will be watching for us. Can we find this Fat Meat Creek? Where is it?"

None of them even looked at her. Then Clem said, "Decide between you who's to go, and plan to be outta here at dawn."

Verity stood in the firelight feeling as useless as if she had two heads. They had no idea of where this creek was and, yet, saw no need to make any sort of plan for meeting up, later. They were idiots, all of them, the children, Zelma, "the boys," and herself most of all for deliberately placing her well-being in the hands of thick-headed, small-minded men. What if they missed Fat Meat Creek? They could wander for weeks while Clem hunted up and down the Ohio and Clark went on without them. She wanted to rush out into the darkness and howl like the wolves, or pound a tree trunk. She'd like to punch Clem right in his dirty, yellow beard. What she did was to pace the area of firelight, gritting her teeth until her head ached, and when the first blaze of temper had bled off, she moved to what was left of the cart and sat down beside Zelma.

Zelma's hand came to rest gently on Verity's. "It'll be all right. Clem'll get you to Fat Meat Creek. He could find his way through a featherbed in the dark. Don't fret."

Verity drew a long breath. "You heard, then. One of them is leaving in the morning to try and find Clark."

Zelma's breathing was shallow, but she patted Verity's hand. "That'll be Abner to go, likely. Don't let 'em fash you none. In the mornin', Clem'll start buildin' a pole cart, like you said. He just takes awhile, sometimes, to work his way around to seein' the right side of a thing."

Her eyes were closed and there was a faintly bluish cast beneath the eyelid. Even in the flickering firelight the veins on her cheeks stood out clear against her pallor. A surge of anxiety flooded Verity's thinking. She hadn't bargained, not really, on the woman's dying. In fact, she'd been so set on going west herself, at whatever cost, that she hadn't thought through what it would mean if she were left to be the only woman in the group.

"You ought to eat more," she said quickly. "You aren't eating enough to get your strength back."

Zelma shook her head. "Your rabbit stew was right tasty, but I can't eat more. Not now." She pulled the blanket up around the sleeping baby. "Has he taken much milk today? He's been awful fussy since my milk dried up."

"Some." Verity thought of the edge of cotton blanket she'd used to dip into the goat's milk for the baby to suck. She said quickly, "He's doing better every day, though," and knew in her heart that it wasn't so. The baby was merely hanging on. She made a mental note to be watchful for a stand of cattails. She could maybe use the hollow stalk to dribble milk into the baby's mouth, a drop at a time.

Verity sat on for a few minutes while Zelma's breath steadied and became more even. She wanted to will Zelma better. If only she could lift the woman with her own hands and shake good health into her. Or share some of her own young strength with the older woman. But there was never enough energy to go around, for any of them. They were all wearing down.

Slowly her anger drained away. She was tired. It had been a long day. She didn't move, however, until she was sure Zelma was asleep.

Sure enough, Verity awakened to the ring of an ax the next morning. Clem had four poles cut and by the time Verity had breakfast set out he'd figured out how to stretch a blanket between them for two pole carts. They discarded a chair and some pewter pots before they left, and winter coats. Verity looked back once and found Zelma looking, too, a gentle grief showing in her eyes.

"That tea pot was my grandmother's," she said and turned her face away.

To her surprise Verity missed Abner, for as Zelma said, he was the one who left before light for Redstone. She discovered only now, that she'd grown to depend on his eyes watching the trace behind. More than once she remembered the stranger in buckskin telling her that it was always safer to know who was following on his trail. Trey Owens. He'd been recruiting for Clark. It was too bad, really. She'd never see him again. Him and that funny dent in his chin. Actually, it was very odd, but she'd had the strongest urge to lay her finger in that little ridge. Just for a minute.

"Ver-ty?" Sally's face was tear-streaked and her mouth puckered. She offered up her arm for examination. "It hurts."

A red, swollen ring on the girl's thin arm showed an angry-looking bee sting.

"It's all right, Zelma," Verity called. "I'll take care of it," and she scooped up a handful of clay from the ground. "We'll paste on a big glob of this mud and the hurt will be drawn right out. See, it feels better already, doesn't it?" She picked up the little girl and carried her for a way, wondering wearily how many more miles it was to Fat Meat Creek and if they'd ever find it, anyway. Even the name sounded dumb. Maybe there was no such place at all. They had only a stranger's word. But that stranger was the man with the cleft chin. Involuntarily she smiled. Fat Meat Creek was there. She didn't know why she was sure, but she was. They only had to find it.

Zelma and Verity's own instincts proved to be right, for by the end of the week they were there. Clem had indeed found his way through a featherbed of a forest in what amounted to near dark, for the hills were so thickly covered with trees the sun was blotted out most of the time. They came out on the edge of a stretch of fine bottom land and hurriedly crossed to get their first glimpse of the mighty Ohio River.

To the north ran a thin trickle of a stream, Fat Meat Creek. Off to their left the forest curled down to meet the river.

They crowded together and looked at the famous Ohio. The river was wider than Verity had expected and the water a dirty brown, heavy with silt from the spring floods. Laying lengthwise in the current was a string of wooded islands so long she could see neither end. It gave her a queer start to know the only thing separating her from acknowledged Indian territory was this strip of rushing river water.

Indians. Her scalp prickled and the taste of old hatred lodged in her throat. She swallowed it down. Not yet, she thought. Not yet. And then, a familiar pull and tug began somewhere deep inside, twisting and wrenching like a live thing. Sometime, somewhere, she was bound to see Indians; she was heading into Indian country. What then? They wouldn't be the ones who'd buried an ax in Papa's skull all those years before and changed her life forever, but still they would be Indians.

Mama always said that hatred ate away at your own insides making us poor imitations of what we might otherwise become. But it was impossible for her not to feel violently about Indians after what they'd done to Papa. Her hatred was a stone in her stomach that had hardened to iron over the years. I'm sorry, Mama, she thought, but I just can't be forgiving like the Bible says. I can't.

She sighed and put the troublesome thoughts from her. It was an old battle and not one that she was likely to solve with a weary body and brain. It was enough, for the moment, to know that the first leg of her journey was at an end. She stood at the edge of the Ohio River, swaying with fatigue, and sent a fervent prayer of thanks heavenward. She was here. Now she only had to wait for Clark and his flatboats, and somehow talk her way aboard.

In the distance, across the river, lay a low mountain ridge. It's no different than home, she thought. Gentle hills to rest the eyes. The air hung in heavy blue drifts across the valleys and an occasional pine tree thrust upward like a finger into the cloudless sky. Verity knew a moment of pure contentment. For the space of a heartbeat she basked in a sense of perfection, of unity between earth and sky and herself. She smiled.

And then, "Whatever it is I'm doing, it must be right. My luck keeps on getting better and better."

She recognized the cheerful voice even before she turned. It was the man in buckskins, the man with a funny little dent in his chin, standing at the edge of that silly creek as if he owned the world. Somehow, she wasn't surprised.

~ * ~

As a matter of fact, Trey wasn't surprised either. He'd planned this encounter with all the deadly accuracy of a diamondback rattler drawing bead on a mouse, and at the same time quarreling with himself about the why of it.

He'd been the length and breadth of Albemarle County, staying well away from Williamsburg, not raising the promise of one sure-God positive recruit and only fifteen maybes. No one was willing to leave their land and loved ones unprotected to fight Indians on a vague plain hundreds of miles away. Even the promise of free land couldn't move them with the threat of the British army rampaging at their own front gate any day now.

Trey had stood on stumps in villages expounding the cause, he'd pleaded in doorways stating Clark's need and he'd raised patriotic sensibilities over a hundred square miles. He'd even hailed a cabin from the limbs of a sycamore where he'd been forced to take refuge from a vicious dog. But, in all his ramblings, he could not forget the determined square of a pair of small shoulders as the young woman—good Lord, he didn't even know her name—as she ordered him out of her path in the fog-shrouded woods. *She* ordered *him* away. As big as a minute, she was, giving him orders with as much authority as General Clark, himself. Danged if she wasn't cute, though. Cute as a spotted pup. Although, and he grinned to himself, he might have to change his language some when he caught up to her again. She hadn't liked some of his best words.

Feeling the need of companionship he took aim on the nearest town of any size and altered course. He'd promised Homer to meet him somewhere in the county, in the spring. If he intended to catch Clark, it was time to make himself visible. By mutual consent he and Homer had connected up the summer they both hunted for Logan's station out in Kentucky. They worked well together. They took an Indian threat seriously, though without panic, and they reacted as one in a crisis, back to back, each instinctively coming to the same decision. Neither of them liked to be crowded.

No one had any idea how old Homer was. He'd never said. He complained of rheumatism, but as far as Trey could see it didn't hamper his movement any. Homer could tree a 'coon as quick as Trey could himself, and then shoot its eyes out before it had time to get scared. While he gave the physical appearance of being falling-down weak, he could outlast Trey on a trail. His long-distance vision rivaled that of a kid still wet behind the ears. His age was immaterial. So was the fact that Trey hadn't seen Homer since last fall. Homer would be in the general area they'd agreed on, and one of these days Trey would look up and see Homer coming toward him.

In the meantime, Trey told himself he had to get the girl out of his mind, but he couldn't stop thinking of her. It was dangerous, he knew. He couldn't afford, didn't even want, to dwell on the rebellious fiery sparkle in her eye, the determined set to her jaw, the assurance that she would get what she wanted from the misty morning, the stupid goat, and the mountain trail. He wished her back from wherever she came, out of Virginia, out of his life. But he couldn't wait to see her again. And therein lay madness. He knew it. His life was not planned around a woman, any woman. His future lay beneath the wide open and limitless sky, unencumbered by responsibility or feelings.

However, if she had connected up with the Dawsons, and he saw no other possibility, she would be waiting for Clark at Redstone along with them. Or failing that, she'd be with the movers somewhere along the Ohio waiting for Clark. In spite of himself he spent a long hour trying to remember what color her eyes had been as he slogged through a wet marsh, waded brush-filled bottom land and negotiated a roaring stream with banks so steep they blocked out the sun. His memory of her was so strong he nearly missed Homer in a crowded tavern at Rockford's Mill.

Trey stood swaying with fatigue, a drink in his hand, staring bleary-eyed at the opposite wall when a familiar slouched figure appeared at his shoulder.

"You find a nice friendly fire to sit beside somewhere's? And maybe a friendly widow to keep you company in front of it? I been waiting here a week."

Trey glanced at the leathery face and slate-gray eyes that missed nothing and the ghost of a smile began and faded. "No friendly fires, and if there were any widows around, you would have found them first. Can a man get something to eat around here?"

With a tired gesture he motioned to a girl in an apron. "Food," he said, bluntly. "At a table with a chair to sit on."

Homer let him eat in silence, patient and watchful. But the minute Trey leaned back, replete, he asked, "Now. What's going on up north? Them ya-hoos doing anything about winning this war?"

"France is still sympathetic to our cause and continues to send aid."

"How sympathetic?" Homer wanted to know. "They throwing in with us?"

"It's rumored that Burgoyne's loss at Saratoga might be what they need to make them do just that. King Louis is apparently ready to declare war on Great Britain, and Spain will probably follow France. Possibly Holland, too. The last word is that the King might sign a formal treaty of alliance any day now."

Homer grunted. "None too soon. It just might save our hind ends. What else? Gates and Arnold still at it?"

Trey frowned. "If you know so much about this, why are you asking me?"

"Because your information comes from the horse's mouth. Mine comes from twice-told stories and guesswork."

Trey drained his cup and thumped it down on the table. "General Gates is a Virginian and his troops trust him. Last year he helped run the British out of New York before he took command of the northern army. The troops like Gates." Trey hesitated.

"Well, go on."

"I'm not sure all that faith is well founded. Gates is jealous of General Arnold. In Gate's battle reports to Congress, he doesn't even mention Benedict Arnold, and Arnold is a brilliant general. Gates is a braggart and a glory seeker." He shrugged. "You asked, that's my opinion."

Homer sighed. "From what I hear, Saratoga was a good fight. Sorry to have missed it. When we heading back?"

"As soon as you can get your old bones together," Trey said, knowing as he spoke that it was his own bones that needed rest, not Homer's. "I have a few things to do here, first. See if I can raise any men for the army. And then we can go. And we'll be traveling fast. Clark's probably already on his way down river."

Three days later they started back, Trey's mission completed. Signs of spring were popping everywhere he looked and the night wind no longer had a cutting edge. Since he had no way of knowing for sure when Clark would depart from Redstone, there wasn't any time to waste if he was to catch him coming down the Ohio. He wondered if the Dawsons made it to Redstone. They'd been cutting it pretty fine when he saw them.

If they hadn't, if they'd foundered somewhere along the way, it was no problem of his. He'd given them all the help he could that morning. Of course, he hadn't known at the time the girl would be traveling with them.

And there his thoughts took off in another direction. She'd lied to him about meeting up with friends. If there had been any plan of waiting for her, the Dawsons would have told him, Trey was sure of it. He'd spent a very thorough hour with them and he'd bet his only cloak that they had no idea they were being followed. Why? What was she so anxious to get away from?

He awakened in the morning thinking that her eyes had been setting off enough sparks to start a forest fire and how she'd stood up to him with that little chin stuck out, defying him. Her hair had looked like a pelt of prime beaver, sleek and shiny with moisture. And her backside as she walked away… He grunted and sat up to check the priming of his gun. In one long, fluid motion, he was on his feet. He had no time for such meanderings. Clark would have his head impaled on a stick if he failed to meet the flatboats at the appointed time.

He punished himself and Homer cruelly on that northerly trek. Swore at his body that wouldn't let him run all day and demanded rest at night, railed at his eyes for not being sharp enough to pick up every sign, and shouted aloud at both the stones and Homer when he missed a trail and put himself five miles out of his way.

He picked up the Dawson's sign at the camp beside the Little Canhawa and followed it like a highway. He knew, from the length of stride and depth of imprint, that it was Abner who'd taken off toward Redstone at the disaster spot. The wreckage of the cart told him why the party had separated like this. The signs even showed him, with a surprising jolt to his midsection, that Verity was indeed traveling with them, and guessed their destination. No, Trey was not surprised to find them barely ahead of him on the bank of the Ohio. He was, however, surprised at his own greeting.

"Whatever it is I'm doing, it must be right. My luck keeps on getting better and better."

But for an instant, surprising him even more, he saw a flash of answering delight in her eyes.

He realized with a shock that he'd hoped all along her eyes would be brown. They were. The color of young walnut bark in the spring. And they seemed to set easy with his own when their gaze met.

And he knew with sudden dismay that the knowledge was not going to bring him any comfort.

Four

With nightfall, a sharp wind drove up river from the southwest. The fire shot sparks high into the air to whirl and eddy brightly before dying in a falling arc against the black sky. The river, which had been such a welcome sight earlier in the day, now sounded alien and angry in the dark.

Sally snuggled drowsily in Verity's lap, and she pulled the blanket tighter around both herself and the child. Earlier, she had bathed them both in the creek and felt wonderfully clean and snug in the heat from the fire. They sat on a rounded log Captain Owens had placed there for them.

Verity had watched while he cast an eye around the edging of trees and made his selection. He braced himself, lifted a section of fallen trunk that would have made another man spraddle-legged with the weight, and then walked to the fire and placed it just so. There was a queer tightening in her chest when he indicated that she was to sit on the log where the heat would drive back the cold night air. He had not looked at her again.

Verity, however, had most certainly looked at him. He appeared to have already fought the war. He wore a dirty, blood-stained rag wrapped loosely around his head and no one yet, had asked him why. His buckskins showed hard wear and some of the fringes were gone completely. His moccasins were molded to his big feet with constant wetting and drying and wetting again.

And there was an ugly bruise on his left cheek. So far, he had ignored his battered condition as if it didn't exist and seemed to be content to answer questions.

Bart and Clem listened to the captain with the concentration of men hungry for vital information. Verity, too, hung on his every word. In an odd way, her heart tripped with excitement and a curious sort of breathlessness hampered her breathing. It was as if she was waiting for something to happen. The scent of burning pine and the restless rushing sound of the river, combined with the snap and crackle of the fire, seemed to fill the night with nerve-tingling expectancy. When Captain Owens turned his head and his gaze fell full on Verity a kind of stunned bewilderment seemed to take hold of her. For a fleeting second she knew an almost overwhelming desire to move closer, to take his battered face in her hands and smooth away the bruise and explore the bandage. He looked so tired she wanted to lay his head in her lap, like Sally, and croon a lullaby. And then a log snapped with a loud crack and the fire settled with much hissing and sizzling, and the spell was broken. Bart hawked and spat into the fire and the captain averted his eyes. The night was the same as it had been earlier, but Verity felt suddenly empty and alone.

Clem turned his face to one side and blew his nose between two fingers. His voice was loud in the circle of firelight. "What makes you so all-fired sure Clark's not already gone down river, and we missed him?"

Using his knife, the captain cut a four inch section from the butt of a hickory stick. "Because he would have left me a sign instead of letting me cool my heels here, waiting."

"What kind of sign?" This from Gideon, his tiredness and boredom gone with the appearance of this experienced woodsman and Indian fighter. "And how'd you know it was for you?"

Captain Owens cut a fine line around one end of the stick and began to work the bark loose, slipping it off the long end before he leveled a hard look at the boy. "I'd know," he said simply, and Verity understood that those piercing dark eyes of his had missed nothing before the light faded and hid their surroundings from view.

Gideon shrank back on his heels, chastised, but the captain did not appear to notice. "Hickory always makes the best whistle, in my opinion. What do you think?" he asked the boy.

Unused to having his thoughts gather notice, Gideon cut his eyes toward his father. "I—uh—sure."

Clem was not interested in the merits of hickory versus other hard woods, or whistles of any kind. He made an impatient motion. "How many's comin' with Clark to fight and how many to settle?"

Captain Owens cut a V shaped notch in one end of the stick and smoothed out the rough edge with a whittling stroke. "Clark is bringing at least three hundred men with him. And he expects Captain William Bailey Smith to meet him at the mouth of the Kentucky River with two hundred Holston Valley volunteers. After last summer, everyone in Kentucky agrees Hamilton has to be stopped."

A curl of chilly air made its way inside the folds of the blanket and Verity drew the wool closer. She had heard all the stories. How the British general, Hamilton, or Hairbuyer, as he was becoming known, launched raid after gruesome raid on the isolated Kentucky stockades. There wasn't a family who hadn't paid a fearsome price for the effort of pushing west.

Bart shoved a log further into the fire. "Old Hairbuyer's dug in good in the Illinois country, ain't he? We hear he's still leadin' them Indians from the Kaskaskia outpost."

Captain Owens nodded. "And Cahokia. And Vincennes. They are all supplied and organized out of Detroit, however. It's going to take a unified campaign against the British headquarters there to finish this thing off."

Verity straightened. Kaskaskia was where Joe was. According to this man, Kaskaskia was an enemy camp. Her voice was sharp, disapproving. "Captain, it seems to me that Clark would do better to spread his troops around and protect the settlers rather than lead them straight into Indian territory."

The captain glanced up from the stick he was shaping. His voice was smooth as autumn smoke, confident and out in the open for all to hear. "The name is Trey. Trey Owens, and I happen to agree with Clark that the only effective protection is a strong offense. Indians have no respect for men hiding behind their women's skirts in a stockade post, waiting to be attacked. If we can clean out the den where they live, it will be a telling blow."

"What makes you think Clark can do it?" Verity challenged, ignoring Clem's glaring command to silence and the captain's proffered use of his first name. "Others have failed."

His voice was soft. "They weren't Clark." He didn't move, didn't blink, but Verity had the feeling that everyone around the fire had stopped breathing as he went on. "Clark is young, only twenty-five, but he's good. He thinks like an Indian. He's been up and down the Ohio scouting out information and fighting Indians for five years, and if anyone knows Indians, he does. His men also know that, and they would follow him into hell and out the other side without a question."

He paused and slipped the bark sheath back on the whistle and presented it to Gideon. "Try it out," he said before his eyes came back to Verity. "He also has the element of surprise on his side. We have two spies living in Kaskaskia, men posing as Frenchmen, and they report regularly. This bold kind of offensive is the last thing Hamilton would expect."

Two men posing as Frenchmen? Verity's interest quickened. Joe and Edward spoke French fluently. She and Joe had learned from their mother and tormented Edward with speaking in the foreign tongue, until he picked up enough to catch their meaning. By the time they were all half-grown they could chatter in French among themselves, as well as they could speak English. This proved to be a satisfying annoyance to her step-father and his wife. Joe and Edward were Clark's spies in Kaskaskia. She was sure of it.

Captain Owens hadn't said, however, that he knew Joe, only that he was there, but it had to be the two boys. It all fit. Maybe the captain didn't always tell everything he knew.

His face was lit now from below, by the guttering fire highlighting his cheekbones and softening his features. Verity found herself wondering where he came from and why he happened to be here in the middle of the wilderness on this chilly April night. He spoke like an educated man, and watching the way he moved, with an effortless ease, she knew there was good breeding and training somewhere in his background. His shoulder-length hair was tied back with a leather thong, and from its glistening wetness she felt sure he'd cleaned himself in the river before coming to the fire. His bruises and the bloodied rag around his head stood out starkly against the sun-darkened skin of his face. He also appeared to be genuinely interested in Gideon's first whispy notes from the whistle.

"Curl your tongue," he advised. "And think the note in your head. You'll get it."

What kind of man hefted a log as he had earlier, to lay near the warmth of the fire for her to sit on, and was also gentle with children? She wasn't used to having things done for her comfort. It left her feeling edgy, jumpy, somehow.

She wished she could remember more of her own papa. The Indians had killed him, leaving her solemn and old before her time. She no longer expected thoughtfulness from men. For years she'd thought her papa had been one of a kind. In the quiet of night, she could remember the hard feel of his body as he cradled her in the crook of his arm and the rumble of his voice deep in the cavity of his chest as he called her his little sweetling. Joe said papa had been a gentle and fun-loving man. But he had died, and Joe had grown up and left her to cope on her own with the man Ma married. Edward had even gone with him, abandoning her to the likes of Old Man Hargraves. Long ago she'd decided that it didn't do to trust a man. When it suited their purpose, they picked up and left. A woman couldn't do that and was always left alone with no one to depend on except herself. Men were invariably a disappointment.

Bart hawked and spat again. "You didn't say how many families," he reminded Trey.

The big man leaned forward with his elbows on his knees. "Hopefully, thirty-five to forty. That many are needed for safety's sake. Any more would be a bonus."

Clem nodded thoughtfully. "That's skinnin' it on the shy side, but I reckon forty'd do it."

Bart asked, "How many guns?"

"A number of the men claim to have sons old enough to carry a weapon. At least Gideon's age and older. We're hoping for a sizable count."

"How many recruits did you raise?"

"Not many," Trey admitted. "Fifteen at the most. We'll know when they show up down river aways." He glanced at Homer sitting quietly, well back in the shadows. The corners of his mouth twitched in an almost-smile. "One for sure. Arthritic and old and mean as a Seneca medicine man, but loyal."

Homer opened his mouth for the first time. He spoke slowly, with studied ease. "And a dead shot."

Verity saw the way the captain's eyes softened in spite of his words when he spoke of his friend and the deepening creases around his mouth when Homer answered. He loved this man, she realized. This insulting banter was the only way acceptable of showing affection between men when their lives depended upon quick-thinking, and nerves were tight as whang leather.

Silence sat on the circle around the fire while Bart and Clem chewed on this information.

Finally Gideon raised a tentative voice. "Captain Owens, you ever killed a sure 'nough Indian?"

"I have," the Captain answered slowly. "And it's the same as killing any other man. Where you're going, you stand a chance of running into a good many Indians, and you don't ever want to forget that they're human. They're men the same as your pa and your uncle and me. Some are meaner than snakes and some are cowards, but the bravest man I ever met was the son of an Iroquois chief and I'm proud to call him my friend."

Verity's head shot up. The marvelous captain about whom she'd allowed herself to think kind thoughts spoke in defense of the red man. Sudden anger clogged her throat, so thick she could hardly breathe. The scene in the clearing ten years ago sprang into her mind with all the clarity of a mid-day sun and she heard the screams, smelled the bear grease, felt a violent trembling jerk her erect. Her lips flattened in distaste.

"An Indian-lover," she said, her voice as hard as her heart. Her lips grimaced in disgust.

Startled, Trey looked up. Her dark eyes were slitted with emotion so intense he could almost hear the vibration humming. He thought of a slingshot whirling around and around before being released. Her face was contorted. What had he said, he wondered, to set her off like that? That Indians were human?

"He was a man," he said simply. "And the blood he shed in my defense was as red as my own."

"What a pity you both lived to tell the tale."

The echo of her ugly words seemed to ring in the quiet of the night forest while Verity and Trey stared at each other as if there was no one else around the fire.

Finally, Homer cleared his throat. "I was about to ask would you take a look at that head of his. It might need pulling together some."

Between clenched teeth Trey said, "My head will do just fine without Miss Philp's healing touch."

"What did he do?" Verity mocked, never taking her eyes from his face. "Stub his toe and fall down?"

Trey spared Homer an angry glance, remembering the desperate way they'd covered ground to get here, and suddenly knew the real reason behind the hurry. A wild pig could have taken one look at himself and Verity and seen what was happening. The curious thing was that it wasn't of his wanting. For the first time in his life, his mind was backing away from a woman while his body seemed to go forward of its own accord.

"You might say he fell down," Homer said, a smile playing around the corners of his mouth.

The memory bloomed strong in Trey's mind of that fog-filled morning yesterday when he had insisted they travel, even though they couldn't see the tips of their own moccasins and he knew Homer was remembering, too. In his wild casting around for a trail, Trey had plunged off the lip of the mountain, down a steep embankment toward a snarling river they could only hear far below, and brought up hard against a granite outcropping of rock. His head had been the only casualty. If Homer laughed, Trey thought, he just might take a shot at knocking him flat. The girl was nothing to him. He'd make sure of that if he had to half-drown himself in the icy river trying not to think of her.

Verity forced her mind to clear. She needed Captain Owens. Besides, who knew when Clark and his army might come down river? It might be as soon as tomorrow morning, and it wouldn't do to alienate the man when she had use of him.

In addition, there was the weight of her own glaring hatred. As long as she lived, Verity's mother had counseled forgiveness of the Indians who killed her husband and babies. "They don't know any better," she had said. "Carrying a hate around only destroys the one who hates. Cut it out of your heart, Verity dear, and go on."

But learning to forgive the Indians was obviously a battle Verity still waged. "*Mama*," she thought with despair in her heart, "*I'm never going to be what you wanted.*" Her mouth sometimes seemed to have a mind all its own and she spoke before she knew what would come out. She'd never be a true lady, and she'd never forgive the Indians for destroying her family and her life.

Deliberately she drew a long breath. There was already water hot on the fire. Verity rose with the limp Sally in her arms. "I'll take care of the captain's head as soon as I settle the child."

Trey rose, too. "Maybe you didn't hear me. I said I don't need your attention. I'm fine."

She lifted one eyebrow. "Are you afraid it might hurt, Captain? Gideon doesn't cry when I patch him up."

There was a taut silence and when he spoke steel hummed in his voice. "Get what you need and be quick about it."

With fingers that were something less than tender she unwound the soiled bandage and cast it into the fire. The blood was clotted and caked over the area, and when she finally got the wound washed clean her fingers gentled of their own accord. It was deep and Homer had been right. A few stitches were needed.

The light of the fire was not bright enough to see clearly and of necessity Verity had to lean close. The scent of body-warmed buckskins rising from him stirred something in her mid-section that she hadn't known was there until this very moment.

She tried, unsuccessfully, to ignore his face upturned to hers as she worked. His breath fanned in rhythmic regularity across her mouth and when that rhythm altered raggedly she was acutely aware that he felt the same rising sensations that confused her.

Slowly she allowed her gaze to lower around a curled ear, across the strong plane of his cheek now dark with a day-old bruise. A rough stubble of beard told her that he'd shaved that morning. His nostrils dilated as he, unexpectedly, heaved in a hefty lungful of air. And his eyes. She looked full into his eyes and felt a strange, compelling pull. His irises were darker even than her own and she could see the reflection of the flickering flames behind them leap in the blackness. His mouth had softened into the beginning of a smile and her hands fell idle on his head feeling the soft spring of his hair beneath her palms. She'd never thought of a man as beautiful, but he was.

She could feel the heat of his body along the full length of her own as she stood beside his knee and was so absorbed in feeling that she forgot to think. Blood thrummed through her entire body. Her mind was blank.

Then, as if he were climbing a steep hill, she could see him pulling himself back to reality. "Are you going to sew me up or let me bleed all the way to Illinois?" he asked softly, his eyes thoughtful on hers.

Illinois. Indians. Iroquois. His words rubbed the raw place in her heart that had never healed. "I'd sew," she said, taking refuge in her pain, "but I'm not sure we have enough men here to hold you down."

His eyes hardened. "You just sew. I'll sit tight all by myself, if you don't mind."

He didn't flinch when she laid down six neat stitches at the edge of his hairline and applied some herbal mixture Zelma said was good for this sort of thing. Without looking him in the eye again, Verity wound a clean bandage around his head.

"Done," she said, as impersonally as a crow landing on the back of a cow. "Now, I have things to do before I can sleep."

Quickly, she checked the sleeping children and Zelma, and rolled in her own blanket. She refused to let herself think about the captain. Instead, she worried about Zelma. Zelma didn't seem to worsen exactly, but she simply faded a bit with each passing day. There was a real possibility the woman would die. It happened all the time, but Verity vowed Zelma wouldn't go without a fight. She wished for comfrey to brew a tea. Brewing a strengthening tea would, at least, be something to do. She didn't like being helpless and vulnerable—the thought shot into her mind like a bullet—like she'd felt with a hand on either side of the captain's face. No. Not helpless, ever again. Captain or no captain.

She didn't want to think of those strange trance-like minutes by the fire while cleaning his wound. She felt almost as if she'd betrayed her father by letting herself be taken in by the deep, dark eyes and the woodsy, heady smell of the man. He was an Indian lover! She'd seen the evidence of Indian cruelty with her own eyes. Evidence she wasn't about to forget. However, he was her key to Clark. And Clark was definitely traveling down the Ohio, where they waited. The captain himself had said so. Clark was set on a course for Kaskaskia—and Joe.

And, of course, Edward, her intended. He was there, too. The only thing was, somehow her memory of Edward slid into the background beside the living, breathing presence of the captain. She couldn't think why this was so. She barely knew the man, and didn't like what she did know. But, something about him drew her thoughts as strongly as bees to honey. Some day soon she would have the time to sit down and think all of this through, but right now she was too tired to think clearly.

Her mouth curved in a private little smile. Joe and Edward had been getting her out of scrapes as long as she could remember. When Edward left with Joe, she was still holding him at arm's length although they had been assuming marriage since they were children.

Her smile dimmed. The captain was harder to hold away. He seemed to infiltrate the toughest shell she could wrap around herself. Heavens, she had been dreadfully rude to him tonight, yet she wouldn't take back a word of their exchange.

And then there was everything else. She didn't know what to do about the nervous stomach that seemed to develop whenever she was near Bart. She didn't dare take her eyes off Sally. The child seemed to live in a happy haze and could wander off within the blink of an eye. Zelma wasn't getting any better, and Clem was impatient with her to do something, anything, to make his wife well.

Her shoulders ached with the weight of responsibility. She had a feeling she wasn't doing very well in handling it all. Wearily, she closed her eyes to the canopy of stars deep in the black of the sky, and as tired as she was, knew she would do far more to get to Kaskaskia. She would do whatever it took.

~ * ~

In the days they waited for the flotilla of flatboats to appear, Verity washed all their clothes in Fat Meat Creek, helped slice and jerk the deer meat Captain Owens brought in, cooked a stew and coaxed Zelma to eat a few bites. She gathered more sweet moss with which to line the baby's blankets, repeatedly milked the goat, thinned the milk and offered the baby the end of a blanket soaked in the liquid, and when she had time to think, nattered frantically in the back of her mind the fact that neither the baby nor Zelma was thriving.

Stubbornly, she refused to allow her heart to soften toward the captain even when the next evening he made Sally an odd little creature which he called a mouse, from a square piece of rag. He spent a few minutes rolling and folding and patting it smooth, and then with a flick of both wrists he seemed to turn the thing wrong-side-out and before Sally could even jump he had the chubby figure resting in the curve of his arm looking for all the world like a mouse with head, humped body and tail.

Sally squealed in pretend fear when he made it wriggle and leap from his arm to hers, but she played with it happily until Bart snatched it out of the air and jerked on the tail making the rest of the body collapse. He threw the rag on the ground and the smile left Sally's face.

"It's gone," she said, her eyes brimming. "You made it all gone."

Trey did not look at Bart. He picked up the cloth and said softly, "I'll fix it. I'll make you another one."

Bart's voice was harsh. "Filling youngin's heads with silliness. Ain't no time to be coddling 'em. Need all their brains to stay alive." His uncaring brutality in destroying the magic Trey had created for the child in the midst of this forbidding wilderness left Verity stunned.

Trey held out his hand to Sally, but she turned away. "It was just a ol' rag, anyways," she said, her voice flat, and went to find her blanket.

Bart left the fire, too, stumbling clumsily and narrowly missing Verity's feet. Trey's eyes followed him into the dark and the hard, unblinking stare sent a shiver up Verity's back. At that moment she doubted Trey's nature was any more forgiving than her own. Soon she, too, went to her blanket.

She was cleaning plates at the creek the next morning when Captain Owens appeared at her elbow. Automatically she glanced at the stitches on his forehead. The wound was healing nicely. His jaw was yellowing out, the bruise not quite so prominent.

He took a plate from her and began to scrape it with sand. “You know, don’t you, that the mother and child aren’t going to make it.” It was a statement, not a fact.

Verity looked up, suddenly defensive. “I know nothing of the kind, Captain Owens. Of course, they’ll make it.”

The lines around Trey’s mouth softened. Those eyes again, he thought. Just like on the forest trail. Warning him off. Telling what would happen and what she would and would not permit. Tiny gold flecks danced in the brown when she lifted her lashes. It seemed as if every time their eyes met and held, there were sparks of some kind. That first morning she’d been wary, determined, ready to do battle. Now she was fiercely protective.

Something inside him turned over. How old was she? She was working so damned hard trying to make it all come out right, but she didn’t know yet that life wasn’t easily molded. She was going to be hurt. Just now she was peering up at him, earnestly trying to prove her point. He wanted…good Lord, he wanted to take care of her. He wanted to make sure she didn’t get hurt.

In an unconscious gesture his head drew back to gaze unseeing at the tops of the trees. What was he doing? He didn’t want attachments. Attachments tied you down, cramped your thinking. What was the matter with him, anyway? A yearning came from somewhere deep inside him to reach out to her. To touch that shining beaver-brown hair of hers. To look down, from close up, into those warm, dark, determined eyes that stayed with him night and day. To run a hand down an arm with silky-smooth skin browned from the sun, and stretched over small bones and firm muscles. She’d fit, he bet, right beneath his armpit—

Damn! He clamped down on the feeling before it went any farther. The path down that trail was dangerous. It would be so easy to allow her to become his responsibility, hell, he was already halfway there. He hadn't intended this. Not responsibility, caring.

"Clem says you're going west to find your brother and another man you're promised to."

"That's right. I've been pledged for years and years."

"That long, huh?" A smile tugged at the corners of his mouth. "Do you really expect to find two men in the wilderness?"

"I do." Her voice was stubbornly determined.

"You've got guts, lady. I'll give you that. Have you any idea how small your chances are?"

"Will it be so hard?" For some reason she didn't want to tell him she thought they were waiting at Kaskaskia as Clark's spies.

He shook his head. "Things change in the wilderness without warning. How do you know they're still alive?"

"Of course they're alive." Her eyes were shooting sparks again.

"And for that matter, how do you know the folks you're traveling with will make it that far? You'll have to bury the woman and the baby somewhere along the way." Brutal as it may be, she had to know where the dangers lay.

"All Zelma needs is rest." In her effort to convince him, her eyes gathered at the corners in an endearing way and he swallowed down the urge to let her think what she wanted. Not to worry her before it had to be. But he believed strongly that it was always better to know, in advance, what you were dealing with. Whether or not she wanted to, whether or not he wanted to make her, she had to face facts.

He hardened his voice. "You must realize, that woman will never withstand the rigors of river travel, to say nothing of living conditions at the stockade once we get there." And, in a softer tone, he added, "And, the name is Trey."

Her eyes narrowed. "I am not a quitter, *Captain Owens.* All I need is a wet nurse for the baby, and hopefully there'll be one on board the flatboats when they come, and a few medicines, some comfrey, herbs…"

He shook his head. "Your determination is commendable, but your common sense is lacking. There isn't enough medicine in this whole country to cure what ails that woman. She's tired, too tired to live. Can't you see that?"

"No!" she blazed.

He shrugged. "Think what you like. I just wanted you to be prepared. And," he hesitated, then amid a confused jumble of conflicting half-thoughts his words seemed to rush forward. "It's hard on the frontier, alone. Clem will need help with the children when the time comes, and you could do worse. Give some thought to throwing in with him. He'll take care of you."

Her horrified look mirrored his own astonishment. He couldn't have been more surprised if he'd stuck his foot in a nest of copperhead snakes. Why had he said that? He wasn't sure he liked the idea of Clem taking care of her. Somebody had to pay attention to what she was doing, he'd already admitted that, but Clem? His breath seemed to clog up his breathing apparatus, but he plunged on.

"Clem is as good as anyone. At least you wouldn't go hungry." And, of course, that which he wouldn't even put into coherent thought: he wouldn't have to worry about her himself. He could relax.

Before he had time to examine the stunned emptiness spreading in his gut, she was on her feet and spitting. "Who gave you the right to tell me what to do? I can take care of myself, thank you, and I don't need any—any Indian lover!—to make decisions for me. From now on, keep your advice to yourself or share it with someone who is interested. Because I certainly am not!"

"And furthermore," she went on when he would have interrupted, "I'm surprised you aren't on the side of the British since you love the Indians so much!"

"Look, lady, I don't understand about you and the Indians, but you must know we aren't any different than the British. Two years ago Congress authorized General Washington to use the Indians in any way he saw fit, and that meant to kill and plunder and pillage their villages. Entire villages, not just men of fighting age. Do you understand what that means? Women and children, too. They even offered a reward for enemy officers and men taken prisoner. So, back off your almighty high horse. We're no better than they are."

She stared at him for a long moment with her eyes widening. "No," she said, but it was without conviction. "They wouldn't."

"They would and they did," he answered firmly.

Clearly she was rattled. He watched her make the effort to pull herself together. "That's still not buying scalps like Hamilton. And it's not standing up for Indians who murder and torture and—and rape and kill babies."

With horror he saw that her eyes flooded with tears. Angrily she dashed them away with the back of one hand. "Nobody decent would be friends with an Indian. Nobody," and she pierced him with a rapier glance, "except vermin!" He looked at her with flat, unreadable eyes and Verity thought wildly, *He doesn't hear me. He doesn't even hear me.*

But Trey heard her. He stood like a pole-axed steer. *Why did I follow her down here to the creek*, he wondered. Because those narrow shoulders of hers looked too frail to carry the burden he knew was coming? Nonsense. Whatever made him think she needed protecting? Frail? Bah! She was frail like a dueling sword. Because of beaver-brown hair and eyes that were full of grit and determination? And there he hit pay dirt, for he admitted the possibility. No, be honest. The probability. He was attracted, certainly, no male with red blood in his veins could fail to be, but he couldn't afford to be encumbered with a female no matter how his gut responded to her. She was a luxury he couldn't pursue at the moment.

And, no matter her opinions on Indians and Indian lovers, the fact was she couldn't make it on the river, or at a frontier station, alone. And Clem would be handy soon. If not him, then one of the other boys. Trey nodded without knowing he did so. Clem or one of the boys. She'd be taken care of. He'd just have to swallow down the squirrely niggle in the pit of his stomach. She was not his responsibility.

He nodded again and had turned to go up the bank when a shout came from the river. It was Gideon, his voice shrill with excitement. "It's them. The flat boats are coming. Clark and his army are here."

Five

An hour and a half later Trey waited beside General Clark as chaos settled into mere confusion. The general, his red hair identifying him at once as belonging to the famous Clark family of Virginia, watched his men help the Dawsons make a place for themselves aboard one of the flatboats.

Men shouted to one another, dogs barked, babies cried and mothers called to their children running wildly in joyous freedom on dry land. The goat bleated in frantic cries and jerked on the rope, getting in everyone's way.

"One of you men," Clark shouted above the din, gesturing with one hand toward the string of large floating platforms, "take charge of that jerky. Put it where it won't get wet."

Without turning his head, his attention shifted to Trey. "I don't deny that jerky will come in handy, with one hundred and thirty men and twenty families to feed. Are you bucking for a raise?"

Trey smiled. Everyone knew Tories got paid in regular hard coin, but the patriots, Clark and his army, were paid in paper money that was virtually useless. The man was laughing though he must be cruelly disappointed in less than half the force he'd expected to accompany him. However, he showed no dismay, neither with the smaller numbers of his tattered army, nor in the scant twenty families joining him. He fairly exuded energy and confidence.

Trey raised his voice. "The meat isn't the best. Mostly stringy and tough at the end of winter."

Clark shouted above the racket. "It will do for jerky. We won't have to stop so often to hunt."

He turned to look up river. "Marvelous land here." Ignoring the confusion around him, he inclined his head toward the far side of the river. "Well-watered bottoms, even if they are a trifle narrow."

Through the milling crowd Trey could see Verity, her arms already full, struggling toward the water with the goat. The frightened creature didn't want any part of the rocking deck of the boat and was giving her a bad time. Bart elbowed his way toward her, but instead of helping he shoved a basket toward her hands, adding to her burden. When she made no move to shift her load and take it, he merely slid the handle over one of her arms. He stood for a full minute watching her uneven progress toward the boat, a half-smile on his face.

For Trey, the zest suddenly went out of the morning. Bart? There had been a vague sense of familiarity in both the gesture and his smile. In his mind, Trey had labeled him the Dumb Ox that first morning by the river. Bart rarely had much to say, but kept busy doing all the heavier work toward getting ready to take to the trail. It was obvious the family depended on him for a strong back whenever needed, but Trey doubted much happened above the man's eyebrows.

The casual attitude of his handing Verity a basket laden with goods to take aboard, galled Trey. The action seemed to make assumptions. It was a homey, somehow intimate gesture, and Trey frowned. But then, it wasn't his affair. None of it was any of his business, was it? However, it was no wonder Verity jumped on him like a duck on a dragonfly when he'd suggested she throw in her lot with Clem. Bart was younger and not encumbered with three children, as was Clem, and he'd certainly not insult her with a lot of conversation she didn't want to hear as he, himself, had done. How she must have laughed when he suggested Clem.

He realized Clark was looking at him expectantly, waiting for an answer to some question he'd not heard. "I'm sorry. What did you say?"

"I asked how many volunteers you recruited down country."

"Only fifteen men agreed to even think about it. And they aren't enthusiastic. Those who come will meet us down river. Everyone is feeling the need to stay home and put in their crops and then too, they're all worried about when the war here along the seaboard will arrive on their own doorstep."

Clark pursed his lips and tilted his head back to look at the sky. "We have to stop Hamilton. It's time. We can't wait."

Trey waited sympathetically for a few minutes and then changed the subject. "How has the trip been so far? High water?"

"High and fast. We're riding the tail of the spring flood. That's why we're in such a hurry. Don't want to lose our advantage."

Trey glanced in the direction of an ear-splitting skirmish aboard one of the boats. A pig was somehow loose from its pen and three little boys chased the confused animal around barrels and through legs. Their screams, and the goat fighting at the end of its tether and jostling the pig, only added to the animal's hysteria. Verity had the goat aboard, he noticed. He was aware now that one of the things she carried was the baby, crying with more energy than he'd thought possible. One of the women came to help her, reaching out for the child. Verity's face was red with exertion and her hair was in tumbled disarray. Actually, Trey liked her this way better than when she wore her hair carefully pulled back. She looked more approachable. Less apt to bite off his head.

Clark's eyes suddenly stopped on Verity. "You! girl!" he called. Verity turned. "You are creating a God-awful ruckus with that goat. I assume you need the animal for your baby, but you'd better keep it out from underfoot and tied securely. I won't tolerate any more upheaval than is strictly necessary."

Verity looked startled and for a second, frightened. Trey realized Clark was holding her responsible for the uproar with the pig, the goat and the baby, and between all of them he could possibly guess at what all else might go wrong in the coming days. The worst of it was that Clark didn't know yet that she had no husband. That would create an additional problem. An unattached female was a burden for the whole party. Maybe he could smooth her path a little.

He said softly, "The baby belongs to the Dawsons. The mother needs help and this girl has been kind enough to lend a hand."

"Well, speak to her and make sure she understands, will you? We have enough to contend with," Clark said.

Trey nodded. "I'll take care of it. Once we begin to move, things will settle down."

Clark agreed. "Beautiful trip, so far. Marvelous river."

"Indians?" Trey asked.

"Passed a Seneca village about thirty miles upriver but have yet to see our first redskin. Makes my skin crawl. We know they're out there." His roaming eyes fastened beyond the Ohio on the hills cutting a jagged line across the sky. His voice lowered as if talking to himself. "We aren't going unnoticed. You can be sure of that. And I can't help but wonder why."

He drew himself up to his full six feet and turned his gaze on Trey. "Captain, I want to be afloat and away from here in ten minutes. See to it."

~ * ~

Verity sat on the edge of the flatboat and dangled her toes in the chilly water. She splashed water up her legs and arms and dabbed at her face with her wet skirt tail. It was nearest to a wash she could manage.

The dawn had been glorious. An early morning mist trapped a quivering shaft of sunlight boring through the clouds and she caught her breath at the unexpected radiance glancing off the river. They had tied up mid-stream last night at a small island and roped the flatboats together for security. Only the night guards were stirring this early, moving sluggishly toward their blankets, and Verity thought she might have been the only one in the world given the awareness of this magical moment.

She smelled the heady fragrance of some early blooming spring flower, smiled at a flock of tiny dark birds vying for space on the same limb of a sprawling pin oak tree in full bud on the northern shore, and marveled at the delicacy of color dancing on the water. A buttery-yellow shimmer spread across the moving surface and faded into cream while she gazed, and an underlay of silver appeared that sparkled in the sunlight like stars in a noon-day sky. Beneath her, of course, was the muddy Ohio in full spate and running like a horse in a race to the death.

All this and she was free! She took a deep satisfying breath and held it. Free of Lena and Otis, free of Old Mr. Hargraves and free to look for Joe. And Edward, too, of course. She lifted her face to the sun. Her whole future was ahead. A whole new unconquered world with unlimited possibilities. She was as free as the river she could feel flowing beneath the flatboat. She firmed her jaw. Whatever needed to be done, she could do. And whatever she needed to learn, she could learn.

Yesterday afternoon they'd passed ten small islands, all sitting higher than the mainland. She'd heard Clark tell Captain Owens that he was mapping the country as they went through it, entering everything in his diary, along with the miles they covered each day. The general was pleased with the fifty miles total of yesterday, considering their stop to pick up the Dawson party.

Zelma had indeed been right. Abner made it to Redstone in time to catch Clark and had been aboard one of the flatboats when they arrived at Fat Meat Creek. For all their slovenliness, the Dawsons had an innate sense of woodsmanship that seemed to pull them through tight spots. She shuddered as she remembered Trey's comment that she could do worse than to throw her lot along side Clem's. The clod! He wasn't even clean. To her knowledge Clem had worn the same unwashed clothing from the moment she'd first seen him on the mountain trail. Clem indeed.

Bart was another matter. He was, at least, inclined to wash his face and hands occasionally. However he made her nervous. He seemed to have his head set singlemindedly on her. Every time she moved, his eyes followed her. He'd had all that time, making their way through the forest, to think, and as slowly as his mind worked she was sure it took every foot of the way. But, she'd observed that once his mind was made up there was no swaying him from the course he'd worked out. That seemed to include Verity. She frowned. It was becoming more and more difficult to ignore him. Every time she turned around, it seemed, she fell over him. She simply tried to stay out of his way.

On shore the pin oak seemed suddenly alive with birds, all of them taking to the air in the same startled second. The newly leafed lilacs and wild grapevine-covered bushes next to the water shook as if a strong wind blew through them and Verity wondered briefly what had caused the birds to take such sudden flight, and then smiled at her own foolishness. The birds were undoubtedly as full of the joy of the morning as she was herself.

She had leaned over the edge of the boat to wash her face in the river when she heard a voice behind her. "Draw some water in a bucket and let it settle. Otherwise you'll bathe in mud and still have a dirty face."

Verity stood up so fast she had to grab for a rope to steady herself. Trey Owens. Again. There he was, in the middle of a wilderness, looking immaculate, as if he'd just stepped from a tub of fresh water beside his mother's fire. Even his hair was combed back neatly and tied with a leather thong. His teeth gleamed white in his tanned face.

She stood before him rumpled from having slept in her dress, hair uncombed, and feeling thoroughly grubby. Her earlier mood was destroyed. However, bitter as it was to admit, what he said made sense. And she did have much to learn about river travel. The words came out stiff and aloof. "Thank you, Captain, I will do as you suggest."

His eyebrows raised in an unasked question, but she turned and was gone, ducking through hanging blankets, stacked barrels of plunder, baskets and chicken crates full of squawking, flapping hens.

She made her way to the little square space allotted to the Dawsons. Zelma's breath seemed, if possible, even more shallow than the night before. She seemed to sleep most of the time. The baby no longer bothered to cry. The poor thing was as skinny as a starving sparrow. Each little rib could be counted and its legs were so tiny Verity was almost afraid to pick it up for fear something would break. She'd had no luck so far in finding a wet nurse.

Verity tried to feed the child, but he showed no interest in suckling so she sat on an overturned bucket and sang to him, silly little no-nothing songs, until the child too slept.

There was no sign of the Dawson men, though their guns were propped against bags of plunder, and she assumed they'd joined the cluster of militia and movers rising now and lining up around the metal slab that served as a base for a fire, at the other end of the boat. Each carried his cup, ready for coffee from the big pot hanging over the blaze. The presence of the few militia, men obviously hardened to the rigors of battle and knowledgeable about Indian warfare, seemed to draw every male aboard. The settlers hung onto every word out of the mouths of the soldiers and then strutted around importantly, pretending they were part of Clark's master plan.

"Old Hairbuyer's going to get his, when we get there."

"Them Indians will run for their lives when they hear the Long Knives are on their way." Clark's men had earned the nickname of "Long Knives" and were known as such from Virginia to the Mississippi. The reason for the name brought a shudder to Verity from where she sat. The boasting continued.

"We don't need no forty families on Corn Island. Twenty's a plenty. We can take care of ourselves."

"Them redskins'd do better to stay home and help their squaws with the plantin' this summer than tanglin' with the likes of us."

They were like little boys transparently huffing and puffing up their own bag of courage. Gideon would probably be doing the same thing soon. Verity determined to call his attention to the soldiers, easy to spot in their home-spun linen, and surely he'd see that they did not have to brag. The militia men wore their deeds quietly in the presence of other men.

Others were beginning to awaken and a bustling busyness began to spread. Children sat up to rub gritty eyes, women carrying kettles picked their way towards the cooking fire, men stretched cramped muscles and kicked animals out of the way.

Verity felt a bubbling excitement build. She was another day closer to Joe. And Kaskaskia.

A canoe pulled alongside and three buckskin clad men climbed out. The night scouts. Their dawn duty, to make sure no Indians had concealed themselves overnight in the bushes beside the river, was completed, and now on the safety of the boat they slapped their friends on the back while exchanging cheerful obscenities. As they passed where she sat, Homer, Captain Owens' friend hesitated.

"Sleep good, Miss Verity?"

She looked up at him. "I did. And awakened to one of the most glorious mornings God ever created."

Homer nodded. "Yup. I reckon God took his hand out of his pocket and made this day 'specially for us." He moved on.

The morning was full of good-natured joshing, ribald comments about the loneliness of the night just spent and the tantalizing smell of boiling coffee. While Verity watched, Homer turned aside and spoke softly to Trey and they both glanced toward Verity. She turned her head. If they were talking about her she would not dignify it with her attention.

She could see the shoreline clearly from where she sat among the boxes and bedrolls. With the exception of a line of ragged bluffs in the east, wide grassy bottoms stretched between the water and the first rise of ground. She'd been a farmer's daughter too long not to recognize good farmland when she saw it.

Ahead of them the river ran straight as a die for as far as the eye could see, but ahead the hills began to close in. Verity eyed the north bank with interest. High bluffs, with the river flowing like a trough between them. It wasn't good. The flatboats would be sitting ducks for anyone atop the bluffs and intent on mischief. Would they see Indians finally? She swallowed against a queer niggling feeling in the pit of her stomach. Thanks to Joe's dogged determination she was a fairly good shot. For the first time she wished she had a gun.

"Don't go a borrowing trouble." Zelma's voice was no more than a tremulous whisper among the blankets. "What's going to happen is generally going to happen and worrying at it don't help none."

"I'm not worrying," Verity said quickly, stung that Zelma had read her expression so easily. "And you mustn't either. I'm taking care of everything." She eyed Zelma anxiously. She looked more weary and drawn than ever. "How are you feeling this morning?"

"Better," Zelma said and lapsed into a silence stretched so long Verity thought she had drifted off to sleep again. But, "Gideon? Sally?"

Verity glanced at Sally's tousled head half-buried in the blankets and then forward to the common cooking fire. A thick sheet of metal was bolted onto the deck and a fire pit built in the center. There must be twenty-five to thirty people on each boat, Verity guessed, and the women took turns at the fire twice a day unless they could safely tie up on shore to cook. Verity scanned the small clots of men.

"Sally is still asleep and Gideon must be with his pa. I ought to go and fix something for them to eat."

Zelma nodded. Her eyes closed.

But Gideon was not with Clem. Nor was he anywhere on the big, square floating platform everyone called a boat. Nowhere that Verity could find. And then, in some obscure pocket of thinking she remembered the birds flocking into the air from the pin oak tree and the disturbance among the bushes. She stared at the pin oak as if it could talk to her. Dear Lord, she thought, and it was a prayer. Surely he wouldn't go ashore alone. But she knew in her heart that he had. Gideon had met another boy yesterday afternoon and the two of them had asked permission to explore last evening. Clem refused and so did General Clark. It was too dangerous, two boys alone. One day soon, they were promised, they could go with the early scouts.

A swift and cold anger surged through Verity. It was a certainty in her mind that Gideon and his new friend had slipped off on their own.

Off to one side Bart stood leaning against a wall of the small cabin aboard the boat. For once she didn't mind his eyes following her everywhere, prying into what she was doing, even she sometimes thought, into what she was thinking. Maybe he'd talked to Gideon this morning. She crossed to him hurriedly.

"Have you seen Gideon?"

He gawked at her. "The boy?"

Of course, the boy, she thought in exasperation. Who else did he know named Gideon? "Yes, the boy."

He shook his head slowly. "Ain't he in his blankets?"

"No." Verity glanced around uncertainly. "I think he may have gone ashore."

Bart gave a negative jerk of his head. "Nah. He's somewheres about."

Verity shaded her eyes and swept the entire boat. He wasn't there. She turned again to Bart and found him watching her with the same expression he always wore. Watchful, unsmiling, dogged patience. Her own patience was worn thin.

"Why do you look at me like that?" she snapped.

He didn't bat an eye. "'Cause I like to."

"Well, I don't like it. Look at something else for a change."

"Why?"

"Because I don't like you always staring at me."

"Wal," he said, "I don't guess I can help what I like to look at."

Verity closed her eyes. Argument was useless. So was asking his help. Stifling a sharp retort Verity turned and made her way to the other end of the boat. All Clark needed was for one of her small charges, goat or child, to make trouble for him and he'd call her to task in a minute. She knew without it being spelled out that she was a burden to the party as a woman alone. She had no one to provide for her except her awkward connection with the Dawsons. She'd seen Clark's brooding eyes on her several times. Her position was tenuous, at least. Well, Gideon would not be allowed to get away with this. He was ashore and she knew it.

Without thinking twice, she reached for Clem's gun, hiked up her skirt between her legs, tucked it into her belt and slipped off the back end of the boat. She permitted herself one gasp as the cold water enveloped her and then struck out strongly with one arm for shore. She carried the gun high, out of the water, in the other arm.

It didn't occur to Verity to take a canoe. She would have had to ask permission for a canoe. Her only thought was to get Gideon back before General Clark missed him and held up the morning departure of the entire flotation of boats.

She emerged beneath the drooping branches of an ancient maple tree and stood for a moment to let the water run off her body. She listened intently, but there was no sound except the splat of droplets from her own wet skirt dripping onto the ground. She couldn't see beyond the green curtain of leaves. Her teeth were chattering and she shivered uncontrollably in the cool morning air, but she forced herself up the bank and hurriedly followed the river in a westerly direction until she came to the pin oak. Sure enough there were signs of a body having lain on ground soft from recent rains, signs clear enough for a child to read. Signs that said loud and clear that whoever it was had watched the boats for some time, accidentally startled an entire flock of birds into the air and then took off, again following the river.

Verity planted her feet in Gideon's muddy prints, stretching her legs to match his long-legged stride. She was seething with anger. Just wait until she got her hands on that boy. She didn't even care if, for once, Clem used the strap on him. She would see to it he was punished if she had to do it herself. Why, the boys must have been up several hours to have slipped away and lain beneath the tree that long. They'd watched her wash her face in the river. They'd seen Trey stop to speak to her and watched while she questioned the ever-waiting Bart. They'd surely seen the early scouts come in.

Verity climbed a gentle incline and found herself on a path worn smooth down to the hard clay. To her left the path dropped away down a sheer bluff to the water's edge. On the right the forest grew in a solid wall, green and thick and utterly impenetrable. It was not a good place to meet a stranger. But then, she wasn't expecting to meet any strangers. Only two naughty ten-year-olds who would certainly get the back side of her tongue when she caught up with them.

She rounded a large outcropping of rock and stopped abruptly as the trail vanished into a willow thicket. The boys had probably climbed an abrupt eruption of shale. Either that or they'd crept into the thicket, for there were no more tracks to be seen.

Verity ground her teeth in frustration. Through the curtain of trees she could see the boats were not yet ready to cast off. She still had some time. Carefully she bent to study the last footprint. Was it Gideon's? She couldn't be sure. Were his legs long enough for that lengthy stride? But if it wasn't Gideon—

From behind the screen of willows came a rumbling growl and the wands began to shake violently. Verity tensed. Her fingers around the gun tightened. A snuffling sound, a sound that could only come from a large animal, seemed to fill the clear morning air. Something moved, something huge, and

Verity froze as the broad, brown face of a bear appeared between the leaves.

Black beady eyes were fixed on hers and its mouth opened around snarling fangs. A roar assaulted her ears and seemed to echo inside her head. Verity forgot to breathe. Sweat broke out on her upper lip.

And then the bear charged in a long, loping stride, straight at her. There was no time to think. No time to even blink. Instinct drew her arms up and fired the gun. She saw the bear stagger with the blow—she had hit it—but it came on. In the split second before it crashed into her, she heard another shot, and couldn't even wonder where it had come from, before the bear cannoned into her.

The great hairy beast fell against her and crashed to the ground with a tremor that seemed to shake the earth. Verity scrambled to her knees, still clutching the empty gun, and stared at the bear.

"A young male. Four hundred pounds, easy."

She raised her eyes to travel up long, buckskin-clad legs and a wide torso, to the cleft chin of Captain Trey Owens. She felt the blood drain from her face.

He helped her to her feet. "Are you hurt?"

She couldn't speak, but twitched her head side to side.

He looked her up and down with that flat gaze of his which was rarely readable, but for once she had no doubt about his thoughts. He was angry. For the life of her, Verity could think of nothing to say.

His lips were drawn in a tight, thin line. "What in the name of all that's holy are you doing out here, alone, confronting bears?"

"I—I can imagine what you are thinking, but I didn't expect to meet any bears."

What Trey thought was nothing he wanted to say aloud, and certainly nothing she would want to hear. His knees were trembling from the shock of finding her with a mother bear almost upon her. The huge animal would have made six of her. And the claws would have shredded her in seconds.

Her mouth, opened slightly in surprise, seemed to draw him like deer to a saltlick and her eyes, not full of angry bees just now but wild with fear, must certainly be the deepest he'd ever looked into. Her face, her bearing, filled him with a need to protect her. Where such thoughts came from he couldn't tell, but he suddenly wanted to flex his muscles and lift a bull ox just to impress her. After he gave her what-for, for being so stupid.

"The—uh—tracks—" She made a weak gesture to the tracks she had been following, mostly blotted out now by the bear lying at their feet.

He grunted, a short expletive of sound. He must have a touch of the sun to be thinking such things of a woman who may have been the prettiest girl in all of the Virginia territory, but also had the temper of a gut-stuck buffalo and the sense of a fruit fly to be wandering alone in the forest. Still at the moment her eyes showed more confusion than anything else. He certainly wasn't confused. What she was doing was about to put him in a bind, again, with General Clark. If he didn't get her back soon, he'd have some tall explaining to do.

His lips parted. "When there are insect trails through a footprint it generally means the print was made the day before. Insects travel at night."

She glanced down at the footprints while her tongue seemed glued to the roof of her mouth. Sure enough, there were faint insect trails clearly visible in the footprints she'd found. Why was he talking about insects? His eyes showed his displeasure in having to pluck her from the arms of difficulty, once more, and his tone suggested that he might be speaking to an infant.

She was trying not to look at the fallen bear. The sheer size of the animal was overpowering. "You killed it?" she asked, breathing normally now. Standing straighter and looking him in the eye. His had been the second shot. "I thought I'd hit it, but I guess not."

"You did. Got him in the shoulder. But, it often takes more than one shot to kill a bear. I've known them to kill a man after they'd been shot through the heart. Just takes time for them to die. If possible, I aim for just under the chin."

"If you hadn't gotten here when you did—How *did* you show up just in time?"

He answered with a question of his own. "Have you lost something?" His eyes narrowed.

"N-no." Verity locked her knees against the urge to quiver and stood her ground. "Not exactly."

He allowed himself the faintest look of skepticism. "For whatever reason, you deliberately separated yourself from the main body of travelers." His eyes raked her sodden form, trembling from the cold and shock of a bear attack and finding him here, inexplicably, within seconds of being needed. She was shaking as if she had the ague. "What if I'd been a Seneca brave?"

Verity clasped her arms around her elbows in a feeble attempt to warm herself, and mutely shook her head.

"Are you positive you aren't looking for something?"

The repeat of the question brought Verity's blood back into circulation. Her thinking focused. He knew! He was playing with her, making her eat crow and glorying in her humiliation. Her own eyes flashed to meet the flame in his.

"Let's stop playing games, Captain. I'm looking for Gideon and you know it. He must have slipped off the boat to explore and I have to get him back before General Clark discovers he's missing." She balled her hands into fists and put one on each hip. "Now, are you going to help me find him, or are you going to stand there full of your self-importance and lecture me until Clark throws me off the boat?"

He spat out a short expletive and leaned back on his heels. "I'm the one likely to be thrown off the boat. I keep making excuses and explaining away your behavior. If I'd allowed you to get mauled by that bear, I might as well have hailed the next canoe going down river and climbed in."

For some reason, Verity saw behind his words and realized that he was as dry as a field of wheat in August. He wasn't standing, like she was, dripping wet, in a cold April wind.

Her voice rose. "Get out of my way. I have things to do." And she moved to step around him.

That was the second time she'd ordered him out of her way, Trey thought, and he'd be damned if he'd let a tiny bit of a woman take command of the situation again. He shot out an arm and stopped her where she stood.

"Gideon is fine. Look." He put broad hands on her shoulders and turned her so she could see the river. She was so close to him she could feel the warmth of his ribcage through the cold, wet of her own clothing. His breath stirred the hair on top of her head and a sudden shiver, from her eyelashes to her toenails, ran through her. It took all her powers of concentration to think about Gideon.

Sure enough a canoe was making headway toward the flatboats and in the middle sat two young boys. One was Gideon.

"The early guards found them but didn't have room in the canoe for everybody. They had to bring the boys home in a relay with the other scout. Homer went back to get them."

Verity's relief at seeing Gideon almost aboard the boat was short lived. She looked up at Trey and her eyes suddenly widened. With the boys back on board the boats might have gone off without her. She could have been stranded here, alone. How had the Captain known she was gone?

He smiled—actually, Verity thought it more a smirk—and read her mind in that infuriating way of his. "I saw you leave," he said. "And my curiosity got the better of me. Now, shall we make the return trip on top of the water? The river is a little too chilly, yet, for my liking."

Verity set her mouth in a grim line and followed him down to the water. She shook off the soft, tanned linen shirt he draped around her shoulders and when he persisted in urging it on her, she flung it in the bottom of the canoe. Freezing was preferable to his laughing condescension. At the flatboat she scrambled aboard and was out of his sight in a matter of seconds.

She had a few things to say to Gideon, however. He sulked and ducked his head at first and then tried to brazen it through. "Oh hell," he said, causing Verity's eyes to snap open wider. "Damn it all, nothing happened. I can take care of myself."

"Enough!" and the hard edge in her voice silenced him. "You will not use that language with me. I won't have it. Is that understood?"

Gideon refused to meet her eyes, but nodded his head finally. General Clark chastised him as well and after Trey took him aside and told him about the bear, the boy was completely repentant the rest of the day. Even Clem thought he'd been punished enough.

When she had Zelma settled for the night, Verity fed the baby and stood, watching the water and shivering in the night breeze. After all, they'd seen no Indians on the bluffs, but Clark remained edgy. The total absence of Indian sign was not natural. Finally, she took the baby and went to sit by the fire for warmth. The talk was of the day's journey and the measly twenty miles they'd covered in a straight run of river. They'd passed nine islands, every one sitting high and rather large, and Clark entered each one in his journal.

She was getting comfortably drowsy when Captain Owens appeared at her side. He sat cross-legged on the hard deck and, despite the chilly edge to the night air, he wore only buckskins. Verity resisted the urge to squirm. With the realization, somewhere in the middle of the day, that there had been only one set of footprints ashore, Verity's anger had evaporated. She no longer wanted to throttle him. She ought to thank him, but couldn't quite bring herself to do it. He was always so insufferably right and she, herself, wrong.

The memory of his hands tight on her shoulders when he'd turned her toward the flatboat that morning and held her snug against his chest, lodged in the back of her mind. Her teeth clenched. How could she possibly think about him with any kind of softness when he was a confessed Indian lover? But he was continually coming to her rescue, it seemed. He had some uncanny way of knowing when she needed him. She didn't like it, didn't want it, but it was so.

She glanced sideways at him and, unbidden, the thought jumped into her mind wondering if his lips would be soft when he kissed. She'd watched his mouth thin out in the firelight as the men told stories at night. She'd watched the quick flash of his teeth as his mouth widened in hearty laughter, and for some crazy reason she still wanted to lay a finger in the tiny cleft of his chin.

Having him this close made her edgy. She felt oddly restless, but wasn't sure if she wanted him nearer or further away. all her senses seemed acutely aware of him. He seemed—hard. Solid and strong. He made her feel vulnerable and safe all at the same time. She wasn't sure she liked the feeling.

Did he think about her? *I must be doing something right, my luck keeps getting better and better.* He'd said that. The words had stuck tight in her head and she took them out, carefully, every so often to go over them, time and again. She examined each word and the tone behind it until she was disgusted with herself for frittering time away on something so trivial. Only, for some reason, it wasn't trivial. How could she admire him and hate him at the same time? It was a mystery that she didn't know how to unravel.

She sighed and pushed those thoughts to the back of her mind. She had to say something to him, something nice, not only about saving her from the bear, but also about General Clark's wrath as well. Finally, after the talk around the fire had died down somewhat, she turned to him.

"I haven't thanked you for shooting the bear. I'm grateful." The words came out stiffly. Not at all the way she'd meant them to sound.

He didn't look at her. "No thanks needed. It's my job to keep all of you safe."

The silence built and grew. Then, "It wasn't Gideon I was trailing this morning, was it?"

He raised his head to look at her, but waited a full minute before he spoke. "No."

"Who?"

"Any guess would be just that, a guess."

"One of your precious Indians?" she asked without bitterness.

"All the slaughter isn't on their side, you know. None of us are blameless. General Clark talks about the time a trader at Wheeling tricked some Mingo braves, a squaw and a baby away from their fishing and into his shack where he and his friends killed and mutilated them horribly. I don't call that particularly civilized behavior."

She had no answer and acknowledged that he might be right. Mama always said that no one side was ever completely at fault.

"Was it an Indian, this morning?" she asked again.

"Could be," he acknowledged, "but maybe not."

Verity knew it would not have been a white man. Any white man would have been so starved for company out here, he'd have hailed them from the bank and wanted news. But she was tired and let it drop. He wouldn't have told her more anyway.

After a while she began to croon to the fretful baby. The moon was a thin sickle, riding high in the sky, and the stars swarmed around looking for all the world like bright fish in the deepest part of the lake back home. Verity lifted her face to search for the dipper.

Trey cleared his throat. "Did you know the Indians call April the Month of the Muddy Moon?"

She turned to look at him, thinking of what he'd said and what he might mean, but he looked straight ahead.

"April's almost gone," she said.

"Still, there's a lot of mud," he answered. "I drew a bucket of water for your bathing in the morning. It's sitting by your pallet." In one swift, smooth motion he rose and was gone into the darkness leaving Verity to stare after him and wonder.

Six

Morning broke low and thick with gray-backed clouds. Verity closed her eyes and lay on her back listening to the splash and suck of the river. She burrowed down in her blankets. The mist was heavy this morning and the late April dawn chilled her all the way through. Even the movement of the water sounded cold.

Actually, she'd come to love the river, rushing, hurrying along, carrying her with it. Carrying her west. Always busy, always changing, the river excited her in a strange way. All of her senses sprang alert when they were traveling. Although she'd never repeat it aloud, she sometimes thought of the Ohio as a "she." As herself really, racing breakneck to go west all the way to the Mississippi.

Reluctantly, she opened one eye. They were tied up, as usual, at a string of islands, mid-river. Mist, rising off the river like smoke, gave the morning an eerie feel. Tree tops were lost in the foggy wetness hovering overhead.

The boat rocked gently in the current, the water slapping against the keel. The sound was soothing and she came out of sleep like a bucket dragged from the bottom of a well. Overhead, birds swooped and dipped in hurried abandon, as if rushing to feed before the sky devoured them as well as the trees. A dragonfly hovered low and darted away. Rain was coming; she could smell it through the fog.

In the weeks they'd been on the water, there had been rain only once and then not enough to more than dampen the bottom of the pans they'd set out. Oh, what she would give for some tallow soap, a nice bath and good clean rainwater to wash her hair. No matter how long river water sat, there was always a residue of silt that turned clothing a dirty yellow and made hair look like that of a molting elk. Verity closed her eyes again and thought longingly of the way her hair felt, like pure silk, after washing and rinsing with vinegar water. She forced the thought from her mind. She was about as far away from vinegar as she was from tallow soap. And it was a long way yet to Kaskaskia. She shrugged off the thought. There was no point in mooning over something impossible.

She'd like, though, just once, for the captain to see her looking nice, freshly bathed and smelling sweet. She wondered, for one confusing moment, how it would feel to lay her head on his hard chest and listen to the beat of his heart. And she had yet to touch a finger to that funny dent in his chin.

With a guilty start she realized her rising interest in the captain and forced it back. How could she allow herself the slightest curiosity about him? He was everything she hated, everything she feared.

And there was Edward. She liked Edward a lot. He and Joe had pulled her out of more scrapes than she cared to remember. The thought of his laughing, carefree face gave her heart a lift. She must love him. Surely she loved him. She didn't have that feeling for anyone else, but somehow she wished there was more fire to it.

She could remember Mama and Papa. There had been times when she was aware of a desperate kind of yearning they had for one another A yearning that made her run across the room to grab them both around the legs so that she could be a part of it. That's what she wanted with Edward. Maybe when she got to Kaskaskia, after a long separation, she would look at him and feel the need to run across the room. Maybe.

In the meantime, there was Clem. Hah! The captain had Clem picked out for her. And Clem wouldn't care if she bathed or not. He wouldn't notice if her hair felt like dried corn stalks beneath his hand. The captain could think again.

A strangling snore brought Verity up on one elbow. Bart and "the boys" still slept, as did Zelma and the children. And that was understandable. They weren't long into daylight, and yesterday had been a hard day. In late afternoon the lead boat had hung up on an underwater snag and the men, those who could swim, took turns diving to try and release it. The entire string of boats tied up, one behind the other, while the men combined forces to fight the current and the cold water. Darkness had finally defeated them and they'd had to give it up for the night. They'd try again this morning.

On the far side of the boat, Homer supported himself on the rail while his eyes roamed the bank. His lean body hung loose between his shoulders and he gave every indication of being ready to collapse on the deck, but Verity knew the appearance was deceiving. Homer was just conserving his energy. Trey had once said there was no man on earth he'd rather have beside him if he got into a tight spot.

Homer was whopper-jawed and ropy-looking and agonizingly shy of women. He turned now, feeling her eyes on him, gave her a brief nod and sauntered away toward the smell of coffee. Except for checking the banks, his guard responsibility for the night was over with the dawn and after he ate his fried hoecake, Homer would roll into his blanket and sleep until the nooning. Homer's vigilance, and that of others who shared the night watch, was a comfort during the wee hours when the shadows deepened and the spirit was vulnerable.

Verity rose on her knees and looked forward toward the west. The unbroken line of trees along the edge of the water was like green walls imprisoning them. A vague feeling of unease stirred in her stomach. The string of islands seemed to float, aswirl in the fog. Unconnected. Separate.

The day didn't look promising. She could see no farther than the small yellow and green flag hanging limp and lifeless on the prow of the lead boat. They couldn't navigate down river, blind. Not knowing when a bend in the river was coming would be dangerous, to say nothing of rapids, small islands, and not being able to scan the tops of bluffs before they passed.

Unless the sun broke through the clouds, the boats might not leave the island today, even if the men managed to free the snag. She fought a surge of irritation at the delay, knowing her impatience would be of no help, and one day more or less was not going to effect whether or not she'd find Joe in Kaskaskia. If he was indeed the man Trey had talked about, he'd already been there for months, passing as a Frenchman while spying for Clark. And undoubtedly, she was sure, thanking their long-dead mother for the French blood that ran in their veins and the language she'd taught them both.

Verity was honest enough to admit, however, that all of her agitation was not due to the delay. She'd been fretting for days about how she was going to talk Clark into allowing her to accompany him all the way to Kaskaskia. She knew better than to ask straight out. He was, after all, going down the Ohio in line of a duty which did not include single female passengers. The only other option she had was that of exchange, and search as she might, she could think of no goods or skill that Clark might use. He certainly had no need of a goat where he was going and no sick wife to care for. There had to be a way. Verity cast about in her mind for an idea. She was going to Kaskaskia. She was. And every day that passed was one day nearer Corn Island where Clark and the militia would leave them. As badly as it would damage her pride, the only one who might be able to advise her was Captain Owens.

She wished they'd started out together on the right foot instead of clashing so soon about Indians. They'd never seemed to get beyond her early anger at his defensive attitude toward redskinned people. Everything she said seemed to rub him the wrong way. And to be fair, he riled her, too, with his bossy and inexhaustible knowledge of the country, the people, the game—everything. She always seemed to come off second best in their skirmishes. Maybe she'd better forget Trey Owens. If only he didn't feel the way he did about Indians, she could see that he'd make a good friend. And it would be nice to have a friend. There was a cold certainty, though, that he wasn't going to like the idea of her continuing with Clark.

Her mind pussyfooted warily around the edges of this problem, for in his own way, the captain was as formidable as Clark. But then, determination must count for something, she thought. She'd try and be nice. Not let him anger her. She'd have to bite hard on her tongue, maybe, but she could do it.

She bathed in water drawn last night and, yellow water or not, she made plans to do laundry while the men worked on freeing the boat. After that she'd take a look ashore for sassafras. The tea just might help Zelma. The ailing woman could do with a day of rest but then, quite honestly, they all could. Not tearing down river as if driven by a hurricane would be a welcome break for them all.

However, they still had to eat, day of rest or not. She edged her way down the length of the boat to the cooking fire and began ladling coffee into a pot. Squinting her eyes against the smoke, she added water to cornmeal, patted out the patties and then waited while the bacon curled in the pan. She then added bear grease and the corncakes. While they sizzled in the hot fat she sank back on her heels and considered the sky. The fog had not lifted. Well, fog or not, she had things to do. The day would not be wasted.

His height caught her eye first, as he made his way toward her. Since the night Trey had drawn water for her, he'd barely spoken. If it had made sense, she might have thought he was avoiding her. When he acknowledged her presence at all it was with a sort of cautious pickiness, like he was trying to sort out a nest of snakes. Yet here he came, making his way purposefully toward her, the fringes on his buckskins swaying softly with his stride.

He wasted no time on greetings. His voice was brusque. "Are you still looking for a wet nurse for Zelma's baby? If so, there's a woman on the next boat who's interested in barter. She has more than enough milk for her own baby, but needs meat." He explained, "her husband died last week of a gangrenous foot."

His tone was impersonal and hurried, but for once Verity didn't notice. "Yes," she said, coming to her feet in relief, for she was increasingly worried about the baby. Her eyes met his in gratitude. His eyes, she thought, were cautious as an unbroken mule confronted with a leather harness. His expression struck her as odd, but she took no time to ponder. Quickly, she set the skillet off the fire.

"That would be wonderful. Let me get the baby and see what meat we can spare."

For two whole days Trey had stayed well away from Verity. He took his stand at the watch, hunted when need be, and deliberately denied himself the joy of watching her move about her daily tasks. However, at mid-morning of the third day, he thought of a perfectly good excuse to talk to her. He set out immediately to find the wet nurse.

Why was he always so prickly with her? He could tease and joke with almost everyone else, but with her he was as spiny as a grouchy old porcupine, and usually she seemed to dart right back at him with pointed barbs. Not this time, however. She was too anxious about the baby to be concerned with him.

With elaborate patience he helped her off the narrow boat ramp, onto the boat behind and introduced her to Esther Hicks. Esther was a big woman, red-faced and hearty but business-like about the arrangements.

"I'd do this for free any other time, you understand that. But my back's fair against the wall, it is, with my husband dying and all. I need to feed my other kids. Can you promise me a steady supply of meat?"

Verity assured her there were three men in the Dawson party, and all of them were good hunters. They had agreed to keep Esther Hicks in table meat in exchange for nursing the baby. The women struck a bargain, and looking as if her burden was considerably lightened, Verity handed her the baby and left the boat with Trey following close behind.

She stopped as they stepped aground and held her breath for a moment. He was instantly suspicious.

"Do you have a minute? I'd like your opinion." Her voice was reedy, thin, unnatural.

"About what?"

Aimlessly, Verity walked toward a clump of aspens and a tangled, dense undergrowth at a slight bend in the river. Slowly, Trey followed. His eyes were never still. They moved constantly along the trees, toward the horizon, the ground beneath their feet, cataloging sights, sounds and smells, sorting and picking through information.

A feeder creek angled off toward the south and a stand of timber marked the head of a wooded gully. He saw a water snake wriggle into the reeds and disappear. He saw the faint prints of a big cat made probably the evening before when it came to drink. He watched the way her skirt swished around her hips when she walked.

Verity looked at nothing but the toes of her moccasins. She stopped. There was no one near. Be nice, she told herself and took a breath.

All of Trey's instincts came rushing forward. What was she up to now? She was gearing herself toward something. It bothered him that he never knew in what direction she was likely to spring next. He tensed.

"I need your advice," she said, concern gathering in her eyes. His suspicions were confirmed. She wanted something.

She wouldn't look directly at him, but fixed her eyes on a spot over his left shoulder. She said it in a rush. "I need to go with Clark. I mean, once he leaves the movers on Corn Island and goes on, I need to go with him. He isn't going to like the idea at first, but—"

"You're damn right he isn't. And he won't take you, so you can get that idea out of your head." He could see a tiny muscle move in her throat as she swallowed.

"There would be a few problems, I understand that, but believe me when I say I wouldn't hold him back. I can keep up with the men. I can shoot, swim, find my way—"

He gave an exasperated grunt. "Forget it! One woman with all those men? He's not an idiot. And if you think you can twirl him around your finger, you're loony. Where'd you come up with this, all of a sudden?"

She hesitated. "I have to get to Kaskaskia."

"Not with Clark you don't."

"Who else is going?"

"Nobody. You'll have to stay on Corn Island. You must have known that when you began the journey," he said, fighting down his anger and trying to be reasonable. After all, surely she could understand why such a thing was impossible. She wasn't simple-minded.

She clasped her hands tightly in front of her. "I can't stay on Corn Island."

"Why not? It will be a hell of a lot safer there than where the army is going."

Verity drew a slow breath and fought for calm. "There's no need to swear at me. I understand the problems, but—"

"No! We're going into battle. Guns. Fighting. Killing. No!"

"But I must go to Kaskaskia." She said it quietly, in an almost conversational tone that made his blood chill. "I *will* go to Kaskaskia. And neither you, nor Clark, nor anyone else is going to stop me."

She was serious. He frowned, a massive pulling together of forehead muscles and then saw how ridiculous the whole thing was. He laughed. A woman couldn't travel with the army. What was the matter with her? But, two bright spots appeared in Verity's cheeks and her eyes were spraying sparks again.

He chuckled. "Are you and your sharp-shooting goat going to take off alone?"

Her grip on control buckled. She would have loved to take that superior smile and bang him over the head with it. Her eyes met his defiantly. "If I have to."

Their eyes collided and held, his piercing, dark and unreadable, hers narrowed, stubborn and rebellious.

"Damn!" he said aloud. She might do just that. He'd never known anyone so hell bent on doing what they wanted. "You'd thumb your nose at the devil to get your own way!"

"If necessary!" She glared at him with a look hot enough to fry bear steak, and stood with her feet apart and her jaw thrust forward. There was no doubt in his mind that she'd do just that if she felt called upon to do so. While his mind was still tumbling over her unrelenting determination to do this idiotic thing, she went on speaking.

"I fail to see why this conversation has to revolve around vile language. Do you find it totally impossible to speak without vulgarity?"

He ignored her and tried logic. "Come on now. Think. It's hundreds and hundreds of miles, not all of it on the river. There will be forced marches across unknown country and illnesses and most probably Indians. That's nothing for a woman to attempt. Be reasonable and pick out someone on Corn Island to settle in with, and—" he stopped. This wasn't easy with her standing there with her mind all made up and confident.

Damn fool woman, but—He guessed he really should watch his mouth since it bothered her so much. No need to deliberately antagonize her when she'd come to him, for once, without anger and looking pretty as a pink posy.

The thought flitted across his mind and was gone so fast it took his breath away. Why couldn't he be the one she settled in with? The idea startled his eyes wide open. She was as easy to look at as any female he'd ever clapped eyes on and damned—darned—if he didn't enjoy matching wits with her, after he got over being mad. He liked the easy way she had with children, her compassion for the other travelers, her care of Zelma in spite of daunting odds. And she wasn't afraid of hard work. In spite of all the trouble she'd caused him, he even liked her feisty spirit that refused to take no for an answer.

What saved him was an expression in Verity's eyes that came and went in the space of a heartbeat. Calculation. There and gone so fast he wondered if he'd really seen it. But, yes, he'd come across that same look twice now over the last three years and to his sorrow he'd paid it no mind either time. He vowed he'd not make the same mistake again. He put a barbed bit on his own thoughts with all the firmness he'd use on a headstrong stallion. He'd risked a lot to get himself the freedom he so craved, and he fully intended to keep right on enjoying it.

"Settle in and…" he finished in a hurry, before it was beyond him. "…and have some babies and plant your crops and take care of your man."

He could see it build. She was so angry she was trembling. And her eyes! Why, he was surprised he had any skin left on his bones.

When she spoke it was as if each word was a rock flung at his head. "If and when I ever decide to take a husband and plant crops and have babies, you can be very sure it will be in my own good time and by my own decision. It will not be because someone—a man—" she made the word sound like a slug-worm, "—dictates my future."

Her eyes were swarming with tiny gold flecks and her cheeks flushed an alarming red. He couldn't take his eyes off her. A flock of butterflies in his stomach seemed to take flight at the same time his chest felt as if it had caved in. He did the only thing he could think of. He kissed her, knowing it was the wrong move even as his arms closed around her.

For a moment she was as quiet as a mouse when an eagle swoops low, and then he could feel her respond. A tremor ran the full length of her body and her mouth softened and warmed under his. Her hands began to travel slowly up his chest. She touched the side of his neck, his hairline, and stilled. He waited, for what he didn't know. But she felt so good, so right, somehow. She fit into the curve of his body just where a woman should fit. A curious feeling of homecoming welled in him and he had frowned with the effort of understanding, when she erupted in his arms like a spitting cat.

"What the—?" he yelled as her fingernails dug into his neck.

Actually, he had the advantage because he was expecting some sort of reaction, but still he had his hands full of elbows, knees and teeth. He was astonished at the wiry strength hidden in the soft and gently curved body. For a second all he could think of was what he held in his arms. The smooth slope of her breast, the clean, fresh scent of her skin like new meadow grass, the feel of her waist, tiny, as it slid around in his desperate grasp. His heart began to pound.

"Now, hold on here. Just a minute." He was afraid to hang on, he didn't want her to think he was trying to wrestle her to the ground, but he didn't dare let go. The way she was throwing herself around she'd fall and be hurt.

"Let go of me, you beast," she panted through stiff lips. Her fingers tore at his as they locked around her body.

"Just calm down, will you? And hold still. Please hold still." He grappled for both of her hands to give himself thinking space, but she managed to keep one arm free.

Another twisting, squirming move and somehow she was facing him. They stood, knees bent and tense, breathing hard, nose to nose, each waiting for the other to give ground. Cautiously, Trey relaxed his arms and braced himself. She'd try to slap his face for sure, and maybe he had it coming, but he didn't intend to take it if he could help it. His left hand inched up, ready.

What he wasn't ready for was a balled up fist at belly-button height with all her weight behind it. It wasn't a damaging blow, but it was a surprise and he took a staggered step backward.

"Hah!" Verity yelped in triumph and spun free. She'd taken three steps when his arm shot out around her waist. He turned her around.

"Let's get one thing straight." His voice was like the blade of a knife as his fingers dug into her arms. "I'm not going to hurt you. And, if you don't want to be kissed, just say so."

He released her and stepped back, still breathing hard. "Now, what's so all-fired important about getting to Kaskaskia?" he demanded.

Verity stared at him as if she'd never seen him. She was frightened and angry and confused and here he stood asking calm questions. When he first kissed her she'd been swept along on a torrent of feeling that left little room for thinking. A sense of melting, weak and exciting and half-fearful all at the same time. And it kept building and building until she hadn't known there was that much feeling in the world.

And then a vivid picture of Otis came to mind, sitting at the table telling her he'd sold her to Mr. Hargraves. Maybe Trey had thought he'd exchange Kaskaskia for the kissing. Another man, but still bondage. And there was her own papa draped over the woodpile with a hatchet buried in his skull, abandoning Ma and Joe and herself to the likes of a stepfather. Then, Joe had left her with no protection from Otis and Lena. For years after Mama had died, she'd had no one. When Trey kissed her and that powerful feeling swept over her it was wonderful, and then she'd felt her entire body back off, panicked. A person had to belong to themselves in order to survive. You couldn't just give it all away. Not when so much was at stake. Feelings that blotted out all common sense and reason were dangerous. She swallowed hard and tried to think.

"I'm promised to a man there, if you must know," she said finally. That ought to hold him. Promised to Edward. Trey'd not be kissing her again.

"Oh," he said, feeling a sudden thwacking ache in his middle. "Promised. Well then." He rallied his thoughts. "Send a message with Clark to have the man come for you when he gets a chance. Maybe by fall."

"And maybe next summer," she responded, tightly. "Or the next."

"Who?"

"Who what?"

"Who is the man? You said you were promised." Even to his own ears his voice sounded short, irritable, like he'd been surprised by thieves and robbed.

"Edward. A friend. A neighbor."

"A very close neighbor!"

"Well…yes. We grew up toge—"

"Never mind. I don't want to hear it. And I don't want to hear any more about going on with Clark. It's out of the question." He looked at her from the corner of his eye. "What does this Edward do in Kaskaskia?"

Verity drew a careful breath. Better tell the full truth here. She had the feeling he'd smell out an evasion at ten paces. "He scouts for General Clark, along with my brother Joe."

He considered this. "The only Joe I know out there is a French speaking man working for Clark. Joe—Oh, I guess it's Philp, isn't it? I thought his name was Phillips. He's a decent sort. Dependable. Clark trusts him." He seemed to speak grudgingly.

"I would hope so," she said with some heat. "He'll never find a better man."

He turned as if to go and then turned back. "Listen. You don't have any business out there. It's untamed country. Untamed men. You don't know what you're letting yourself in for."

"I'll manage." Her chin came up defiantly. He thought she was a child, ready to cry and run home at the first scare. But she wouldn't. She'd show him. "Other women live in the Illinois country. Indian women, at least. And Joe is there. He'll take care of me. And Edward," she added hastily.

"But you'll not be joining your brother. Or this Edward-person, either. Not right away, at least. Best to just settle in here and wait."

He was giving orders, for all the world like Otis in one of his worst moods. She wouldn't stand for it. She'd gone to some pains to get away from all that and she would not allow it to begin all over again out here in the wilderness. She drew herself up and looked him over coolly.

"I can see I'm wasting my time. Very well, I'll merely thank you for thinking of the baby."

Irritably he waved away her thanks. But he waved to her back. She didn't see. How did she manage to aggravate him with practically every word out of her mouth? Maybe because she looked vulnerable, though when he tried to help, she seemed to sling it back in his teeth.

He called, "Why in blazes didn't you just say no?"

She didn't turn. But with smug satisfaction he knew she'd liked the kiss. Before she turned on him. What had happened? It was as if, all of a sudden, she was fighting for her life. Carefully, he touched his neck where her nails had dug in. His forefinger came away with a drop of blood on the tip.

Verity stopped by the river's bank. Stung by his question she pretended not to watch as Trey swung away and headed toward the prow of the lead boat where the diving was already beginning. The man was impossible. Friendly and helpful one moment and cross and downright rude the next. What scared her was that, if she'd let herself, she might have enjoyed his kiss. With one hand on her waist where he had caught her, she remembered the feel of his arm. It had been like running into a rail fence. She was just a little in awe of his strength.

But, his language. She sighed with the memory of the words he'd used. *Mama*, she thought, *you'd have been disappointed in me. I try to be a lady, but I always seem to end up yelling. You always said my tongue would get me into more trouble than my hands.*

And she guessed she'd ruined whatever chance she ever had of Trey Owens helping her go down the Ohio with Clark. After this he'd be more likely to run the other direction if he saw her on the next boat. *But worst of all*, her thoughts rambled on, *Mama, I almost like him even if he does have a vile mouth. He sometimes uses awful words. And, of course, there's the way he feels about Indians*. But, in an effort to be fair, she remembered that he was respected by everyone and good with children, and helpful to anyone on the flotilla needing a hand. Mama would have approved, she was sure, but then Mama had been special. The whole thing seemed terribly complicated.

Verity pulled herself up straight and looked toward the line of boats where the diving was already beginning. Trey seemed to be helpful to everyone but her. He wasn't going to help her get to Kaskaskia. That much was clear. And that left her course ahead in doubt. Her chin came up. Who needed his help? She could take care of herself. She'd managed to run away from Otis and Lena, and she'd taken up with the Dawsons, and come this far down the Ohio on her own. She could do the rest, too.

Seven

Head down, for once not scanning the woods as he went, Trey headed back for the boats. He'd been a fool kissing her like she was a tavern wench. He'd made an awkward grab for her like a twelve-year-old and was rewarded with an uproar that surprised him as much as he'd surprised himself. If Homer ever found out, he would never let him forget such simple-mindedness. But then, he'd make sure Homer never found out. He didn't want to dwell on it, too much, himself.

And that was what worried him. Trey couldn't seem to get her out of his mind. Her image invaded his dreams at night, her voice, soft as it usually was with other people, seemed to cut through the daytime din of pigs and goat, and men and shouted orders on the boat, and thoughts of her wet dress sticking to her like the skin of a wild persimmon as she'd emerged from the river that morning did nothing for his concentration while he was out scouting.

Half of him said that laying with her would solve the problem and why didn't he just do it, or make the attempt—as prickly as she often was he couldn't be certain of the outcome—and get it over with? But the other half was honest enough to admit that he was just as intrigued with her grit and determination and quick wit as he was with her outer trappings.

It worried him that he spent so much of his time thinking about her. Why the hell did he feel responsible? Her fate wasn't any concern of his. She had surely included herself in the trip by her own wishes and had ingeniously put herself in the position of having all three of the Dawson men to protect her. He couldn't think why it was impossible to shake this absurd feeling that no one was as competent to watch over her as himself.

He snorted in disgust and whacked at a stand of willow weeds growing in his path. *Put her out of your mind, man. You get close enough to the fire and you're bound to get scorched pants!* He'd misread deer tracks only day before yesterday and it cost him an hour of tracking time to find the stupid beast and kill it, and another two to dress it out and get it back to the river. Half a day gone, all because he couldn't get rid of the feeling that in some vague way Verity occupied a place in his life and that her problems were his to solve.

Today he'd allowed himself to be taken in by a whole host of things he hadn't stopped to pick apart at the time: the smoky depth of her eyes, her gutsy determination no matter how wrong-headed and certain of defeat, an odd vulnerability he sensed rather than heard, and the one wondering breath she'd drawn as he pulled her close.

And now this. Thank God the decision to take her down river wasn't his to make. Clark would never countenance such a plan. Not for a minute. He could depend on that. The expedition would be on Corn Island soon, and that is where Verity Philp would stay, her determination squelched. She couldn't be allowed to travel with the army. The implications of Verity along on such a journey were enough to make his head ache.

His thoughts gathered like a thundercloud. After all, he would be nearby on the island to keep an eye on her because Clark had decided to leave him behind, riding herd on the farmers, keeping them in fresh meat and guiding their settling efforts.

He gritted his teeth and irritably hoisted his gun to settle across his shoulders. The decision wasn't to his liking and he'd made it known. He and Clark had had it out nose to nose, the way they usually settled things, red-faced and yelling at the top of their lungs, but this time Clark convinced him that someone who knew the ways of the wilderness had to stay behind.

Of course, the idea did have an up side. Verity would be there. But maybe that wasn't a plus. Maybe all he would accomplish would be waiting while the frying pan got hot.

He shook his head. No. His reason for staying was simply that these families were not yet Indian fighters. For the most part they were unused to the kind of constant surveillance necessary to survival. In his spare time Trey was teaching the men the art of using their eyes as they would an arm or leg, instinctively, constantly moving, collecting images and information, storing them to be drawn out later when needed. Gideon was his best pupil. He was young, but not too young to learn the tricks that gave him an edge over death. Instruction was, at least, a foot in the right direction.

Trey came to the river and stopped to look over the flotilla of boats moored to the bank. They had hit the snag while trying to negotiate the channel between a string of islands and the southern bank, and those boats caught in the narrows were in a bad spot, tied to the shore. Trey didn't like it. Every minute the boats remained in that position increased the chance Indians would find them. No Indians had been seen, so far, but that didn't mean anything. They could be thick as fleas on a dog's back and a whole army of white men would never know they were there unless the Indians chose to show themselves. Homer reported drums had been talking for several days now, but there was no sign to put a finger on. The only sure thing was that they were near, somewhere.

Divers on the lead boat were preparing to go overboard. He spotted Homer, stripped to the waist, with skin across his chest as white as a fish's belly and ribs sticking out like those on a carp's skeleton. Most of the men ready to go into the water were soldiers. The farmers, landbound as they were, likely couldn't swim. He was needed, yet he hesitated.

It would go down hard standing on the bank waving goodbye to these men, his friends, as they headed downriver toward Kaskaskia and all that awaited them there. Clark had promised Trey could follow later. The issue was how much later. Too late, in any case, for the fighting. Bah! His only hope was that Homer might be convinced to keep him company baby sitting the farmers and their families. A forlorn hope, but one he clung to.

With a sudden clarity of vision he knew that a lifetime of military duty was not for him. He didn't know what would come next, nor when it would appear, but he did know he was no more willing to confine himself to a lifetime of taking orders than he was to taking a wife. In the meantime, however, there were twenty some odd families left in his care for the summer.

But, still, the decision to be left behind had been hard to swallow. True, he'd agreed of his own free will to wait on Corn Island for word from Clark, but that didn't make it any easier. Nor, now that he dwelled on it, did the thought that Verity would be nearby all summer, plaguing his dreams and his hunting and invading his thoughts like he'd never expected any female to do. He didn't necessarily like that either. Not completely.

Right now he was nattering away at the fact that she hadn't followed him back to the river. The scouts had been out early as usual, but the southern bank of the Ohio was acknowledged Indian country and who knew what could happen in an hour's time? A whole war party could be hidden behind the ridges a quarter mile inland. A young woman, alone in the spring morning, might be too big a temptation to pass up. Where the hell had she gone?

He decided to go on down to the boats and, if she wasn't back soon, send someone after her. She'd been warned often enough not to stray. Surely she wouldn't wander far with a storm building in the west. Purposefully he strode down the embankment and headed for the prow of the boat.

~ * ~

Before plunging into the trees, Verity paused to assess the sky. The fog had begun to lift while she bargained with Mrs. Hicks, and during the heated exchange with Trey she was aware of a queer hushed intensity growing around her. There looked to be a huge bruise on the western sky, greenish around the edges and spreading as she watched to take in the bluffs on both sides. Rain, for sure. Maybe some wind, too. Birds, dozens of them, filled the forest, flitting from limb to twig to leaf as if trying to find a safe spot to ride out the coming squall. The morning swelled with expectation. Verity quickened her step. If she hurried, she could take a quick look in the woods for comfrey. A nice comfrey tea would do wonders for Zelma. She wouldn't go far, and she'd be back before the storm broke. She couldn't possibly be so unlucky as to meet another a bear. Not again.

She spared another glance at the sky. The rainwater would certainly be welcome, but a storm would impede the diving process. No one in their right minds would dive while lightning threatened. Not that Clark would allow it, anyway. For all his youth, he knew what he was doing as commander, and the men all but worshipped him. Even Trey.

Her thoughts hesitated to consider the fact that she called him by his given name in her mind, but wouldn't give him the satisfaction of using anything but the military title to his face.

She seemed to stop a lot to consider one thing or another about Trey Owens. Captain Trey Owens. She didn't even have to close her eyes to see his face in profile, the way it had been etched against the sunset last night as he gazed shoreward looking for a place to tie up. His dark eyes had been hooded with even darker eyelashes, his lower lip was full, jutting forward slightly as he concentrated on the riverbank, his hair still tied back with a leather thong. She closed her eyes then, remembering the way the buckskin drew tight across the breadth of his shoulders and how the pants fit snugly over his hips. One hand had been on a bale of stacked hay and the other gripped his rifle.

Even his hands intrigued her, long broad fingers set in a wide, take-charge hand. Covertly, she had watched those hands heft a heavy log, patiently carve a whistle for a child, efficiently gut a deer. She'd felt them around her waist, on her back, gentling on her hair, insistent as they pulled her closer—A hot flush of the cheeks made her realize what she'd been thinking and she snapped her eyes open and frowned.

Not counting Lena's babies, until now she'd never kissed anyone except Edward and that had been a long time ago. Although she wondered, after the way Trey had held her, touched her, even briefly, if that quick smearing together of the lips with Edward could really be called a kiss. Edward had liked it well enough to want to do it again, but she would have none of it. It was disgusting. But not with Trey.

No, whatever Trey did called up an entirely different set of feelings. Anger, maybe, that he thought he could kiss her without so much as a by-your-leave—curiosity certainly, and a queer quivering in her nether regions, but not disgust. And—she was embarrassed all alone in the woods—if she really hadn't liked his kiss why did she still have this ridiculous sense of well-being? Why did every nerve in her body still zing like a released fiddle string? Irritably she wiped the smile off her face. It wouldn't be too hard, too easy in fact, to start liking him.

Don't think about him, she commanded herself. He's just a man, after all, and in this case it appeared that if she let it happen he would stand in her way of traveling with Clark. Instead, concentrate on the comfrey. *Concentrate on comfrey.* She looked around.

The land stood high and proud, away from the water, aswarm with wild grape vines, white dogwood and purple mountain laurel, and trees so thick it would take three men with arms outstretched to span them.

Feeling the solid, unmoving earth beneath her feet was heavenly. She hadn't noticed how tired she was of the constantly shifting boat until she felt the firm, black loam of dry land. But more than anything else, she appreciated the solitude. Privacy could not be found aboard the boat, and not having a place to be alone was probably the hardest thing of all to endure. Actually, while a piece of her chafed at the delay in her plans to reach Joe with all speed, another part of her mind considered the snagged boat and early morning fog a stroke of fortune, after all, for providing her with an hour of quiet.

Verity hummed under her breath as she identified the elegant, stately heads of tall pines, oak, walnut, elm and cedar. She wandered through a tangled grove of hickory and black walnut trees and stopped for a long moment marveling at a huge white oak tree, whose large fluted trunk soared upward like an engraved column. The solid, spreading branches didn't even begin until thirty feet up the tree. Her curious fingers traced the grooved trunk in wonder.

A low rumbling of thunder sent her on, searching the thickets for sassafras or evergreen needles or skunk cabbage. Any of the three would do to brew a tonic tea, if she could find any comfrey. Her mother used to say such teas cleansed the body of winter's waste and purified the blood. She'd like to find enough to make tea for the entire family. And Trey, although she knew better than suggest he drink it.

At the thought of him there was a queer flutter in her chest, a flutter which she squashed firmly. He was more mulish than any of them. Besides, what did she care if he wasted away from the winter? Him with his arbitrary orders, his "yeses" and "nos," which he expected her to accept. His only thought of her was that she find a man to care for her. Well, she'd taken care of that with the mention of Edward. Maybe now he'd stop talking about Clem, at least.

Freedom from the squalor of the boats, even for an hour, made her happy enough that she could forget Trey's flat-out forbidding answer and even laugh at the less than subtle hints the Dawsons dropped from time to time about her and Bart. They would find out what stubborn really was if they kept on trying to link her up with him.

Carefully, she stepped around the exposed roots of a fallen tree and stopped with a small gasp of surprise. Before her lay a tiny meadow carpeted with exquisite purple violets. The sight was so unexpected and beautiful that her breath stopped in her throat. She wanted to open her arms wide and hug the vision to her. And then she realized that violets made a lovely tea, too. Accidentally, she had stumbled upon the perfect thing to brew a strengthening tea for Zelma. And she'd gather a handful to take back. Maybe a bouquet would perk up Zelma's spirits.

More than anything she wanted to sit down among the soft ferns and steep herself in the tranquility and beauty that filled her senses, but thunder growled again, closer now, urging her on. Hurrying, Verity flung herself into the glade of violets, stripping the delicate petals from the stems and filling both pockets on her skirt. And then, with a wistful glance at the peaceful meadow, she turned and ran for the boat.

Thunder boomed again near at hand, and it seemed that the world stilled. Nothing moved. No birds called from tree to tree. No chipmunks skittered through the bushes. Even Verity's feet made no sound on the deeply needled forest floor, and suddenly the silence itself made her feel queer. As if the trees had hushed their rustling branches to watch her progress and the animals had stopped on their homeward way to peer from behind bushes. She ran on, leaping a frothing creek, the water curling around smooth stones in a clear streambed. She skirted a patch of brier bushes and passed once more the sentinel white oak trees towering far above her. Then, with no warning, she rounded an outcropping of slanted slabs of rock and stepped squarely into the ashes of a still-warm fire, thin tendrils of smoke curling upward. A fire hurriedly abandoned. She couldn't have stopped more suddenly if she'd run into one of the giant tree trunks.

The hair at the base of her neck felt singed by a bolt of lightning. Each individual hair on her arms stood separate, trembling. A campfire where there should have been none. Her scanning gaze pinpointed no stick or rock displaced, no footprint, no sign at all of human attendance upon the fire. One word blazoned itself on the inside of Verity's brain and lodged. Indians!

Energy poured into her legs. She sprinted for the river as if an entire tribe of howling braves was hard at her heels. She ran until her lungs swelled to bursting and her legs were staggery tired. She ran like she and Joe had run through the buckberry thicket. Her heart seemed to be trying to force itself from her body. Papa sprawled on the woodpile, a hatchet buried in his head. Ma trying to straighten her twisted skirts. The echoing whoops and hollers. Berry-stained hands. A dirty heel. She ran, sides heaving and wild-eyed until she could see the river through the trees.

She stopped, gasping, at the tree line, her arms flung around a knotty maple trunk for support. Frantically, she looked back over her shoulder. There was nothing, nobody behind her. Hanging on to the tree, she closed her eyes and gave way to a wash of relief, forcing herself to breathe deeply, naturally. She consoled herself that her fright was not born of imagination. There had been a campfire. A campfire so recent, and abandoned so swiftly, the embers were still warm. Who to tell? Clark surely, but he was not as approachable as Trey. And even though she knew he was angry, she didn't hesitate. She'd tell Trey.

By the time she gained the flotilla of boats scattered along the water's edge, churning, black clouds were rolling toward them, one on top of the other, and a queer darkness settled over the river. Verity leaped aboard the flatboat just as the heavens seemed to split wide open with a ragged slash of lightning. Thunder crashed from the skies and a sudden, violent wind rushed down the river, bending everything in its path.

Men aboard the lead boat called to those in the water to come aboard, and a half-dozen crawled gratefully over the side. Mothers gathered children into shelters and others tried to tie down blankets and household paraphernalia. Children cried. Chickens squawked. The goat bleated frantically.

Verity collected the baby from Esther and made a dash for her own boat. She found Zelma huddled in her blanket, worrying about Sally and Gideon. Verity handed her the sleeping baby and emptied her pockets of violets into a kettle and ran to find the other two children. She found Sally and Gideon hanging over the rail, watching the water.

"Trey Owens is still down," Gideon yelled above the roar of the wind. "He's going to get sizzled by the lightning if they don't get him out!"

Suddenly interested, Verity leaned farther over the water. She could see a sandy head come up and bob back under again.

"That's not him," she screamed back at Gideon.

He nodded. "That's Homer. He won't come in until he brings Trey up."

"Is he lost?"

Gideon's head went back and forth. "Says he's almost got it."

Mind-numbing claps of thunder rolled over one another, too close to separate, and blue-white tongues of lightning danced across the tree tops. Verity could hear another onslaught of wind coming down the river and the boat began to toss as the wind drove the water before it. Rain came then in a sudden deluge and they were drenched to the skin before she could do more than draw breath.

"Gideon," she shrieked, "you take Sally back to your mother. Don't let go of her hand. And stay there."

"I want to watch," he began, but Verity cut him short.

"Now!"

With a sullen glare for Verity, Gideon pulled Sally's arm roughly and headed back toward their shelter.

Verity turned again to the river. All thoughts of Indians and campfires were gone. The heavens seemed to be slinging sheets of water at the earth. She could barely see the front of the boat where the men were dragging someone over the side. She stepped onto a roll of coiled rope and shaded her eyes against the rain. Homer. She knew by the hair color. He seemed more dead than alive.

But where was Trey? Surely they wouldn't just abandon him to the river and the storm. A vicious blast of wind nearly tore her from her place and rain blinded her so that she turned away and covered her eyes with one hand. Her hair came loose and blew across her face, her skirt billowed between her legs threatening to topple her over the side, but she could breathe again facing away from the storm.

What she saw stole her breath from her body, for Trey was in the river, riding the crest of a wave with one arm outstretched and tangled in the branches of a small tree. She yelled and turned to the men still hanging over the pitching prow of the boat. She screamed again, but her voice was lost in the fury of the storm. Wildly she cast about for something to do, some way to help him. The coil of rope where she stood! Trembling and fumbling in her desperate need to hurry, she hefted the rope and flung it with all her might into the river toward the rolling branches of the tree.

The rope caught in the upturned roots and with an almighty heave Trey managed to catch the end. His arms looked to be heavy, dragging, and he barely had the strength to keep his head out of the water, but somehow he got the rope around his body and managed to knot it.

"Wait!" she screamed into the storm. "Hang on."

Verity anchored her end around an iron cleat and with one frantic glance to make sure Trey was still there, she ran for help. She had to claw her way into the center of men before they would listen, but when they finally understood she was nearly trampled as they rushed to pull Trey in.

As quickly as the storm came up, it died. By the time Trey was on deck and had spewed out the water he'd swallowed, the rain had stopped, the wind was gone and a watery sun was sliding through the clouds.

He was safe. The huge bulk of his body was firmly on the deck and, while he sat with his head supported on his hands looking as gray as the ashes of a cold fire, he was definitely not near death. Suddenly weak, Verity sat on an upended barrel and watched as the men pounded Trey on the back, gave her a glance of half-admiration and half-embarrassment, and then went to see about their own families. Homer was the last to leave. He flicked Trey lightly on the shoulder, as if they'd parted after a leisurely afternoon stroll, and turned to Verity.

For the first time ever, he looked her full in the eyes. His head jerked in Trey's direction. "His head don't work too good, sometimes, less'n he's in the shade. Times are, he needs taking care of. And since he's not likely to be grateful, I thank you, ma'am." Without a glance at Trey, he turned and slouched out of sight behind a stack of crates.

Trey was still fighting to control his breathing. He eyed Verity uncertainly. "Believe it or not—he likes me."

Verity couldn't seem to sit up straight. All the stiffening had gone out of her spine.

Trey flexed his arms and tested his body slowly, stretching and hunching. He pulled his sodden leather shirt over his head. "Everything seems to work," he said finally. Then, his voice tight, grudging, "I guess I owe you."

That straightened her spine. In the blink of an eye all her fear turned to anger. The ungrateful wretch. "You don't owe me anything. Do you know how close you came to being dead? And killing Homer at the same time, just because he wouldn't leave you in the water alone? Have you any idea just how thoroughly stupid that was?"

Her voice was rising. The whole day seemed pent up inside her and had to come out. Her relief at finding a wet nurse for the baby, Trey's arrogant remarks of the morning, her violent response to his kiss, the campfire and her own Indian scare, her joy in the violet patch, the magnificent and frightening storm, and her terror when she saw Trey being carried down river. "You owe this whole expedition an apology. Every man, woman and child aboard thought you were drowning. Why—"

His voice was deadly quiet, but it cut through hers like a knife. "Wait a minute, lady. I owe nobody an apology. The boat is free now and we can move as soon as Clark gives the word. You had best curb that tongue of yours, because my loyalties are to Clark and nobody else. Now, until you know what you're talking about, you'd better close your mouth."

Verity rose from the barrel where she sat. She was breathing as hard as Trey. "Maybe, captain, I should have saved my breath and my energy and let you drown. You might not have been missed as much as you'd expect. And I'll simply tell Homer, instead of you, about the Indian sign I found."

With as much dignity as she could manage, given a dress that slapped wetly at her calves and hair that hung in dripping, lank strings around her face, Verity followed Homer around the stacked crates and out of sight.

Behind her she heard an explosive "Damn," and the sound of wet buckskins hitting the deck.

Eight

During the night Zelma died. Verity found her cold and stiffening when she went to collect the baby for his early feeding with the wet nurse.

Verity was more angry than grief stricken. She'd been half-way expecting the death. For all her efforts to cure Zelma, the woman had just given up. She'd faded a little with each day until finally there was nothing left. Verity pounded a futile fist against her thigh. How could the woman just quit when her children needed her, when the entire western push was in front of them, when each morning brought a new and exciting array of possibilities and all the freedoms she could dream of?

But, of course, this was what taking a man did to women. Marriage wore them down and used them until their juices dried up and all they had left was dry dust, of no good to anyone, even themselves. Her own mother had been vivid proof. Verity knew she had not died of some illness, but of overwork and broken dreams.

She, herself, could talk all she wanted about being promised to Edward, no one need know she had serious doubts about the whole man-woman thing. Men seemed to take what they wanted as their due and were surprised when a woman objected to being handed only what was left.

Their departure was delayed for a brief hour while they buried Zelma. A shallow grave was dug, a few words said and rocks piled on top so scavenging animals could not dig up the blanket-shrouded body. Almost without drawing breath, Clark gave the order to load up and move out. Verity stood briefly at the grave site, holding the baby, and thought with some bitterness that it was hardly decent to end a life with such haste, and yet she knew as well as anyone that it wasn't safe to linger. The memory of the campfire, still warm beneath the sole of her thin shoe, spurred her to glance over her shoulder as she moved behind the others to the boarding plank.

She had told Homer of her foray into the forest and discovery of the cooking fire. She couldn't quite bring herself to speak to Trey, although that is what she really wanted to do. He'd avoided her the remainder of the day and confined himself to another boat. To her disgust, Verity found she missed raising her head and finding his watchful gaze on her at unexpected moments. The knowledge of his attention, even though she refused to admit it in so many words, was reassuring. Satisfying, in some obscure way. It was as if a sort of contentedness was attached to Trey's presence, and that was stupid. The man was as unpredictable as the river and had never given her one reason to think she was anyone special. A man could scatter kisses thick along his back trail and not have it mean anything at all. Trey had made it plain that his concern was for the entire flotilla. In fact, he seemed to reserve his rudeness and anger for her alone.

But she did wonder what he might have said about the campfire. Her conversation with Homer had been typically short and unsatisfactory.

"Do you think it was Indians?" she'd asked.

"Could be," he answered, his eyes searching her face intently, even though she could tell he was uncomfortable in her presence. "It was foolhardy, ma'am, you being that far away from the boats and alone," he said finally, his eyes not meeting hers, but shifting toward the shimmering stretch of river before them.

"I wanted herbs for a strengthening tea for Zelma. And I wasn't really a long distance off. Because the storm was coming," she added. But she had been farther away than she should have been and she knew it. She'd been warned several times.

When he spoke it was as if the words were pulled from him and he still didn't look at her. "Trey, he's not going to like it. He's going to be madder'n a gut-stuck grizzly. Clark, too."

"Clark needs to know, I realize that. But there isn't any reason the captain should be told, is there?"

He turned his eyes on her then, carefully, and Verity wondered suddenly what he was thinking. Out of the corner of his mouth he favored the broad expanse of river with a half-smile. "Yup. I reckon there is."

And she watched in frustration while he walked away from her in a measured, rolling gait, matching the changing pitch of the flatboat. All twenty-three of them aboard the boat had become experts at keeping their footing aboard the craft by learning the same rocking cadence. But, Homer was the only one among them who didn't appear awkward and ungainly while making his way from one end of the boat to another.

When would he tell Trey, she wondered, since Trey was on another boat? And what would Trey do about her breaking the rules yet another time? She shrugged. He could hardly put her ashore and leave her to the Indians. Nor was he likely to throw her off the boat and make her swim. Maybe he would just ignore it as of no consequence. But, as of the moment the flotilla shoved off from shore and left poor Zelma in her lonely grave, he had done nothing. He hadn't even looked at Verity with those black eyes so often flat and unreadable, even while they leaped with a watchfulness that missed nothing. She put it from her mind. There were things to do and vistas to watch unfold. She refused to worry.

She even managed to ignore the calf-eyes Bart made at her when he handed her the string of catfish he'd caught.

"Ain't nobody fries a mess of fish like you do," he said gruffly as he swung the line for her to grab, and Verity looked up, startled, at what she supposed was a compliment. "Corn pone?" he asked.

"Yes." They ate corn pone twice a day, every day.

He nodded, satisfied. "My woman's got to make passable corn pone." He walked away, his bulk swaying easily with the rock of the boat.

Verity hadn't moved, the fish still dangled from one hand. She ran his words over again and again. "My woman." What did that mean? She wasn't his woman. She had never given him any reason to think in those terms. In fact, she'd been all but rude in answer to his incessant staring at her and following her about. His woman? Bart's woman? Never.

She skinned and filleted the fish with quick, angry strokes. Bart was almost as bad as Old Man Hargraves. Not quite, maybe, but almost. Never. No matter what he thought. No matter what they all thought. Not Bart. No one could force her to marry anyone. She was free of all that. All she had to do was get to Kaskaskia and Joe, and the rest of her life stretched before her. Uncomplicated. Smooth. She talked herself into a better mood and by the time she began to fry the fish, she was humming to herself and smiling.

The previous day they had passed lush and lovely islands. On both sides of the river the country was rich and level with high, steep banks falling away into the river. From mid-morning to evening they fought a strong head wind and the entire company knew Clark was unhappy with the mere twenty miles they'd made after passing the Hochocken, or Battle River, as some of the men called it.

With the late start they'd made because of the burial, Verity was afraid they'd not do any better this day, but the wind had died down at mid-morning and they skimmed down the river like a drift of blossoms torn from the trees and scattered on the water's surface.

Spring seemed to have arrived overnight. A warm wind swept up the river. Tight buds had appeared on trees and swelled with ardent promise. Willows along the bank waved graceful plumes of lacy green. Fruit trees blossomed creamy white beside the frothy pink of redbud bushes. Clouds of ducks and geese filled the southern sky and the very air swelled with their honking and squawking. That morning she'd awakened to a pair of mourning doves complaining energetically above her head.

For once she sat idle and watched the river go by. At mid-afternoon, thirty-five miles below the Hochocken, they entered a beautiful country chock-a-block with buffalo, bear and deer—so much game and so fearless that they could be killed right from the boats. On the western curve of the bank they found a broad bottom land, instantly christened Buffalo Bottom.

The day took on the quality of a holiday with men cheering one another on, guns firing and children screaming with glee. Several canoes were set ashore with men to gather the meat and then follow the boats downriver. Men shouted and waved their hats in the air, women flapped their aprons, chickens and pigs squealed. Verity laughed aloud at the party-like atmosphere. Tonight they would have plenty of meat. She'd use some of her precious store of dried herbs along with the cornmeal and they would have a feast.

Bart had been one of the hunting party and that evening, after leaving a buffalo haunch with Esther Hicks, he came to his own fire swelled with importance and for once, talkative. Verity was alone.

"More deer than I could count. Never seen such a passel of game in my life. Not all in one spot, anyways. Buffler and even bear in plain view." He paused and shifted feet. "Course, for someone who's a good shot it warn't much of a thing. Gideon could've done as well. However," and his voice took on a tinge of something that made Verity lift her head. "I disremember a year when we'uns went hungry. I can always find game, and it don't do no more runnin' once I take aim."

His eyes homed in on her with single-minded intensity. He almost frowned with effort. Verity realized he was telling her what a good provider he would be. Promising her she would never go hungry. Horrified that she'd allowed herself to get trapped into having to listen to a near-proposal she averted her eyes.

"It's this river," she said quickly, cutting off a hunk of meat for the pot. "Full of surprises and beauty and—and—I'm surprised ducks don't simply fall out of the sky into our boats." She could hear herself prattle on, breathlessly filling the air with talk so that he couldn't say anything more. "The azalea bushes, flowering crab apple trees, daffodils. I hope the Indians appreciate it all since they're the only ones who see it. 'La Belle Riviere,' that's French for The Beautiful River. It sounds beautiful in any language. My mother spoke French. Do you suppose—"

He cut across her chatter with a heavy voice. "I want you to be my woman."

Verity shut her mouth. She couldn't seem to drag her eyes away from Bart's hooded, unblinking gaze. Words failed her. Mutely she shook her head.

"Don't wag your head at me," he said, harshly. "A woman needs a man to take care of her and I aim to be that man." In an almost unconscious gesture he shrugged and the muscles in his heavy shoulders flexed. He was, indeed, strong as a bull ox. "You got nothin' to worry about when I'm around. I'm your man," he repeated.

"No." Verity said at once and then again with conviction. "No. I'm pledged to a man in Kaskaskia. You know that."

Bart's mouth drew up in an indifferent sneer. For a man who rarely spoke he seemed bent on talking now. "Kaskaskia's a long way and you might not ever get there. Besides, who knows? Your man may be killed already. There's no use in your goin' on when I'm here."

"You don't understand." She spoke slowly, taking pains with the half-lie. He must believe her. "We grew up together. We've been promised since we were children. I can't marry anyone else."

Her refusal made no difference. His face relaxed in confidence. "He's not here. I am. You'll see. I'll build you a strong cabin on Corn Island and keep you in plenty of meat. You'll give me sons to help in the fields. It'll be good." He turned to go.

"No! Wait!" What could she say to penetrate that stubborn will of his? "Bart. Thank you for offering. I'm honored. Truly I am. But, as long as there's a possibility of finding Edward, I can't. Don't you see? I gave him my word."

Her word. He understood that. A man's word was sacred. She watched the struggle cross his face before he spoke. "One day," he said harshly, poking a dirty finger at her, "you'll be mine." He left the fire without a backward glance.

Verity felt limp with relief and sat for a dazed moment, unmoving, beside the fire. How long could she hold him off once they reached Corn Island? She would have to take great care not to insult him. Bart could make her position in the family very uncomfortable. With Zelma gone, it could get that way in any case. She blinked hard to clear her head. She *had* to go down the river with Clark. She had to get to Kaskaskia.

A loud clatter and flurry of feathers and squeals drew her attention. Clem was making his way toward her, kicking a sluggish pig and a basket of chickens aside. He would be hungry. Verity drew a long breath. Trey's words echoed in her head. Surely Clem wouldn't expect her to take Zelma's place, would he? Surely that had all been in Trey's imagination. Clem wouldn't… O Lordy. She'd think what to do later, when the boat settled down for the night. In this confusion she couldn't even call her thoughts her own.

The feast Verity had envisioned was enjoyed by everyone except her. She barely tasted the thick, rich stew flavored with wild onions, and herb-flecked corn cakes. Clem, Abner and Bart ate with noisy gusto, licking their fingers clean and smacking their lips with appreciation. Gideon tried his best to imitate the men. Verity struggled with where to put her eyes. Bart's gaze, dark and heavy with meaning never left her. It was hard to ignore him. To her surprise Clem was loud with raucous bursts of nervous laughter and many stops and starts in his conversation. She stopped serving Sally to watch Clem—what on earth was the matter with the man—until he met her eyes with a quick look and shied away. She dropped the wooden spoon. He was making eyes at her! Her mouth almost fell open.

Abner shoveled stew in his mouth while watching his brother with a bright and interested look. He was all but laughing out loud, his head swiveling back and forth between Clem, Verity and a smoldering Bart.

To Verity's horror, Clem spoke suddenly. "You got a better touch with corn pone than anybody, even my mother," and when she stood speechless he eyed her, up and down, with a disgusting leer and went on.

"Fine figure of a woman, too. One a man takes notice of. But you got no need to fear," he said raising his voice and glancing around threateningly as if warning off unwelcome guests. "There ain't no need for nobody else around here as long as you got a real man to take care of you. That's me."

Verity gasped. Zelma hadn't been dead yet for twenty-four hours.

Bart lunged to his feet. "You're forgettin' yore wife ain't cold in the grave yet!"

"I ain't forgettin' nothing. Like who's boss here. Like who needs a woman the worst. Like somebody who knows what a woman wants."

Verity had to almost scream to make herself heard. "I am not chattel and you'd best remember that." She poked herself in the chest with a thumb. "I don't belong to anybody except myself. And when I get to Kaskaskia and marry Edward, I'll still belong to myself. So, you're both wasting your time."

She turned her back on the sudden silence and began cleaning up. To say anything more might create an even greater problem. Maybe this would be enough. By morning maybe both Clem and Bart would have other things to think about. But, maybe, too, she ought to give serious consideration to sleeping elsewhere, even on another boat, now that Zelma was gone. Not only for the sake of propriety, but to ease her own worries. Between Bart and Clem, life hadn't been pleasant at times, and was likely to get worse now that another woman, a wife, was no longer there to hold them in check just by her mere presence. She'd talk to Esther Hicks about it, she decided, soon.

She collected the baby from Esther who had her entire brood underfoot, waiting to be fed. This was not a good time to talk. Returning to her own boat, she settled the children for the night. When the men wandered off toward the main cooking fire she, too, moved away toward the rail. The baby could be heard, if he cried.

She wished she could get away, off the boat and onto the shore, and be alone for just a little while. How nice it would be to be able to *think* without interruption. All day Sally had followed her around, clinging to her skirts. Gideon would be all right without his mother, but Sally wore the bewildered expression of one who had been cast adrift on the sea. Her mother's presence, frail as it had been, was an anchor and without it she was lost. But now, Sally slept and Verity was free of her tugging hands for a few hours. The rest of the movers were still awake, however, and stirring around. With so many people crowded into so small an area, it was like living in each other's pocket.

She found a sheltered space between baskets at the rear of the boat with a stack of bound hay snugged among them and sat, hunched and hidden in the dark, promising herself a little while all to herself, not long, and then she'd go back to her blankets.

The stars hung low in the sky, heavy and fat as pears on the trees back home in Albemarle County. The dark form of an owl glided silently through the night toward the trees. A breeze freshened as it swept down the river and she lifted her face to it gratefully. Thoughts of the pear tree brought a small wave of homesickness, but not for people. She wished only for the land, the hills and the familiar river, not grand and splendid like the Ohio but pretty on a smaller scale with rocks and rapids and fast water, bound by purple, hump-backed, thrusting mountains on both sides.

However, it wasn't likely that she'd ever go back; she'd made her choice. She grimaced into the night. Not that there had really been any choice, Otis and Lena had made it impossible to stay and she'd done the only thing she could. And so far, she'd managed.

A smile creased the corners of her mouth. She'd been kissed by the most handsome man she'd ever seen. That had to count for something. Of course, he was an Indian lover and that rankled deeply. And at times he made her madder than any man she'd ever met but, in any case, the kiss had been nice.

She wedged herself deeper into the baskets and watched the river. The days had passed, rolling as relentlessly onward as the river, since they'd taken to the water. Even now, she could feel the way the water pushed at the sides of the boat, tugging at its moorings and urging it to move. Everything on the river was in a hurry to go west, herself, the movers, the militia—the captain. Captain Trey Owens.

The handsome, maddening, dictatorial captain. And, suddenly, out of the night came again the wondering thought that it was certainly odd how she called him by his given name in her head and was careful, in his presence, to use his title at all times. She couldn't explain it and frowned. How very odd.

And then, as if it came directly from her thoughts, she heard his voice. She almost sat up, startled, before she realized that Trey, himself, in the flesh, was walking on deck carrying on a conversation with someone else.

"...stubborn little minx," he was saying. "I've told her and told her it isn't safe to wander. She can find more trouble than any two females I ever knew. A campfire, that near the river!"

Verity's mouth flew open in silent surprise. He was talking about her! A minx he'd called her. A stubborn minx. Finding trouble! Heat rose in her face. Why, why, the ornery—polecat. The only thing was, she could hardly get to her feet and confront him. It would look as if she had been eavesdropping. She had to sit and listen in silence while he called her names!

He went on. "Indians. And, up to no good, I'd guess."

The other man answered with a snort. It was Homer. "Does a Shawnee like horses? Of course, they're up to no good."

"Pass the word to keep all eyes peeled from now on. We've known all along they were out there, but this is our first proof."

There was a comfortable silence and then Homer spoke softly. "You got other things to worry about, too."

"Like what?"

"Like the biggest thing any man's got to be afeared of. A good woman. And she's one of them, for sure."

Another silence and Trey's voice came on a sigh. "Yeah."

"There's times I get to wondering. Times when you get to acting like a gopher in soft dirt, and then—"

A grunt.

"—and others when you behave like a coiled diamondback rattler."

No response.

"Well?"

"You're beginning to talk like an old woman."

Verity waited. Who were they referring to? Could it possibly be her? Was she the good woman? Who else could it be?

Finally, "You better find your blanket. Early watch will be on us and you'll still be here flapping your jaw."

A heavy sigh. "Have it your way. You're the one going to get singed."

She could hear the unmistakable sound of Homer's rolling gait as he moved away. Trey didn't stir. She waited, her anger building. Talking about her. Ordinary gossip, like two women at a wake. Still she waited. He'd called her a trouble-maker. And stubborn. She fumed with her lips pressed close together. Her legs began to cramp from staying in one position.

And then, suddenly, a strange pulse began to beat through the night. So soft the sound seemed only a memory, it was borne on the wind and carried to her ears down the trough of the river. It beat in her skull, vibrated in the pit of her stomach, tingled in her fingertips. In an instant her anger drained away and was replaced by an icy spread of fear.

Drums! Indian drums. Her heart plunged and then reared. Without conscious thought, Verity scrambled from her place behind the baskets and looked wildly around for Trey Owens.

He straightened from where he leaned, not three feet away, against a stack of crates, and she could see the white gleam of his teeth as he smiled.

Verity's eyes strained toward the shore, through the black of night. "Shawnee?" she asked, through teeth clenched so that they wouldn't chatter.

Her throat was so tight she could barely make a sound.

He inhaled through his nose and nodded. "Talking to one another," he said. "They're not close. Don't worry."

"I'm not," she denied, although she had to lock her knees to keep them from shaking.

The silence stretched as the drums swelled and faded on the breeze.

"What are they talking about?" she asked, trying to force her tone to sound normal.

He shifted and blew out a breath. She could tell he was making out it was nothing in an effort to ease her fears. "Treaties, illnesses, peace, war."

"Us?"

"Maybe."

She shivered in the warm night. And as naturally as if he'd done it every night of his life, he stretched out a hand and she moved into the shelter of his arms. It was warm there and she burrowed closer.

Trey signed and bent his head to rest his cheek on the top of her head. She smelled faintly of violets and wood smoke, and he thought he'd never smelled anything better. Nor held anyone that felt as good or fit as perfectly.

"You knew I was there, behind the baskets, all the time, didn't you?" Her voice was muffled against his neck and he could feel her mouth draw up in a smile.

"I always know where you are," he said.

"Then why did you say I was stubborn? And a trouble-maker?"

"I was wrong. I should have said you are the prettiest, stubbornest, trouble-maker I ever knew." His tone was caught between tender and teasing and Verity pulled away to look up at him.

In the lantern light his eyes held hers. Verity's breath stopped in her throat. One hand slid down her arm and his fingers entwined with hers. "I want to show you something. Are you game?"

"Game?"

"Are you willing to come with me? I found a place today. A real pretty place, and—Wouldn't take a half-hour if you'd come with me."

Without even needing to think she nodded. It didn't occur to her until much later that she would feel safe with him anywhere. Maybe she didn't always like him, but she trusted him with all her heart.

He led her off the boat and onto dry land, still holding her hand, and into the forest. The sky with all its stars disappeared. The darkness enveloping them was nearly complete and Verity could see nothing but vague shadows, a subtle lightening or darkening of the blackness.

"Where are we going?" she asked. "I can't see."

"Don't worry, I can see for both of us."

"What about the Indians? Or are they your friends?"

"The drums are across the river."

The ground was fairly flat and free of the rocky hills they'd left in Virginia. Yet because she stumbled several times, he pulled her close to steady her. Her shawl rode up her arm and his buckskin shirt was smooth against her bare skin. His grip around her waist strong. She plunged along blindly with full confidence in his lead. They hadn't gone far when the forest opened suddenly and the sky appeared once more. Trey pulled her to a stop beside him and stood quietly.

There was a lake lying smooth and unruffled in the starshine. Verity gasped at the unexpected beauty.

"Why," she said with a catch in her throat, "it's like the sky fell in the water. I can see every star and every bit of light that's in the heavens."

Trey nodded. "It's just about the prettiest piece of water I've ever seen."

He led her around the near edge of the lake to a fallen tree and settled her beside him. His arm was warm around her shoulders and she seemed to fit in the cove of his body as if she'd been carved for just that purpose.

There was no moon, but the sky was alight with fat, white stars hanging close to the earth.

He pointed. "See up there? Venus. It's called The Lamplighter of the Western Sky because it's the brightest of all the evening stars. There's The Queen's Chair. And Seven Sisters."

She tipped her head back in awe. "They've drained all the light from the day and saved it to make the night shine."

His arm was warm around her shoulders. "Over there's the Milky Way, that swooping river of stars." He bent his cheek to hers to better focus her gaze.

Verity tried to take in the multitude of floating pinpricks of light in the vast dome of the sky.

"I only know the dippers and the North Star by name. Where did you learn about all the others?"

"On board ship. The sailors," he hesitated and went on. "When my parents and brother and I came to America, the sailors on the boat told Billy and me. Mainly as a distraction I think. Both our parents died during the crossing and they sort of took us on for the remainder of the trip. Gave us something to think about besides wondering what would happen to us once we got here."

"What did? Where did you go?"

"A good man named Thomas Stone took us on as indentured servants and taught us the bookbinding and printing business. Billy's still in Williamsburg. His service will be over soon."

Verity looked at the dark silhouette of the trees against the sky across the water and thought about Trey Owens bending over a printing press. The picture wouldn't come.

"I can't see you content to be inside walls all day," she said looking up at him.

He laughed. "Neither could I, but I stuck it out for almost all of my time. I was shy only a couple of months when I left. Billy says Thomas Stone won't hold it against me. He made it legal that I fulfilled my contract because of all the extra things I used to do for him. He's a good man."

"You've seen Billy then?"

"A few times. He's almost a man now." He smiled then and asked slowly, "What about you? Are you ever going to tell me why you were fighting the mud and rain and a goat on that hillside the first time I saw you?"

Verity looked out at the lake without speaking for so long Trey had begun to think she wasn't going to answer his question.

When she spoke it was in a voice so soft he had to lower his head to hear. "I had to leave in a sort of hurry. There was a man who'd spoke for me and Otis—my step-father—had bargained long and hard. He was set fast that I was going to marry Old Man Hargraves but I just couldn't do it. I couldn't bring myself to accept to do it. I couldn't," she finished in a rush.

He raised an eyebrow. "Are you telling me that you were running away when I found you?"

She nodded without looking at him.

There were enough holes in what she'd told him to keep him awake at night for a month. "Just how old was this Old Man Hargraves," he asked.

"Old," she said flatly and with enough distaste to tell him what he wanted to know. And then she chuckled, a delightful gurgling sound like a fast-running stream, and smiled up at him. "To myself I called him a smelly old goat and that's what made me think of the Dawson's needing the goat for the baby and how I could possibly earn my way west."

He was charmed. He'd never known anyone with as much sheer force of will and just plain guts, and all of it wrapped up in a tiny slip of a girl no taller than his armpit.

She had trusted him after all. The knowledge humbled him. For all he knew, her Pa was out combing the hills for her, still. She had taken a risk of some magnitude in telling him. He felt as if something priceless had been given him.

He realized she was looking up at him with a steady and thoughtful gaze. She said, "Do you know that your eyes are as black as coal and just about as hard looking?"

"As bad as that, huh?"

"It's deliberate. You don't want folks to know what you're thinking. I can't ever tell."

Ah, so she thought about him during the day. "Out here, it's what we do that proves our mettle, not what we think."

"What do you think of me?" And to his surprise her eyes slammed shut and she ducked her head. "I'm sorry. I shouldn't have asked that." And to his dismay she moved to get up.

"No. Don't go." Instinctively his arm tightened. "Stay here. Right here." One hand slid up and into her hair.

She turned and it seemed that every nerve in his body sang out. She smelled fresh like the woods. Every star in the sky seemed to be reflected in her eyes. Her lips were only inches from his. He could feel her trembling, or was it he that trembled? She sat, unblinking, unmoving, trapped like him by whatever it was that flowed between them.

Slowly his head came down. *Take it easy boy*, he thought, *don't rush it. Give her time to back off. Don't bungle this one.* But Verity waited for him, her head resting on his arm. She tilted her head so that her chin moved forward and her lips reached for his, ever-so-slightly, but ever-so-definitely. Gently he rolled his mouth across hers, and then again, with more urgency.

He turned her body into his and tightened his arms. And was lost. There was a roar in his head like a towering, rushing flood and at the same time he felt a desperate need to tear himself away and run. All his instincts gathered and rushed forward but he could no more push her away than he could outrun the flood and he felt a curious sense of knowing that this was like nothing he'd ever find again. *Hold on here,* he told himself, *This is white water country. Be sure you know how to swim before you plunge into the rapids.*

But what he did was something else. With rising triumph, he rode the crest of the wave. To hell with the danger.

Nine

They camped the next night on the banks of the Little Guyandotte River, thirty miles down stream from the confluence of the Ohio and the Great Conhawa River. Throbbing drums the night before had made them wary, but their passage had been uneventful until early afternoon when two buckskin-clad men in a canoe rounded a curve in the river before them.

A shout went up from the lead boat and Verity paused from changing the moss in the baby's blankets to look up. With much broad waving of the arms and pointing, Clark signaled that he wanted to meet on shore and, obligingly, the canoe pointed its prow toward land and the entire flotilla of flatboats did the same.

Verity had settled the baby in its blankets for a nap and was hanging garments to dry on ropes stretched across the boat when Homer appeared on shore, calling to her. "Cap'n wants you. Come now."

"Captain Owens wants me? Whatever for?" She stopped with an armload of blankets unable to think why in the world Trey would send for her like this, in the middle of the day, when all the men were obviously engrossed with the occupants of the canoe.

Homer jerked his head toward the gathering on the river bank. "Them's two Frenchies. Ain't nobody can understand a word of their gibberish. Cap'n says maybe you can."

Still she hesitated. Clark wasn't likely to welcome her presence in a group of men, no matter what Trey said—unless he had urgent need of her. Clark needed her. A smile spread across her face.

"Of course," she said to the waiting Homer and carefully laid her armload of dry garments over a stack of boxes. She called to one of the other women to listen for the baby and in a minute was on shore, being hurried along as fast as her legs would carry her. Homer all but dragged her by the arm with a firm grip, separating the men and steering her in front of him as if he were guiding a slow-moving cow, until he fetched up next to Trey.

"Here she be," he said quietly through the din of what sounded to be every single person there talking at the same time. "I hope you know what you're doing. If she can't talk Frog—"

Trey glanced at her with relief and took her arm. Verity stiffened. First Homer pulling at her and now Trey hauling her forward. She was, after all, about to do them a favor. They didn't need to manhandle her.

Without looking at her, Trey muttered from the side of his mouth. "I hope you really can speak French because I crawled out on a very shaky limb, lady."

The Frenchmen were not overly tall, but slim and straight and pleasantly dark complected. They were dressed for the frontier with fringed buckskin and knives, and had the darkest and most active, glittering eyes Verity could remember. The hands of both men hovered uneasily near the knives at their belt. Clearly they were not comfortable being so vastly outnumbered and surrounded by men armed for war, speaking a language they could not understand.

"Sir?" Trey stepped forward, his hand still gripping Verity's arm so that she moved beside him. Clark's head turned.

"Miss Philp speaks French. Maybe she can be of service." He gave her a slight push so that she stood in front of him, alone.

Suspicious, General Clark looked Verity up and down. She thought about the damp hem of her skirt from the washing and her hair was probably in wind-tossed disarray. She must look nothing like the kind of woman he would expect to be able to speak two languages.

He seemed to make up his mind. "I need to know where they're coming from and where they're going."

Verity's chin came up. It wasn't a request; it was an order. He was treating her as if she were one of his men. Resisting the impulse to smooth back her hair and straighten her skirts, she turned calmly to the Frenchmen and welcomed them warmly in their own tongue.

The effect was astonishing. Broad, white smiles broke out and answers came thick and fast. One of the men, the taller of the two, inclined his head in a respectful bow.

"They come from far to the west, a place called the Shining Mountains, a place of unsurpassed beauty, meadows and mountains, clear streams and virgin forests, more game than one could imagine. A paradise, they say."

Clark nodded. "I've heard of the Shining Mountains. Did they come by way of Kaskaskia?"

Under Verity's questioning the two men spoke, although not quite as freely, and with cautious glances at Clark and all his men.

Verity translated. "They traded four canoes full of furs with the Chateau brothers in a place called St. Louis."

Clark frowned. "What about Kaskaskia? Were they there? How many men? What sort of defense have they mounted? Guns? Canon? Ask them."

With her hands clasped carefully in front of her and trying to keep her face emotionless, she said, "General Clark, they are understandably anxious about these questions. Kaskaskia is peopled by their own kind. By friends. They aren't going to give you information enabling you to go in and slaughter those they care about." She drew a breath and her chin came up a fraction farther as she looked directly at him, without apology. "It isn't fair or even gentlemanly of you to ask."

There was a sudden and absolute silence. From behind her she heard a muttered oath from Trey. She knew she had committed the unthinkable in both questioning Clark's orders and in accusing him of not being a gentleman, but suddenly respect and fairness was more important to her than whether or not she got down the Ohio. Clark rode roughshod over everyone and everything in his way and granted, his men adored him, would follow him into any situation, but her honor in presenting these questions to the Frenchmen was at stake, too.

The General's hand clenched and his mouth hardened into a thin, flat line. He had to take two long breaths and expel them before he could speak. His voice was leashed with restraint. "Will you tell these gentlemen, *Miss Philp*, that we await imminent word to the effect that France has entered the war on our side. My superiors have assured me of this fact. It is only a matter of days, perhaps, until it happens. And, for your information, I do not intend to inflict wholesale slaughter upon Fort Kaskaskia. It is my fervent hope and prayer that we can take it with a minimum of bloodshed on both sides. My prior knowledge, before attack, will enable me to make that hope a reality. Now, would you be so kind as to translate and get me some answers?"

With all the dignity Verity could muster she turned to the Frenchmen and began to speak. After a whispered conversation between themselves, the Frenchmen came to an agreement and began to talk.

"It appears the fort is not heavily armed, either with men or guns. No canon," Verity said, finally. "The people, as good French persons, are not happy under British rule, but are too fearful of reprisals by both the Indians and Hamilton's forces to attempt to free themselves. If they knew France had entered the war on the side of the Americans, it might make all the difference in the world in the ease with which you take the fort."

A collective breath of relief seemed to sigh from the throat of every man there. Clark strode forward to clasp the hands of the Frenchmen and wish them Godspeed and then turned away. The taller of the Frenchmen, who had not been able to keep his eyes from Verity during the entire exchange, leaned forward and took her hand. To the surprise of everyone there, he did not shake it, but bowed deeply and kissed it!

Verity blushed to the roots of her hair, a soldier in the ranks laughed, and Trey straightened slowly from the deceptively loose-hipped slouch he had maintained for the last few minutes.

The Frenchman was still talking to Verity with a warm look of promise in his eyes, when Trey stepped forward and removed Verity's hand to hold it himself and put his other arm around her waist. It was a clear declaration of territory, which the Frenchman did not miss.

"Auguste Fauconnet," he said to Verity in mellow tones rich with accent, and that was the only thing Trey understood for the man continued in French, not at all bothered by Trey's tightening grip on Verity's waist or the glowering look Trey bent upon him.

He apparently asked a question, for Verity hesitated and then said slowly, "N-non," upon which he nodded once in deep satisfaction, turned to Trey, smilingly executed another bow and strode purposefully to the canoe and shoved off.

When they moved into the current, he turned once to salute Verity with his paddle and a flash of white teeth, and was swept away.

Verity didn't move until Trey forcibly turned her. "What did he say?" he demanded, his voice gruff and unnecessarily harsh.

She didn't look at him, her eyes still following the disappearing canoe. "He asked if you were my husband," she said, moving away slightly, forcing him to release his grip on her. "And he vowed to see me again on his return trip."

She turned and walked away, toward her own flatboat, without a backward glance. Trey stood for a moment looking with slitted eyes up the river, after the canoe which was no longer in sight.

"Damn!" he exploded. The hand-kissing Frenchie had enough slick charm to grease the bore of a cannon. Women liked that sort of thing. And he was coming back up river, likely sometime this summer. But at least he, Trey, would be here waiting with the rest of them. Verity wouldn't be unprotected.

~ * ~

To Gideon's disgust, Verity set him to helping her air their bedding in the fresh air of the golden afternoon. By evening they were finished, with everything back in place and rolled up, Zelma's pitifully small pile of belongings given to others who needed them.

Clem, the straggly yellow beard on his chin working jerkily for a moment, nodded and said it was good. With steady eyes he complimented her on her handling of his domestic affairs. In sudden fear that he was going to suggest a permanent arrangement, she made an excuse to leave and spent the rest of the afternoon on the far end of the boat. It wasn't unusual for a widower to find a new wife immediately. The frontier was hard and even two weeks was a long time to remain single if there was an available female nearby. However, Verity had no intention of marrying Clem. And she didn't know how to get out of it without hard feelings. Feelings she couldn't afford until Corn Island, at least. She rummaged around in her mind all afternoon for an answer.

There was also the constant problem of trying to avoid Bart's watchful gaze. She had developed a permanent itch between her shoulder blades. Just the thought of his flat, dark eyes homing in on her could make her squirm. Her feelings were far different when she raised her head and found Trey watching her. Confused, troubled, maybe, but not fearful.

Thoughts of Trey were never far from her mind, no matter how firmly she tried to chase them away. She told herself she would *not* remember the way his hair gleamed in the sun. Or the curious habit he had of standing hip-shot with one hand braced against a tree or the rail of the boat. She did her best to also forget the way she'd felt when he kissed her, but she could do nothing to stop the jolt of excitement that leaped along her veins when their eyes met accidentally. The worst of it was that she saw an answering thrill in his eyes. She didn't dare let herself think of him in the way a woman thinks of a man; she had all she could handle getting herself to Kaskaskia. Besides, men weren't dependable. They let you down just when you needed them the most. No, she wouldn't think of Trey Owens at all.

In spite of her efforts, however, there was one thought that nagged at her worse than the persistent buzzing of the swarms of flies that plagued their evening camps. His eyes had crinkled in that endearing way he had on the day they'd reached the banks of the Ohio. "I must be doing something right. My luck keeps getting better." And she'd known then and there, whether she wanted it that way or not, that this man was special.

Trey labored under his own black cloud of uncertainty. He shouldn't have kissed her the way he had, like a winter-hungry wolf. For a certain kind of woman it would have been fine, even expected, but Verity wasn't that kind of woman, and he'd barged into the whole thing with all the finesse of a buffalo in a dry canebrake. "Edge too close to the fire and you'll get your pants scorched, boy," he told himself. In the clear light of day, and with Verity nowhere in sight, he swore that he wanted no ties, on his person or on his time, and yet he'd deliberately gone out of his way to ensure ties of all kinds. For a few moments last night, his brain had gone as spongy as a mud-wallow, and he hardly knew what he was doing. No more. He'd have to keep a tight rein because it seemed all the girl had to do was look at him slant-wise and his knees turned as soft as his brain.

He blundered around the flatboat all day, knocking into crates, elbowing people aside, growling irritably and in general, sharing his foul mood with everyone aboard.

Clark raised his voice as the boats were drawing to shore, readying to tie up for the night. "You've been acting like a wounded bull all day. Have you been gut gored, or are you fit to scout around?"

Trey scowled at him in a manner that would have frightened a lesser man. "Scout," he said, shortly.

Clark frowned. "Scout then, but put away that nasty temper first or you'll be no good to yourself or me."

Trey showed him his back and left, jumping into shallow water and wading ashore. Homer followed close on his heels. "Where're you going?" Trey called over his shoulder.

"With you. The mood you're in, you're liable to mistake your big toe for an Indian and shoot if off by accident."

"I don't need a nursemaid!"

"Don't intend to nurse you. Just foller you around some."

"Well then, make yourself useful. Wander up that creek a way and see what you find." And nodding toward one of the several streams feeding into the Ohio at this point, Trey loped off up another, his gun cradled in the curve of his arm.

Six strides up stream the entire Ohio disappeared, flatboats, people, mouth of the creek and all. He was dwarfed by high bluffs on both sides, bluffs so high they swallowed the sun, leaving him in a murky green dimness much like being underwater. The stream angled southwest now and he followed the edge of a rushing creek with frothing water curling around jagged, moss-covered rocks in the stream bed. He slogged through a swampy area, waded a brush-filled bottom with the stream now a thin line splitting the clearing, and forded countless numbers of small feeder creeks. Nothing. Not a blade of grass bent, not a twig broken. Nothing. He saw not a sign, anywhere, to indicate a human had ever been close to the Little Guyandotte River.

He was negotiating an abrupt curve in the stream at the foot of a rocky cliff where the current had washed out a deeper channel, when an alien whiff on the breeze brought his head up. Instinctively his hand went to the knife at his belt and he crouched where he was, behind a dense thicket, and concentrated on the forest.

Somewhere nearby there was the throaty croak of a frog, the noisy scampering of a ground squirrel, and high overhead various tweeps and twerps of birdcalls. The bright blue wings of a wild canary twinkled briefly and disappeared in the treetops. He inhaled deeply, searching for the scent, but it was gone. He swore silently. There had been something, he was sure of it. He'd smelled Indian just as surely as his right hand was closed this moment on the stock of his gun.

Where was Homer? Not that it was likely Homer would walk into an Indian camp, surprised. Nor that the help of one man would make a difference if the Indians were already in place, circled around him and ready for meanness. But he and Homer thought alike when it came to Indians, and two heads might make better sense than one if it came to figuring out which way they might jump next. However, calculating swiftly, Trey figured he'd come at least two miles up stream from the Ohio and Homer wasn't likely to be anywhere within hailing distance, even if he dared hail. He might as well have at it and track them down alone. He had shifted his weight to one foot, ready to move, when a whisper came over his shoulder.

"Where'd you think they be?"

Trey spun around, hurling his gun up to deflect a blow as he came. Homer had one hand on the barrel, angling it away from himself, before the weapon reached waist height.

"Might ruin my aim if a hole was to be blasted through me." His voice was soft with laughter. "Got you that time."

"You addle-brained yah-hoo," Trey whispered fiercely. "There are Indians somewhere around, and you're playing jokes."

The twinkle in Homer's eyes didn't give way. He nodded. "Nearly fell over 'em pow-wowing in the middle of the trail." He jerked his head toward the south, as an invitation for Trey to follow, and set off through the brush and trees.

The two men ran quietly for another mile through the needle-carpeted forest before Homer slowed and put up a hand. His voice was a whisper. "We're close. There's only three of them, but don't get careless. They look about as friendly as a nest of rattlers in tall grass."

Cautiously, they crept toward a clearing and peered through the underbrush. Three Indian braves crouched around a pile of stones, muttering softly to themselves. They were naked except for loin cloths hung around their waists, reaching almost to their knees, a limp feather dangling from their hair and fringed knee-high moccasins.

"They know the flotilla's here?" Homer asked, quietly.

Trey nodded. "Near enough. They've been watching the boats come down river. They're impressed with the size of our party."

Suddenly, one of the Indians leaped to his feet and gestured fiercely toward the river. His oiled body was lean and ropy with muscles, and high, prominent cheekbones accented the black recesses of his eyes. A fanatic light gleamed there. He chopped the air viciously with his fist and gobbled like a turkey angry with his mate.

Trey sank back and flattened himself on the ground. "Can you still throw that tomahawk?" he asked under his breath.

Homer grasped his gun in one hand and pulled the short-handled ax from his belt with the other. "I still got all my hair, ain't I?"

They listened, holding their breath almost, to what was obviously an argument between the three Cherokee, and then looked at one another with unbelieving eyes when the Indians went suddenly silent and then trotted off into the forest, away from the river.

"Well, what do you make of that?" Homer sat up slowly. "And here I was just spoiling for a good fight."

"Two of them had good sense," Trey said, getting to his feet. "My orders were to scout out any Indians. Not kill them. We're trying to get down the river as fast as possible, with as few people knowing about it as we can manage. If we'd killed those braves the entire Nation would know about it in a matter of hours. We would never make it to Corn Island. As it is, they know we're here, but no blood's been spilled."

Homer shrugged. "What's better is that you ain't so besotted with that pretty beaver-haired woman that you can't think what to do in a hurry. I had my doubts for a while."

Trey glared at him. "It's a good thing you don't fight with your mouth. Otherwise, you'd have been bear-bait a long time ago."

Homer grinned happily. "At least we know now where the drums were coming from."

"My guess is they're south, in the hills somewhere, waiting for a good excuse to come out and snipe away at river traffic. But, they don't outnumber us or they'd be hanging from the trees in warpaint. Clark will be glad to hear that."

What Clark did was to set out extra guards that night and keep the fires built high. Everyone except the children slept with one eye open and both ears straining to hear the drums thudding away in the distance. Verity was no exception. She lay in her blankets until dawn listening to the steady rhythm and prayed they wouldn't stop. As long as she could hear the drums, she knew where the Indians were. Trey had said so.

A shudder rippled through her, beneath the blanket. How could Trey defend the Indians? If it was one thing she knew, it was Indians. Hadn't she seen with her own unwilling eyes, heard with disbelieving ears, the results of befriending Indians? Hadn't they murdered her father and baby sister, injured her mother so badly that she lost the baby she was carrying, and destroyed her entire family? Even Mama having to bring Otis into their lives had been a result of have-to, survival, for Ma and Joe and her. And then, Mama died, too. And Joe went away. None of it would have happened, just like that, if it hadn't been for the Indians. They were the fault of it.

And Trey had the gall to say she should see the Indian point of view. That they had every reason to fight. No! She'd never see it. Never. And to think she'd let him kiss her last night. *No*, she told herself, *be honest.* She'd even kissed him back.

And there is where the argument broke down, for even thinking about the feel of his mouth on hers brought the swarm of butterflies back to her stomach. You weren't supposed to feel that way about a man unless you had something permanent in mind. But what did she have in mind? She didn't know. Oh, she could say straight out that she was not interested in a man. Any man. But with the first pressure of his arm around her last night, as they stood listening to the drums, all her determination had drained away.

Her heart had fluttered at the touch of her cheek on his neck. The skin was soft and yet slightly scratchy with a whiskery roughness. She'd never touched a man's neck before, never imagined how soft the skin could be below the line where his beard grew. Never imagined how hard the beat of his heart would be, pounding against the flat of her hand on his chest. And, until that very moment, she hadn't realized that her own heart was thumping away like she'd been running up a mountain.

She had never, that she could remember, been afraid with the same mindless, frantic need that had driven her into his arms. When the drums had begun again, by the lake, she'd all but thrown herself at him. The ebb and flow of the drum beat gave substance to every shadowy fear she'd ever harbored. And, after he'd kissed her, Trey had seemed to sense that and merely held her tight against his chest, murmuring softly into her hair. "It's all right. Sh-h. They're miles away and as long as we can hear them we know the Indians are still only talking."

One hand stroked her hair with the same gentle touch she had used herself with Lena's babies, while the other traveled up and down her back, soothing, quieting. "It's their land, see? Not that they live on it, but it's their hunting ground. All of their lives depend on it. Their food, their clothing, the next generation. They're scared. And they have to fight. What kind of men would they be to roll over and play dead? They would shame their ancestors and their children's children would never speak their name again. They would be cursed. If you understand, you won't be afraid."

And when one hand again guided her mouth to his she forgot to be afraid, and gave herself up to feeling. Such a coursing, fiery energy as she'd never known seared through her veins. Without conscious thought her arms went up and around his neck drawing him even closer. She might have been standing there still, locked in his arms, if he had not pulled away. He'd drawn a ragged, steadying breath and leaned his forehead against hers for a long, silent moment. Then, "We'd better go back."

"But, what if…"

"There won't be any trouble tonight. You can sleep. I promise." And with a gentle push, he urged her toward her bedding. Curiously enough, she had slept. Soundly.

It was odd to know someone cared. She didn't quite know what to do with the way it made her feel. Expectant and yet, at the same time, anxious, ready for flight.

There had been a queer buoyant feeling when he'd admitted to knowing she was resting among the baskets.

"I always know where you are," he'd said. "Always." What did that mean? Could it possibly be that he was aware by some inner, unexplainable sense of her presence at all times, just as she seemed to be aware of his? Surely that was more than mere butterfly wings beating against the wall of her stomach.

And what of her own reaching response? She couldn't pretend, even to herself, that he had taken her by surprise, for she'd been thinking of kissing him, really kissing him, every day since he'd landed that little chicken peck the day she'd found the violets.

She smiled into the darkness and then sighed, deeply. The kissing mustn't go any further. It was as if her heart was divided in two parts. One side was trilling with the captain's obvious interest, and the other more than half-angry at herself because she couldn't forget what he represented—a soul in sympathy with the Indians. And what was worse, now she knew what it felt like to have his arms wrapped around her, pulling her closer and yet closer to his body. Not for the first time she wished with all her heart her mother was still alive. She knew an urge to whimper for her mama, like Sally. She needed to talk to her.

Maybe it was because she had yearned for someone to confide in during the night, but the next morning when she carried the baby to Esther, the big, bosomy woman took one look at Verity and said, "You look more in need of mothering than the babe."

Verity could have stood insolence, anger, being ignored and even cruelty, but compassion was her undoing. She'd just spent an hour ignoring Bart, who didn't talk, but dogged her footsteps until she wanted to scream; another sparring with Clem, who did talk and sent Verity's heart into her mouth with every word he uttered for fear he'd declare himself an available husband; and intervening between Sally and Gideon.

At Esther's kind words tears sprang to her eyes and balanced there ready to flood down her cheeks while she tried to deny that she was troubled. "No…I'm fine…really. Now that the baby is feeding…"

Esther shook her head. "I've been Ma to too many not to know pretending when I see it. What's the matter? To look like that, it's got to be a man."

Verity could only stand, mute, with the tears hovering and clench her teeth together to keep from crying.

Esther took the baby and put it to her breast, all the while talking to Verity. “Mostly I’d say they ain’t worth it. Men that is. But if you find one that strikes your fancy and he’s a good man, to boot, you’d better set the hook fast.”

“What if you don’t know if he’s a good man or not? What if you’re not even fishing.”

Their eyes met and held in instant understanding. Esther’s large red face was intense. “What if you realize too late that you should’ve pulled him in while you had the chance?”

Verity shook her head. “He’s not—I’m not—” She stopped. She didn’t know what she wanted to say. If anyone had asked her a month ago what kind of man she wanted she’d have spit in their eye, but now that she’d met this particular man all she could do was cry. “There’s something about him that gives me…a good feeling. Even when I’m so mad at him I could strangle him, just knowing he’s here gives me a sort of heart’s ease. I know that doesn’t make any sense—” She sniffled and dashed tears from her cheeks with the palm of her hand.

Esther changed the baby to the other breast. “Maybe this isn’t the right time. Sometimes things just don’t match up. Like times when people are on opposite sides of the river. But I can tell you he’s a good man. You don’t need to wonder none about that. And, maybe he don’t know, yet, what he wants. Men are slow, sometimes.”

Verity stood up. “I need to get back, but before I go I wondered if—” All of a sudden it seemed too much to ask of Esther to take her in, along with Sally and the baby. She had enough children of her own to bed down at night.

“Wondered about what?”

“Nothing. Tomorrow is soon enough.” Maybe by tomorrow she’d have everything straightened out. She just needed to be able to clear her head and think clearly. “I’ll talk to you tomorrow.”

Verity went back to her place in the bow of her own boat and sat studying the water rushing by the sides of the flatboat. Where had the river been? What strange and beautiful sights had it seen and left behind as it flowed past? And where was it going? For she was going along with it, as fast as ever she could. She and the captain and Clark and his Long Knives. That's all she would think about now. Not kisses, nor tender touches of her hair. Nor the vulnerable, soft skin of a man's neck. She'd think of the journey.

Overhead a turkey buzzard cut lazy spirals through the sky. It was a huge bird, a five-foot wing-span she guessed, with the feathered tips of his wings folded inward to catch the air currents. He rode the sky like a warrior. Beneath her feet the sun the earth was warm in the spring heat. The sun spread itself benevolently on the flatboats and threw quiet shadows behind them across the water. Blackberry winter had come and gone, those four days of bitter cold without which the blackberries would not bloom, and now the cypress willows were unfolding precious buds to greet the new season.

Everything, it seemed, had its time. Purpose was set, definite. The dogwood, blackberries, wild plum trees blossoming. Even the buzzard. All of nature was slotted into patterns. Everything but her. She still didn't know how she was going to get to Kaskaskia. She would ask Trey one more time to help her, to speak for her with Clark. Surely Trey would see how important this was to her. She had to go to Kaskaskia. She would *make* him help her. If she was important to him at all, he would understand.

It didn't occur to Verity until much later that without mentioning any names both she and Esther had seemed to know exactly which man they had been talking about.

Ten

Verity felt as if she might explode, scattering bits and pieces of herself over the whole river.

She couldn't seem to get away from Clem. He had followed her around the entire day, his belly preceding him like the flag on the prow of their lead boat. He stood so straight trying to balance his belly that he bent slightly backward and the arrogant, determined expression on his face kept Verity's eyes active every minute. She had the feeling that if she lost sight of him for a second, she'd hear his voice over her shoulder telling her he had the preacher in tow.

To her added disgust, Bart again had his eyes fixed on her. Between the two of them, the constancy of being watched so closely was beginning to rattle her.

Her fear was ridiculous, of course. There wasn't a preacher for five hundred miles in any direction. Not that a preacher was always considered necessary. If a man and woman were of like minds, they just took up with one another and everyone realized that the first preacher to come along would be asked to say the proper words. She was not of a like mind, of course, but the thought did nothing to reassure her. What kept her unease simmering was Clem's one-track determination to make up his mind to a thing and then hang on to do it. It seemed to be a Dawson trait.

She remembered the night on the trail when she'd tried to get the three Dawson men to make a cart from what was left of the wagon. Neither Bart nor Abner had argued with Clem, only Verity. They knew from experience how useless it was to try and change his mind. Clem wrestled his mind into some sort of decision and then proceeded to bend facts and events into a conforming shape.

And Bart, in his own quiet, stubborn way, was proving to be just as annoying as Clem. A dozen times a day she looked up to find him staring at her, unblinking, waiting. She sometimes had the feeling his considerable bulk was held on a straining leash. What was the most unnerving of all, however, was the occasional flash of anger that was there and gone so quickly she almost convinced herself she'd imagined it. Was he angry at her? With Clem? With circumstances? Verity felt as if she were balancing on a rope over rapids. Both men disgusted her, but she feared Bart.

When had this happened? All along the trail he'd been almost indolent, plodding through the days, always in the background so that for hours on end, Verity would forget that there were three men in their group and not two. Now, while his eyes remained flat, the dullness was gone and Verity had the idea he was ready to pounce. She shuddered.

Her decision to stay out of the way for the few remaining days until they arrived at Corn Island was easier said than carried out. All morning she'd managed to keep one step ahead of Clem, joining the women's gossip groups, feeding Sally early and then leaving before the men came to the cook fire, hiding in her favorite place among the baskets. At the nooning she watched Trey and Homer leave the boats to range ahead, scouting, to be picked up farther down stream later in the afternoon. She waited until the last moment to board, and then slipped unnoticed aboard the second boat. She spent the afternoon with Esther Hicks.

The baby was filling out nicely with Esther's abundance of milk, and even had the promise of a wrinkle around each wrist. He smiled happily now and waved his hands around, his little blue eyes following the antics of the tethered goat.

"Having goat's milk for my young'uns is a real blessing. I'm indebted to the men in your party."

"As long as Sally and Gideon get some every day, we have no use for the rest. You're welcome to it."

"Between your party and your young man, we always have a good supply of meat, too. When Mr. Hicks sickened, that's the one thing I worried about most. It seems I got a passle of young'uns, all wantin' their bellies filled every night. That nice young captain of yours, he brought me meat regular before I made the bargain with the Dawsons. And every few days, he still does. He brought me a brace of ducks this morning. He's a good man."

A good man. Two days ago, Verity had used those same words saying that she didn't know if Trey was a good man or not. Here was Esther assuring her once more that he was, indeed, a good man. Verity had turned those words over in her mind a dozen times since, worrying them, wondering what kind of man he really was. This information only added to her confusion. He provided for a woman with no man to hunt for her, and yet Verity knew for a fact that he loved the murdering, torturing, life-threatening Indians she hated and feared with all her heart. How could the two go together and still be part of one man? And now Esther was telling her the answer, with no question in her tone, and perversely Verity was irritated.

Her voice was sharp. "He isn't my young man. I hardly know him." *Hardly know him*, her heart echoed. *You know him well enough to kiss him as if nothing else in the world mattered. Well enough that your pulse leaps, even catching a glimpse of him on the far end of the boat. Well enough that you dream in the dark, of his heart beating beneath the palm of your hand. How well do you want to know him?*

Esther raised a set of knowing eyes. "If he's not your man, maybe you have your heart set on Bart, then? He's carrying a powerful hankering for you."

Verity's head snapped up. "I'd as soon jump off the boat into the river!" It wasn't until Esther smiled she realized the woman had been joking. "No!" Verity sank back on her heels. "It isn't Bart. If I lived long, like Methuselah, it would never be Bart. Or Clem."

"Bart I can understand. Pulling in a yoke harness with him would be an uneven load. But what's wrong with Clem?"

A gleam of interest in Esther's face sharpened Verity's wits. Esther and Clem? What a lot of problems it would solve! Esther and Clem! But some inborn sense of fairness brought her up short.

"He's got to have his own way," she said slowly, "and a woman doesn't count for much in his life. He'd be a hard man to be married to, I think."

Esther's smile only broadened. "So was Mr. Hicks. But a smart woman can get around any man that ever walked. I ain't worried as long as he don't hold with batting his woman around. I'll not stand for that."

Verity shook her head. "Zelma wasn't ever afraid of him. He just ignores women, mostly."

Esther nodded thoughtfully and shifted the baby to burp. She seemed to have gotten the information she needed, that Clem was available and did not abuse his woman. She dropped the subject.

"Those big rivers we've passed today. Wonder what they were?"

Verity shrugged. The rivers were all beginning to look alike. "The men say we'll come to an even bigger one this evening. Clark hopes to camp near the Scioto."

"Hope it's clear water with a lot of rocks. I need to wash."

Verity agreed. Everything they wore was becoming the same shade of dirty yellow and felt grainy from the silt the river was carrying. They all wished for clear, clean water.

But even before they got to the Scioto, Verity knew they would not find clear water in this river. In the afternoon the boats followed another great, sweeping bend in the river to the south and when they'd angled back to a more direct westerly direction the river began to show traces of even more muddy, grit-filled water. Their first view of the Scioto was that of a wild rushing spate, gushing out to join the Ohio in an angry brown torrent. It took every hand they had to maneuver the boats to the northern bank and secure them against the current.

Verity couldn't wait to get away from the confines of the boat. She bundled up soiled clothing in a blanket while the ramps were run across to shore and was ready to cross at the first word.

It was sundown and they had come to a place where the river was broad and the water was smooth. To the south, sheer, low cliffs rose. In front of them, a lovely little meadow lay in the evening sun. On one side stood a small grove of willow and elm like an island in a sea of waving grasses. Back where the land began to lift sharply upward, a dense green forest began.

In the heat and hush of the late afternoon, the air above the bluff seemed to hover, sentinel-like. Verity couldn't make up her mind if the feeling was one of protection or menace. The red clot of sun against the horizon to the west was like an inflamed eye and she tried not to think of portents and meanings and possible, terrible, bloody things that could happen.

"Don't go out of sight." The command came from behind her elbow in a firm tone that brooked no argument.

"What?" She turned to find Trey standing so near her sleeve brushed his buckskins. His eyes were as hard as his voice.

"Don't get out of sight of the guards." His eyes didn't quite meet hers, they probed a spot over her right shoulder. "Your clothes washing can wait."

Verity stopped dead in her tracks and tucked the blanket under one arm. They had stopped to pick up the scouts barely an hour earlier and already he was giving her orders.

"Why?" she asked slowly, eyes narrowed against the setting sun at his back. "Indians?"

"Just do as I say." He stood there like a total stranger talking to a slow-witted child. She had difficulty remembering the hour they'd shared by the lake and the kiss that still seared her memory when she thought of it. He was about as changeable as the river.

"Is there an Indian threat?" she persisted. Surely they all deserved to know if they were in danger.

"Are you having trouble with the language? I said—"

"I heard you." The man had gall. She turned back to her place in line and moved along, across the planks, her chin high. Inside she fumed at the freedom he took to spout directives. He was no better than Clem. Or Otis.

The minute she let herself soften toward him, the very second she allowed herself to feel a smidgen of trust and attraction, he took advantage of it. Perversely she wanted to put him in his place.

"Bart said only this morning that he thought the Indian threat was exaggerated."

Trey's neck seemed to swell as his face reddened. "Bart said that, did he? What intelligent reason did he give for that stupid conclusion?"

It didn't make any difference that she agreed with him, she only wanted to goad him as he goaded her. Bart's logic sounded hollow even as she said it.

"Where are they then? We haven't found so much as a footprint, or—or—a feather—for days. There aren't any Indians in this part of the country."

"Haven't found—" Trey began, stopped and looked at the sky as if for Divine Guidance. *That jackass. That ignorant, stupid, small-minded excuse for a man thought that just because you didn't see Indians, they weren't there.* "Your friend," he began coldly, "your *friend*, Bart, couldn't find his butt with both hands and you would do well—"

Suddenly there was a commotion in the rear and Trey was catapulted forward, his hat flying from his head. Instinctively, she reached out to grab it before the river claimed another trophy. He apologized to the lady he'd bumped forward, then growled at the twelve-year-old who'd butted him in the back and turned to Verity.

"There are reasons why I can't allow you to—"

"Oh really?" She was angry. So angry she trembled from her eyelashes to her hemline. *Allow. He'd said he wouldn't ALLOW her to wash her clothing* "You don't want me to wash my clothes. You don't want me in the forest. You don't want me to go to Kaskaskia with Clark. Well, let me tell you something. I'm tired of hearing what you don't want me to do. Since the day I left home—me and my *goat*—no one has given me orders. And, in case you're interested, I am getting along just fine making my own decisions."

Trey's eyes went dark and his mouth flattened into a thin line. Verity wasn't the only one angry. He watched one of her eyebrows cant upward as she forced a placid expression on her face. The new feeling playing over her features was worse than the fury had been. He said, "I want your word to stay close by."

"And now, *Captain Owens*," she said, as if he hadn't spoken, "I suggest you go find someone to order around who might give you a hope of being obeyed." She slapped his hat across his stomach hard enough to make the muscles contract and marched off, leaving him in the middle of two lines of people departing the flatboats. Some of them were laughing, some tried not to. One thumped him on the back and said cheerfully, "Nothing harder to handle than a mouthy woman."

"Agreed," Trey replied, with a false grin, trying to put the best face possible on the situation. It would not be good to lose his influence with these people since he was to lead them while they stayed on Corn Island. "Or more dangerous," he laughed good-naturedly, and then forced a smile to stay on his lips while he watched Verity's progress up the bank and her angling aim toward the Scioto.

The woman was worse than the plague, he thought, feeling tormented by his lack of power over her. And she could get into trouble faster than a tumbleweed in the wind. She taunted him. Even when she wasn't anywhere near, he could feel a tangible awareness of where she was, what she might be doing. And when they were standing elbow to elbow, his tongue seemed to tie itself into knots. Simple cautionary words turned into orders given in a tone that even his men would resent. He could hear what he was saying and couldn't seem to stop.

And her! Instead of having even a few of the understanding graces women were supposed to have, she took his well-meant words and flung them back in his face like stones. He'd thought it before: she had the tongue of a viper. And—and, damn it, why couldn't he get her out of his mind? His thoughts softened as his gut seemed to slip sideways. She had a body that turned warm and soft in his arms, and a mouth that tasted of honey and mint leaves. And enough courage to stand off an angry bear. And while he admired her grit, she'd made life harder for him than he'd ever known a woman to do. Hell, he had the feeling he was losing some battle that he didn't even know he was fighting.

Standing there on the plank mid-way between boat and land with the mighty Ohio swirling under his feet, he knew he had to gather himself together or he'd make a fool of himself, for sure. He was sweating and on edge, and he'd be damned if he'd think of her any more. Her eyes alternately spat more fire than any wildcat he'd ever tangled with and looked at him with the trusting, dainty gaze of a yearling fawn. Her hair, beaver-brown and soft, smelled of the wind and leaves. Her body, stronger than her size would make you think, had gone all loose with passion when he kissed her. It was enough to drive a man crazy.

Ah-h, he was doing it again. He seemed to be overcome with some sickness that he couldn't get out of his system. It was frightening, the amount of time he spent remembering every little thing about her. Things she said, the way her ears lay snug to her head. Her courage in standing up to Clark, letting him know that she didn't consider him a gentleman, even though it might have far-reaching complications for her. The sheer guts of starting on this westward trek at all. Everything. The way the tie of her apron twitched from side to side as she walked. It was like a madness he couldn't run fast enough to shake.

When had he begun to have such strong feelings for her? Was it when she stood up to Bart's badgering of Sally, or on the river when she'd defied all advice and got herself aboard, anyway? Or maybe, even before then, before he'd realized it, when she'd stuck out her chin and dragged that stupid goat along the side of the hill.

She wasn't at all the kind of woman that usually took his eye, a soft-spoken, flirty-eyed female who catered to his every whim. Verity hauled her own water, made her own decisions, and had the gall to face down the Dawsons at every meal. More than that, while she seemed to be curling her way into his thoughts with increasing regularity, she seemed to pay no attention to him at all. Never looked for him, never turned at the sound of his voice, never seemed pleased to find him at her side. It was a damnable situation.

Finally his legs began to work. He went down the planks to shore and stretched to look above heads for Homer. Someone had to keep track of her, he thought, and if she saw him one more time she might just take it into her head to do the opposite of what he'd said. He'd have Homer range a bit farther afield tonight, just to satisfy himself.

~ * ~

Verity strode up the bank and turned inland. There was so much energy chained inside that she could not—could not—stay on the flatboat one minute longer than necessary. She'd taken one last look to pinpoint Clem before she left the boat and another as she disappeared beyond the rise. He was still there, talking to Abner and apparently unconcerned with her leaving.

Maybe she could have an hour of peace. It had been a dreadful day. Hiding and making herself both invisible and unavailable had also made her nervous and cranky. She felt ready to snap at anything that moved. She'd had to get off the boat in just the same way she had to have some privacy now. No quarreling people, no fretful babies, no pigs squealing or chickens squawking. And no Clem stalking her relentlessly. The scouts had not reported any Indians, none that she knew of, but Trey's warning hummed in her head. She most definitely didn't want to meet any Indians. But, oh, the prospect of being alone, even for a few minutes.

She groaned, wondering how much longer it would be before they raised Corn Island and just how long she could keep up the fancy footwork with the Dawsons. But here, now, was her golden opportunity. She threw back her head and laughed aloud in childish abandon. The whole forest, well this part of it anyway, all to herself. The feeling was glorious. And she wasn't all that far away from the boats, there were vague sounds in the distance, over the bluff, that identified the location of the flotilla.

She could hear the Scioto off to her right and, hitching the roll of dirty clothes higher, she wandered in that general direction. As she thought, however, the water was worse than the Ohio and unfit for washing. She hesitated for a few precious minutes enjoying the solitude, and then, hoping to find a feeder creek that was clearer, she followed the river bank gathering a handful of delicate, pink spring beauties and running her fingertips around the furled green frond of some willowy weed. She stopped in a sunny glade to admire the bronze-leafed sundrops sprinkled at random—heaven could be no more beautiful—and wandered on. She crossed a wide shallow creek where a dense litter of driftwood all but strangled the flow of water on stones slick with moss underfoot.

The river bank had been almost flat, but after following the stream for a bit she found herself in a small grove of trees surrounded by tall ferny fronds and dense undergrowth. The clearing was so peaceful and unspoiled that she couldn't resist and she sat down in the dappled sunlight and lay back.

The thought crossed her mind that Trey wouldn't like her being alone. However, she really wasn't very far away from the boats, just a few steps, more or less, from the feeder-creek that led to the river. And the quiet was so blissful. There were times when she thought she simply couldn't bear the crowded conditions on the boat one minute longer. The smell of unwashed bodies, the constant noise of animals and shouting people, the sight of unrelieved squalor all around her was deadening to her spirit. Not that she would ever complain, the flat-boats were carrying her closer to the West. But oh, the thought of an hour of peace and quiet was too much to ignore.

She'd take an all-over bath in the river, she decided, before she went back. After she'd washed their clothing. She'd sink down to her chin and let the water pour over her and be all-over clean, really clean, for the first time in weeks. If Trey found out, he'd surely scorch the air with some of his terrible words, but it would be worth it. She smiled, remembering the day the goat had chewed the tethering rope in two and caused mass confusion aboard the boat as it bucked down the river on a strong current.

He'd cut loose with words she'd never heard before, while scrambling after the illusive animal, and the look on his face had been beyond description when he'd risen with the bleating goat in his arms to find himself right in front of her, the sound of his swearing still echoing in her ears.

His face had reddened, his jaw worked and he'd inhaled a lungful of air before he opened his mouth again. "I'd say I was sorry if I was, but this da—this four-legged creature is enough to make a saint swear. And we both know I'm no saint." And he'd stalked off, juggling the still bleating goat.

She could hardly be angry with him for the bad language. With all he had to do, the goat was a pesky bit of trouble most of the time. And he was the one who bore the brunt of Clark's anger when a fracas came to his attention. No, she couldn't be upset with him for that. He'd looked much like Gideon did when caught in some mischief. Frustrated, guilty and embarrassed all at once.

She squirmed around to a more comfortable spot and removed a stone from beneath her back. The silence filled her senses and her whole body began to ease into the earth. The sky rode high above the treetops, embroidered with delicate, lacy leaves and downy-soft clouds. Verity rested her head on the blanket-bundle, closed her eyes and listened to the sounds of the forest. She'd move on in just a minute. Get the washing done and her bath and go back to the boat before the captain had another reason to scold her. But, oh, the peace was so wonderful.

With her eyes closed there was a sensation of floating, the motion of the boat still in her bones, and it was a moment of pure bliss. She couldn't allow herself to fall asleep. That would be foolhardy in the extreme. But, just to rest her eyes and her body in tranquility was so nice. There was the gentle twitter of birds and a furtive scurrying of some small woods animal. A hint of a breeze stirred the trees. She smiled.

And then, eyes still closed, she became aware of a smell that didn't belong. Spring beauties and sundrops had a sweet fragrance, pine needles were spicy, the earth had its own scent, deep and pungent and powerful. This was—This was—Her heart kicked once and she knew she'd made a mistake even as her eyes snapped open.

Bart stood over her, his lips split into a satisfied grin. "Knew if I waited long enough, old Clem'd run himself half to death. Now it's my turn."

Verity fought down the sickish fear that flooded her senses and forced her eyes to meet his. Bart with shoulders broader than an ax handle, neck like a tree trunk, hands like…like… She fought the urge to close her eyes. When she'd left the boat Clem and Abner had been talking on deck, neither of them paying her any mind. Why hadn't she had the sense to look for Bart?

"I saw you first," he was saying. "You're mine. I told him, but he says he needs you more'n me."

She felt beads of sweat pop out on her forehead. Bart could tear her apart with his hands, like a chicken ready for the pot. Or worse. Oh God, much worse. No! It would not happen. She'd not let it happen. She was smarter than he was. Slowly Verity rolled to her side and sat up.

Careful, she thought. Be very careful. Pretend innocence. "Were you looking for me?" She stood up and dusted the leaves off her skirt. "I've been busy all day and have a pile of laundry yet to do."

She had taken one cautious step backward before Bart's hand shot out and gripped her shoulder like the talons of an eagle.

"You ain't goin' nowheres," he said, his jaw thrusting forward.

"Just to check on Sally," she said warily, doing her best to be natural. "And it's about time to begin the cook fire."

"Not until you tell me you ain't hitchin' up with Clem."

"Clem?" A wash of relief flowed over her so strong her knees almost buckled. "No. I am not marrying Clem. Or anybody. Remember I'm pledged to a man in Kaskaskia. I gave my word."

He looked at her uncertainly, reluctant to believe her. "Clem says he's goin' to have you."

She could feel her blood flowing through her legs again. She could handle Bart as long as she didn't get rattled. "Nobody, not even Clem, gets their own way all the time," she said.

A sly smile came over his face. "That's right. Ma used to tell him that." He pulled her closer. "And now it's my turn. Nobody'll know, 'cause you won't dare tell."

"Wait. Bart. You don't want to do this." She hung back trying to make him meet her eyes. But the force of his pull was greater than her strength and slowly she was dragged closer.

"After this, it'll be done. You'll be my woman."

The coarse stubble of his chin scraped across her cheek as she twisted her face to the side. "No!" Her voice rose. "Stop it!"

The fire in his eyes flamed brighter. "Nobody'll else'll want you then. Not Clem and not the man in Kaskaskia."

He had her by both shoulders now in an iron grip. She smelled his sour body odor.

Suddenly, it was as if all the pent up energy of the long day came unleashed. She erupted twisting, scratching, biting, kicking. She fought in panting, grunting silence, as if saving her energy for the battle. The only sounds were Bart's as he growled and swore with the effort to subdue Verity's surprising resistance.

It didn't last long. The sleeve of Verity's bodice tore from shoulder to wrist and the sound of tearing loosed a jolt of anger from the pit of her stomach. She tasted blood as she bit into Bart's arm. He reared back in an effort to shake her loose and she flung up her head, hard, connecting with his lower jaw. The crack sounded like doomsday and brought Bart to a standstill. In that instant, Verity turned and rammed her knee upward with all the remaining strength she could muster and was gratified with a groan of agony as Bart went to his knees on the pine needles.

Forgetting her blanket-bundle she ran, not daring to look back, not thinking of her torn dress or even where she was going. And the tears, which she had not shed in the heat of battle, now flooded down her cheeks and hoarse sobs were torn from her throat. She didn't see the flowers, was heedless of the brambles that caught and tore at her skirt, didn't even look where she was putting her feet. She stumbled and fell to her knees, scrambled up and ran again.

If she ran fast enough, maybe she could outrun the ugliness. Bart was ugly. What he wanted to do to her was ugly. The way he continually possessed her with his eyes was ugly. She felt ugly, herself, just having had his hands on her. Seeing the forest through a sheen of tears, she rounded an outcropping of rock and ploughed headlong into Trey striding purposefully along the river.

The force of her forward rush carried him back two staggering steps until he brought up hard against a rocky bluff. He took one look at her, pale with fright, crying with exhaustion, her dress torn, mouth smeared with blood, and pulled her into his arms. "Good God in heaven. What's the matter? Who did this?" He held her away long enough to look at her once more and then crushed her close again.

"Answer me. Where are you hurt, Verity? How badly are you hurt?" His hand was on his knife as he scanned the trees behind her.

"He was going to…" She tried but couldn't seem to stop the racking shudders that ripped through her body. "Just like old Mr. Hargraves… And I wouldn't—couldn't—let him." The sobs threatened to split her mid-section and she gripped his shirt with both hands.

"Hargraves?" Trey looked confused, but he took both hands in his and held fast. "The old man in Virginia? He's here? Did he do this?"

She shook her head, her eyes squeezed shut. "Otis sold me to him, but I ran away."

Trey seemed frozen in place. His eyes were hard on hers. He hardly breathed. "Your father sold you to this man? Your father?"

"My stepfather." She hiccuped. "For twenty acres of good bottom land and the use of a mule."

"But you ran away instead. With the Dawsons. That's what you were doing the morning I first saw you with the goat." He looked as if he'd been blinded, the way he stared at her. He hadn't fully understood when she told him the story at the lake. The word "bargain" had been used, but "sold" was another matter entirely.

The tears had stopped now, but she couldn't get her breath. She pulled at her torn sleeve and wiped her nose on the remnant, then made an effort cover her bare arm. Trey still stood with one of her hands in his. Absently he caressed her knuckles with his thumb. There was a white line around his mouth.

"Did Hargraves do this? Is he back there? Are you hurt?" The grip of his hands was so tight she thought the bones might snap.

"No." Should she tell him it was Bart?

"Your Pa? Out here?" His eyes were as dangerous looking as a rattler Joe had once cornered in the barn.

"No. I'm just—scared."

Angrily, he shook her hands. "Look at your face and tell me you're fine. Did he hit you? He is a dead man."

She swiped at her chin and cheek, saw the blood, and couldn't help a quick flash of satisfaction. "Nobody hit me. I—I bit him."

"Bit him? That's his blood? Whoever he is, he'll have quite a wound." His voice went soft and deadly. "Who attacked you? Verity?"

She stepped back and pulled her sleeve tighter into place. She had to think. If he knew what really happened he might slit Bart from neck to navel. He certainly looked capable of it at this moment. And that would complicate everything. She had heard Clark say, several times, that the stockade at Corn Island was going to need every man, every gun, they could muster. He would be extremely displeased with the loss of even one gun. And if Clem found out that Trey and Bart had fought over her, she would no longer be welcome at their fire. What would become of her? She would have to swallow her pride and her guilt and ask Esther, after all, if she would take her in. But, more important than anything else, she thought honestly, was that she couldn't bear the shame of Clark being right in his blind assumption that she'd cause trouble between the men. No, she couldn't tell.

Roughly Trey gathered her close against him and she could once again feel the steady thrum, thrum of his heart. "Verity.

Tell me. Now." He was back to giving orders again. Only this time she couldn't take offense.

"It would do no good and a lot of harm if I told you," she said softly, her voice muffled against his chest. "And if I make sure I'm not alone until we get to Corn Island, it won't happen again."

He was rigid with anger. He wanted to kill the man who would terrorize her in this way. Or kill any man who would sell a precious young girl for any reason. And, he couldn't forget that ripped sleeve. With his own fingers he would tear the throat from the man.

"Did he put his hands on you?"

"Not—not quite. Not in the way you mean."

"Who?" In his frustration, he shook her gently. "You have to tell me!"

"No," she said softly. "It's over and I'm not hurt."

"I want to know!"

She shook her head. "You warned me. I didn't listen. I had Indians on my mind, not white men. I won't make the same mistake again. You can be sure of it."

She stepped away from him and wondered if Bart would have had time to get away by now. Well, she'd done her part. If he was still there, it was his own fault. She had the satisfaction of knowing that he would at least be walking with a limp for a few days.

Trey watched her move away, over the hill and toward the boats. He would not rest until he found out who was responsible for this. And he would have that satisfaction. It was a vow.

He turned his head and spit. As for her stepfather, he hoped there was a particularly uncomfortable corner of hell reserved for men like him. And where in tarnation was Homer? He was supposed to have been trailing her. Yet, if Homer had found her, he would not have been here himself to hold her, comfort her.

And he wouldn't have learned the painful secret that had sent her down the river to begin with. Maybe there was a God in heaven, after all.

As he stared at the spot where her head had disappeared behind the bluff, he realized that freedom no longer meant the same things to him that it once had.

An evening breeze blew upriver, and he turned to it gratefully. How could it have happened that everything he'd ever wanted from life had changed because of one small, stubborn woman? He'd seen prettier women, maybe. Had good-times girls, certainly. But Verity was different. How this was so escaped him. They didn't agree on anything. They didn't want the same things out of life. They rubbed each other the wrong way, in every way but one.

He exhaled mightily with the memory of the feel of her in his arms. The one way they did agree was worth hanging on to, however. But why, of all the women in the world, would he be drawn to this one? And, the knowledge hit him in the breastbone with enough force to drive the breath from his lungs.

He was in love with her. The thought skewered its way through his gut and into his brain. It was true. How it happened didn't matter, only that it had. He felt dazed. Bludgeoned. He loved her. She was his. And whoever had attacked her was still out there, somewhere, skulking around in the forest. Whoever had hurt her would not be allowed to get away with it. It was a vow.

He started down her trail at a ground-eating trot.

Eleven

Verity slept well. But then all her life she'd slept well. With the exception of the night she'd lain awake planning her escape from Otis and Lena, she couldn't remember a night that she hadn't slept fast and hard and long. Her mother used to tease her that such sleep was the mark of a person with nothing on her conscience, but Verity knew today that it more likely meant her conscience was in such bad shape it was numb. Because she knew for a fact that hatred was a mortal sin.

First there had been only the Indians. She'd lived with dark thoughts about Indians for as long as she could remember. What they'd done was horrible, unforgivable, and she would never forget as long as she drew breath. More recently came Otis and Lena, and she hadn't known for a long time that what she felt for them went beyond disgust and fear. Now she'd added Bart to her list and was probably damned for all time. Mama would simply despair.

She had wanted Verity to be a lady in all senses of the word. In a way, Verity was glad Mama wasn't there as witness to her unladylike behavior. Stealing a goat, plotting to get to Kaskaskia by whatever means it took, relieved about the possibility of foisting Clem's attentions off on Esther. And constantly trying to outsmart General Clark and the captain. She wondered what Mama would have thought of Captain Trey Owens.

Still lying in her blanket, Verity felt a sweet thickening of the blood running through her body. Lord a'mighty but he was a handsome man. And he'd called her his sweetling. She, who had promised herself to good old Edward in Kaskaskia, went all warm and soft at the mere thought of Trey's arms around her, crushing her tight to his chest as he cried out, "Are you hurt? Who did this?" And then, "He is a dead man."

She remembered the springing softness of his chest hair through the laces of his buckskin shirt, she felt again the hard band of muscle as his arms scooped her up, she tasted the saltiness of her own tears mingled with the slight sweatiness of his neck. Scrunching her eyes shut, she pulled the blanket up snug to her chin as if to protect herself from this invasion of her senses. Her conscience was going to have more to answer for than she'd ever dreamed. If Mama was right, she'd never have another good night's sleep again. But oh, it was fun thinking of Trey Owens.

Not so Bart. He was just a dumb old pig of a man. Verity's smile disappeared in a scowl. No. Bart was big, surely, single-minded and an absolute swine, but not dumb. Neither was she. The only reason he'd laid hands on her yesterday was because she was caught unawares, and that would not happen again—not now that she knew where the real threat lay. Knowing your enemy was half the battle, she thought. The better half.

However, given the way both Clem and Bart looked at her, she couldn't delay leaving their section of the boat. Today, she would definitely speak to Esther about moving her belongings and Sally and the baby to Esther's fire. She wouldn't ask Clem, she'd just do it. She would still cook for the three men and Gideon, but she'd be careful not to be alone with Clem or Bart.

She arose from her blankets fresh and eager for the day and determined to use her common sense so that there would be no opportunity for either Clem or Bart to force a confrontation.

The first thing she saw was her neatly folded blanket-bundle, placed carefully beside her resting place. The bundle of clothing she'd left in the glen with Bart. For a moment her mind went blank. Who? Bart? No. As angry as he'd been, he would have flung it at her head. If not Bart, then who? Trey? If so, he'd surely have some questions to ask later. Questions she'd just as soon avoid.

Bart squatted in silence and eyed her through the smoke of the community breakfast fire. His face told her plainly that he wasn't forgetting what had happened. With satisfaction, Verity noted that he used his left arm carefully and wore the sleeves of his shirt fastened snugly at the wrists. She hoped her teeth had torn a hole through his arm all the way to the bone. Verity kept her eyes on the corn pone and fatback she was frying and tried to ignore him, but he sat and stared in silence until she became so agitated she wanted to heave the cooking pot, grease and all, at his head.

Worse yet, Clem had a fawning, fixed look on his face that set her teeth on edge. And he wasn't silent.

"Mighty pretty hair-do you got this mornin'."

Startled, Verity looked up. Her hair was combed the same way she always wore it, pulled back from her face and braided. She didn't answer.

Clem tried again. "For a young'un, you sure can cook. Your mama taught you good."

This time Gideon looked up, the question full in his eyes. None of them had ever heard Clem use this tone of voice. The boy stopped chewing.

Verity turned the pone.

With a mighty hawk, Clem turned and spat over the edge of the boat. He stuck both thumbs in the waistband of his pants and smiled with the air of a man who, once having begun, was determined to hang on to the end. "Don't know what more a man could ask. A pretty gal that can cook, too."

Bart's eyes swung toward his brother. His voice was heavy with warning. "She's promised. To a man in Kaskaskia."

"Don't make no never mind to me," Clem drawled. "And this is none of your business, so you just shut your trap." His eyes never left Verity.

Verity rose to her feet with the spoon dripping in her hand.

Clem rocked back on his heels and picked at a tooth. "A man'd be a fool to pass up a chance to wrap hisself around pone like that ever' mornin'." His words were one thing, but the way his eyes roamed over her made the back of her neck crawl.

Her hand ached from the grip she had on the wooden spoon. "If you want this corn pone every morning, you're at the wrong fire. Esther taught me about it. You'd better be making up to her." And she turned her back on him to dish up breakfast for Sally.

"Well, uh—" He spoke to her back, doggedly going on. "You still make a fine figure of a womaaaa—." He didn't finish because he suddenly had two hundred pounds of brother sitting on his chest.

From a squatting position Bart had leaped across the fire, sending sparks flying and the cooking pot skittering. The two men rolled across the canting deck and into a crate of chickens.

Bart hauled Clem to his feet. Clem staggered and squinted unbelievingly at Bart.

"What're you—wha-s—"

"Ever'thin'…always…yours." Bart buried his fist to the wrist in Clem's gut. Clem sagged as his breath rushed out. "Got to be…first…"

Verity snatched Sally out of the way and backed against the railing. Still clutching his corn pone, Gideon seemed paralyzed as the fight rolled and stormed around him.

Elbows flying, knees gouging and breath coming in short, wheezing grunts the two men seemed to Verity to be one animal, pulling apart to growl ferociously and then joining again to pummel and jab.

A crowd gathered. Men cheered encouragement.

"Go for his eyes. Gouge 'em out."

"A bear hug. Get him in a bear hug."

The Long Knives, for the most part, stood quietly and watched, leaning on the butts of their rifles. The outcome wouldn't affect them. They were only interested in the fight.

At the rail, Verity stood frozen as men converging on the boat by land, from prow and stern. General Clark stood a full head taller than most of the men as he stopped, still on the island.

"Separate them," he commanded. "I can't afford to lose any able-bodied men. And bring them to me later." He watched while two of his men waded through the crowd.

By this time Bart had Clem down, knees clamping one arm close to his body while he pinned Clem to the deck with his own weight. His teeth were bared and his face was contorted with effort as he pressed a thumb relentlessly into Clem's eye. Clem's body bucked desperately to rid himself of Bart's hulking poundage.

Three of Clark's men laid hands on Bart but it was futile; one wrapped an arm around Bart's neck, set his feet and pulled. Nothing. A shout went up for help and two more men joined the effort, and yet another. Finally, his face purple with rage and arms straining, Bart tumbled backward with a terrible shout of frustration, carrying all the men with him. A half-dozen jumped to sit on him so he couldn't get up and resume the fight. His shirt had ridden up, the sleeve high enough to see an inflamed wound on his left arm. Verity recognized it as the place she'd bitten the day before. Angrily, Bart shrugged his shirt back in place and sat seething, eyeing his brother with a hard, waiting gaze.

Clem rolled to his stomach and vomited. Verity swallowed and covered her mouth with one hand to keep from doing the same thing.

Breathing heavily the brothers glared at each other. On his knees now Clem held one hand over an eye and pierced Bart with a venomous stare from the other. Bart made no move toward him, but braced himself with one elbow and panted, "She ain't yours."

Verity felt the full force of every eye on the boat. There wasn't any doubt who Bart was talking about. Or what they had been fighting over. She'd never been more humiliated in her life. The question was in every eye. Who was taking her away from whom? She wanted to sink into the river and disappear. She wanted to take back the whole morning and start over. She wanted to explain to everyone there that she was innocent. And suddenly, with a straightening of her spine, she realized that she wanted most of all to spit in the eye of every suspicious, lusting face there, mentally accusing her of playing off brother against brother. Her chin lifted.

"I belong to no one," she said loudly, looking defiantly from face to face. "No one!"

Slowly, the crowd began to disperse, men wandering slowly back to other groups, speaking to one another, glancing back over their shoulders. Verity watched them go.

Softly, from just over her left shoulder, came Trey's voice. "You certainly do make an entrance to the morning. Every man here is thinking you have got to be some kind of woman to have brothers at each other's necks, and every woman within earshot is jealous, wondering how you do it."

Verity froze. None of them mattered. Not really. The only one who mattered stood so near the fine hairs on her spine tingled and even her heart seemed to wait on his words. Without turning she asked quietly, "What do you think?"

There was a gravely hoarseness to his voice. "I was thinking on which one it was, sneaking through the woods yesterday. Now I know."

When she looked, he was gone.

~ * ~

No one had to tell Trey he was floundering in deep waters. He didn't yet understand how his life could have taken such an abrupt change without his willing it to do so. He was still having a hard time believing the change was permanent.

Was it truly love he felt for Verity? He hadn't had a whole lot of experience in the field, maybe it was lust pure and simple. If so, he was hit a lot harder than he'd ever imagined possible. He knew he wanted her, from the beginning he'd accepted that, but this seemed to be different somehow. When she wasn't where he could see her, he *missed* her.

There was the quick flash in her eyes when she was set to take him down a peg or two, the way her chin lifted as she pulled her courage about her and committed herself to a course, and the cute little swish of her skirts as she passed by. Even the sound of her voice was special and the way she used her hands, capable and efficient with an economy of movement. He liked the way her hair grew away from her forehead and the way her lashes lay on her cheeks when her eyes were closed. And—he swallowed hard with the memory—he'd liked a lot the way her hands felt on his chest, resting and trusting, when he found her running from Bart in the forest.

Yesterday, he'd carefully backtracked her and found her blanket roll and read the signs. The ugly sore on Bart's arm during the fight with Clem told Trey all he needed to know. The thought of another man's hands on Verity sent an icy-hot shaft of anger spearing through him. This, because he knew what she felt like in his own arms. He ground his teeth together so hard his jaw ached.

A muscle in his jaw twitched. Oh Lord, he liked the way she felt in his arms. He'd never held a woman who seemed to fit in all the right places like she did. His knees trembled at the memory of her arms around his neck, her mouth on his, her hands in his hair, and a pain shot up under his ribs for all the world like a long-bladed knife searching for his heart.

And that's what made him uneasy. He didn't like feeling vulnerable. He felt as if he was at the mercy of a windstorm. This unknown, powerful force could be dangerous. It more than half frightened him. And so, for three days he went out of his way to avoid Verity. At the same time, not even trying to conceal his actions, he set himself to knowing Bart's every movement, waiting for the time to come when the man would be alone. Trey didn't want an audience for what he had in mind.

On the fourth day, his careful scrutiny of Bart's actions led him into the woods after the man. As Bart rounded an outcropping of granite he came chest to chest with Trey, waiting.

"You filthy, sneaking son-of-a-bitch, the only thing that's keeping me from skinning you an inch at a time, Comanche style, is that you and your gun will be needed on Corn Island."

Bart hadn't time to utter a word before Trey's foot caught him in the ribs and a right fist connected with his jaw. Systematically, Trey attacked him with fists, feet and head butting. This was no gentleman's fight. The man was lower than pig leavings. He had hurt Verity and he would pay. Trey knew an unexpected glimmer of respect in that Bart didn't try to deny that he knew what the beating was about. He made a valiant effort to fight back, but Trey had the edge of total and complete, dedicated hatred on his side, and did not give the man time to collect himself between blows. Bart went down several times before he stayed in the dust, bleeding from cuts on his face, one eye closing, and grunting with every breath he drew.

"You—danged—bastard. Busted—ribs," he gasped, spitting a bloody tooth into the dust.

Trey stood over him panting. "If I had it my way, you'd be dead, you sniveling coward. You'd rut on your own mother."

Bart gently lifted himself to one knee and looked at Trey through his one unswollen eye. "This ain't the end," he said finally through gritted back teeth. "She ain't yours, either." He sucked in breath. "And it's still a fur piece—to the Mississippi."

Trey hung over him, weaving slightly, his arms hanging by his sides. "For you it's done. If you ever lay a hand on her again, you'll wish I'd finished the job today. I promise."

~ * ~

Late in the afternoon Clark sent for Trey. He found Clark pacing the deck of the lead boat, hands clasped behind his back and nose thrust forward into the wind.

"Wonderful country!" he said, not taking his eyes from the mulberry trees lining the banks. "Wonderful. It's been a great trip. Would have made better time, of course, without the settlers, but they're necessary."

"I've kept them busy with their rifles," Trey said. "They'll do to hold the outpost on Corn Island by the time they're needed."

Clark nodded. "I want a stockade built as fast as possible and crops planted. You'll be in charge. See to it that they practice with those rifles every day and insist they post guard every minute, day and night. Who knows what will happen when the Indians find them all dug in and fields sown with grain. I want them ready for anything."

"They're scared enough of Indians that I don't think I'll have any trouble."

"I'm leaving Mason as second in command. He's a good man. A bit green, but good. You can count on him."

Trey knew Mason. A personable young man, willing and eager to do his share. "We'll make out. When will you be leaving?"

"The minute the stockade is defensible. The summer is wasting away while I ride the deck of a flatboat! And every day that goes by sees the English more firmly entrenched in Kaskaskia. Damnation! I wish we knew what was happening back east. I expect a messenger, daily."

Clark's shoulders relaxed slightly and he turned to Trey. "I know you'd rather come along, there isn't any glory in tending a group of farmers, but," he clapped Trey on the shoulder, "I need you here. I will be totally dependent on the settlement here for my information from the east. Without a stable outpost here, my position in the west would be untenable." He interrupted himself to ask, "What's wrong with your hand? Looks like you tangled with a grizzly."

Trey flexed the reddened hand with split knuckles and swollen joints. "Nothing serious," he said gruffly. "It'll heal."

Clark gave him a hard look, but nodded finally and went on. "Just take care of my relay station on Corn Island."

Trey frowned. He would indeed rather go on down the Ohio and be part of the routing of the English. However, "I agreed to stay for awhile," he said, "but don't forget me here."

Clark smiled. "I won't forget. I have complete confidence in you, and in Mason. My only worry is whether the settlers will function as a group. It is, after all, an island, and if the squabble the other morning was any indication, by fall they will be grating on each other's nerves. You might have your work cut out for you. That Philp woman seems to be a troublemaker."

Trey hesitated, for he knew Clark was still smarting from Verity's insult during their conversation with the two Frenchmen, but this was probably as good a time as he'd get. "In all fairness, sir, I doubt the woman had much to do with that. The Dawsons didn't seem to have consulted her about whether or not she wanted to become a Missus."

"Any time you add a woman to three men you're asking for trouble. I should have known better."

This was not the time to go into a long-winded explanation of why Verity was part of the Dawson party. Nor did Clark need to know of the glade in the forest where he'd found Verity's blanket roll and read the story the signs had left. She'd put up a good fight, but it wasn't hard to tell what had happened. And, as of the moment he'd seen the teeth marks in Bart's arm during the fight with Clem, there was no longer any doubt about who Verity had been running from. However, Bart was his problem, not Clark's, and he'd already handled it. If Clark knew, it would only set his mind harder against Verity. Maybe he could do something to alter the man's opinion, however.

"She has a brother in Kaskaskia, Joe Philp, as well as a fiance. A man named Edward something. She wants…"

Clark's eyebrows shot up. "Of course. Joe and Edward. Invaluable fellows. Infiltrated the town some months ago and are smuggling out information. Speak French like natives. Without them we'd have no idea of the size of the garrison or the political situation. The Frenchmen in the canoe only confirmed what Joe and Edward have already told us. One of them is the Philp woman's brother?"

Trey shifted feet. "Joe and Verity's mother was French. The thing is, Verity is bound and determined to get downriver, to Kaskaskia, and join her brother and his friend."

Clark's eyebrows went even higher, but he didn't answer.

"She wants to go with you."

Clark's eyebrows disappeared beneath his hat. "With me? You mean march with my men?"

Trey nodded.

"I wouldn't think of it. Encumber myself with a woman? With that woman? Out of the question."

Without realizing it, Trey had been holding his breath. His mouth relaxed in a small, relieved smile. "That's what I told her you'd say, but she's hard-headed enough to try and talk you into it herself."

"Tell her what I said. I don't want to be bothered by her. Momentarily I expect to come to the mouth of the Kentucky River and find Captain Bailey waiting with at least 200 Holston Valley volunteers. After that, Corn Island is directly in our paths. I've no time for trivialities. And no women. Especially her."

Trey tried not to grin too broadly. "I'll tell her. She won't like it, but I'll tell her."

He left Clark feeling smug, knowing Verity wasn't going to be allowed on the last leg of the journey. For one thing, he didn't trust her on her own. She found too much mischief. And Verity being nearby might be the one bright spot in his having to stay behind. At least this way he'd be in position to watch out for her. He didn't trust the Dawson men any further than he could heft a pregnant buffalo.

How could he ever have considered either Bart or Clem as possible suitors for Verity? Bart was arrogant, stupid, overbearing, crude and, above all, he had a mean streak. Clem was even worse in other ways. Verity would dry up and die being tied to either of these men for life. They would stifle her laughter and her independence and work her until she dropped, with not a thought to her comfort or safety. What an idiot he'd been to have suggested such a thing back at Fat Meat Creek. He must have been out of his mind. It was a wonder she hadn't taken a hatchet to him in his sleep.

The thing was, there was this Frenchman, going now in the opposite direction, but avowed to be back, and as if that wasn't enough, this Edward-person was waiting in Kaskaskia. The threat from Edward was unknown. Clark thought highly of him, praised his valor and cunning. He and Joe, both. Trey shifted uncomfortably. What if Verity was really set on having Edward as a husband? He'd just have to change her mind, that was all.

He approved heartily of her decision to move her things to Esther's fire and made a habit of searching her out every evening. He looked forward, all day, to the way her eyes quickened as she caught sight of him coming toward her. When the day was done and the fire glowed brightly, it was astonishing how easily they laughed together. The antics of a confused opossum wandering into camp, Gideon's attempts to mimic the militia swagger, Verity's own experimentation with new and strange herbs—some worked well, some not. Nothing seemed too trivial to share.

Verity wanted to know about his past. He knew much of hers.

"Once I'd heard George Washington talk about the land out west—the endless plains, streams so clear you could count the scales on fish—nothing but land and trees and sky, I simply had to see it for myself. I had to. Thomas Stone is more fair-minded than most men. If he hadn't pardoned the last two months of my indenturement—But he did and I'm free."

"But your brother is still there?"

"Almost finished. He'll join me then, out here somewhere."

"What's General Washington like?"

He thought a minute, his thoughts far away. "He's a fine man. He opened the door of politics for me. I enjoy discussions with men who are in position to change the course of history. And I find what Clark is doing in Kaskaskia, intriguing. He's changing the course of our country."

Trey began looking forward, every evening, to the time when he could sit next to her, talk through his day and hear about hers. They argued at times, but laughed more. He found himself storing up thoughts, sights, sounds all day to tell her at night. It became very important to bring that special sparkle to her eyes and watch her mouth soften into a smile.

"The goat's in trouble again."

"The goat?"

"She ate a hole in a blanket while one of the soldiers was sleeping under it. He woke up to find her chewing, while his butt was getting cold. I hope you aren't sentimentally attached to her. She may not last out the day."

"We no longer need her, since Esther is nursing the baby, but others do."

Her eyes fascinated him. In an endearing way, they often telegraphed her thoughts before she spoke. When her eyes went dull and she turned away, he lay awake long after to wonder what sorrow or problem she was keeping from him. The three days he had avoided her had been difficult, to say the least.

Deliberately, he didn't probe the sore spot of having avoided her, nor did he question his intense relief that she would be confined on Corn Island for months, maybe, where he could be near her. He figured time and distance was on his side. And anyway, he didn't know yet what he was going to do about the place she was building in his heart.

Twelve

The 200 Holston Valley volunteers failed to materialize. The mouth of the Kentucky River yielded only 25 men and Clark was visibly daunted, then angry.

"Where are the rest?" he shouted at Captain Bailey. "Cowards all?"

Standing at weary attention Bailey answered, "Sir, they elected to mount their own offense against the local Indians and head south."

Clark's color went from red to purple. "They're squandering their manpower, diluting it so as to be useless."

Captain Bailey risked a glance at Clark. "Most of them have families, sir, and don't want to get too far away. By staying in Kentucky they can put in their crops, be gone for a month or so and come home again."

"Don't they understand that one telling blow against the viper's head will kill the whole British snake and end the war once and for all? This stupid scattering will only prolong the bloodshed!"

"Yes sir," Captain Bailey answered miserably. Trey, standing beside him, felt equally betrayed as only three out of his possible fifteen eastern volunteers had shown up with the Holston Valley group.

"Twenty-five men," Clark muttered, turning away. "What can I do with only twenty-five more men?"

By morning, however, he had shrugged off his disappointment. "Back in Williamsburg," he said to Trey, "I convinced Governor Henry that we ought not wait to be destroyed. We should attack at a time when surprise is on our side. I believed we could do it then, and I believe it now."

"It's a long shot," Trey said.

Clark nodded. "From the beginning. The House of Burgess granted me the money with which to buy boats, weapons, and ammunition even though I felt I needed at least three times that amount. They empowered me to muster three hundred and fifty soldiers, although they frankly didn't think a single man of gun-bearing age was available because they were all serving with Washington. And in spite of it all, I assured them I would see the British colors presently flying over Kaskaskia, Cahokia and Vincennes replaced by our own flag." He squared his shoulders. "I intend to make good my word."

Trey found himself standing taller to match Clark's confidence. Somehow the man made you feel bigger and more powerful than the facts warranted.

By the time the boats reached Corn Island, the flotilla considered itself an army. Trey stood on a hillside and watched the unloading with something akin to pride. There were no uniforms, only the usual frontier garb: buckskins, moccasins and fur caps. Weapons ranged all the way from short-handled axes and long-bladed knives to tall rifles kept clean and ready. They weren't real soldiers, most of them were farmers, yet down to the last man they were young and strong and eager to follow Clark. Even as he searched out Verity, making sure she reached land safely, Trey found himself, once again, grinding his teeth at the unfairness of being left behind.

Before night fell, the construction of blockhouses had begun and before the week was out, reasonable protection from the Indians and the elements had been erected. Trey had not seen much of Verity all week. He was busy leading a small group of men to explore farther downstream. The only noteworthy finding was a parcel of rugged ground at a narrow part of the river which erupted in a series of wild waterfalls. He reported to Clark that there might be a need to portage.

Clark pressed him for details, which he gave, but found to his discomfort that his mind was wandering to the possible whereabouts of Verity. When he didn't immediately see her moving about the camp, he had to make a conscious effort to keep dragging his eyes and attention back to Clark and the conversation. He knew, for instance, that Verity was sleeping with Esther Hicks and her children, even though she cooked for the Dawsons and took care of the children, as usual. He also knew that Bart still moved with one arm close to his body, protecting sore ribs and that Clem could once again see out of his still-swollen, multi-colored eye.

What he didn't know was how delicately Verity walked through the days and what a toll the strain was taking. She sensed a deep-seated drive in Bart that made her mind go cold when their eyes collided. He was black and blue in every exposed portion of skin visible and he moved gingerly, but his attitude toward her seemed to remain unchanged. She puzzled over how he could be so battered. She hadn't realized Clem had inflicted that much injury; the fight, as brutal as it had been, hadn't seemed to last long enough to have produced such damage. The brothers no longer spoke to each other. She avoided contact with both of them when at all possible and after a few days the fight was no longer important.

Verity had never worked harder in her life. With the strong smell of new resin from freshly felled logs in the air, and sawdust thick on the ground, they all worked at settling in, raising barns and cabins, planting gardens and sowing corn. Even Gideon came to the fire at night with his young arms and legs trembling with exhaustion. The exhaustion wasn't entirely from building and planting, however. Clark kept his rough, young army drilling when they weren't cutting trees and fitting logs, and slowly but very methodically, he whipped them into fighting shape. Verity had overheard him mutter to an aid, "Thank God, frontiersmen already know how to shoot straight." Gideon spent every moment possible drilling with the army and, with Trey's supervision, learning to hit what he aimed at with his rifle.

Verity, also, was learning new things. Trey came for her one afternoon, explained that he felt it important that she know one end of a canoe from the other, and took her out on the river. She disgraced herself before they even got away from shore by refusing his offer of a balancing hand, stepping into the canoe and tipping it over instantly to end up sitting waist deep in the shallows.

Trey, trying hard to keep a straight face, extended a hand to help her up.

She scrambled to her feet, wiping her hands on her dripping skirt, her mouth spread in a wide smile. "You may as well laugh. I'm sure I look a complete ninny. Maybe you'd better tell me if there's some trick to getting in. It seemed so easy."

"No trick," he said, continuing to hold her hand in his. "Just make sure you step into the very middle of the canoe and center your body weight directly over your foot. Keep your knees loose."

She made it into the canoe without mishap and stood balancing in the middle with both hands outstretched. "Now what?" she asked.

"Now make your way to the far end so that I can get in back here."

Carefully, slowly, Verity turned and inched her way forward and crouched, finally, looking over her shoulder at Trey.

He grinned. "You're a natural. Now, pick up the paddle and hold it across your knees while I get in."

When she got the paddle positioned, she turned to find Trey already in the canoe and raising his own paddle. "How did you do that? The canoe didn't even rock!"

"Practice," he said, and proceeded to show her how to hold the paddle, to move the canoe forward, backward, fast and slow.

When Verity looked up, they were out of sight of the camp. She realized that even though she probably should, she didn't feel threatened by the possible presence of Indians with Trey along side her.

As if he could read her mind, Trey looked off into the hills and said, "I wish there was some way you could know the Indians like I do. You wouldn't be so afraid."

She was suddenly defensive. "I'm not afraid of them. I hate them."

"Why?"

She couldn't answer. She didn't want to remember. He wouldn't understand.

Trey dug in with the paddle and held it steady against the current, heading away from the center of the river and toward the shallows. Verity glanced inquiringly over her shoulder, but he was concentrating on the willows along the water's edge.

The nose of the canoe gently eased into the bank, making its way through a six-foot stand of green reeds swaying in the light breeze and sheltering the shore. They might have been the only two people in the world, hidden as they were from everything except the birds. Trey put down his paddle and eased forward until he was directly behind Verity.

"Tell me why, Verity. Lots of people, who don't understand, hate Indians, and there's always a reason. Sometimes more than one." His hand rested light as a bird's feather between her shoulderblades and began to stroke slowly up and down her back. He felt the tension ease and a slight quaking shake her frame. "Tell me, love."

'*Love.' He'd called her his love.* She forgot to breathe. Had he meant it, or were the words merely an idle expression? The thought that he might truly care deeply for her sent a quiver shimmering up her spine. She wasn't entirely sure she liked the feeling, but there was, strangely, a reassuring sense of comfort behind the unsurety.

She was quiet for so long he began to think she wasn't going to answer. Then, in a small, flat, expressionless voice she began. "When I was little, very young, our family was attacked by Indians. My mother, Joe and I were the only ones to survive." Thick tears clogged her throat and she began to shake her head. "I can't..."

He pulled her back against him and cradled her gently. Wrapping his arms around her, he gently caressed her arms. "Tell me. I want to know. What happened?"

And, as if her heart had overflowed after all these years, she told him. All of it. The hideous ax in Papa's head, Mama losing the child she was carrying, Lissy, who had cried—poor Lissy—and the necessity of Mama marrying someone, anyone, who could provide a roof over their heads. Then there was Otis and Lena and all the babies. And the tears came. She could never remember weeping like that, with total abandonment. Through it all his arms enveloped her, holding himself steady and her safe. She was not aware of turning in his arms, but at the last she was crying into his shirt with the steady, reassuring drum of his heart beating in her ear. She cried until she was dry and limp.

"Sh, sh, it's a long time ago. I'm sorry about it all, but it's over. Nothing will happen to you now. I won't let anyone hurt you."

"There is no protection from Indians," she said wearily.

"Evil walks in the world, Verity, no matter the color of a man's skin. Indians simply live by a different set of rules than the white man."

She attempted to pull away, but he held her fast. "I forgot. You like Indians!"

"Well, one anyway."

"But, you just said—"

"I said I have an Indian friend. I don't love them all. There are a lot of white men I don't love, either. I've killed my share of men, both white and red. But Indians can be as kind and loyal and brave as any white man you ever knew. Each one is different. You wouldn't judge all white men by Clem and Bart, would you? And there's something else. Don't believe everything you hear. Small men brag and even lie to make themselves appear big. Indians are frequently given credit for things they didn't do."

"I know what they did once," she whispered, but the hard core of anger she'd carried for so many years was lessened. While she was weary with crying, she no longer felt weighted down by the burden of her hate.

Quietly he rocked her in his arms. "I would give anything if it had never happened, if I could have spared you that. But I can't. Remember, it was one Indian party, not the entire mass of Indian nations living in America."

"That's what Edward says, but I can't seem to make it stick."

His heart skipped a beat and then picked up again. Edward. It was always Edward. He was getting damn sick of the man and he'd never even met him. In fact, he was beginning to wonder about his own firmly held convictions. What had seemed dawn-clear and firm was now clouded and the edges were vague. What did he really feel for her? Maybe it was time he found out.

He coaxed her from the canoe and they walked up the bank in the sunshine and through a meadow dotted with daisies. Listlessly, she pulled one blossom free and held it to her nose.

"What's that little ditty you girls always chant about daisies?" he asked.

Slanting her eyes at him and smiling, she pulled the petals from the daisy, one by one. "He loves me, he loves me not. He loves me. He loves me not," until one last petal was left on the stem. Slowly she pulled it free. "He loves me," she said.

He cupped her hands in his and forced her chin up so that her eyes met his. "Who were you thinking about?"

"It doesn't matter. It's just a silly child's game." She threw the stem away.

"Was it Edward? Were you thinking of Edward? Or is it the Frenchman?"

And because she wasn't ready for his question, because she was suddenly frightened of the tenderness in his eyes and the sudden swelling of her own heart, she said, "It's your turn," and snatched another daisy and held it out to him.

"No." He put both hands behind his back and shook his head.

"What's the matter, Captain Owens? Do you already know that your true love loves you?"

Trey almost winced at a painful catch in his chest. "I couldn't begin to guess," he answered, fascinated with the playful toss of her head, the frank teasing in her eyes.

"Maybe you're afraid to find out."

He realized she was challenging him. “It’s just a game,” he said, lamely, echoing her earlier statement.

“I did it.”

“Ah. But we already know who you love, don’t we?”

“I thought the object was to find out if *he* loved me.”

Her eyes crinkled in the most endearing way when she was laughing. Trey couldn’t help laughing back. “You win,” he said and accepted the daisy.

Quickly he stripped the flower. “She loves me, she loves me not. She loves me,” he declared, tossing the stem away.

“You cheated! You tore off two petals at the same time. What happened to fair play?”

He didn’t bother to deny it. “I believe in winning,” he said with a smile.

Her smile faded. “At whatever the cost?”

He reached for her. “It depends on what is at stake.”

There was a simmering warmth in his eyes that warned her he was no longer teasing. Her heart quickened as his hands tightened on hers.

“Are you determined to marry him, then, as soon as you get to Kaskaskia?”

Edward. He was talking about Edward and he deserved an honest answer. Still, she floundered, hunting for words. “I’ve known him for most of my life. We’ve always planned to wed.”

“I’m talking about love. Do you love him?”

“I—I—I’ve known him for—”

“I heard. For most of your life. But do you love him?”

She looked deep into his eyes trying to find something, anything that would explain the turn in conversation, when without warning, his arms went around her, crushing her against him.

His hand plunged into her hair and dragged her mouth so close to his that she could feel his warm breath on her lips.

"Does your heart nearly burst when he kisses you? Do your legs go weak and your head go mindless? Can you think of nothing except him every hour of the day? Does the thought of someone else holding him make you want to commit murder?"

His voice was hoarse with emotion and he shook her lightly. "Does it? Because that's the way it should be." And his mouth came down hard on hers, sweeping away any possibility of thought.

Her pulse began to race as his mouth moved across her lips leaving a trail of tiny hot kisses. His attention seemed to leave her lips, then, and traveled across her cheek to her ear and then down to her throat. Her knees did indeed go oddly weak when his hands moved hard on her back, up and down and around, trying to mold her more firmly to him. She made an involuntary little sound of need deep in her throat. Abruptly, he pulled back. His breath was coming in harsh, ragged puffs.

"Does it feel like that when he kisses you, Verity? Does it?" And his mouth was back on hers again, slanting first this way and then that. He was carrying her to a place she'd never been before.

A sudden jolt shot through her from toes to head and her whole body went slack. Was this love? If it was, poor Edward had never come close. Verity felt as if she was filling with some unnamed liquid that threatened to burst into fire at any moment. With a small sigh of surrender, her arms went up and around his neck and, without willing it, she was kissing him back. She had never felt more alive in all her life. Every sense she had, seemed to be heightened almost to the point of pain. She wanted more, tried to press herself closer and was so far lost that she didn't even think of protesting when she felt his hand at her breast.

The thought of what might have happened next kept Verity awake for weeks afterward, for at that moment a huge elk came lumbering through the undergrowth. The snapping of wood and breaking of bushes, combined with a roar of alarm brought Trey to his senses. With one movement he thrust Verity behind him and faced the danger with one hand on his knife.

After one startled second, the elk disappeared back the way he'd come and Verity and Trey both took a step apart to compose themselves. She fussily tried to smooth her hair and rearrange her clothing. He looked at the sky and gulped a large lungful of air. Together they made their way back to the canoe.

Before she stepped into the craft, Trey put one hand on her arm. His voice was harsh. "I won't say I'm sorry. I'm not. But you'd better think again about Edward. The only thing I know about him is that Clark respects him. But I promise you, there is no way you could have kissed me like you just did and love another man."

Verity closed her eyes and, because she could not find her voice, she merely nodded. She had to admit that he had not taken anything she had not freely given. And if it hadn't been for the elk, she might have given even more. It was embarrassing. She would do some thinking, all right. A lot of it.

They were silent all the way back to camp and Verity could think of nothing else. Not then, nor in the days following. Even though Trey made no effort to seek her out, she knew he watched her and when their eyes met, a spark seemed to flame between them. A flame with a life all its own. She remembered that he had asked if she thought of Edward every hour of the day and she had to be truthful and say that she did not. Whole days, sometimes many days, went by without a single thought of Edward.

There were times when she couldn't even remember what he looked like. When his image did come, she knew a pang of guilt. Edward, with his sandy hair and open, trusting eyes, would never have kissed her like Trey had. He deserved more than what she could offer him. It was confusing.

Even though she hadn't really wanted a husband, she had always thought that eventually she'd marry Edward. What else was there for a woman? Now the picture was blurred and vague. For, while Trey was always near by, he was rarely with her. He was always directing the labor, pointing out what needed to be done, giving orders and just being in charge. So, while the building continued, and the days took on a familiar pattern, it was now Homer who took her out in the canoe. Annoyingly, she couldn't put Trey out of her mind. He stuck there like some glutinous mass she couldn't go either around or through.

~ * ~

Verity never worried about Gideon. She always knew where he was and what he was about. But Sally—Verity couldn't trust her to do anything—clean the dishes, stir a pot at the fire, even watch the baby—and she finally gave up. It was enough when Sally would sit contentedly, lost in watching a hill of ants or counting the clouds in the sky and not go wandering off as she was want to do. This particular morning she was carefully picking dandelion fluffs and pinching off the little fuzzy wands one at a time. A small smile played on her face, and she didn't even notice when the baby rolled off the blanket and into a patch of sawgrass. His screams brought Verity running, but Sally didn't even look up.

Verity stood for a long minute watching the last of the logs being wrestled into place at the blockhouse and counted the days. It was now late June and she knew that soon, maybe even tomorrow, Clark and his men would be gone. She had already scraped together her remaining courage and politely requested the General's permission to accompany him and his men down river and overland into the Illinois country.

Clark had been civil, but curt. The answer was a non-negotiable no. Days ago Trey had relayed Clark's previous response, but she'd stubbornly gone to the General anyway and asked him herself. The steely flint in his eye left no doubt that if she tried to sneak in with the troops in spite of his orders, he would abandon her where she stood. She left him with a long, steely look of her own.

His words followed her from the tent. "Orderly, keep an eye on that woman. She is to remain on the island."

If she could think of anything else, she would most certainly try it on the General, she thought, stomping back to the Dawsons' fire. The only thing was, she couldn't come up with one single excuse or ruse or trumped-up reason that would gain her a place aboard Clark's flatboat flotilla.

There was nothing for her here. It was increasingly difficult to be near Clem and Bart. Esther had taken over complete care of the baby, and Trey would be leaving one day. Whenever he left for Kaskaskia, she would be completely alone, with no protector, no one to care. She really had no choice. She had to go on to Kaskaskia. Angry, she slapped her hand against her skirt.

It was maddening to be thought of as a burden, unable to make your own decisions, go your own way. Not for the first time she envied the glory, the freedom, of being male. Of course, if she were a man, she would have missed Trey's kiss. And that would have been a shame, because it had been very nice. Kisses, however, didn't get her past the need to leave the Dawsons. Buried in her skirt, her hands knotted into fists. Well, she hadn't given up. Not by a long shot. Not while there was a single hour left in which to hope.

Two days later, however, the taste of defeat was bitter as she stood a mile downriver on the bank at the Falls, Sally's small hand holding to her skirts, and watched Clark and his rag-tag army paddle toward the west. The water was, after all, high enough that the boats floated through the rocks and rapids, and Captain Owens grimly watched the flotilla depart before he turned to look over the band of farmers he was to lead safely through the summer. Unshed tears burned behind Verity's eyes and she averted her face so that he couldn't see. She squared her shoulders. She would not, would not, stand here and let Trey Owens say, "I told you not to count on going." Never.

"Come on, Sally." She forced a cheery note into her voice. But when she reached for the child's hand, Sally wasn't there. Her quick glance through the thinning crowd failed to pick up the bright curly head. Where had she gone? Was she with her father? Not likely. Esther? No, she could see Esther shepherding her own brood back toward the boats.

And then she saw her, picking something at the edge of the trees. Verity had taken two steps in that direction when Trey's long strides carried him to her side. "Did you send along a message for Edward?" he asked, not unpleasantly, blocking her path and most of the sun with his bulk.

"No," she answered with more spunk than she felt. "I figure on taking it myself some day soon."

A muscle in his jaw clenched and his face took on a hardened set. "I'd gladly have taken it for you."

He was badly disappointed, she could see. And it didn't require any great insight to know that a man like him would rather be where the action was, than stuck at home with a plow and harness. In spite of herself, a surge of sympathy welled in her at the bleakness in his eyes. She put out a hand and touched his arm.

"I'm sorry. I know you'd rather be on the river."

He drew a long breath. "Yes, well... Last night Clark revealed a set of sealed orders from Governor Henry. He intends to take not only Kaskaskia and Cahokia, but Vincennes and Detroit as well. Corn Island is to be his supply station and information relay. We'll grow corn here as a staple for the army. And, of course, do all we can to stay out of the hands of the

Indians until he breaks the back of the British. The day he sends Hamilton through here in chains will be the day I can leave and join him."

Looking over Trey's shoulder, Verity could see Sally. The child was still bending over, reaching for something, closer to the trees than before. She called, "Sally, we're leaving," and turned to Trey.

"But, you must feel a sense of satisfaction in doing what you can to help America win the war for independence!"

"Maybe so, but I'd far rather do it in the wilderness than on 70 acres of island, shepherding a bunch of farmers who might not know an Indian if they saw one."

She looked up at him solemnly. "Then I guess we're both cheated out of what we want, aren't we?"

His gaze was soft on her face for a long minute and Verity's stomach seemed to slip sideways. A curious warmth in his gaze leaped at her. She'd seen that look before and felt the answering leap in her own body. "I guess what we both want will have to wait," she said.

"And you still want Kaskaskia?" he said, leaving unsaid that Edward was in Kaskaskia.

"I know my position here is worsening."

"You have my protection. Anything I can do—"

"I know and thank you, but you aren't always nearby."

He bent his head to hers and stepped between her and the crowd to shield her from their eyes. "Have you thought about what I said the last time we talked?"

"I've thought of little else," she answered.

He flushed and his voice was bitter. "And you still want to go to Kaskaskia." It was a statement of disgust. "I can't believe you'd... Why?" He threw his hands wide. "I don't understand."

She only shook her head and refused to look at the pain in his eyes. Then, "Hell and damnation! You're more stubborn than a two-headed mule, do you know that?"

She kept her head bowed so that he couldn't see the sudden sheen of tears threatening to flood down her cheeks.

And then he seemed to pull into himself as he glanced around at the others and remembered his duties. "I think we'd better head for the boats. We're losing light. There might be a storm coming up and I want us all across this section of water and back on the island before it strikes."

The settlers who had come along to send Clark off were drifting away to make their way up the bank toward the spot where the canoes had been beached. Verity looked at the sky and while the light was not as bright as it had been, there was no sign of a storm. She'd better collect Sally and leave, too. The last of the boats were ready to pull away. Trey was already stepping into the prow of a dugout drifting away from shore.

"Sally!"

But Sally was not at the edge of the trees. Verity couldn't see her little head bobbing anywhere. She must have wandered into the forest. She could not have gone far.

She called to Abner to wait for her and Sally and he waved absently, involved in conversation with one of the men.

A dozen strides took Verity off the bluff and into the woods, screened from the view of the others. The light filtering through the dense overhang was murky and tinted a dull green. The day was definitely fading, storm or no storm. However, there was a strawberry patch at hand and, sure enough, there was Sally, her hands full of ripe berries and a red stain around her smiling mouth.

"See Ver'ty, what I got? They're good."

"You had a special treat, didn't you?" Scolding Sally would serve no purpose so she took her by the hand and turned back to the river, visible only in patches through a screen of bushes and trees. But—she could barely see. Frowning, she straightened to tip her head back and look upward. What she could see of the sky was almost dark! What had happened to the sun?

A shaft of unease knifed through her. There had been no thunder. No lightning. No wind to send warnings. What could it be? A cold spot in the pit of her stomach flowered and spread.

"Sally," she said, "We have to go. Now." But even as she turned she realized Sally wasn't there.

In her place stood a stunningly savage-looking red man with half his head shaved and a single eagle feather hanging from his scalp lock. Verity's heart seemed to stop beating. The top portion of his face was painted black and the bottom red. Faster than a snake could strike, his hand shot out and gripped her arm in a painful grasp.

Verity's breath stuck in her throat and refused to go any farther. Here was the object of fifteen years of nightmares. Living, breathing, embodiment of all that was evil and cruel and murdering in the world. The Indian wore nothing but a breechclout and carried a wicked-looking, short-handled tomahawk. His coppery body shone bright with oil as he crouched over her, undecided.

Verity tried to pull free but he only tightened his grip. In a sudden frenzy of fear she clawed and kicked and fought with her one free arm, but he merely held her at arm's length, too far away for her to reach him. They lurched back and forth, trampling the berries underfoot until the sharp tang of their sweetness filled the air. In some deep pocket of her brain, Verity knew this had happened before. Her bucket had been full of berries when she'd heard the screams from their cabin, and she and Joe had run… She tried to bite, but he pulled her against his greasy chest and crimped her jaws together in a painful clamp. She could move only her eyes, could see only into his.

His eyes were as black as bits of charcoal and open so wide she could see the whites in a circle all the way around, and full of some strong emotion, which he didn't bother to hide. Verity's own eyes opened wider. He kept glancing up at the sky and then back at her. He was afraid! No, not afraid, but definitely uneasy about something. She wished she could see clearer, but the light was almost completely gone. He jabbered something, short choppy words given in a commanding tone, and before she could draw breath, the clearing was full of Indians, all with the same half-frightened, wild look in their eyes.

For a full minute it seemed that they all talked at the same time, casting anxious eyes first at the sky and then at her and then her captor jerked her chin up toward him. In the deep twilight he leveled a long look at her and then at the sky, now almost black, and then slowly drew his free hand over his own eyes.

Verity didn't understand, for surely he was trying to tell her something, and tensing her jaws to keep her teeth from chattering in fear, she shook her head and raised her shoulders in mute appeal.

He didn't waste time in repeating, but twisted a hand in her long hair and started off at a run, dragging her along behind. She stumbled, half-sprawling, after him and for the first time opened her mouth in a defiant "No!"

He stopped instantly, gave her two hard blows along each side of her head and wordlessly started off again. She tasted blood and knew her teeth had broken the skin on the inside of her mouth, or maybe she'd bitten her tongue. Her whole mouth felt as if it were on fire. But she'd be damned if she'd go along like a scared rabbit. She dug her heels into the soft pine needles underfoot and threw her body to the side.

With an angry grunt the Indian whisked her skirts up over her head, wrapped his hand in the folds, and set off again. Her legs moved without her will, following. Her head buzzed and her vision was skewed in the darkness of her skirt-enshrouded, shrunken world, but she ran with him. If, in her blindness, she wavered at all, he simply towed her along the way he'd drag a side of deer. The other braves fell in behind.

She wanted to cry, both from pain and from terror, but was more afraid of crying than she was of the hand forcing her stumbling progress after him. She wanted to whimper aloud. She wanted to scream. She was afraid to think of Sally. Had they—God forbid, had they used the ax on her bright curly head and left her little body back in the glade? And where, oh where, were they taking her? What were they going to do?

A cry rose in the back of her throat, but she swallowed it and concentrated on accommodating her feet to keeping her balance and her own legs to his gait. Somewhere she'd heard that if you gave Indians too much trouble they simply killed you because they didn't want to be bothered. Her only chance lay in staying alive long enough to escape. Grimly, she clung to that hope.

Thirteen

Verity fought her way clear of an enveloping nightmare that swooped about her like a huge black bird. Something was very, very wrong. Her head hurt, her chest felt as if it were caved in and nothing about her would move. Her arms and legs had no feeling whatever.

The cool damp air told her there was a ground mist hanging low and a faint wind stroked her face but—and then, in a rush, she knew exactly what was wrong and her eyes snapped open.

She had slept the sleep of exhaustion, without caring about comfort or food, only grateful that the headlong scramble through the forest had ended, finally, with the fall of night time darkness. The last thing she remembered was sinking down where they'd halted with the Indian's fist still knotted in the skirt over her head. Her trembling legs had simply given way and she felt herself slipping into some gray, silent peaceful place of the mind.

A dim and watery dawn filtered through the leaves casting the little glade where she lay in an eerie half-light. By turning her head carefully to the right she could see three braves sprawled carelessly in sleep, like so many garishly painted wooden figures.

No sign of Sally. Where was she? What had they done with her? Verity turned as far as she could. Her mind screamed the word, *Sally*, but the child wasn't in sight.

To her left lay two more Indians, one being The Fist as she'd begun to think of him. Instinctively, she pulled as far away from him as she could get.

Pulling, however, proved painful to various parts of her body and she realized for the first time that she was trussed up like a prized pig ready for roasting. A sturdy limb lay across her stomach with each of her hands tied to an end. The weight wasn't unbearable, but was definitely uncomfortable and she lifted her head to see what could be done about it. She saw then why there was no feeling in the lower part of her body. The same thing had been done to her legs. A pole stretched her feet wide apart. A grapevine had also been tied around her neck and cross-tied between two trees. She was firmly anchored where she lay.

Swallowing hard against despair, Verity dropped her head back onto the pine needles. Her heart set up a frightening thudding in her breast. How long would it be before she was missed back at the island? And what would they do then? What could they do? Was anyone there capable of tracking the Indian party?

Trey.

Trey could track. Trey would come after her. Just the echo of his name brought a measure of calm. Oh, please God, let him come soon. She needed his stubborn strength and knowledge of Indians which until now she'd so fiercely resented. She didn't care how mad he was with her for, once again, straying from the main body of settlers. If only he'd follow and get her out of this mess he could yell all he wanted.

And what about Sally? What had they done with her? Would she ever see any of them again? Sally and Gideon and Esther? Trey? Verity had heard stories all her life about how Indians treated captives. Never before had she had reason to know if she was a brave person or a coward but, and her heart gave a queer flutter, it looked as if she might find out soon.

Trey would surely be looking for her by now, she thought. He wouldn't just let her go without a trace. She allowed her thoughts to soften slightly as she considered the way he'd looked day before yesterday when they'd met unexpectedly, him with an ax over one shoulder, a wrist slung carelessly across the handle, and his rifle carried in the other. His long stride carried him over the uneven ground and a smile lit his eyes as he caught sight of her and altered his direction to cross her path.

An admiring glance had whisked from the top of her freshly washed hair to her moccasin-clad feet. He liked what he saw, it was obvious, and a shiver had run up Verity's back all the way to her hairline. But he only said, "Glad to see you're sticking close to camp. Until we know what the Indians are up to, don't leave the fort."

Verity's eyes hardened. He wasn't going to tell her she looked pretty. He was back to giving orders. She said, "We'll sicken without greens and fruit in our diet."

The look he gave her may as well have been a tolerant pat on the head. "Let me worry about that," he said, nodding at the armload of wood she carried. "Need any help?"

Verity bit back a sharp answer and hitched the wood higher. "If you move anything, the whole mess will tumble. Are you about finished with the roofing?"

"Ought to be done by nightfall and Clark will be gone within a day or two." He cut an anxious look toward her, a look he tried to conceal and failed. "You've given up on the idea of going along, haven't you?"

She smiled sweetly and nodded. It was the biggest lie she'd ever told, silently or aloud. "Apparently this isn't the time, Captain Owens."

A white line of tension disappeared from around his mouth and he fell into step beside her. "Trey," he corrected automatically, tempering the rest with a fond smile. "It's hard to believe you're finally using some common sense. What is this? Miss Verity Philp acting responsibly?"

Common sense had nothing to do with it, Verity thought, but he could assume whatever made him happy. The first boat pointing its nose down river after Clark left, the very first, would have her in it. It would serve no good purpose, however, to have him know what she was planning and become watchful.

With a smile of her own, she said tartly, "If an order is reasonably intelligent I see no reason to step around it." And then quickly, while a frown gathered on his face, she went on, "Trey isn't an ordinary name. I've never heard it before. Is it a family name or does it mean something special?"

His jaw tightened and he glanced through the trees toward the river. "A name is only a means of identification. It's not important."

"I disagree. A name is very important."

"Trey's enough."

Verity didn't even try to hide her smile. Actually it was more of a smirk. "You're avoiding the question."

His shoulders slumped a fraction of an inch and then he squared around. "It's Frederick Herkimer Owen, The Third."

And then, when she didn't react, he repeated, "The Third. Trey. Three. Understand?"

She shrugged and raised her eyebrows. "Why all the secrecy? It's a perfectly respectable name. And Trey is very efficient, considering—well, considering."

He resumed his walk toward the Dawson cabin, picking his way through people, calling a greeting here, an order there. Shouting above the hammering.

Without looking at her he answered, "It's not acceptable when you're ten-years-old and small for your age and all the other boys call you Herky Jerky."

"Oh." And then with elevated eyebrows and a glance at his long legs striding out in front of him, "Small?" she asked.

"Everyone else I knew got their growth at about twelve and I didn't shoot up until I was fifteen. I'd given up by then." He chuckled. "I learned to fight during those three years. Used to dare them to make me cry." He cocked his head to one side. "Maybe I wasn't too smart, though. They sure tried hard to back me down."

Grimly, lying on her earthen bed, with the morning sun breaking through the fog, Verity refused to let herself cry. She would learn that much from Trey. Tears were a luxury she couldn't afford just now when she needed all her wits about her. If she just weren't so tired! After yesterday she felt as if there was no strength left in her, anywhere. She was wrung dry.

The day before had been a nightmare of unimaginable proportions. The Fist, her captor, seemed to be the leader, for the others obeyed his commands instantly. At the first waterway they'd come to, he'd released her skirt long enough for her to drink. In one brief glimpse, she'd seen Sally riding high on the shoulders of a painted brave, and then Fist had given a cross-armed gesture and sent half the Indians up stream, and the others down.

Miles later, leaving the stream, she realized with dismay that there were only six of them left. They'd been dropping out by ones and twos all along the way. Sally was not with them. Nor was the brave who had been carrying her.

Now, in the light of dawn, her spirits sank even lower. Trey would never find her. No one could unravel the many trails they'd left.

A pine cone dropped from a nearby tree with a soft plop, causing all her senses to spring alert. A jay screamed from the forest heights and a cool breeze lifted the short hair on her neck. Her legs still ached from the unrelenting pace the Indians had kept for most of the day. And her head! Every single, individual hair hurt! A hatred welled in her so deep she thought she might be sick. Indians!

They had gabbled as they ran in the growing dimness, Verity could hear them, their voices shrill with fear. Several times the Indian's grasp loosened and she saw glimpses of the sky. The sky had turned a strange greenish hue, then ash gray and finally darkened until the forest was almost a midnight black. In a small clearing they stopped briefly to gaze upward at the sun. A stricken look came into each face, replaced quickly by undiluted terror. The sun looked as if a large bite had been taken from it. There was only a small sliver left and it disappeared while they watched.

The chatter stopped, then. They ran silently. In a rotating cycle one Indian ran point and one at the rear, constantly alert. They'd plunged headlong in the dark through thickets, waded shallow channels of swift moving water, crawled over rotting logs and scaled small mountains of loose rock. Verity's knees and thighs had taken the brunt of the punishment from the brush and were whiplashed raw from thorns and shin tangle and brambles.

Only when a tint of light pinked the heavens did the Indian's anxiety lessen. When the brightness of a normal day began to strengthen they slowed the frantic pace and stopped looking back in terror as if expecting to be overtaken by some slobbering, clutching apparition from the spirit world.

Verity recognized the terror in their voices and in their panicked pace. Triumphantly, she clutched at a spear of satisfaction in that she knew what happened to the sun had nothing to do with the Indians' spirit world. They'd witnessed what her father's books called an eclipse: when the moon hid the sun from view. Strange, certainly, but not a forecast of doom as the Indians seemed to think.

However, the respite from their headlong dash gave way to a punishing, steady pace that had Verity gasping within a half-hour. The coldness of icy streams as they plunged through them revived her from time to time and one long, downhill stretch of plateau rested her cramping leg muscles. Apart from that, it had been a matter of grinding her teeth with the determination not to give in, not to give up and provide the Indian reason to split her head open and leave her to die on the floor of the forest. When he'd finally come to a halt, she stood swaying with fatigue in the moonlight and then slowly crumpled at his feet.

She lay on her back now, deep in the forest, in some God-forsaken place she knew not where, and hoped in a spot too deep for tears or prayer, for Trey to find her. Trey and Homer. They were the best. Everyone said so. And finding her, she thought, would certainly be the test of their skill.

It would serve her right, however, if Trey was relieved by her absence rather than worried. She'd gone out of her way to give him a bad time, and be obstinate and difficult, when all he'd asked was simple cooperation.

What if he remembered only the trouble she'd caused and decided he was better off without her? No. She told herself that thoughts like that did him an injustice. Her plight was no fault of Trey's, but he would come after her. He would attempt to rescue anyone. But the way he loved Indians, she knew better than expect him to leap into camp with guns blazing. He'd probably walk in smiling and try to charm The Fist out of his prized captive and that would get them absolutely nowhere. For if yesterday had proved nothing else, she was sure, by the way he'd snarled at the others—and once even raised his tomahawk menacingly—that Fist considered her to be his possession, and his alone.

A sudden muted grunt brought her head around. The Fist was awake and sitting up. He stared at her with bright, black eyes, apparently making up his mind about something.

By this time the others were awake. With a minimum of fuss, they scooped water into their mouths from a nearby stream, and then set about making repairs on their paint from small containers carried on their belts.

Verity's feet were untied and the noose removed from her neck, but the limb stretching her arms was left in place in spite of her plea for them to release her.

After more primping than any females Verity had ever seen, the Indians seemed to judge themselves ready. The Fist freed Verity's hands and allowed her the brief opportunity to squat behind a scrubby bit of brush to relieve her bladder. If she hadn't been in such dire need, she thought she would have died of mortification. Then, he yanked her skirts over her head once more, and they were off. Again on the trail, running blindly behind Fist, she tried not to cry out as feeling began to flow back into her arms and hands.

Thankfully, the going was not as rough this morning. They were on a well-traveled trail. No brush slapped back from Fist's progress to sting her flesh and there was no tangled undergrowth to stumble through, with Fist yanking her upright by the hair whenever she lost her balance.

They ran for maybe an hour at an easy lope and then stopped. He dropped her skirt and once more attached a vine around her neck. Verity could at least see more than a brief glimpse around her. What she saw, however, caused her blood to run cold.

A quarter-mile in the distance, teepees fringed the lower end of an elongated lake from which a wide river flowed westward.

Dozens upon many dozens of men, women and children squatting, working, smoking, playing, moved around between the teepees. A pall of smoke from the cooking fires hung low over the settlement, and even though her mind was almost numb with fright, it registered the stunning sight of the colorful Indian village nestled against the backdrop of a tree-fringed hillside with a clear lake sparkling at its feet.

One of the braves lifted his head in an earsplitting announcement of their arrival and started around the lake with the rest following, shouting cat-calls and shrill yip-yips of their own. Fist followed at a more sedate rate as befitting one who was bringing home a trophy. The vine around Verity's neck was shortened and held in his fist at thigh level, so that she was forced forward into a submissive pose.

By the time they reached the outskirts of the village, it seemed as if most of the residents were running to meet them. A fearful babble of cackling laughter and piercing shrieks broke in waves around them. Dozens of naked children ran everywhere, round-eyed, hooting, touching. Dogs barked and snapped at her heels. Women and children poked their fingers into Verity's ribs and pulled her hair. Little boys stuck sticks between her legs trying to make her fall. The noise was deafening. She twisted frantically trying to avoid sticks and fingers and moccasined kicking feet. Then, slowly, fear gave way to anger.

They would not get the better of her. She would not allow them to see that they bothered her in the least. She pulled together the fringes of what dignity she could muster and forced herself to stare straight ahead and ignore the surrounding pandemonium.

Fist stopped in front of a particularly large teepee with a V shaped opening at the top where smoke rose in a faint curl from between large flaps. A stooped and beady-eyed older woman in a long-fringed skirt and braided hair waited with eyes squinted against smoke from the cook fire. Fist said something in a respectful tone and handed his end of the vine into her waiting grasp. Then he walked away without looking back. The woman—was it his mother or his wife?—shifted her gaze to Verity and studied her with black, glittering eyes.

With effort, Verity stood tall and returned the questioning look. The squaw turned then and walked away from the village and up a grassy slope, leading Verity like a hound on a leash, and bent to tie the vine to a small sapling, leaving Verity with a short tether. The remaining vine she cut off and used to tie Verity's hands before her. She stood back then, with lips folded tightly as if considering what the Fist had brought home.

Finally, still expressionless, she walked back to her teepee where the women had gathered. They turned to peep backward at Verity and titter into their hands. One even mocked Verity's bent-necked walk through the village. At last the novelty wore off and they returned to their work.

In spite of the heat, Verity stood shivering until it became apparent that no one else was coming near her. She'd been staked out like a goat on a hillside. She sat down and composed herself to wait.

The day passed uneventfully with the regular goings-on of the village carried forth as if it was a play being presented in the bowl of the valley. She sat beneath the tree and saw women tending fires and cooking, young girls dyeing porcupine quills, men gossiping in front of their teepees and children racing back and forth in violent play with a deerskin ball. If anyone got curious and approached her too closely, the old woman suddenly appeared at the teepee flap, screeching a raucous warning and the offender veered off immediately.

Apparently, Fist had left orders that she not be disturbed. Or even, she began to worry by evening, fed. No one came near her, and by twilight the rumblings in her stomach were becoming difficult to ignore.

However, if hunger was a problem, her full bladder was a crisis. All day she'd determinedly refused to squat in plain view as did the Indian women, but by sundown she was in misery. Finally, in despair, she crept as near the thicket as her tether would allow and, fighting tears of humiliation, spread her skirts wide and relieved herself. In disgust she moved away. At this rate she'd soon smell as strongly as the Indians.

At last the old woman came bearing a bark tray with slice after slice of some round sausage-type roll, a glutinous pile of ground corn and honey, and several chunks of meat which Verity had watched her fish from the common cooking pot. She didn't stay, merely placed the tray and a bladder of drinking water within reach and left. Gratefully, Verity ate all there was and licked the drippings from her fingers. She was astonished at how tasty the food was and would have welcomed more.

An hour later the woman was back, this time with a small, gaily painted pot which she carried in one hand. With the other hand she signed that she wanted to smooth the contents on Verity's arms and legs.

Verity tried to make herself smaller. Was this some new torture technique? Would the stuff infect her wounds, give her poison ivy, or would it heal? Nothing could be read from the woman's face, it was as inscrutable as the tree trunk behind her. She simply stood patiently and went through the motions of soothing on the ointment, again. Cautiously, Verity extended one leg in answer. She gritted her teeth against flinching when the old woman touched her, but after all it wasn't hard. The salve was cool and took the sting out of her scratched and bleeding skin with a speed that almost brought tears to Verity's eyes. And then the woman left, ignoring Verity's call of thanks.

After that she simply sat, alone and uneasy, waiting for what would happen next, but nothing did. Eventually, darkness covered the valley, the fires died out and the voices quieted down. Verity covered herself the best she could with her skirt and lay down at the foot of the sapling. There was nothing to be done about the mosquitoes and she was sure she wouldn't sleep a wink out in the open and unprotected, but she did.

She awakened with the sun bright in her eyes and a sharp kick in the ribs. The Fist stood over her. His huge hand reached for her hair and a stab of stark terror rushed over her. She scrabbled away from him to stand, panting, with her back against the tree.

He smiled then, a horrible showing of teeth, but obviously pleased that she understood and was willing to obey. He beckoned a small gathering of men closer. They clustered around her and with eager eyes looked her up and down, commenting in short, guttural spurts while Fist turned her this way and that, for all the world as if he was preparing to sell a prize horse!

Verity's fear solidified into hard, concentrated hatred. They were uncivilized, ignorant savages. They were vermin. She put everything she was feeling into her eyes and was rewarded when one of them, stepping too close, took an uncertain step backward.

There was a short debate with a short, stocky young brave making what appeared to be an offer and Fist shaking his head, and then another brave trying to top the first, and Fist again shaking his head, emphatically this time and in derision. Finally, he again reached for Verity's hair, this time snagging the ends and wrapping his fingers securely in the brown strands, and delivered a violent tirade with much waving of his other hand and rude gestures. The braves drifted away with much hooting and apparent disgust, and finally Fist released her hair and stalked away himself. Verity sat down once more and waited.

The day stretched on. The heat grew, became oppressive, and cooled finally at sundown.

Despite her discomfort, Verity was interested in the life of the village. Children were petted and loved, and never once did she hear a voice raised in anger against them, no matter how provoking their antics. In late afternoon, they sat beneath the shade of a tree while an ancient woman seemed to be telling stories. Given their rapt faces, Verity wished she could understand.

At evening the old squaw again brought a tray of food which Verity consumed greedily. No one came near her except for another group of braves who stood twenty feet away and discussed her merits with loud voices and obscene body motions. Fist opened the flap of his teepee and looked out, called a warning and went back in. They left, apparently disappointed by their inability to provoke a scene. By dark, Verity was resigned to spending another night in the open.

She was less afraid now and, by Indian standards at least, conceded they had taken care that she not be physically tormented and that she was fed and watered. But she worried about Sally. If the rest of the warriors had come in after the Fist and his group, she hadn't seen them. Had they taken Sally captive, maybe got tired of carrying her and turned her loose, or was she lying in some glen forgotten and dead? The thought made Verity sick. Maybe Trey had found her, wandering on her own, and taken her back to Corn Island. Weak as it was, she comforted herself with this possibility.

For hours sheets of lightning had played across the sky, but it was almost full dark before thunderheads began to build and rumblings drifted over the mountain and into the valley. No one paid any attention to her. Apparently, she was to spend the night in the open, Verity thought, resigning herself to a night of sitting out a thunder storm. Wind and hail maybe, but no stars.

The village had begun to settle down and brace for the storm when three other braves came to stand at a distance and stare at Verity. Her skin crawled. They wore bristling scalp locks and carried razor sharp tomahawks at their belts. She found it hard to ignore the tomahawks. She had decided to turn her back on the three young men and pretend disdain, when Fist came striding up the rise from his teepee. She sat up. Not her hair again!

He yelled a warning at the men to stay where they were and came toward Verity with a scowl that said plainly he was tired of the bother. He towered over her, blotting out what remaining light there was in the sky, and said something in a loud tone. The others fidgeted, one laughed uncertainly, but no one moved when Fist struck her fiercely with the palm of his hand across first one cheek and then the other.

Her head jerked violently to one side and then back again. Her ears rang. She blinked to clear her vision and braced herself on both elbows for whatever he might do next.

What he did was to squat down directly in front of her, knees apart, breechclout swaying and ask quietly, "Long Runner's woman? When she just looked at him, utterly bewildered, he repeated urgently in a harsh whisper, "Long Runner. O-an's woman."

O-ans? Trey Owens? she wondered, blinking and trying to focus on the two figures of Fist that were wavering before her. *Long Runner?* Fist had spoken in English. Heavily accented, but still English.

Desperately trying not to look beyond Fist to where the three braves discussed her fate with full attention to Fist's intimidation, she whispered, "Yes." She would be Trey's woman if the Indian wanted it that way.

He peered into her eyes for a full minute and she scarcely breathed. Then, subtly, the look in his eyes shifted. Something had been decided. So smoothly that she detected no movement, a knife slid down from between his legs and landed with no noise whatever on the hem of her skirt. She stared at it in fascinated wonder, and then furtively moved her foot so that the knife was hidden.

"Hear me," he commanded, still in a whisper because the three braves were inching closer. "When tears fall from sky and moon hides face, go beyond canoes to water. Go like smoke through treetops. Good?"

"Yes," she whispered, grasping at this new hope. "Smoke," she said.

He stood, rattled off another string of gibberish, gave her a kick in the thigh with the flat of his foot and walked off, waving at the three men as if to say, *Go to your blankets, she isn't worth it.*.

Verity moved one knee slightly, pulling her skirt more fully over the knife. The braves laughed as if the joke was indeed on them and then calling loudly to Fist's back they wandered off, too.

Verity's chest burned like ten thousand fires smoldered there and she cautiously let out her breath, afraid that when she looked again the knife wouldn't be there, after all. But it was there, nestling in the folds of her skirt, she could feel it with her ankle. And when she looked the blade gleamed wickedly in the slashes of lightning.

None of it made any sense. Her jaw still throbbed from the chop Fist had given her and her hip would surely have a bruise the size of a cooking pot in the morning. He'd put her through the agony of that hair-yanking, exhausting, blind scramble through the forest and the humiliation of being tied like an animal to a tree—and then stealthily slipped her a knife and told her which direction to run!

Was it a trick? If she used the knife and tried to escape would Fist's long, outstretched arm be waiting and would he give her to the women to torment and punish? Maybe she ought to just stay where she was, sit out the storm and wait and see what tomorrow would bring. After all, no one had actually harmed her yet.

However, and her heart did an odd lurching slide at the thought, what would happen when one of the braves finally met Fist's asking price? Becoming an Indian squaw, a slave, degraded and carrying no more worth than a beast of burden, or dying in an escape attempt: that was her choice. Surely there was an alternative. There had to be another way.

As yet she had not dared touch the knife. She would not risk calling attention to herself. Her brain scurried in ever narrowing circles. What other way? Where? How?

She was alone. The village was deserted now, everyone inside, braced and ready for the storm. Even the dogs were quiet. Clouds boiled overhead and thunder crashed around her ears. Even the earth shook as if the very air itself were moving.

And still Verity waited. She waited for her heart to stop its pounding, for the old woman to come screeching out of the teepee, for Fist to come back and take a stick to her for somehow having a knife.

But, and she didn't know how it was so, her mind was made up. Whether it made sense or not, she was going to use the knife.

Verity waited for the moon to cover its face.

Fourteen

Trey eased back from the knothole and his view of the Indian village, and leaned against the crumbling inner wall of a hollow tree. He'd been standing on what amounted to barely more than a toehold inside an ancient elm since dawn and now that dusk was falling and the time for action was nearing, he could relax. Anyway, it was no longer possible to see through the overlay of branches and leaves. The far hillside where Verity waited, tethered, lay veiled in mist as the storm moved closer and the camp itself receded as darkness flowed into the valley. This was all the rest he was going to have, and he needed to make the most of it.

Without moving so much as an inch, except for a grimace of sweet, piercing pain as his body came to life, he concentrated on every muscle he could activate from the soles of his feet to his eyebrows.

"Damn fool woman," he muttered under his breath as he flexed his left calf. "Trying to do it all alone, as usual." He'd read the signs. The Indians had gotten Sally first and when Verity gave chase, she'd given them a good fight. He'd seen no evidence of Sally after the initial grab. The question wasn't who; he could see plainly that it was Indians that had taken them, but where they had gone.

If only Verity had come back to the fort for help. But with her usual bullheadedness, Verity had not asked anyone, had gone her silent way and gotten—what? Captured is what she'd got. And she had gotten him up a tree, with spiders down his back, and bark dust in his nose and cramping muscles—and only half a chance of coming through this with both of their skins intact. But from the moment he'd discovered her absence, found the trampled berries and read the signs, he'd had an idea he'd end up with a lot of problems and no choices.

At first Homer had insisted on coming along. "We think Indian style, you and me. And if you're dead set on going after her, it's liable to take us both."

"You're needed more on the island," Trey answered, sliding a knife into his belt and reaching for a small bag of smoked meat. "The settlers are green as grass. If somebody isn't here to lead them around they'll get themselves killed by the time I get back. I'll go alone."

Homer didn't deny the farmers' vulnerability. He scowled. "You oughtn't go at all, even if you are addle-pated about her. Don't make no sense, taking off into the wilderness after one woman and a child that's already been gone half a day. You know what you're likely to find."

Trey knew. At the first sign of trouble, the Indians would have dispassionately knocked Verity and Sally in the head, taken the scalps and gone on. If the captives couldn't keep up or if, and here his breath stuck in his throat, if Verity fought—and he couldn't imagine her going peaceably—if she had rebelled in any way, she'd already be dead.

The gorge inside him had hardened at the thought. He couldn't stop the instant picture of that lovely length of beaver-brown hair, dripping red, hanging from some savage's belt—and a pain like he'd never known sliced upward, tearing at his vitals. Violently, he wrenched his mind away from the image. He wouldn't think of it. She was healthy and strong. She could keep up. And if her stubborn streak came to the fore, she could probably last out the most strenuous Indian trail. He had to believe that. And he had to find her. There was no alternative.

He only glanced at Homer. "I'll be back in three days or most likely I won't be back at all."

Homer regarded Trey with the eyes of a man resigning himself to a bad decision. But all he said was, "Seems to me you're gol-darned set on chasing trouble's tail, but if that's the way your stick floats—"

Trey nodded and picked up his gun. "Any ideas which way they would have jumped at the eclipse?"

Homer hawked and spat. "Hell, take your pick. As superstitious as an Indian is, a black sun could mean anything from bad medicine to a return of wandering spirits. This is the time of the Raspberry Moon for the Shawnee. They'd see it as a bad sign, for sure, with most of their men away at war. Hunting them, you'll be all over the forest like a dog smelling trees."

It was a long speech for Homer and Trey had nodded his agreement that this was so, raised his gun in a half-salute and disappeared into the woods, leaving Homer standing on the bank of the river, shaking his head.

Carefully, forcing his cramping muscles to move, Trey raised himself the few inches necessary to see out of the knothole. It was a good six-foot drop to the forest floor and he didn't want to make that leap until he was ready. A sprained ankle would change the odds from just about dismal to none at all.

By squinting for focus he could barely see Verity. There she was, still in the same spot she'd lain in since Blue Wing had kicked her and left. She'd made some effort to cover herself, probably as protection from the mosquitoes, by pulling her petticoat down as far as it would go and her skirt up over her arms and head. It looked as if she had every intention of waiting out the storm without complaint. He knew a ridiculous swell of pride. She'd done the right thing all along. He'd known she was tough, but he hadn't known she was smart, too.

He couldn't see the knife, but was confident Blue Wing had slipped it to her as he'd said. The next question was: Would she come? Blue Wing said no, but Trey thought she would.

"Too many things go wrong," Blue Wing had said, his topknot bristling fiercely in the moonlight, last night. The Indian had dropped onto the trail dead center in front of Trey as he trotted along, nearly startling him into shooting before he realized the painted red man was his old friend.

"She's not a coward," Trey answered, frowning.

"Not coward," Blue Wing agreed readily. "She make good mate for Long Runner. But, still—to come alone and in dark, not knowing where or who awaits—She is after all, only woman."

Mate? Trey closed his eyes as a powerful gust of wind shook the tree, filling the air with a blizzard of fine dust. Mate? An image of Verity as she'd been the day he'd watched her come from the river, hunting Gideon, exploded behind his eyelids. Water dripping from her hair, clothes clinging to the soft curves of her body—and then, when she'd discovered he had been watching and Gideon was already on the way to the flatboats, her bottom lip had come out in a way that had him laying awake at night. She gave away all her emotions through that lip. He could tell when she was hurt by the tiny quiver that she tried to hide. When she was angry, like that day at the river, the lip firmed up like granite and she was just as apt to flay the skin off a man with the sharp side of her tongue. He smiled, even as he blew dust softly from his nostrils.

But—mate? Was he ready for marriage, settling down, children? And wasn't that, after all, where love led with a woman like her? But, just the thought of being hampered with the need to consider someone other than himself and a hard lump formed in his stomach. He knew it wasn't fair, knew it didn't follow his personal code, but even though his mind stuttered at the thought of wedding her he knew he'd never let anyone else have her without a fight. Not as long as he had breath left in his body. What was it about her that affected him this way? He no longer knew his own mind.

Maybe it was the contradiction that intrigued him so. She was all softness and sweet smells and eagerness one minute and the next she could stand, tough as buffalo hide and stare down a pack of curious warriors, as he'd witnessed this very afternoon. When he thought of her, there was the same sense of building excitement that always came before battle. She was some woman. And she *had* to see the opportunity Blue Wing had given her with the knife as a challenge. She had to. There wasn't any other way to get her out of the village.

Blue Wing had come up with the plan. Not that it was a good one; it was, quite simply, the only one. He had explained to Trey in minute detail that he had taken pains from the first, from the very moment he'd realized who the woman was, to make sure she was treated the same as any other captive. He hadn't dared raise curiosity by special treatment. Such behavior would have endangered them both. At the same time he'd gone to some trouble to see that she would not be badly hurt by simply claiming her as his own. Without it being said, Trey knew Blue Wing had placed himself in a position of possible dire consequences if he was discovered to be protecting a prisoner.

However, in spite of everything, it was probably the eclipse that saved Verity. The Indians believed that she'd been sent to them as an omen. They were in awe of the woman and child they'd found at the same moment the sun began to blacken its face. It was still necessary, though, that until they knew for sure, she be treated as an ordinary captive lest they be made to feel foolish.

The urgency of getting her out of the village tonight began with the arrival of bad news at midday. The feeling had turned ugly toward the captive when news was brought by a runner that a small raiding party of ten young braves had been ambushed and killed. She was going to be burned.

"This village many gray hairs," Blue Wing had said matter-of-factly as they hunkered down together in a small moonlit clearing. "The man of my sister gone with other braves."

Trey didn't question where they'd gone. At this time of year, for an Indian brave, there was only one activity. Hunting. For either game or white men. One was as necessary to their way of life as the air they breathed, and the other was a threat to their very existence.

A sudden gust of wind blew up the hollow shaft of the tree bringing the scent of rain and the stale smell of the village.

Burn her.

Trey had seen a captive burned once and the anguished screams of the unlucky brave from another tribe rang in his ears to this day. The thought of Verity—her sweet skin charring, hair flowing about her shoulders and igniting instantly, her screams—His palms broke out in a sweat. No, he wouldn't think of the possibility. He needed all his senses about him tonight. It wouldn't happen. He'd kill her himself before he'd allow it.

He put his eye to the knothole once more, but the world had darkened so that he could no longer see the teepees or Verity. The rain came slashing at the earth, bending trees and flattening grasses. He could feel the vibrations of thunder through the trunk of the elm as the sound crashed overhead.

Where was she? In sudden panic, now that he couldn't see for himself that she was all right, he pressed his eye even tighter to the hole. Nothing. What if she didn't come? What if she caved in to the fear and the not knowing and indignities of the last three days and just stayed where she was, rolled in a ball of misery and at the mercy of the elements? She didn't know her choices were reduced to running or burning.

Trey contemplated the idea of sneaking into the village himself and stealing her away. But the chance of his going undiscovered in the midst of an Indian encampment, even during a storm, was slim to nothing. The dogs would smell him out, if nothing else. By now, there was a possibility that Verity might be able to move among them. His scent, however, would be totally alien and they'd alert the camp in minutes. Maybe Blue Wing—but no, Blue Wing had gone about as far out on a limb as friendship could take him. A simple visit to his sister in the west had landed him in a spot where he had to compromise the tribe's hospitality and put his own life in danger in order to do the honorable thing for his friend's woman.

And that brought up an interesting question. How did Blue Wing know Trey had any special feelings for Verity unless they had been under surveillance? It was clear that Clark's trip down the Ohio hadn't gone without notice. Whether or not they had seen any Indians, the Indians had certainly seen them. Blue Wing had known all along where he was and what he was doing. What they were all doing, for that matter. Trey wished Clark knew he was being watched. It could make all the difference in the world to a safe trip to the Mississippi.

He shifted uneasily. Where *was* she? The rain pelted down relentlessly and the wind forced its way through the valley. And though he couldn't see them, he could hear teepee flaps fluttering wildly. His immediate vision was filled with the lake whipped into froth by the wind. Damn! A simple little rain would have been enough. She'd never find her away around the shoreline in a gully washer like this.

But the rain was not what was keeping Verity. She sat huddled in miserable indecision against the trunk of the tree where she was tethered.

Rain slashed at the earth and thunder rattled overhead. Lightning rent the heavens in knife-like strokes that brought the village into vivid relief. Most of the teepee flaps had been tied, but there were a few left to crack in the wind. No life was visible. Even the few war ponies tied at teepee entrances stood without moving, their rumps to the wind, necks drooping, tails blowing between their legs.

Still Verity sat, narrowing her eyes against the torrent, trying to convince herself she could make her way around the edges of the village without being seen. The logical time to make her move was now in the midst of thunder and wind which would cover any noise she might make. However, the slashing lightning illuminated the whole valley like the brightest of sunny days. If anyone chose that time to look out of the teepee, she might as well lie down and wait for the hatchet. She clenched her teeth.

Besides that, who or what was waiting for her beyond the canoes? Fist hadn't said, only that she was to go like smoke. Maybe no one was waiting. Maybe she was just to flee, aimlessly, into the forest. She'd never survive the night, alone, in the wilderness. And if there was anything waiting by the canoes for her it could conceivably be worse than what she was enduring now. After all, she hadn't actually been hurt, only humiliated beyond belief. And frightened. As a captive, life would be difficult, but she would still be alive. Once she used the knife and cut the vine from her neck it would be too late to go back. If she was captured, it would go hard for her.

But just sitting here, waiting for Fist and the morning to come, waiting for the rain to end and the mosquitoes to come back, meant giving up her one chance at escape. It meant not going on down the Ohio to find Joe and Edward. It meant never having the opportunity to become a lady, as her mother always wanted. It meant becoming an Indian squaw!

And Trey. She would never look up from her work and find his gaze searching for her, never again know the feel of his arms around her, never get the chance to lay her finger in that dent in his chin. She would never know whatever it was that might have been.

She fumbled for the knife in the folds of her skirt. Whatever the future held, she wasn't going to just sit here and wait for it to find her.

The vine took only a second to cut and she was on her knees the next, trying to remember how the village was laid out. If she went to her left and stayed fairly near the trees, it would bring her out a hundred yards above the boats. And as nearly as she could remember, there wasn't a shrub or blade of grass between the forest and the water. No cover. Only a marsh at the edge of the trees. And maybe two dozen canoes laying overturned at the water's edge. She wouldn't let herself think beyond the canoes. She'd deal with that when she got there.

Repeating a prayer like an incantation, she ran between the lightning flashes, holding her skirt up with one hand and clenching the knife in the other. The knife was her only protection and she knew with gut-wrenching certainty that she would not hesitate to use it.

At the first flash of lightning, she flung herself flat on the ground and stayed there until the sky darkened again. Then she rose and ran again. She made no attempt to shelter in the trees, it would have taken time, and suddenly she was possessed of a frantic need to get to the canoes. The smell of rancid oil filled her nostrils as she passed a teepee. The coppery bite of the storm lingered on her tongue. She thought fleetingly that if she got out of this, she would never, ever, forget the smells of the Indian village.

Somewhere off to her right a dog barked, a shrill yap of warning that soon escalated into an annoying din. Must be the only dog in the village that hadn't come sniffing around her during the last few days. Her heart beat wildly as she alternately ran, flung herself flat and ran again. The dog was telling the entire population of the village that she was escaping! She expected to feel arrows in her back at any moment. And then the racket broke off sharply in a yip of pain as a guttural voice interrupted. The barking ceased.

She stopped, her breast heaving, at the edge of a marsh. Just beyond was the beach, and then the water and the canoes. Rain streamed down her face through straggles of wet hair, and impatiently she slicked her face clean so she could see.

No one was there. The shore was swept clean by the wind and the rain, and only the ribbed bottoms of the beached canoes gleamed in the flashes of lightning. She didn't know who she had expected, Fist maybe, but there was no one.

On her knees in the tall grasses of the marsh she could look around the crescent of water to the village and knew that half way up the hill the tree stood where she had been tethered like an animal for the last two days. Over there lay slavery. At least here, without a vine knotted around her neck, she had a chance, slim though it might be. She clutched the knife tighter and hurried toward the canoes. Maybe she could steal one of the birchbark boats and get away before anyone knew. She refused to be beaten until she was tied to that damnable tree again. And she vowed she'd go down fighting if they caught her. This time she had a knife.

Darting from canoe to canoe she worked her way down the line of boats, hiding behind each prow as she came to it. At the last canoe she hesitated. This was where Fist had told her to be.

And she'd done her best to come like smoke as he'd commanded. She looked at the forest, forbidding in its total darkness, and knew she would be hopelessly lost in minutes. Whipped by the storm, the lake was almost as formidable as whitecaps crashed and foamed in powerful disarray. But she was a good swimmer and, thanks to Trey and Homer she could handle a canoe. She didn't know much about finding her way through a forest.

In the next flash of lightning she looked back at the village for her bearings and back the other way, toward the juncture where the river emptied into the lake. It would have to be the water.

~ * ~

Trey was beginning to think he would have to go into the village after her. He couldn't, wouldn't, leave her and she obviously wasn't coming. He had just set his head to working out the best of all the poor choices of ways to infiltrate the camp when, as a brilliant flash of lightning split the sky, he saw her feeling her way carefully around the beached canoes, trying to shield her eyes from the rain, looking anxiously in both directions as she crouched behind the last boat.

For the space of two heartbeats he froze in place, wanting to make sure she was real and not a specter he'd wished up just because he wanted so strongly to see her, and then he dropped straight to the forest floor, crawled out the low opening and ran into the rain. In less than a minute he had an arm around her shoulder, pulling her back into the protection of the trees.

"Good girl! I knew you'd come! Are you all right? You aren't hurt?" She only looked at him with dazed, unbelieving eyes.

He could feel a silly grin spreading across his own face. "I told Blue Wing you'd use the knife. I told him."

She raised a tentative hand and touched his chin as if assuring herself it was really him and her mouth moved silently beneath the roar of the storm.

He raised his shoulders to indicate that he couldn't hear and moved to lead her deeper into the trees when she put a hand on his forearm to stop him. He frowned as a pressing need to get her to safety crowded in on him. Safety was a long way off by anyone's reckoning, and he tugged her none too gently into the shadows.

She lifted her face to him and smiled as if she knew the most exciting secret of all time and drew her finger lightly along the line of his jaw. A sweet zinging in his blood jolted him from his heels to his ears as lightning crackled around them and the hills cupping the valley threw the thunder back and forth. He felt rooted to the spot. But it wasn't the lightning, it was her. Her touch.

Gently her finger nestled in the cleft of his chin with a touch as light as the brush of a feather. With infinite patience, as if there weren't an Indian village within shouting distance, as if a mighty wind wasn't tearing a path through the forest, as if needles of icy rain weren't flinging themselves at the earth and sluicing down their bodies, she raised on tiptoe until her mouth was inches from his.

"I've wanted to do that for the longest time," she said, her eyes still on his chin. He wasn't sure that he heard her voice, he wasn't even sure the words weren't born of the lightning and thunder and rain for they branded themselves on his heart. What he was sure of was that he loved her with all of his being and a world without her by his side wasn't worth contemplating.

An awareness, sudden and slashing, ignited between them, traveling instantly along nerve endings, tingling, prickling, consuming. In the wind-driven rain, Verity lifted her face. The feelings that roared through her might have been part of the storm, but she would never know.

He shook his head. "This isn't the time or the place, my Sweetling but one day, I promise you, we'll finish what we started."

Verity pulled away, shocked by the headlong way she'd flung herself at him. She tried to step back, not looking at him, but he refused to let go of her arms. "Oh no. You're not going to go all skittish on me and stick out that lower lip. We'll finish it, my dear, and when we do we'll make our own thunder and lightening."

As if she could, in a million years, forget what just happened, Verity thought. Ladies didn't leap on a man and invite him to have his way with her. Oh, her mother would have been so disappointed. Her eyes smarted with sudden tears. It was just that she had been so surprised to find him waiting for her, and so relieved after having been frightened for so long… But, no excuses, she thought, firming her lower lip. She had been wanting to lay her finger in that funny dent in his chin forever and ever, and there for awhile it seemed as if she might never have the chance to touch him again, or anything else maybe, and she'd grabbed at the opportunity.

She made an effort and swallowed the giggle that tickled the back of her throat at the thought that she really had grabbed at him, and then sobered when he gently cradled her face in both of his large hands. His eyes were tender.

"As much as I'd like to kiss you again, it's time to see what a tough little lady you really are. We have a long way to go and not much time to do it in. The storm is beginning to move off and we need to make use of it. Are you game?"

"Yes, but you're forgetting about Sally. I can't leave without her and I never did see them bring her in. I don't know where she is."

A flicker of something, an irrelevant thought maybe, crossed his eyes, but he answered smoothly. “Sally is fine. Don’t worry about her.” And with a pointed incline of his head and an elevated eyebrow, he asked again, “Are you ready for this?”

She nodded with confidence and tucked her hand in his. What was it the Bible said? Something about ‘Wither so ever thou goest.’ Yes. Well, that seemed to say it. She wasn’t about to let him get away from her as deep as they were in Indian country and especially after a kiss that made tomorrow seem like a definite possibility.

She cocked her chin. “You can’t be any worse than The Fist. Just don’t reach for my hair.”

Trey nodded once, took a deep breath and plunged forward. She scrambled to catch up, startled at his abrupt move, and vowed that if it killed her, she’d not hold him back.

It was a vow she broke at once.

Fifteen

Verity hadn't taken six steps before her senses registered the direction they were taking. Her toe caught in a twist of gnarled creeper vine and she sprawled headlong, knocking the wind from her lungs in a startled grunt. She was on her feet before Trey turned around.

He grabbed an elbow to steady her. "Got to do better than that," he said, his eyes on the village. "Look where you're putting your feet."

She pointed across the lake toward the fringe of teepees along the water's edge, in a direct line from where they stood. "I am not going back there."

He made an impatient forward movement. "It's the first step out of here."

"If you think I'm going back in there, you are crazy." Unconsciously she touched her neck, still tender from the chaffing of the vine.

He squinted at her through the streaming rain. She had that stubborn set to her chin, again. "We aren't going *into* the village, only past it."

"No." There was an edge of panic in her tone.

He reached for her arm again, anxious with the sense of passing time, and felt her tremble through the sodden fabric of her sleeve. She tried to pull away, but he hung on.

"I won't go. You can't make me." Her head swung away from the Indian town and the lake. "You came through the forest, we can go back the same way."

"And do exactly what they expect us to do? That's not smart."

"But Trey," and he could hear the tremor in her voice. "I can't do this. You don't know—Don't ask me."

He swung her around to face him, steeling himself to do what he knew best. Thank God, it was too dark to see the fear in her eyes. What he wanted to do was cradle her in his arms and assure her everything would be all right. He knew she had been through a bad time, worse than he knew, maybe, and he wanted to soothe her and comfort her and make the hurt go away. Instinct warned him of the folly of such a waste of time. In a quiet, calm voice he said, "Trust me. I know what I'm doing. I didn't come this far to lose it all now."

The forest was full of sound: rain-sound, wind-sound, rumbling thunder dying away into the east. They stood nose to nose, breathing hard, hair flattened by the rain, trees whipping and twisting about them while Trey wished he could infuse some of his own will into Verity, demanding that she be strong, and not weaken now, just when the going might get really rough.

Her answer, when it came, was a question. "Does it have to be this close to the village?"

"Please, just trust me, Verity." He could sense her struggle to accept the promise in both his words and in the stolid, firm body that she felt beneath her own hands. He could all but read her mind. Trust him when there wasn't another thing in the whole world to put her faith in? Trust him, when she just lived through the worst nightmare of her entire life and he was leading her back in that direction?

He stood, unmoving, and watched her make up her mind, until her head tilted forward so that her forehead came forward to rest on his chest. His heart swelled at the faith she placed in him and he pulled her close in a quick hug. "Good girl. We're going by water—and I know you can swim, I've seen you—because the storm and the darkness are on our side at the moment. Now, let's get going. We've lost time."

Five yards down the bank they came to the water's edge. While keeping a watchful eye on the village, Trey uncoiled a length of vine from around his waist. "Take off your skirts and petticoat," he said, softly.

Verity leaned forward to pull her skirts between her legs. "I can hike them up and tuck them into my—"

"Drop them. They're too heavy."

Verity straightened indignantly. She whispered, "I've swum like this before and it worked very well."

"Not well enough for what I have in mind. Get rid of your skirts."

"I will not crawl into the water in my drawers!"

He stopped fiddling with the vine and glared at her. "And who is going to care when they find you at the bottom of the lake with your skirts modestly around your ankles?"

"Who made you an authority on modesty?"

"I did! So shuck the skirts, woman, before I get tired of arguing with the most bullheaded buffalo that ever walked the Greater Miami River basin."

His neck was thrust forward with the intensity of his hoarse whisper and Verity had the sudden feeling he might very well walk off and leave her where she stood. Buffalo?

Bitterly, she looked him in the eye and loosened her skirts. They fell in a soggy splat to the ground and she stepped out of the circle of wet clothing without taking her eyes from his.

His gaze swept down as far as her ankles and then back up, and a slow smile spread across his face. Verity swore to herself that if he said a word, one word, about her capitulation, she would not speak a single syllable until the moment they made Corn Island and then she would announce to the entire community what he'd done. He'd likely be tarred and feathered, and run out of camp. One word. She waited.

But he was silent. He slid his buckskin shirt over his head, retrieved her skirts and petticoats from the ground, swiftly wrapped them into a roll, tied them with a length of vine and looped it over one shoulder. He signaled her to follow and crept out over the water on a fallen log. Silently he rolled off the end and into the water, and motioned for her to follow.

The water was deep and cold. It rose up around her like a black, smothering blanket pressing in from all sides, tucking into every nook and cranny in her body.

With a series of sharp tugs Trey loosened the log from the bank and turned it parallel to the shore. Even in the darkness, she saw that the log had been selected with care and many of the branches removed. The ones that were left made good handholds and thick cover for their heads.

The water swirl around them as Trey's legs scissored and he headed the log into the current. Verity had to allow, in spite of her anger, that he'd planned well. Behind the log they were effectively hidden from the opposite shore and the current did most of the work. All they had to do was keep the log headed in the right direction.

Verity's heart beat thickly in her chest. Water rose and fell around her shoulders and neck. Somewhere across the lake were hundreds of Indians, all of whom were hopefully sound asleep. She tried to make her mind a blank, not to think of the far bank. But, without looking she knew exactly when they floated past the Indian village by the taint of smoke hanging in the air at water level. She found herself breathing in short, shallow gasps until they were safely past.

"Now for the mouth of the river," Trey whispered and altered the thrust of the log.

Verity didn't answer. The water was choppy and she had her hands full balancing so that the log didn't roll. She had long since admitted to herself that Trey had been right about her skirts.

A heavy mantle of darkness pressed in from all sides as the rain continued to fall. There was no longer lightning to occasionally illuminate the night and the blackness was oppressive. She felt suddenly alone and confused. Her hand crept along the log until she touched Trey. The hard muscle of his forearm was reassuring enough that her breathing returned to normal. He was still there. She wasn't alone. And, he knew what he was doing. He said so.

Her arms had begun to feel like leaden mallets when she noticed the change in water temperature. The river? Peering over the top of the log was useless, the night was too dark, but Trey seemed to know where he was because every few minutes she could feel the log change course.

"Do you have five minute's strength left?" The whisper came softly from the front.

Pride made her answer quickly. "I'm fine," she said, aloud.

"Hush!" His voice came right at the end of her nose, soft and tight. "Sound travels over water. Let's not give them anything."

And a few minutes later, while she was still stinging from the rebuke, his voice came again. "Put your feet down. You can stand."

Thick, oily mud seemed to grab at her ankles. Reluctantly, she stood and took the few necessary steps at Trey's heels. He stepped into a stand of cattails that grew as tall as his head and his shadowy form was immediately lost. A flutter of panic rose in Verity's throat. She parted the thick-stemmed rushes and hurried after him.

At the bank he reached back a hand to haul her up the incline and then kept a firm grip on her as he set off through the brush and trees.

"Wait," Verity said, hanging back. "I want to wash off the mud before it dries."

"No point." Trey didn't alter his long stride. "We'll be back in the river soon enough."

"Then, where are we going?" Why were they leaving the river at all, Verity wondered, if they were coming right back to it.

"Got some business up ahead. Won't take long."

She scrambled along after him as best as she could, trying not to hold him back, trying to keep up on her own. However, the pace he set was ridiculous, she thought. No one could track them through the storm. Probably no one would even know she was gone before daylight. She said so, aloud, but softly.

He nodded. "And we have to take advantage of every minute we've got. Because when they come, they'll come a-running and we want all the head start we can get."

"If they had any suspicions that I was gone, the whole village would have been aroused. And you saw, it was as silent as a stone when we went by."

"You're arguing again. Now listen, damn it. Indians aren't stupid. You can always count on them to do the unexpected. I make it a point not to deliberately rile an Indian as I've just done by stealing their prized captive, and I never, never, sell him short. Any more questions?"

"No." The thought of meeting up with any riled Indians was something she'd rather not consider at the moment. Her heart beat faster at the spoken threat and her scalp tingled at the memory of Fist's fingers entwined in her hair. She'd have to take

Trey's word that it was necessary to punish themselves like this in a midnight flight, through a storm.

"Look, I know this is hard on you, but it's necessary. Believe me. Now hang on so you don't get lost." And he was off again, through the rain-sodden, black of night.

She clutched a handful of his shirt with panicked determination and pushed on praying that her second wind would show up soon, and then her third. At last, he came to a stop. He stopped so suddenly that she slammed into his back and nearly bowled them both over. Before she could right herself, he said something in the Indian language and there was an immediate answer. A surge of horror shot through her and she recoiled at the sudden, overwhelmingly familiar smell.

A patchy hole in the clouds allowed a brief glimpse of a clearing in the trees. An Indian stood in a small glade, his war paint streaking in the rain, and the bristling roach of hair on his head wilting to one side. Fist! It was The Fist! He'd tracked them, somehow, and found them and he was going to reach out with that powerful hand and grab her hair again, and she couldn't stand it. She would not let it happen.

She didn't even think, she snatched the long knife from Trey's belt and with a whooping holler she didn't even know she was capable of, leaped straight at Fist with the knife held low, ready to stab and rip upward.

For one long second the two men were too astonished to react. Then, in a heartbeat, the entire clearing seemed to erupt in motion. Fist dropped to the forest floor and rolled forward on his shoulder knocking her feet from under her, a mighty gust of wind hit the tree tops slinging tiny pellets of hail into the clearing, and Trey came at her from behind roughly wresting the knife from her hand.

"It's him," she screamed at Trey as he bore her to the ground. "It's him!"

Then his hand covered her mouth and she was shrieking garbled nonsense into his cupped palm and the knife was gone. Fist stood looking at her, his expressionless face for once shattered by surprise.

"I know," Trey said, straddling her as he held both her hands over her head. "I know it's him. Blue Wing's a friend. The one I told you about. Take it easy."

His friend! Verity felt her eyes widen in disbelief. The Fist, Blue Wing Trey had called him, her captor, her tormentor, was Trey's friend. After all he'd done to her, Trey still called him friend. She bucked beneath him like a wild mustang and in a flurry of legs and arms and teeth they fought like snarling dogs. Before she was finally exhausted Verity was trapped between his legs as they sat upright on the wet pine needles, and his arms were wrapped tightly around her from behind. One hand still covered her mouth.

"If you don't shut up," he said, breathing hard, "you'll bring in every Indian for a hundred miles." And to Blue Wing, "How did you ever haul her this far in two days? She's worse than a wildcat."

Blue Wing's composure was restored and he didn't blink an eye when he answered in slow, but understandable English. "Hair easy. She make no trouble." And his hand reached forth in the old gesture.

Verity stiffened against Trey's chest, but she refused to let Fist, or Blue Wing, see her fear. Since she couldn't speak she tried to put all her hatred into her eyes. Hard gusts of Trey's breath moved the hair over one ear and the heat of his body seemed to quiver into her own. She tightened her hands over his.

Blue Wing nodded wisely without ever having looked directly at her. "Long Runner's woman make damn good warrior. But maybe no good in teepee. How many ponies do you ask for her?"

Verity's throat seemed to close off. Ponies! He was asking her bride price! Against her back she could feel a rumble of laughter in Trey's chest, and then he took a firmer grip on her.

"Well now, let's see. I guess the issue isn't what she's worth to you as much as it is what she's worth to me." The warmth of Trey's breath in her hair stopped as he tilted his head to look up at Blue Wing. "She's a stubborn woman. Argues all the time. Your teepee would sound like a nest of quarreling crows."

Blue Wing grunted and closed his hand around his tomahawk handle. "She learn." He spread his feet further apart and crossed his arms. "Maybe one pony enough."

"Maybe too much," Trey laughed softly and removed his hand from her mouth. "Don't talk," he warned.

"You swine!" Verity hissed, and struggled again to free herself, but he now had two hands with which to hold her.

"No, my friend, I guess not." Verity could feel the force of his breath again and his voice was right at her ear as he answered Blue Wing. "Counting all three of your herds, you don't have enough ponies."

Abruptly, before Verity had time to decide what he'd meant, Trey got to his feet, lifting her with him. He kept tight hold of one wrist. He spoke rapidly and under his breath. "Hang on for a few more minutes. Just stand quiet. What happens right now is important."

So Verity waited, forcing herself to stand quietly while Trey and Blue Wing conversed in guttural sounds. Sentences were short and clipped, the tone hard. Blue Wing seemed to be giving directions, for at one point his hand went out in a sweeping motion toward the river and then back in toward his body in choppy zig zags.

The talking stopped and for one long moment the two men stood regarding each other in silence. Then Blue Wing stepped forward and clasped Trey's forearm and wrist in a firm grip. He said something in a tone almost of sympathy and was gone. Verity blinked and looked again, but Blue Wing had vanished into the mist and the shadows. He was gone.

"Well," she said, turning to Trey. "What was that about?"

A smile played around Trey's mouth, bringing the little dent in his chin into sharp focus in the moonlight. His eyes crinkled at her for a moment. "He wished me good luck and said he thought maybe I was trying to cut down a tree with a dull ax."

"What did he mean by that?"

"Just a joke," he said. "Hang on." And he was off, again, at a dead run through the night and the forest, pulling her with him.

By the time they reached the river bank once more the rain had stopped, though any disturbed branch or leaf loosed a deluge of heavy raindrops to shower down on them. At the edge of an embankment Trey fell to his knees while Verity tried to pull air into her burning lungs and peer at the rushing water through the overhang of bushes. She could hear him muttering softly, but didn't have the breath to ask what he was doing. He had disappeared into dense, dripping brush and all that was visible was his heels.

"—here someplace. Blue Wing said—Ah!" And then he was backing out dragging something heavy from it's hiding place.

"A canoe!"

"We'll make better time with this," he said, pushing it prow first into the river. "Come on. In with you."

Wet leaves slid under her feet as Verity held onto a dogwood branch and inched her way down the steep bank to the water level. "I can help paddle," she said, crawling over the side and silently blessing the hours Homer had devoted to instructing her. "Homer says you are good with a canoe."

"Good enough," he answered, shoving off and easing himself in. "There's only one paddle so just set easy while I put my back into it."

"You were going to tell me about Fist. Or Blue Wing, whatever his name is," she said. He wasn't going to weasel out of it. She had an explanation coming.

"And I will," he reasoned patiently. "But we have a lot of miles to put behind us before daylight and I'm not apt to have a lot of spare breath for talking. What I have to say can wait until dawn." And he bent forward to dig the paddle into the current.

For awhile she sat upright, straight and tall as a sapling, with her eyes anxiously scanning the darkness along the banks. Gradually, however, as her eyes began to dry from staring and her back to cramp from its rigid position, she relaxed and allowed her weight to lean against a backrest. Even if the bushes were alive with hostile Indians, she couldn't see them in the inky blackness, she reasoned, the tops of the trees were only shadowy outlines against the dark sky. She might as well rest while she could. Who knew what more Trey would demand of her before morning.

Trey continued to reach into the river with the paddle in regular, deep strokes. The canoe seemed to be shooting through the water. Relax, he'd said. Did he know how many miles they were into Indian territory? Well, the answer to that, of course, was yes. After all, he'd come after her. But he didn't seem overly worried. There might be a dozen of those flat, black expressionless eyes watching them this very minute from the banks and waiting in ambush. Her heart thudded against her ribs and she waited for a barrage of arrows.

When she turned, she could see the shape of Trey's shoulders as near as the reach of her hand, and though her fingers fairly trembled to know the reassurance of that solid muscled shoulder, she did not move. It seemed that sitting still was the only contribution she could make to their journey so she would try her best to do that well.

The canoe surged through the water at each powerful stroke. She wondered how long could he go on at this pace, without wearing out? And another thing—for all she knew, he was as lost as she was. How could anyone follow directions as vague as Blue Wing's waving of the arms in this wilderness of trees and brush and rocky streams and storms that cut and slashed like a lancer's blade?

But Trey showed no signs of tiring. The rhythmic dip and pull of his paddle did not change. She wondered briefly how long it would be until daylight, and how many miles they could possibly make before then. She sat up a little straighter, forced her eyes wider open, so that she would be in position and ready to see when the sky began to lighten, and then fell sound asleep.

She roused sometime later to find herself alone in the canoe and struggled upright in alarm. "Sh-h-h," Trey's hand was on her shoulder.

He was in the water, shallow water apparently, for he was walking and towing the canoe along beside him. "We're taking a little detour through an old channel. If Blue Wing is right, and I can find it, there's a small creek we can get through back here."

The clamor in Verity's chest subsided at the sound of his voice. She swallowed the thick pounding in her throat, but at the same time there was a flash of anger at the Indian's name.

"Where are we?"

She looked out over a broad expanse of water thick with stumps of dead trees, ten to fifteen feet tall, scattered like ghostly sentinels in a gray mist rising from the river. Behind them, under a sky that was no longer black with lowering clouds, lay the main channel of the river. She shivered.

"Cold?" he asked. "Your skirts are in that bundle in the bottom of the canoe. They'll be damp, but maybe you could wrap them around your shoulders."

She merely glanced at the tidy roll. Her skirts had lost importance, somehow. "Aren't you tired?" she asked. "You've been up all night and paddled down a river most of that time. You must be ready to drop."

"Not quite," he answered. "Not until I find the right spot. We have a few hours to go, yet."

"Blue Wing again?" she asked, her upper lip curling in distaste.

Carefully, Trey threaded the canoe through the maze of dead trees. "He knows all the good hidey-holes."

Verity shivered again. Their creeping progress was agonizingly slow and the stumps rising through the swirling fog to appear and disappear released a raft of fluttery wings in her stomach.

She shifted her weight to ease her cramping back and Trey steadied the rocking motion she'd caused. She felt grumpy and resentful of the fact that while Blue Wing had slipped the knife to her in the Indian village, practically under the nose of an audience, and seemed to be responsible for guiding Trey back to Corn Island, he had also been the cause of all her problems. She didn't understand. Her scalp was still tender and her jaw sore from Blue Wing's clouts, and yet Trey trusted him!

"I'm waiting until the sun is up, and no longer, for my explanation," she said stiffly. "You and your Indian."

He made a small sound of disgust. "You are the most unreasonable woman I ever met. You talk like your tongue is going to fall out tomorrow and you have to get all the nasty stuff said tonight. You'll wait until we get to where I'm going, until I can think about something other than keeping us alive past sunrise. Then we'll talk about Blue Wing, and not a minute before."

She flounced back in the canoe and then wished she hadn't. Dignity was hard to maintain when the least movement resulted in chaotic tipping from one side to the other.

Well, she'd succeeded in making him mad again. It was something she seemed to do without trying. She couldn't keep the smile out of her voice, "And, so far, you've only seen my good side."

He didn't give her the satisfaction of an answer, only a grunt she wasn't sure she heard after all. She leaned back and stretched her legs around the roll of her skirts and his shirt.

Gray, rotting stumps seemed to float toward her in the almost-dawn-light and slip silently past as more took their place. The canoe might have been suspended in clouds of shifting, swirling fog. Occasionally, she could feel Trey pushing the canoe against the current and her body began to feel heavy. Her eyelids drooped. Once there was a sudden splashing near the far bank. She started forward.

"Bass," Trey said softly. "Must be feeding time."

She lay back and looked up at the sky. Stars spiked pin holes in the night and a gentle, warm breeze stirred the treetops. The storm was a memory. Why, if it weren't for the liquid feel of the river beneath her, she could almost imagine herself back at home in the cabin with Otis and Lena. She could see those same stars from her window there. But with a curious sense of contentment, she knew she'd rather be where she was, fleeing from Indians, afraid for her life, with Trey. Always there was Trey.

She didn't want to think it, but there wasn't any use in pretending. What would she do when he left? For there wasn't any doubt in her mind that he would. They all left. Maybe in different ways, and for different reasons but you couldn't count on a man for staying. Why even Trey had talked with Fist about selling her for some ponies. Surely he hadn't been serious, she thought, but still…it didn't do to depend on a man.

An all-goneness spread through her stomach. This wasn't like her father being killed, or like Otis who'd been halfway decent until Mama died, or like Joe who'd taken off after Clark the very minute he could. This was Trey, who made whistles for little boys and hunted game for a fatherless family and drew water for a girl who didn't know any better than to wash her face in a flooding river. This was Trey, who had come, for whatever reason, through a fair stretch of Indian territory to snatch her from beneath the noses of an entire village of hostiles. Trey, whose touch put a quiver in her stomach like the ping of a tuning fork and whose presence by her side this night seemed only natural, after all. His leaving might not be all that easy to take. She'd have to think on it some. After all, it wasn't likely that Clark would send for him anytime soon.

With her last conscious thought, she realized that Trey had rolled into the canoe and once again picked up the paddle.

Sixteen

Trey leaned on one elbow and stared down at Verity, still asleep in the faint glow of near-dawn. Her hair flowed in a dark mass on the soft bed of moss and he could faintly see her lashes lying in smudged shadows on her cheekbones. He thought he'd never seen anything prettier in his life.

Careful not to wake her, he touched one cheek with the back of his hand. A slow smile stretched his mouth. Her skin was as soft as a mink pelt and he wanted desperately to fold his arms around her and feel her warm, soft body melting into his own.

She'd held up well last night. Better than he'd expected. It was something he couldn't comprehend, how she could be so totally female that he had the urge to stand up and bellow like a bull buffalo in rut, and at the same time have the stamina to stay at his heels all night long. She was as gutsy as any man he'd ever ridden with.

When he'd finally found the creek Blue Wing had spoken of and navigated its meandering length, they'd managed to cut off a good hour of river travel. They still had, however, a five-mile run across rough terrain without much cover. Trey insisted it was necessary to cover this stretch of country, when they would be especially vulnerable, in the dark. By the time he'd pulled up, here at the river—and it had better be the Ohio or Homer would never let him forget that he'd gotten himself lost—by the time he'd pulled up at the river and this giant willow tree, Verity was rubbery-kneed with exhaustion, but she was still on her feet. She was tough, and he admired that.

He guessed he'd never know how it had happened, but what he felt went a lot deeper than admiration. For as long as he could remember, all he'd cared about was the freedom to move around as he pleased, meeting up with all kinds of people and traveling the length and breadth of the wilderness. He'd taken up with General Clark because he'd never met a man quite like him, a man who could inspire other men to perform deeds greater than they knew, and a man who was determined to open this new country to settlement. Now, even his dedication to Clark was not quite as sharp. He was dedicated to the taking of Kaskaskia, he'd given Clark his word, but beyond that? Other priorities clouded his earlier vision.

Verity still slept. The curtain of willow fronds dipped into the water at its outer edge; nearer at hand they dragged the ground. As the day brightened, it was as if the two of them lay in their own private, green-shaded cave. Verity's breath came in shallow, even intervals, her breasts rising and falling gently with each breath. This wasn't the kind of girl a man loved and left. She wasn't a saloon girl or a gambler's whore. She was the forever-after kind. She deserved commitment and home and children. And he wasn't sure he could deliver all that. But, God help him, he wasn't sure anymore that he could leave, either.

His smile flattened and a frown took its place. A plow, land, becoming a farmer, held no allure for him. He'd be bound to the land as tightly as any prisoner chained in his cell. He could never again point his nose into the wind, pick up his rifle and turn his back on what had grown stale. Homer would one day check his priming, step into a canoe, and lift a paddle. Then what would he, himself, do? This was the reason he'd left his brother Billy and Thomas Stone and his apprenticeship in Williamsburg. It wasn't that the printing business didn't suit him. He had enjoyed his work immensely. But the larger world called. Bigger men. Wider places. Would Corn Island or Kaskaskia be enough, without the challenge—even with Verity?

Lord, what a dilemma! Each moment he spent with her made him appreciate her more. Want her more. Heightened his need to make her his own. An ache deep in his gut threatened to double him over. And, there was still this Edward person in Kaskaskia. To say nothing of the Frenchman on the river that day. He'd seen the way the man looked at Verity. The Frenchie had even had the gall to kiss Verity's hand. In spite of knowing that it was his own indecision he railed against, he felt an anger build. She would not go to another man. He'd see to it. How, he didn't know, but that he would was a fact he was as sure of as the sun beginning to filter through the willow wands.

~ * ~

Verity awakened slowly, reluctant to let go of the bliss of lying still without Trey urging her to run yet another mile, swim yet another river, climb yet another rocky incline. Her feet were sore and she was stiff all over, but it was the kind of stiffness that would work itself out when she arose.

Though the morning was still fresh, the air held the promise of noon-day heat. At the water's edge, outside the cocoon of the willow, she caught glimpses of Trey bending to some task. She could barely recall the ending moments of their journey last night, but she remembered distinctly Trey gently helping her to the ground and pulling the moss for her bed. After his unreasonable demands of the grueling night, he could not have been more tender when they reached the river. She had a vague memory of his bathing her feet in cool river water.

She sat up and pulled her fingers through her hair, trying to subdue the wild snarls. She gave it up finally, as useless, but decided to go down to the water and wash her face. Before she could move, however, her attention was caught by Trey's odd behavior. He was methodically spitting into the water.

Verity rose to her knees and peered through the overhang of branches to see better. Trey held what appeared to be a fishing line in one hand and was slowly allowing spittle to drip from his lips into the water, waiting a few seconds, and then spitting again. In no more than a minute he'd landed a fat bass, and in another, two more. The next minute he came striding up the bank toward the willow canopy with three beheaded fish on his line and a self-satisfied smirk on his face.

"I'm impressed," she said, "but what was all the spitting about?"

"Good morning. Fish are curious. A puddle of bubbles lying on the surface just might be something to eat." He looked at her, a direct and intent stare. "How do you feel this morning?"

She flexed her shoulders. "Fine, unless we have to run all the way back to Corn Island this very minute. I'd rather eat first." She eyed the fish he was scaling, hungrily.

He glanced up and around at the willow room. "Your drawing room, madam. We'll rest here until dark. Too much chance of running into a war party in the daylight."

"And then what? Do we swim, paddle or run?"

"Paddle. We ought to raise Corn Island by moonrise."

While he talked he had scooped out a depression in the sandy soil and lined it heavily with leaves. In this hole he laid the three gutted fish and covered them with more leaves. Then he took out his flint and struck a spark. In minutes, a fine spiral of smoke came from the tiny oven and was lost in the leafy branches overhead.

"Now let's just pray there aren't any lone warriors roaming around, eager to prove their manhood by finding us before the rest of the party comes up."

She laughed. "You don't seriously think anybody, Indian or otherwise, could have tracked us though that miserable night and could now find the smoke from this tiny fire."

His eyes were serious. "I do. They won't see the fire, but they might very well smell the smoke. You're selling them short again. The Indian's senses are honed much sharper than ours."

Her laughter died and she couldn't help a furtive look up the bank. "Then why take the chance?"

"It's called a justifiable risk. We have to eat, or at least I do, or I won't have the strength to paddle half the night."

Verity sat up straighter. "What are you going to paddle? We left the canoe a hundred miles away."

"Not quite, but there's another close by."

She didn't doubt it. At this point she wouldn't question him if the fish had walked up from the river and lay down by their fire. And somehow, naturally, they would have been provided by his good friend, Blue Wing.

"About Fist. Or Blue Wing…" she said, and left the sentence dangling.

"All right." He nodded. "Fair enough." He leaned back against the tree trunk and lifted one knee, resting a wrist across his leg loosely.

"He *is* a good friend of mine. I mentioned him to you a long time ago. Once, I did him a good turn and then a couple of years later he had the chance to return the favor and did. Put simply, at great risk to himself, he saved my neck."

He stopped and for a moment didn't go on. Verity couldn't stand the suspense. "Well," she prompted, "what happened?"

"Since then, I have sat at his fire many times, and his wives feed me the same choice bites of meat they save for him. He is my friend."

"But, what happened? What great risk?"

He went on as if she hadn't spoken. "He's far away from his own village now, visiting his wife's family. As a courtesy they took him hunting with them the day they stumbled onto you and Sally. They have been spying on our flotilla for weeks and he recognized you as—ah, my friend and—"

"He called me your woman," Verity interrupted.

"That's—what he said, yes. Anyway, the best thing he could do was claim you as his personal prisoner. He had, after all, captured you at the beginning of the eclipse. That fact carried weight, and he could control what happened to you. If he'd turned you loose at the moment of capture, or later on the trail, the other braves would have killed you both. He did what he could do for you. He convinced the rest of the war party that you and Sally had some mystical connection with the sky darkening, and he saved you. He saved you for me. That's what he said."

"I'm getting a little tired of being sold. At least Otis got the promise of twenty acres and a mule."

"Blue Wing was very impressed with you. He thought you'd make a good warrior, although he wasn't sure how good you'd be in the teepee."

"He offered only one pony!"

Trey's eyes twinkled. "That was after you'd tried to slit his throat. On consideration, he thought maybe even one pony was too high a bride price!"

"And is that what you think?" She made the comment softly with an arch lifting of her eyebrows, but her heart did a funny little side-step. She'd thrown down what was definitely a double-edged challenge.

He sobered. "I think," he said slowly, "that this Edward-what-ever-his-name-is in Kaskaskia, had better have a lot of ponies in his corral."

Their eyes met in a strange and powerful pulling together. They were sharing something, Verity wasn't sure what. The air was charged suddenly with a magical wonderment.

An underlying uncertainty made her avert her eyes. What did she know about him? Nothing much. *But*, sounded a voice loud and clear, *what do you need to know? The man came after you, through miles and miles of hostile Indian territory, risking his life every step of the way.* "No greater love hath any man than that he lay down his life..."

He had, indeed, gambled his life. But why? It was enormously important that she know why he'd risked so much. He hadn't moved, hadn't even blinked. He waited another long minute and then lifted his weight away from the tree and stretched out a hand.

She stared at his fingers, a scant six inches from her own, and found she couldn't even breathe let alone place her hand in his. She was fascinated by the callused palm waiting in silent supplication. There was a smear of new blood—fish blood?—on the pad of one finger but she was powerless to ask about it.

Slowly his hand rose, reached and closed behind her neck, pulling gently until she leaned forward. Verity's heart thundered in her chest while his mouth hovered over hers, and then his lips brushed hers in a feathery promise.

"Sweet," he whispered, "so sweet," and threaded his fingers through her hair, pulling her closer.

Somehow, her hand was on his chest, feeling the pulsing throb of his heart that matched her own. Her fingertips recorded his lungs pumping hard for air. He tipped her head back with his kiss until she rested on his arm and then he pulled her hard against him. A long, slow, curl of excitement twisted through her.

Of their own accord her arms raised to cling around his neck, and she knew how easy it would be to give herself to this man.

He pulled his mouth away, fractionally. "Verity. Verity." He murmured her name into her hair, her neck, into her mouth. "When you were missing I thought I'd go crazy. Homer thinks I already have."

"I've never been so scared." She was breathless and giddy as his mouth covered hers again.

Never breaking the seal of their lips, he turned her so that she was cradled in his lap, leaning against his raised knee, as they both settled against the willow trunk.

"I thought I'd lost you." The words slurred together as his lips never quite left hers.

"I knew you'd come," she murmured at the same time, admitting to her hope and her trust.

"I'd have stomped hell out of the whole village if I'd had to." And with a low, pained sound he hauled her to his chest and rocked her back and forth as if she were a baby.

Her whole body seemed to shimmer in answer. She was floating free, like the river in flood tide. "If only I'd known that Sally was safe," she began, and felt him suddenly go still.

She drew back and looked into his face. His eyes closed and then opened. His arms around her suddenly felt as if they were made of wood. His body seemed to sag.

"What? What is it?" She put a hand on his chest and held it taut. "Sally? Where is she? You said she was safe."

"She is—safe." He swallowed, unable to go on. He looked at her, knowing that this was going to be bad. She'd never understand.

She tried to push away, but he held her where she was. "Trey? You have to tell me. What's the matter?"

"She's—Sally is—" He took a fortifying breath. "I couldn't bring you both out."

Seventeen

Verity sat in rigid anger, her skirts gathered tight around her ankles. The ribs of the canoe dug into her body unmercifully and her back ached like a bad tooth, but a red blaze of fury carried her beyond superficial pain. Even beyond speech. Her screaming was done.

At first she hadn't believe him. She'd pulled back in his arms, "You didn't leave her with the Indians!"

When he didn't answer immediately she sat, while a cold numbness settled over her. He meant it. He had left sweet little Sally with the savages.

"Look," he said, bracketing her shoulders with his hands, "I had to make a choice. A runner came in with the news that a small war party of young braves had met with bad luck. They lost ten men and, according to Blue Wing, the attitude toward captives was turning sour."

Verity just looked at him for a long moment, her tongue lying silent in her mouth, waiting for assurance that Sally was being traded, or promised in some way to be returned for ransom. But that hope faded with his next words.

"Sally is with a childless couple who just lost an infant daughter at birth. They were grief stricken since this was their second child to die in the same way, and they're delighted with another little girl to love."

Verity's voice was stiff with disbelief. "You did leave her."

"The Indians adore children," he reasoned. As if she were floating somewhere above the treetops, she heard him explain patiently that Sally would be happy in her new home and that Verity need not be concerned about her. An annoying buzzing filled her head. His voice came from a distance. "The fact that she's a little slow to learn won't matter in their way of living. She'll have a good life."

Verity jerked herself from his arms and stood up. She put a step between them. "A little girl. An innocent baby. And you left her with a pack of savages. You're no better than they are!"

A nerve jerked in Trey's jaw and his eyes flattened. He hadn't wanted to tell her Blue Wing's deciding information. Her eyes were huge with horror as it was, but he'd had no choice, after that.

"They were going to burn you," he said, one hand entreating her to understand. "The eclipse saved your life at the time of capture, but it was a very bad omen to loose ten braves in a minor skirmish and it was decided to sacrifice you. The medicine man was already mixing black clay."

Black clay. Plastered to the top of the victim's head to preserve the scalp during burning. The sound of her mother's screaming suddenly echoed in Verity's ears and the sight of the baby being clubbed against the side of the cabin filled her vision. Horror shuddered through her in violent ripples. Sally—

He was still talking. "She's fine. From what I've seen of her life with Clem, she's probably better off. She'll be well treated and loved." He reached for her. "Remember, you were able to come to me, on the lake, and try to escape. She couldn't. You were in danger of being burned. She's in no danger whatever. My sweetling, I had to—"

"Don't-touch-me." Her voice carried the underlying threat of a wolverine's snarl making him draw back instinctively, and her eyes bored into him. "How *could* you leave that baby with those heathens? I don't understand how you could possibly do that. Just—don't touch me. I don't even want to look at you!"

They raised Corn Island at moonrise. The trip was accomplished in stony silence except for the faint dip of Trey's paddle into the water. Verity clenched her jaws together so tightly they ached.

The entire station roused to greet them. Their story had to be told time and again, and Verity hugged by every woman there before anyone was interested in retiring again for the night. When the women and children finally went off to bed, the men were still slapping Trey on the back and congratulating him on Verity's safe recovery.

Still reeling from what she considered to be Trey's betrayal, she had said little about Sally, only that she had not seen the child since shortly after their capture. Trey's eyes questioned her across the room, but Verity noted bitterly that he didn't volunteer information. He answered direct questions, one of which being the fact that no, he had not seen any sign of Sally. He allowed them to assume he knew nothing of Sally's whereabouts. Coward! she branded him with her eyes. Coward! Traitor! Cheat!

Neither, she realized later as she lay in her blankets, had he mentioned Blue Wing's help. She could certainly understand why. If it were known that he had friends among the Indians, Trey's leadership on Corn Island would be over. Cowards, Indian lovers and Tories were hated all the same.

And yet, Trey's foray into the wilderness had not been the actions of a coward. There had been the possibility of danger of the most violent kind every single moment. Blue Wing's secretive actions, Trey's own haste at getting away, and the care he took to remain undiscovered made that plain. He had encouraged her when she was so tired she thought she couldn't take another step, he had carried her when she was too exhausted to go any farther, and he'd bathed her bruised and aching feet in the river when he thought she was asleep.

But, he had not told the others it had been a deliberate decision to leave Sally with the Indians. He had not told them of his strange friendship with Blue Wing.

None of it made sense, she thought wearily. How could she love an Indian sympathizer and a coward? It wasn't something she was proud of, but the fact remained that even when he didn't announce to the gathering that he'd chosen to leave the good-natured, six-year-old with the Indians and she was so angry she could have spit right on the floor and stomped her foot on the spittle, she still couldn't bring herself to betray him. It would have been throwing him into the lion's den, like in the Bible, and she just couldn't bring herself to do it. It was dawn before she slept.

Trey had no such problem. He knew exactly what he was doing. Clark would have understood, but he knew better than to think any of these settlers would. No one on the island, except Homer, would know why he'd left Sally, would acknowledge that it was the only thing to do. Trying to get her out might very well have meant certain discovery and death for all three of them. Indians were unpredictable when riled. He doubted even Blue Wing could have saved them.

And he'd told the truth about Sally being happy. Indian children were happier in their freedom than any white child he'd ever seen, anywhere. His conscience was clear. Now if Clem had been a doting father and likely to be grief-stricken at her loss, that would have been another matter. The only time Clem seemed to even realize Sally was present was to aim a cuff at her for upsetting something, or yell at her for not doing something else. Incredibly, he hadn't been as upset as Trey'd expected when they returned without her. Clem had accepted Trey's assurance that children were rarely mistreated. Rather, they were petted within an inch of their lives and adopted into the tribe. *No*, he told himself, *Sally was definitely better off with the Indians. In a few months, she'd never remember another life.*

That Verity didn't understand bothered him. The look in her eyes when he'd remained silent about Sally's whereabouts had cut him deeply. It was something he'd have to work on later. Just now he was exhausted and dawn wasn't far away. He had duties to see to on the morrow and lying awake worrying would serve him no purpose.

It was noon before he's taken care of the dozens of details piled up during his absence. Mason had done a good job as commander and Trey's praise was justified. The families were settling in as scheduled, the cabins and blockhouse were up and the corn planted. Women had garden plots under way and the men had been divided up for hunting duties and a rotating watch.

"No news from the east? Nothing about how the war is going?"

"No sir, nothing." Mason stood erect before him, his back ramrod straight, and his eyes properly trained on a spot just off Trey's left shoulder. "But some of the men are getting to be crack shots, sir. They practice every day."

Trey lifted his gaze from cleaning his rifle. "Willingly?"

Mason's glance slid off Trey's eyes and back to a corner of the cabin. "No sir. In fact, one of the men discharged his gun accidentally and shot Homer in the foot. Just a flesh wound, but he's temporarily hobbling about using a stick. He's not too happy about it."

Trey's mouth relaxed into a smile. "I guess not. In the foot, huh? I'd imagine the man got a quick and loud lesson in gun safety."

"Yes, sir. And one thing more. One of the Dawson men is ready to take up with that widow woman, Esther—something."

Mason looked uncomfortable. "Just for your information, sir," he said.

"Which one of the Dawsons?"

"The one with the kids. The one whose little girl is still out there."

Inwardly Trey winced. The Dawsons would forever more be known as the family whose little girl was still "out there."

"That'll be Clem," he said. "Very well. And you're right. I need to know these things." He leaned the gun against the wall. "That's all for now, Mason. You've done well."

Mason hurried out, intent on business of his own, and Trey stepped to the door. The day was clear and hot with high white clouds clotted together in a sky so blue it almost hurt his eyes to look at it.

Clem and Esther, huh? He'd better check on the story. He wished it wasn't his business, but since Clark had left him in charge, everything about the settlers was his responsibility. If it was true, there would be one less thing for him to worry about. Verity would rest easier, too. Clem's romantic thoughts would be directed elsewhere.

The air was full of the sound of activity. Everywhere he looked, someone was busy stretching an animal skin, hanging strips of raw meat on a willow meat-drying rack, hoeing or chopping wood.

Trey's ears still rang with the sound of an ax being driven into a tree when he rounded the corner of the Dawson cabin. Verity was stirring a pot of stew over an outdoor fire. Beyond Verity, at the edge of the trees, Bart lounged against a stump and watched the pull of her dress across her shoulders and the rhythmic swath of her arm as she stirred. Her hair was freshly washed and drawn back loosely at the nape of her neck. Stray tendrils escaped to blow about her face as she moved.

She had on a different dress than the one she'd traveled in, something with blue sprigs of flowers on a white background, and had rolled the sleeves up to her elbows. Around her waist she'd tied a length of material as an apron. He was fascinated by the way that knot rode the contour of her swaying hips as she stirred the thick stew.

But then his gaze fastened on Bart. The man squatted behind a tree, outside of Verity's vision, with a faint possessive smile turning up the corners of his mouth. His eyes, heavy-lidded and only half open, seemed to devour Verity where she stood. Trey's face went stiff. With Clem out of the picture, Bart would feel his way clear to pursue Verity. That might go hard for her. He'd have to ask Homer to help him keep track of Bart. If he touched Verity again, Trey knew he would kill him without a second thought. And, as their eyes collided, he knew Bart knew it, too.

All of a sudden his skin felt too tight and a hot flood of anger threatened to swamp him. He wanted to place himself in front of Verity and glare Bart down.

Without thinking he crossed the ground between them and, ignoring her frown of surprise, put an arm around her Verity. She leaped away as if she'd heard the warning rattle of a diamondback. She held the long-handled, wooden spoon in front of her like a dueling sword.

"What do you want?"

What did he want? He could hardly tell her his thoughts. "Does the contents of that pot extend to hungry trackers?" He ignored her unfriendly words and tried to make his voice ordinary and smooth, but he could hear the tightness of his tone.

Bart stepped out into the open. "Hell no, it don't. I got that prairie chicken myself and it won't stretch no further'n us Dawsons."

Verity started and went white as she swung toward Bart. A three-day-dead buck could tell she hadn't known Bart was there, watching. And that same dead deer could see she didn't like it. She took a quick step backward, away from Bart, and then visibly pulled herself together and turned back to Trey, lowering the spoon.

"Surely—" She swallowed and began again. "Surely, you didn't expect to be invited to share our meal."

Trey's anger dissolved as fast as it had developed. At least she was talking to him. Her absolute silence of the night before still rankled. He'd never known anyone who could say as much as Verity could without opening her mouth. He smiled.

"Ah," he said, and an eyebrow went up in a teasing quirk. "but an empty belly won't be ignored."

With surprising agility, considering his bulk, Bart moved forward until he was even with Verity. His stance was wary, like a man waiting for trouble. "You ain't invited. Why don't you just move on?"

Trey's voice was smooth as cream. "Mr. Dawson, sir, I came to see your brother. Now, if he isn't here, I'll be happy to oblige you by leaving."

"Abner or Clem? Who you wantin'?"

"Clem. I understand congratulations are in order." The damn bully. Standing there like the family guard dog.

"Well, he ain't here, so goodbye."

"What congratulations?" Verity asked. Her color was coming back and she appeared to be herself again.

"Clem," Trey answered. "Clem and Esther, I hear, are about to tie the knot, so to speak."

"Without a preacher?" Her eyebrows went up.

He shrugged. "They can make it legal the next time a preacher drops by. It happens all the time."

"Not to me it won't," she vowed. "I intend—"

"Captain! Captain!" Mason rounded the building, red-faced and sweating. "A messenger has arrived. France has come in on our side. The French are with us, after all."

Mason seemed to have brought a crowd with him. Homer was close at his elbow, leaning heavily on his stick, and Abner came puffing up an instant later. Settlers pushed in close. A roar of approval went up.

"The French!" Trey smiled. This was good news. News that Clark needed to know, immediately. If the French at Kaskaskia knew their country had joined the war on America's side, they wouldn't be hostile to Clark and his men when they arrived.

He turned hurriedly toward Verity. "It seems I have business to take care of. Have a good evening." He swiveled on a heel. "Where's that messenger? Bring him to my office."

He made plans rapidly, accepting some and discarding others. He was at his make-shift desk when he heard footsteps.

The sight of the Frenchman coming through his door brought Trey to his feet. "You!"

"Auguste Fauconnet," the man said, his black eyes snapping. "Returning as promised."

Trey's teeth clenched at the man's cocky grin. "But, I thought—a messenger—" He looked out the door as if expecting someone else to enter. This was the Frenchman they'd met coming downriver. This was the man who'd kissed Verity's hand and—and promised her he would return.

"I am the messenger. Since I was coming back, I volunteered to bring the good news. France has entered the war. Victory is ours, my friend, as the garrison at Kaskaskia is peopled with French."

Trey tried to pull himself together. How could he leave to carry the message to Clark with this man here to dance attendance on Verity? He'd already seen how he'd charmed her upriver. The man could likely talk birds out of trees. Verity was no match for him. If he would only stop grinning as if he'd single-handedly won the war!

"I understand the lovely lady I met earlier is still with families who are staying here on the island."

Unconsciously, Trey's hand balled into a fist. Damn it. The man was all but licking his lips. He itched to wipe that smile from the Frenchie's face.

"She's had a bad time. Only got back from being kidnapped by the Indians. She's in no shape for visitors."

"I will comfort her. A terrible thing for a lady to have suffered at the hands of the savages."

Trey spread his legs for a firmer grip on the floor. "I went in after her. I got her out. I'm responsible for her safety." It was a blatant declaration of territory and the Frenchman understood perfectly. His eyes lost their shine and turned hard and brittle.

He stood for a long minute, considering Trey, up and down, from shoulder to shoulder. Then, with a dismissive tone he said clearly, "You are a backwoodsman. A hunter. You cannot give her what she needs."

"And what would that be?"

"A home, children. And a man who would be there every night to show her how much she is loved."

That brought Trey up short. Fauconnet was absolutely right. Trey was a backwoodsman and a hunter. Verity deserved at least a home and a family. His thoughts faltered.

The Frenchman went on. "She is a lady. She is—" His hands waved expressively through the air. "She is—magnifique! A beautiful flower among a tangle of weeds. And you, my friend, do not even know the difference." His lip curled in faint disdain as he eyed Trey.

"And I suppose you think you are the man who deserves her?"

"Auguste Fauconnet knows women. Yes, I am that man."

Trey squared his shoulders and pinned the Frenchman with a steely glare. "The lady knows her own mind. I expect she can make her own choice. And now, I have work to do. Make yourself at home. You can bed down with the men."

He sat at his crude desk for a long time. He didn't like the idea of leaving Verity with Bart dogging her footsteps, and he liked even less leaving her with that damn Frenchie sniffing around her skirts, but Clark desperately needed this information. Time was of the essence, and with Homer out of commission there was no one else to send.

Clark's confidence in him would be sadly misplaced if he failed to get the news downriver as fast as humanly possible. He would just have to trust Homer to care for Verity's safety in his absence. He had trusted Homer with his own life many times. He could trust him with Verity's. His mind was made up. He called for Homer and Mason.

"I'll leave to carry the message at full dark," he said. "Mason, you'll take over again."

Homer shifted his feet and hooked a thumb in his belt. "You'll be needing company this time," he said.

"I can move faster alone," Trey said absently, his mind already working on things to do before he could leave.

"They's Indians up and down this river as thick as hair on a buffler's back," Homer said slowly. "And two can make a canoe cut the water quicker'n one."

Trey dismissed Mason and motioned for Homer to stay. "In a canoe you'd be invaluable. We both know that. And your eyes might get us where we're going, still wearing our hair. It's happened before. But there will be lots of miles to go on foot." He motioned to Homer's wrapped foot and shook his head. "You'd hold me back.

"Besides, I need you here. You still have some training to do if that foot is any indication of just how good the settlers are getting with their guns. And I want you to keep an eye on Verity. She's vulnerable with that snake Bart creeping around. I saw him today, hiding in the bushes watching her at the fire. I don't trust him. He's already been at her once and I took care of it, but if I'm not here…" He left the sentence unfinished.

Homer spat out the open door. "I guessed as much. That's what happened to his face. I didn't reckon his brother did that much damage. You're hooked on her for sure, ain't you?"

Trey hesitated and then said simply. "Yes. Yes, I guess I am. And I ask you, as my friend, to protect her in my absence. Will you do it?"

"Shore. Is it too much to ask if she feels the same way about you?"

Trey grunted. "She wouldn't throw water on me if I was afire, right now. Maybe later, when she's had time to think things through."

"Then, you might have a problem. That oily Frenchie left here making a bee line for her cabin."

A nod conceded the point. "I'm depending on you to keep that arrogant, stupid ox, and the damned Frenchman, away from her until I get back."

Homer cocked one hip and shook his head at the impossibility of the task. "You got a feel on just how I'm to do that?"

"Hell, I don't know. Drown them both for all I care. Just watch her."

~ * ~

Verity had not moved as Trey turned away and went to meet the messenger. She forgot Bart standing beside her and the stew she was supposed to be stirring. Her mind worked furiously. Trey was going to Kaskaskia. She could see the thought in his eyes before he left her. She didn't even consider asking him to take her along. She knew what the answer would be.

But, standing with the stirring spoon still in her hand, Verity made up her mind that he wasn't going without her. She couldn't stay here much longer. Esther would be moving in and there was never room enough in a cabin for two women. Bart would—she didn't even want to think about what Bart would do with Trey gone. The community would press her to take up with Bart, justly so, as no one else was fixed well enough to take her in. Her position would be impossible. There would be no place for her on Corn Island. Besides Joe was, after all, in Kaskaskia. That's where she intended to go all along. And Edward. He was there too, of course.

She ground her teeth together. Somehow, she was going along with Trey. Somehow.

Eighteen

At dusk, in a show of normality, she'd gone to the river for water. Trey's canoe sat ready for his departure in the shallows along side several others. She eyed them all carefully, deciding which would best suit her purpose when the time came. Then she filled her pail. As she struggled up the bank with the bucket sloshing at her side, Bart suddenly appeared at the top of the hill. He had simply reached for the bucket, and she had recoiled instinctively.

His face flushed red. "You'd travel day and night with that Indian lover, but you won't let *me* carry water for you!"

"Get out of my way." She held the bucket in front of her like a shield.

"Like hell I will. We got some unfinished business, you and me." Bart advanced a step on short bandy legs and grinned, a red slash in his matted beard. "And all the time in the world to get it done, now your friend's leaven'." He reached for her. The same hand that had once grabbed under her skirts, now tore at her clothes.

Her breath came fast in her throat. He was not going to touch her again. She couldn't bear it. His fingers closed on her wrist and she screamed, one long wild yell, at the same time throwing her weight into the bucket and onto Bart.

She caught him by surprise and they went down in a snarl of tangled legs and arms and sluicing water. Fear gave her the strength to get to her feet first, but she hadn't taken two steps before his hairy arm circled her ankles and she went down face first in the dirt and pine-needles.

She twisted in his arms, kicking and bucking, but he held on and rolled, taking her with him, over and over until she was dizzy and he was sprawled on top of her.

He grunted as her knee caught the inside of his thigh. "You want to fight, huh? Well, you won't pull that one on me again." He was breathing hard through bared teeth. "I'm goin' to have me some fun teaching' you manners." He sat up astride her middle and gazed down in triumph. His eyes were cold.

Verity went still. "I'll have you flogged," she said with all the steel she could muster.

He bent closer, his breath sour in her face. "The way I figure it, Clem and his new misses and you and me can set up together."

"Never!"

"When I get done, you won't be in any shape to argue no more."

"I'll take a knife to you. I swear it. You won't dare go to sleep for the rest of your life."

His eyes widened and he chuckled. "This is goin' to be a real pleasure, missy. I promise you that."

He gazed at her for a long minute, her eyes, her mouth, down her neck to her breasts and beyond to the point where he straddled her. Suddenly he threw back his head and laughed. "Yes, a real pleasure." And he lowered himself against her, searching for her lips.

Shock knifed downward through her stomach. He was going to put his mouth on hers. She felt her skin crawl. In one blinding bolt of anger she tensed her fingers into talons, and clawed frantically at his eyes.

His bellow of rage and pain momentarily deafened her. She saw a line of blood well beside one eye and begin to run down his cheek before he let her loose to cover his face.

With strength born of sheer terror, she twisted to her right and caught him off balance. Before he could recover she was up and running, her breath coming in harsh, sobbing gasps. She slipped on wet leaves and went down on one knee, but regained her feet and ran on, not looking back, frightened with every step that she would hear his heavy breathing behind her. She stopped at the edge of the woods and held to a young sapling until her knees stopped shaking. Bart did not follow.

Just before bedtime she'd seen him, one eye covered by a red rag bound around his head. So, she had hurt him. Her heart beat faster, wondering what he would do. He'd been watching her all afternoon, like a greedy dog waiting for a bone. Then, he'd caught her at the river. She now knew, for certain, he'd never let her alone. She could expect trouble at every moment, without warning. For weeks, the only time she felt safe was at night, asleep near Esther and her children, and soon even that would no longer be available to her. Her knees trembled, but she kept her chin high as his one eye met hers.

She paid scant attention to the conversation as they ate the evening meal. Bart's eye, heavy-lidded and brooding, never left her. A shudder racked her body. Trey was due to depart at full dark, and after that she would be alone. Had she overlooked any argument at all that might make him reconsider and take her with him? Ruthlessly, her mind squirreled over every option she could think of. Nothing.

She had to go.

It wasn't until she realized Clem had called her name twice that she focused on what he'd said. The messenger was the

Frenchman they'd met that day on the river. He had volunteered to retrace his steps back down the Ohio, carrying the word that the French had come into the war on the side of the Americans. He'd volunteered, Clem said with a smirk at Bart, just so's he could get back to Verity. He'd been asking for her.

Verity stopped eating to consider what this might mean to her plans. Would the Frenchman be of any help? At the very least, his presence in camp might keep Bart at bay. Might. She wasn't sure about that. Could he be talked into taking her after Trey? Maybe catching him downriver.

A knock at the door silenced her thoughts. Clem opened it to the sight of the handsome man who had kissed her hand so gallantly at the water's edge weeks ago. The Frenchman. His eyes found hers instantly.

"Ah. The lovely lady is here. I have been looking." He bowed from the waist and stepped into the room, uninvited.

Bart had not stopped shoveling stew into his mouth.

Verity stood. "Mr—ah—"

"Fauconnet," he said, his smile showing rows of white teeth beneath a very black moustache. "Auguste Fauconnet, a man who has come many miles just to lay eyes on—"

Bart interrupted, trying to talk around a full mouth. "Now just a minute. You got no reason a'tal being here." He swallowed noisily. "Nobody here b'longs to you, so you can leave the same way you come in."

Fauconnet spared Bart not so much as a glance. "Would you," and he nodded to Verity, "do me the honor of walking with me around the camp?"

Bart came off the chair. "She ain't goin' to do no such thing. Get out."

Fauconnet's eyes never faltered from Verity's. "Does this man speak for you?"

She shook her head. "No. No, he does not." And then, pulling herself together, she said, "As a matter of fact, I was just leaving for a friend's fire, Esther, a woman with whom I sleep. You may walk with me, if you like."

He bowed again and flashed a smile. "It will be my greatest pleasure."

Bart bellowed. "She ain't goin' nowhere with you. I told you to get out. Now go!"

For the first time Fauconnet turned to Bart. He didn't blink. "The lady speaks for herself, I believe." Verity realized that, without seeming to move at all, his hand was on a long knife at his belt.

"I said she stays!"

"She apparently prefers the company of someone without the manners of a pig and who does not smell like his pen. Now, if you will excuse us?" Without taking his hand off the knife, he crooked an arm to Verity and she took it.

Verity's eyes met Bart's only for an instant, long enough for him to glare some sort of wild promissory threat before they left the cabin. If Verity had any doubts about going after Trey, they vanished in that instant. Bart was dangerous. He would do her harm. As angry and betrayed as she felt about Trey's leaving Sally, he would never hurt her. He'd proven that. She'd trust her luck to the river. And to Trey.

At this moment she was trusting herself to the Frenchman with the wide, white smile, who had kissed her hand so gallantly in the morning sun, and who now carried a knife with a long curved blade at his belt. He had stood up to Bart rather nicely, she thought. He was no coward. Maybe he really would take her down river after Trey.

He placed his other hand on top of hers where it lay on his arm, and they walked in silence as far as the water.

"I'm sorry Bart was so rude," Verity said eventually. "He's that way with everyone. It's just the way he is. But, if it hadn't been for him and his brothers, I could never have come down river. They brought me to take care of Clem's sick wife and his children. I stay with them during the day, and cook and take care of things. But I sleep with my friend and her children on the other side of camp at night."

"Ah, but he, the loud one, wants more than that."

"Well, yes. But he isn't going to get it." Verity turned to walk along the path at the river. Fauconnet followed, his hand at her back. "I'm going on downriver."

"Oh?" He flicked an interested glance at her. "You are leaving this place?"

"Yes. I have—uh—someone waiting for me at Kaskaskia."

He turned her to face him. "I must be bold and ask who is waiting for you, so far away."

"I have..." she hesitated, feeling a pang of guilt. She was using Edward. He didn't deserve that, and she didn't like the way it made her feel. "I have a fiance there."

"A fiance? A man to whom you are promised?"

She couldn't look at him. "We've had a sort of understanding since we were children."

"And, does this tracker, this scouting person who is in charge here, know this?"

"Trey? Yes, of course, he knows about Edward. Why?"

"When he talks about you, his eyes are the same as that barbarian we just left. If he ever knew about your fiance, he has forgotten him." He gave a short bark of laughter and went on.

"Neither do I think, myself, that you feel as if you belong to this Kaskaskia man. You do not have the—what is the word—the passion in your voice when you speak his name. No, he is not for you."

Verity stood, wordless, as he kept talking. "You should not be in a crude cabin on the frontier. You should live in the civilized world. I would like to show you a place where you could laugh and be happy. Have pretty dresses, eat fine food." He waved a dismissive hand. "You do not belong here in the dirt and at the mercy of the elements." He fingered the fabric of her skirt. "Nor wear clothing that feels like the skin of a tree."

Verity stopped just outside the light of Esther's dying fire. Tree skin? Bark. She smiled. "You are very nice, but I plan to go downriver."

"You would blossom in my country. Paris was made for you."

"Paris, France?"

His hands gripped her shoulders. "The City of Love. Yes, Paris, France. I will lay it at your feet like a string of jewels. My father has vast holdings there and will be delighted to have me return home to the family business. Come with me. My family will consider me the most fortunate of men to have you by my side."

"But I don't know you."

"All the more exciting. I promise you I have no bad habits. I have traveled long and hard to get back to you before I lost you forever in the western wilderness. I will make you the finest lady in all of Paris. La Belle Parisienne. Say you will come."

Her thoughts skittered wildly. She'd barely spent a half-hour with this man—total. But he was exciting in an adventurous way she hadn't dreamed would intrigue her. She'd never considered the possibility of traveling to another continent. Paris. Dresses. Jewels. She could certainly be a lady, in France. Just like Mama always wanted.

But this man would come with it. And as nice as he seemed to be, as civilized as he put it, and as bold and daring—he wasn't Trey. He wasn't Joe, or even Edward. She could never go to Paris, France and not ever see Trey again. Never to see his hands, gentle and sure as he cut Gideon's hair. Never to hear his voice, tender and soft as he named the stars in the night sky. Or Joe. The brother who didn't even know she was on her way to him. She didn't want to leave her life right here. As bad as it was at this moment, she wasn't ready to trade it for another.

"Would you…" She turned to face the Frenchman. "I need to go downriver. My gratitude would be boundless if you—"

"Go down the big river after that scout, that tracker? You do not wish to do that. He is another lout. Not good enough for you. Auguste Fauconnet is the man you want. I will take you on the river with me, but we will go east toward the future. Toward your fortune."

She knew, then, that she would go alone. The Frenchman wouldn't help, Homer had to stay here, and there was no one else. So that was the way it would be. Her mother had always said her first words were, "Me do myself." And she would.

Two hours later, after the disappointed Fauconnet had gone to his blankets with the single men, she crept away from the sleeping Esther to watch from the willows on the bank as Tray left with only Homer to bid him goodbye. Then she waited for time to pass so she could follow. Her heart beat hard in her chest like a wild bird trying to get free and her hands trembled holding her small bundle, but her resolve never faltered.

She saw Bart standing in the half dark at the river's edge, methodically looking over the settlement, while she crouched in the reeds near the string of beached canoes. She closed her eyes, shivering, afraid that her gaze would somehow draw his to her hiding place. Finally, he wandered away, up toward the cabins.

She couldn't stay. It was that simple. Bart would find her in the end and take her with stealth and superior strength, no matter what she did. Fauconnet would try and defend her honor, she was sure, but Bart didn't play by any man's rules. He would win.

Trey had a half hour start. It ought to have been more, but she didn't dare let him get too far ahead. Besides, if she didn't go soon, fear would strangle her determination and she'd simply stay where she was out of weakness.

She closed her eyes and held her breath for one long minute and then she crept into the water and felt for the nearest prow.

For all her certainty that Trey was out on the water ahead of her, her heart still thwacked against her chest wall as she slid the boat into the water and rolled over the side. She grunted as the canoe dipped sharply and she flung her weight across the fragile craft. Her hip landed on the ribs at the bottom. It wasn't a smooth entry, not like Trey who slid up and over as if he weighed nothing, not even like Homer's clumsy efficiency, but she made it.

She picked up the paddle and hesitated. The settlement was quiet, not even a dog barked, and the dark pressed close all around her. She hated to leave without telling Esther, who had been a friend. And Gideon was just learning to be a man. She would miss him. Yet, her future did not lie here on Corn Island, she was sure of that. She was pulled to the river, after Trey, toward Joe and Edward, and Kaskaskia, and Clark.

Borne on a slight breeze, the scent of the Ohio, illusive and exciting, filled her senses as a swell of current moved her toward the channel. She deliberately turned her back on the settlement then, rather than let a curve of the river take the sight from her, and faced the west.

Instantly she was swallowed up in the black of night. The flutter of fear grew stronger. She didn't have any idea what was out there, whether by some miracle she could paddle downriver without an Indian scout spotting her, or if she could indeed catch Trey sometime tomorrow when it would be too late to take her back. For that matter she didn't know if she could catch him at all. She, above all, had cause to know he was good with a paddle.

The lonesome yelp of a distant coyote drifted on the wind. Wild animals. Indians. What else? She felt with her foot for the reassuring hard barrel of the gun she'd stolen on her way out the cabin door. Mama would never approve, but then Mama had never headed into the wilderness on her own, either.

The gun, the knife Blue Wing had given her, a fresh loaf of bread and a few strips of jerky stuffed in a sack were her only preparations. And, of course, the little bag with Mama's needle and thimble. She'd changed into Joe's clothes once more, because they were easier to travel in, crammed her hair under his old hat, and was ready.

Tentatively, she dipped the paddle into the water and stroked. The canoe glided forward on the black, slick shimmer of the river. One stroke nearer to Trey. It was odd, but as angry as she was at him, and her anger was perilously close to hatred, she didn't consider for a second that he might abandon her when she caught up to him. If she caught up to him, she amended. No one knew better than she the depth of his stamina, the hard and enduring sheath of muscles across his shoulders, and the will of iron that drove him on when others would quit. He would still be going strong when she herself was exhausted. She lifted her head and firmed her jaw. She could do this. She must do this. The paddle dug deeper.

The spring flood had long since passed and the Falls were no problem. The river was so low that if she'd had anything heavy in the canoe, she'd have had to lighten it to get through. She passed on the north side of a small island laying in the middle of the river and by the time the moon rose, the banks on both sides stretched up high and forbidding. Because of the cliffs, she was grateful for the night hiding her from watchful eyes. For miles she paddled close to shore in the shadow of the bluff, rather than risk the faster current in the moonlight.

Dawn was just pinking the eastern sky behind her when she passed the mouth of a large river coming from the north. She hugged the southern bank in spite of the possibility of Indians, because the current was more powerful on the north and she was afraid the canoe would capsize. Homer had once said that the next river of any importance was the Pidgeon. When, she wondered had Trey passed? How many hours earlier and at what speed?

Her shoulders ached from the unrelenting pace she'd set herself and her knees seemed to be frozen into place where she knelt. She doubted if she could move if she'd had the opportunity. Looking up at the bluffs still towering above her, she swallowed a rush of anxiety. She'd never been so alone, or so frightened. When it became light enough to see, she would be an easy target if Indians were watching.

Calling on everything she'd ever heard about wilderness and river travel, Verity knew that the sensible thing to do would be stop for the day and take cover. But she didn't dare. Trey would be moving too fast and she knew he wouldn't stop for anything short of disaster. The news he carried for Clark was too important.

She ate some of the bread, chewed a few bites of jerky, washed it down with river water, and went on. Now, however, she stayed in the middle of the current. In some places the river was so wide she would be out of rifle range from either bank.

By mid-day she knew she would have to stop. She was falling asleep with the paddle in hand and the pain in her shoulders had settled into a steady throb. Still there had been no sign of Trey. At every bend in the river her eyes seemed to reach ahead, around the curve, searching for a glimpse of a canoe.

High banks had eventually given way to flat lowlands and she felt more secure having distance vision once more. Mulberry trees lined the banks in lush profusion, and in the heat of the day she paddled into the shelter of a cluster of trees with low hanging branches and slept for a couple of hours.

She awoke with a start to find the sun lower in the sky and a squirrel scurrying along a limb over her head. Rotating her shoulders and stretching vigorously loosened her muscles, but her stomach was like a lump of stone when she pushed her way out of the bushes into the river. Please God, she prayed, let all the Indians be busy somewhere else this afternoon.

"Even the sparrow shall find a home." That's what the Psalmist said, and that's where I'm going, she thought, aiming the prow of the canoe downriver once more. To find a home. There was some confusion in her mind about how this was to happen. A home with Joe, of course. True, she'd pledged herself to Edward, but how could she honor that promise considering the way she was beginning to feel about Trey? Not that there was any future with him, she thought, even if he were willing, not after he'd left Sally with the Indians. But still, how could she think of home as a place without him? Trey, with eyes that spoke to her without words and hands patient enough to whittle whistles for young boys. A man with courage and commitment enough to hunt her down in hundreds of miles of forest and lead her to safety under the very noses of hostile Indians. The world seemed steadier when he was near. And yet—fiercely she put more of her back into the paddle—she had to get over him, somehow, because she had no intention of yoking herself to a man who deserted little girls in Indian camps.

It was becoming more difficult, however, to stay mad at him. He'd risked his life for her every foot of the way on their trip back to Corn Island. And, being fair, she'd seen for herself how happy Indian children were. She remembered how the little girls had played a game with fruit pits in the village. And other games with rolling hoops. Adults had been unfailingly patient and gentle. Never once had there been a voice or a hand raised in anger toward a child.

Was Trey right? Would Sally be happier with the Indians? Clem certainly hadn't raised much of a fuss when Trey told him that he was certain she'd been adopted by the tribe. He hadn't lied, only not told the full truth, that Blue Wing had told him of Sally's new and happy family.

Verity grunted in disgust. Clem's own flesh and blood and he'd barely made a showing of asking about Sally. He had quoted a Bible which Verity would have taken an oath on that he'd never opened, saying only that the Lord giveth and the Lord taketh away. Verity took a grim satisfaction that she'd seen the last of the Dawsons.

She paddled just short of exhaustion and then rested, always hoping for the sight of Trey, then paddled again. The plain seemed barren of life, nothing moved all day and into the evening. Not a deer, not a rabbit. She ate the last of her bread and jerky at sundown and it revived her enough to go on. Her back felt as if it were broken in a dozen places and her arms moved in jerks and spasms. By full dark her mind was wandering.

There were whole stretches of time when she was sure Trey was by her side, urging her to keep going, telling her she was tough enough to do what had to be done. At other times, he seemed to be calling to her from far away, always urging her forward. One more stroke of the paddle, one more bend in the river, one more hour before she rested.

The moonlight brought her to her senses. She leaned over the edge of the canoe, splashed water into her face and forced herself to concentrate. The northern bank was safest. More Indians to the south. Hunt for a stand of trees or low-hanging brush. Where was Trey? She could have passed him in her daze. But no, she knew better than that. He was probably still paddling tirelessly, already in the Illinois country. Whatever had made her think she could catch him?

She pushed the canoe close to the bank and hid it in a swampy patch of sawgrass, staggered on stiff and wobbling legs back out into the shallows and up the bank on a smooth slab of rock. Her wet tracks would dry in minutes. With the last of her energy she climbed a rough-barked tree and sprawled in a nest of limbs close to the trunk, twelve feet off the ground. Her last thought was of Trey, hoping he had been as lucky as she, safe, with no Indians sighted.

She awakened in those last few minutes before full dawn when the earth seemed to be holding its breath, gathering itself for the momentum of the day. She sat quietly for a while contemplating her plight. Her food was gone. She still didn't know where Trey was, or where he would leave the river and strike overland. The only thing she knew was that, if she stayed on the river, eventually she'd come out where the Ohio emptied into the Mississippi. And what then? North or south? She had no idea. It was a bleak picture.

To her right, through the trees and lifting mist, she could see a creek meandering away from the river between brushy banks and wandering around the contour of a bald, knobby hill beyond her gaze.

And, berry bushes! A dozen strides away! The creek bank was covered with berry bushes. Her stomach twisted in hunger at the thought of the sweet purple-black berries melting on her tongue. She scrambled down the tree heedlessly scraping elbows and knees and ran, clutching the rifle in one hand, through the woods to the creek. She stripped the fruit from the bushes and crammed them in her mouth as fast as she could swallow.

When her first immediate hunger was satisfied she stopped to wash her hands in the creek and saw by her reflection that the juice had run down her chin, too. The water was swift and clear and cool, and only about knee-deep. Suddenly her whole aching body longed to be submerged. She could almost feel the satiny coolness of the water caressing her skin, making her slippery and sleek, carrying away the loneliness, the fear and the aching muscles of the night.

Yet she hesitated. What if an Indian, or wild animal—a bear, God forbid—should happen upon her? Her eyes made a quick circuit of the surrounding forest. Nothing threatening that she could see. She listened. No sound except that of birds high above and the scurrying of squirrels or small critters in the underbrush. Still… But oh, the bliss of being clean again. Clean all over at one time. To wash in water not thick with silt and river debris. The temptation was too much. She stood to slide off her pants and shirt and shift, and stepped into the pebble-bottomed stream.

In a near trance of ecstasy she scrubbed her skin and massaged her legs and flexed her shoulders as the current flowed around her. She couldn't remember anything, ever, feeling as good. Her aching muscles relaxed. Her nerve endings came to life slowly, tingling and expanding in the icy water. Lowering herself into the stream she felt its hurrying, bubbling force, the chill of smooth rocks shifting beneath her, the tug and pull of the tiny current. In the freshness of the breeze, a hint of night lingered, bringing a rush of goose bumps to rise on her bare skin. Her deep sigh of pure pleasure echoed in the clarity of the early morning.

Verity pulled her hat forward to shut out the light and rested her head against the bank. The mossy smell of decaying leaves wafted up from the earth. A blue jay screamed from the sky. A sun, yellow as butter, cleared the trees and shone full in her face. From the woods the jay screamed again and Verity's eyes snapped open. The small hair on the back of her neck prickled beneath the crown of her hat. Something had startled the bird. Something unfamiliar. The jay called again, a raucous cry of warning and, swooping low over the creek, fell from view behind a stand of juniper. Slowly Verity stretched out her right arm until her hand closed on the stock of her gun.

The sound of the rushing stream covered her movements as she gathered her legs under her and stood. Water streamed down her arms, her stomach, her legs. Her breath caught in the back of her throat. To her waiting ears, the crack of a twig sounded like canon fire and she swung the gun to her shoulder. She sighted down the barrel, and her finger tightened on the trigger even as she turned into the danger.

Trey stood there his eyes incredulous with surprise. His hands, holding the rifle ready, fell limply to his sides. He looked like a steer that had been poleaxed, one who was dead and didn't yet know it. "My God," he said, the words coming out in a thick rush of disbelief.

He blinked once and then again. She was still there, looking as fresh and pink as Eve in the Garden, and not a fig leaf in sight. "My God," he said again. He was incapable of coherent thought, let alone speech. It was like seeing lightning dance on a lily leaf. His mind refused to accept what his eyes saw.

A hat. That's all she had on. A hat. Stupidly, his mind kept repeating the phrase. And a gun.

He had to try twice before his voice worked. "Would you mind pointing that thing the other way?" he asked, striving for an even tone. "I'm partial to being in one piece."

Without taking her eyes from his, she lowered the gun and let it dangle from one hand. Her face suddenly drained of color, leaving her eyes too big, too dark, in the small planes of her face. And then suddenly the color flooded back, burnishing her entire body with bronze. For a moment her eyes glittered dangerously and then she bent to gather her clothes and with a back as straight as a rifle barrel, she stepped behind a clump of sprawling mountain laurel.

Trey's eyes remained fastened on the place where she'd been. *Hang on, boy. Take it easy. You're thinking things it's safer not to think.* He'd promised her that one day they'd finish what they had started, but he was in a hurry to get down river. This was not the moment. With difficulty he slowed his breathing.

Verity. Here. Bathing.

It wasn't possible. And yet, the mountain laurel was atremble with movement. Crushed leaves at the water's edge were still wet with her footprints.

How did she get here? How in hell could she possibly be here, on the Ohio River bank, two nights and a full day from Corn Island? If it had been Homer now—but Verity! Maybe something terrible had happened on the island and Homer had chucked Verity into a canoe and made off. With vivid clarity he remembered his charge to Homer to take care of her. Had Indians… Where was Homer?

She stepped from behind the bushes in the same baggy pants she'd worn that first day he saw her back in Albemarle County. How in thunder could the sight of her in pants so loose she may as well have been draped in a tent, make his blood race as fast as when he'd seen her clothed in nothing but the morning light?

She wore the same pants, the same hat—good Lord, the hat had hidden only her hair—and the same defiant look in her eyes. A fine sheen of sweat broke out on his neck. He felt like a twelve-year-old boy in the grip of something he didn't understand. He noticed then that her cheeks were a rosy shade of bright pink and in spite of her lifted chin, she was biting the inside of her bottom lip. She was unsure of herself. Embarrassed. He said the first thing that came into his mind.

"What, no goat?"

He could see a rapid pulse beating in her throat. The pink in her cheeks heightened. "I was looking for you," she said in a voice that tried to be big and failed.

"What for?"

"To—to go downriver."

His eyebrows raised. "Alone?"

"Yes." The fingers of one hand picked at a pant leg.

"You don't really expect me to believe that you somehow got yourself down nearly one hundred miles of river all by yourself?"

"Yes." Her gaze clung to his.

He studied her carefully. There was no evidence of anyone else within earshot and he knew for a fact that she was strong-minded enough to attempt what others would never consider. But still—"

"To be honest," she ventured, "I'm surprised to see you so soon. I'd—"

He laughed, an amused bark that interrupted her, and then thought better of what he was going to say. "An understatement, surely. And, the question is why you're here at all."

She flinched at the double meaning of his words, but answered calmly. "To go with you, of course. To Kaskaskia."

Kaskaskia! The damn-fool woman was willing to risk her life to get to that Edward-person. After he'd forbidden it about as forcibly as he knew how. He swept off his hat to slap it smartly against his leg.

"I told you—how many times did I tell you?—to wait on Corn Island and I'd send him back. This is madness!" His voice rose to a near shout. "Will you ever learn to listen?"

She ducked her head and was still for so long he found himself waiting on edge for her argument. "Well?" he demanded harshly, waving an aimless arm at the river. "You could have been killed a dozen times, in two-dozen ways, out there. In the dark, and my God, in the daylight. What were you thinking?"

Her voice was soft. He barely heard her. "I couldn't wait. Please believe me, it wasn't possible."

"Why couldn't you wait? Because you had to have your own way!"

She raised her eyes finally and shook her head. "I might not have waited anyway, I wanted to come that bad. But at the last, I couldn't. I was afraid."

He frowned. "Afraid of what?" And when she didn't answer, his brows gathered in deeper lines. "You may as well tell me. We aren't moving until you do."

Her mouth went loose for a brief second, as if she was going to cry, and his gut tightened like a clay brick in the hot sun. Except for that one time, on the Scioto, when she'd been running, he'd never seen her any way except spitting angry fire if she didn't get her way, or else soft and sweet in his arms. He would have guessed there wasn't anything much she couldn't handle.

"Well?"

"Bart."

One whispered word and he knew all there was to know. Bart. Of course.

"That day with your washing?" he asked, and she nodded.

He felt like he was choking. "He did—hurt you, then."

"Not the way you mean. But he wouldn't stop trying." Her eyes flooded with an unspoken plea and she looked suddenly like a frightened little girl. "That last night, after you left, he—I didn't know what else to do."

Trey threw back his head and drew a long breath. Clem was bringing Esther into the cabin. There would have been no safe place for Verity. And the runt was set on having her. He'd known it and left Homer to do a job that was his.

He sighed. "Are you all right?"

She nodded and a smile pulled at the corners of her mouth. "He'll be looking out of only one eye for a while, though."

His chest swelled with pride. She was a gutsy one all right. "Good for you."

Trey's vision filled with the sight of her as she'd stood moments before, feet in the noisy stream and her brother's hat on her head, drawing a bead on danger with a borrowed gun, naked as the jay that had given away his presence and the most beautiful thing he'd ever seen. Bart? He felt like ramming his fist through the nearest tree. How could he *ever* have considered Bart as a possible husband for her? Even in his ignorance back in Virginia, he should have seen that Bart and his crude ways weren't for her, as fine-boned and courageous and—and good as she was. And neither was the damned Frenchman.

And as if she'd read his mind, she said, "The Frenchman, Mr. Fauconnet, wanted to take me back east with him. I could have done that."

Trey swore under his breath. "The Frenchman, did he know you left the island alone?"

She shook her head. "I asked him to bring me after you, to Kaskaskia, and he refused. He will have been angry to find me gone."

A wash of relief flooded over Trey. She turned the Frenchman down. In order not to show his feelings, his voice was rough.

"You could have gone to Homer." But he knew instantly why she hadn't. Homer could not have been with her every moment. He had a bum foot and other responsibilities, as well.

So had she. She would have needed a guard, day and night, and he hadn't been far-sighted enough in his rush to get to Clark to see that.

"Whatever made you think you could catch me?"

"I had to," she said simply.

He wanted desperately to take her in his arms, and ease the fear he heard in her voice. He wanted to hold her, if for no other reason than to reassure himself that she was safe. My God, she'd come through Indian country alone. Country that Clark and his entire army traveled through with every eye peeled and guns primed.

But he wasn't blind. He could also see a readiness to bolt just beyond the surface of her thinking. And he could guess what was going on behind those incredible eyes. What had just happened, what he'd seen, was something that in her eyes was shared by only husband and wife. If he made one move now, she'd be certain for all time that he was no better than Bart.

And was he? He loved her. He'd admitted that. Surely it was love when the need to be near her had clouded his duty to Clark. He'd come close to sending the message with someone else, just so he didn't have to leave her behind. Love was one thing, but he wasn't at all sure what came next.

"You know what I'd like to be, right now?"

His gaze jerked back to hers. "What you'd like to be?"

She nodded. "A bird, so I could fly anywhere I wanted and not be a burden. I hate this."

He groaned inwardly. There was no point in struggling against the inevitable. "You'd never have caught me if I hadn't run up on a submerged log in the dark. Busted the whole bottom out of my canoe. I slept the night a few hundred yards away and found your canoe this morning in the rushes. I knew it wasn't made by any Indian, so I took the time to look around. That's when I found you."

He held out a hand and the corners of his mouth quirked upward. "No burden. You will never need anyone as badly as I need you right now. You and your canoe."

Her smile of relief caught him smack in the breastbone and hung there. Her hand in his was trusting. What more could a man want? And as for tomorrow, maybe when it got here he would know what to do with it. In the meantime, Clark was marching overland by now, and a canoe was at hand. Left unsaid was his biggest fear, that of the unknown Edward-person waiting at the end of their journey. He'd just have to deal with each problem as it arose.

"Daylight's wasting," he said. "Let's go."

Nineteen

The river had begun to feel like home. It was good to be back on it again. Verity hugged the knowledge to her that Trey would be near for the next few days. Near enough to lay her eyes on, if not her hands. Lurking Indians, current-borne trees swinging and slashing in violent arcs, the fear of hidden falls and whirlpools all receded to the back of her mind. Together, she and Trey would manage. Joe, Kaskaskia, tomorrow—and Edward—could wait.

Verity sat in the prow of the canoe scanning the river's surface for obstacles. Trey paddled tirelessly from the rear. What a comfort it was to know he was back there, that she was no longer on her own. Not even Bart was a threat. He'd been left far behind. There was no possibility of his heavy-lidded, brooding, waiting eyes seeking her out. Not at this distance.

Once more the Ohio had saved her, carried her away from bondage and those who would make of her something she didn't want. She trailed one idle hand in the water. Low sandstone bluffs rolled by on either bank. Occasionally, they passed a sunny canebrake or a meadow of long grasses whispering in the late afternoon breeze. After months of a general westward progression, ahead of them the Ohio flowed south in an almost straight line broken by vast, sweeping bends. The river made a soft, shushing sound as it purled against the thin bark of the canoe. For long minutes Verity basked in a glow of complete contentment.

"This won't last. We'll be headed into the setting sun before long." A smile hovered on Trey's lips when his gaze caught hers, and then moved on to the banks on either side. Every line in his body seemed poised, alert and yet his eyes when they rested on her gave their full admiring, seeking, attention for long seconds at a time. She could no more stop the leaping response of her heart than she could make the Ohio run backwards. She drew a long steadying breath before she spoke.

"Where are we? Do you know?"

"Near enough."

"You said there would be Indians or renegades. You said there are caves along the river where robbers hid and attack movers."

"We have to pass the Wabash River before we come to Cave-In-Rocks. It can't be far ahead. The entire country around it is supposed to be full of white and red mulberry trees with high and smooth banks along the river. I'm seeing a lot of mulberry."

"How do you know what to look for?" She was amazed at the multitude of things he seemed to have stored in his head. "Have you been down the river before?"

"Clark. He reads everything he can get his hands on about this country. At night he'll stay up, talking, as long as he has a listener." One shoulder shrugged. "And I'm interested. St. Louis is across the river from Kaskaskia and, who knows, they might need a printer there. Maybe even a newspaper."

Trey was almost as surprised as Verity. Until the moment he voiced the words, he hadn't thought of seriously of starting his own business. Oh, he'd run the thought around in his head, but hadn't tried to build on it. The more he thought about it, however, the more he liked the idea. He could send word back with the first of Clark's messengers and ask Billy to join him.

He flexed his shoulders. The notion set fairly comfortably. He hadn't run away from the work in Williamsburg, after all, only the confinement. He had wanted to be a part of whatever was happening in the west. In St. Louis, the wilderness would still be as near as the edge of town.

And it was a wonderful wilderness. A dark flock of smoky blue pigeons wheeled against the sky. Gray herons with mottled blue feathered their heads stalked stiff-legged along the bank. Turtles, black as coal, perched atop waterlogged limbs jutting into the shallows. Along the water's edge, a constant fringe of small trees and brush angled out over the water. And in the prow of the boat, Verity sat with her hair shining in the sun and one graceful arm hung loosely over the bow.

Every day she became more important to him, more dear. He wanted to protect her, sleep beside her—he even wanted to argue with her. He wanted the right to cherish her, to run his fingers through her hair, down her body. He almost laughed out loud just for the hell of it.

He'd always been able to make decisions quickly and decisively, but for some reason it was as if he'd been slightly off balance for a long time. He'd had chance after chance to squint at the target, but couldn't seem to hone his aim. Now, for the first time, he knew exactly what he wanted and who he wanted to go there with him. And he, like an idiot, was delivering his beloved into the arms of another man. That would have to be remedied.

His eye followed the flight of a soaring hawk, its fringed wing tips feeling for the air currents. The hawk dropped, swooped low, and climbed again towards the sky, broad and blue and without a cloud in sight.

He leaned forward and touched Verity's arm and nodded toward the hawk. She smiled, knowing somehow what he meant her to know without words. Maybe that had been the problem. He'd kept trying to go it alone and was stumbling over his own feet. It's been her from the beginning, he thought. From the first moment he'd laid eyes on her in her brother's hat, fighting with a goat on a hillside. What to do about it was another matter. Maybe, after Kaskaskia—

"There it is!" Verity called, pointing ahead. "Oh Trey! It's so big!"

And the Wabash was indeed big. In a matter of moments they were caught in the added force of its current. Two hundred yards across at its mouth, muddy water poured into the Ohio in a foaming torrent. Before they had time to do more than draw breath they were caught up in a powerful westward sweep and the canoe shot forward as if driven by a high wind. Trey paddled vigorously just to keep the canoe upright as it bucked and slipped sickeningly sideways through the water. Verity clung to the sides. Water flattened her hair and whipped it across her face, soaked her clothes and plastered them to her body and yet her face, when she turned to him, was not fearful.

Another woman would have cowered in the bottom of the boat. He found himself shouting a challenge to the river as the prow rode up the crest of a wave and pointed itself at the sky before pitching downward at a dizzying angle. He threw his back into the paddle with dedicated concentration.

Verity balanced her body for the next wave. She was like no other woman he'd ever known. She seemed to leap forward into life and he felt a surge of energy to match hers.

In minutes they were through the worst, and while the canoe still lurched and slid as if shoved by an invisible hand, it was possible for Trey to maneuver for position.

Verity shifted her weight and leaned against the gunwale, weightless and limp, and watched him still driving the paddle deep. Sooner or later he was bound to wear out. No one could keep up this pace for long. They rounded a bend and the river opened once more before them.

"Cave-In-Rocks is coming up. Look sharp," he said, "and you might see the Great Manitou. The Indians believe this cave to be his dwelling place."

"Their God?"

He merely nodded and changed the paddle to the other side.

"Are we going to stop?" Verity wanted to see this well-known place.

"Too dangerous. Everyone going west passes down the Ohio and river pirates have a hey-day waylaying them. We'll cut to the far side." With the calm acceptance of a man who prepares for the worst, he was aware of the reassuring pressure of his rifle against his knee. He was as ready as he'd ever be.

The bluffs grew more ragged and the hills steeper. Great sandstone abutments jutted out a hundred feet or more over the river. The water showed traces of reddish silt. And then as they rounded a gentle bend, above a brushy base of tangled overgrowth, the low, yawning mouth of a deep cave hove into view.

"There," Verity whispered, a hand blindly reaching for his buckskin covered knee. "I see it. It's deserted."

"Maybe." The broad stone shelf in front of the cave was empty, true, but there was no way to tell for sure whether men hid in the dark recesses untouched by the setting sun. Trey angled for the far bank; he didn't intend to take any chances with Verity in the canoe.

To Trey's relief, they passed without incident, and he paddled on for another hour through the slower current, before he began looking for a spot to leave the river.

"I don't want to stop for the night until moonrise, so we'll hole up somewhere for a couple of hours." He tossed her a bag that landed with a solid thunk at her feet. "Chew on this if you're hungry."

The sight of pounded corn and jerky reminded her stomach that she hadn't eaten all day, but she had to admit that the traditional trail food couldn't compare to the pounded corn cakes and dried meat slices she was served in the Indian village. Silently, she admitted that the Indians must know something the white settlers had yet to learn.

Trey found what he was looking for in a long finger of dense reeds separating the main current from a shallow stand of water at the edge of the forest. Abruptly, he turned the canoe into the bank of reeds and rolled over the edge. Verity was so tired and sore she didn't even ask how he knew what to find behind the swampy, reed-choked area. It was enough that she could trust him to do what was best.

Verity did, however, sit up when it appeared he was leaving the canoe. "What are you doing?"

"Just covering our tracks." He pushed the canoe forward and painstakingly straightened the reeds behind him as he went. "No point in leaving a map for anyone to follow."

He waded forward, guiding the canoe through the tea-colored water of a grassy swamp. Suddenly he grunted, a sound of satisfaction, and to Verity's amazement pushed the prow directly toward a solid bank of sprawling bushes.

"Get down," he said and when she didn't move he placed a hand on her head and pressed hard enough that she flattened herself on the bottom of the canoe. They seemed to pass straight through a wall of trees and brush and emerged in a narrow channel that led away from the river at a parallel angle. Trey beached the canoe on a fallen log and, smiling, stretched out a hand.

"Your quarters, my lady."

Verity stepped out onto a carpet of pine needles wincing as sharp nettles of feeling came back into her legs and feet. She straightened slowly, favoring her back. The setting sun fell in golden shafts between the trees. They seemed to be surrounded by a tangled forest of hickory, pecan and black walnut trees. She saw a persimmon tree, one which her Mama had called "paw paw," and a wild pear. The pears tended to be the smallest and most sour of all wild fruit trees, but Mama always said they made the best preserves and jams.

She sank down on the soft earth, groaning in pleasure. "I may never be able to straighten my legs again. How do you keep on hour after hour?"

His eyes were busy at the edge of the forest. "Don't think about it. Now, you stay here while I take a look around. I'll be right back." And he seemed to fade into the trees and was gone.

For an instant, it seemed to Verity that she was alone in the forest. Then activity resumed. Birds twittered fussily. A ring-eyed raccoon peered around a log and disappeared. A pair of striped chipmunks scurried from a downed tree to a pile of dead leaves and disappeared into a hole in the forest floor. Verity felt the tension draining away through her toes and into the earth. Smiling, she took her hair down and shook it loose around her face. She leaned back on her elbows. The quiet was so profound she heard leaves whispering overhead as a breeze passed through the treetops. It was a restful, waiting silence. Peaceful. And yet, what if he never came back? What if something happened to him, an Indian, a snake, some horrible, unthinkable accident? The quiet was all of a sudden oppressive. She couldn't breathe. Her heart seemed to be clamoring to get out of her throat.

She got to her feet, ready to run, but where would she go? They'd come from the creek and everything else was trees.

Suddenly, there was a great rumbling off to her left and then a savage roar of sound that seemed to shake the very earth. Her heart beat even faster. It came again, a dreadful, angry grumbling. The sounds seemed to be moving closer. She was shaking, her hands at her mouth, her eyes darting in every direction.

As quickly as Trey had disappeared into the forest, he was back. She threw herself into his arms so fast he barely got the gun out of the way.

"What is it? What's happening?"

He wrapped his arms around her in a satisfying clinch. "What? Are you complaining about the bear?" One hand travelled down her back and then retraced its path. His voice went soft and thick. "Two old fellows are having a shoving match, is all. Arguing over the same territory. Or a female."

He felt her hair silky and soft spilling over his hands. Her breath was warm on his cheek. The petal-soft skin of her neck shot a fire into his gut that nearly bent him double. He wanted to touch her, needed to touch her, feel the velvet of her skin next to his.

Verity stopped thinking. She was shockingly aware when Trey's hand went behind her neck and his fingers tangled in her hair, and her body involuntarily stiffened. In an instant of clarity she knew a moment when she could have pulled away, declared that she hated him still for leaving Sally, but in another moment she knew it was a lie.

She didn't understand, but whatever she felt for him was not hatred. And it would be hypocritical to pretend otherwise. He was the rock she could brace her back against, the one man who made her feel, for the first time ever, like a woman. She could feel herself watching him like Mama had watched Papa. He was all that was important. The world.

Abandoning all thought, she gave herself to sensation. Her body went limp. Boneless. The hard length of his body leaned into her, pinning her against a tree and warming her body with the heat of his.

Her hands found their way around his neck to knot in the hair at his nape and then moved down to explore the solid breadth of his shoulders.

Her eyelashes fluttered at the feel of his breath on her temple and a queer throbbing began in the pit of her stomach when his mouth hovered a hairsbreath away from her own and hung there. His lips moved against her cheek and it seemed such an exquisite torment to have his mouth so close to hers without contact, that she turned her lips into his.

For a brief instant he hesitated and then the light flickering in his eyes flamed. With a low moan he crushed her to him. She clung to his solid strength while he left a trail of kisses from her ear to her eyes and across the tip of her nose. "I must be doing something right." He'd said that, she remembered. And, oh my, she had to agree. As far as she was concerned, this was probably the rightest thing he'd ever done.

One hand slid down her back and pressed her even closer. The other lifted to the back of her head.

His lips were hard and insistent, searching. The forest seemed to swim around them. A yearning welled in Verity like a hungry tide. Her arms tightened.

And then, in a sweeping motion he picked her up in his arms and moved into the forest. "I've found a spring," he said his words coming in spurts. "Warm, fresh, clear water—not three minutes away—like our own private tub—here, right here."

Still holding her close, he set her on her feet. There was indeed a gurgling spring so clear it sparkled as it gushed from a nest of rocks on the ground and flowed into a shallow pool. His hands were shaking as he helped her out of her pants and shirt and then while she stood in only her shift, he quickly removed his own clothing. Verity's body seemed to lack any will to resist and he lowered her into the spring. The water enveloping her was wonderfully warm and Verity almost groaned with ecstasy as her sore and aching muscles responded to the heat.

"You've had a hell of a few months, starting all the way back in Albemarle County. Not only did you have to fight a stupid goat and the river, but you had that sick woman and her baby, and Clem and Bart and—and me. I've been as much to blame as anyone."

The words were floating over her thinking. His tone told her all she wanted to know. He cared. Her heart soared. He was still talking.

"—never been very good at promises, but…"

She looked up and locked her eyes with his. Some ancient instinct told her what he was trying to tell her. Lightly she laid her finger in the little indention of his chin and then cupped his face with both hands. "It's all right," she said.

"No, listen. This is something I need to say." And he realized it was so. He could no more stop his heart from spilling over than he could stop the run of the river. "I want you to be my wife. I want to wake up mornings with you beside me. I never thought this time would come with any woman and I don't even know how it happened now, but I don't want to face the rest of my life without you."

An hour ago, a week ago, he'd had no intention of saying anything like this and yet once the words were out, he knew it was right. In fact, in some silent recess of his brain he felt pride in his supreme intelligence of being able to sense what was ordained.

He realized his hands were shaking. He was afraid. He was a tracker, a woodsman, a hunter. He'd lived on the fringe of danger and faced down men and wild animals and never known fear like this. What if she said no? What if she declared her undying love for this Edward fellow in Kaskaskia?

He'd rushed her, damn it. Women needed courting time. Women like her, anyway. And that's just what he didn't have. Speed was essential to get news of the French to Clark and here he was running at top speed to destroy the only thing he had going for him with Verity—time. Time for her to forget Edward, waiting in Kaskaskia. If she'd stayed on Corn Island he wouldn't be in this fix. But then, when had she ever followed orders?

Of course, if she'd stayed, the damned Frenchman might have taken her upriver before Trey could get back. Or Bart might have gotten to her, in spite of Homer. It had been an impossible situation she'd faced. Hell and damnation. What was he to do except finish what he'd begun?

"Will you?" He rushed on before he lost what momentum he had. "Will you stand up with me in front of the priest in Kaskaskia and take the marriage vows?"

Her eyes had gone wide in surprise. Not letting himself guess as to what she might be thinking, he went on. "I know you're promised to this man in Kaskaskia, but I'll talk to him. He'll have to understand. I'll make him understand." Hell, he'd talk a grizzly into nodding agreement if he had to.

Roughly he pulled her to him and buried his face in her hair. "Say yes. Say you don't know. Say you'll think about it. Just don't say no. Please."

The trees echoed the pleading he heard in his voice and he scarcely recognized it as his own. So he was reduced to begging. So be it. This was Verity and he loved her with all his being. Life without her would be unspeakably barren and bleak. She had to feel the same. "I want you for my wife. I need you."

"Now?" she asked, her voice almost lost in his shirt front. "Do you mean right now?"

He was aware that he held her head in a vice-like grip against his chest and released her. What was she asking? She wasn't saying no. She wasn't declaring passionate love for anyone else. His heart skittered into a frantic race. "Not this very minute, no. But yes, as soon as we get to Kaskaskia."

"I'll talk to Edward."

Frowning, he crouched down to look into her face. "Are you saying yes?" A smile began and spread across his face. "Is it yes? Say it. Say it aloud. I want to hear the word."

"Yes," she said, looking at him solemnly, "but I have to know—"

"What? Anything." He shook her slightly in his joy.

"Trey, tell me. I still can't make it right. If Sally had been one of our babies—if one of ours was taken—would you let her go without trying to bring her home? I don't think I could bear that, Trey."

He held her two hands in his large ones and looked, unsmilingly, into her eyes. "I pledge you my solemn oath, I would give my life to bring our child home to you. Do you not understand, yet, why Sally is better off with the Indians than with the Dawsons? Gideon is a boy, half grown. He'll fare better. But Sally's life would have been hell as she grew older. Clem would have given her to the first man who took a fancy to yellow curls and, ready for womanhood or not, she'd have had to go."

He conceded, "Esther may have some influence on him, but I didn't know until we got back to Corn Island that they were going to set up together. Her life with Clem would have been one of being cuffed about, working like a horse, and used by rough, uncaring men. Please don't worry about Sally. I promise you on my word of honor that she is happy. I'll make contact with Blue Wing and make sure, if that will make you feel better."

Verity looked deeply into his eyes as if searching for the answer there and finally, with a sigh as soft as ashes collapsing in the fire, leaned her forehead on his chin. "Do we have to wait until we get to Kaskaskia?"

A jolt speared through his gut like a hot iron. He swallowed hard. "I don't want any woods colts of mine running around. I won't do that to you. You deserve better. We'll be at Kaskaskia in a few days."

She peered up at him through her lashes. "Could we not take our vows, here, now? To each other. God is listening. I know he is. And the priest could bless them when we get to the fort." She smiled at him and his head went suddenly light.

She took her eyes from his to look around. "In a forest glade, lit by a golden shaft of a setting sun. It would be a prettier wedding than most women have, even without the priest's blessing." She held out her arms.

For a long minute he was stiff beneath her hands and then she felt a tremor run the long length of his body. He was lost and she knew it. She pulled his head down to hers.

His kiss was soft at first, gentle, and then urgent. She felt herself meeting his need with her own until finally, breathless, he pulled away.

"I love you, Verity. As God is my witness, I love you." His voice was triumphant, for after all, he had won. "I will cherish you and protect you and honor you with my life and my body forever. I swear."

And, as the sunshine fell around her in a soft haze she smiled up at him. "And I, too, will cherish you with my body and my life for always. In the eyes of God I marry you now. Today. This minute."

That was all she had time for because he was kissing her and laughing and kissing her again. And she was kissing him back, and thrilling at the pleasure she could give.

Mindlessly, they pulled each other from the water, laughing, stroking, touching. She felt as if she held in her possession a very rare and precious knowledge and was as complete as she would ever be, joined by invisible bonds of oneness to this man before he ever touched her in passion. The feeling was too fragile for thought. Deliberately, she pushed everything else from her mind. The future—Edward—would take care of itself. This would be enough.

And then there was no room for thought. His hands were caressing, touching, her shift fell away and she arched her back against the hardness of his body. She could feel the ripple and bunch of his muscles and for one brief second saw his eyes brimming with tenderness before she closed her own.

And then a slow, mountainous tide began to swell, lifting her, carrying her, exposing her to a soaring, searing height. And all the while his voice whispered in her ear, teasing, loving, demanding, giving his all in return.

They lay quietly in the darkening glade. Trey held her head on his chest, against his heart, and ran a hand down the small of her back.

"My sweetling," was all he said, his voice not quite steady. "Oh, so sweet." He pulled her closer and held her as if he would never let her go.

His heartbeat kept time with her own and she turned her head slightly to lay her lips against the wall of his chest. "I know," she said. "I know."

She felt that she had been wandering in the wilderness for a very long time and finally found a place to call home. She put an arm around the comforting vastness of his rib cage and sighed. "I know."

Twenty

Trey was a happy man. Contentment coursed through his body like the slow-moving summer river itself. He was aware of why this was so. He had made Verity his own. All of his earlier hesitations and fears were suddenly as nothing. He felt renewed and invigorated and intoxicated like a man given a reprieve from the gallows.

He lifted on one elbow and gazed down at Verity, asleep in the dappled and fading sunlight. He knew he had a foolish grin on his face, but there was no one to see, and he didn't care anyway. She was as sweet and soft as a kitten's ear, and as exciting and courageous as any Seneca brave, although he could hardly tell her that considering the way she felt about Indians. And she was his.

He wasn't even astonished that all thought of a life apart from her had disappeared. It was as if the last hour had been planned from the beginning of time, only he had been so consumed with himself and his precious freedom that he had been unaware. Any ideas of freedom, from now on, included Verity or he would be free from nothing. He would be simply alone in bondage to her memory.

Thoughts of Edward, the man she had been so hell-bent to marry in Kaskaskia, shoved their way to the fore. He dwelled for quite a while on what he considered to be his own breach of gentlemanly conduct. He had, after all, known very well that Verity was promised to another man, and she had all but moved heaven and earth to get herself to him in the Illinois country.

The smile gave way to a massive frown. In spite of all this, he'd talked her into marriage. Hell, be honest, he'd never thought of Edward once during the past hour. A curl of unease threaded through his thinking. They had exchanged marriage vows, yes, but in the aftermath of their lovemaking, in the clear light of day, would she consider them binding? He certainly did. In his mind they belonged to each other now. Edward boy—he directed his mental speech to the man he'd never met, a man who Trey admitted with a wince was honorably serving Clark in his own capacity just as Trey was doing—I'm sorry, man, but you lost. Quickly, he took back the last thought. He wasn't sorry in the least. Not a bit.

He was concerned, however, about how Verity would feel concerning her broken promise to Edward. She had a black and white version of what was right and wrong that occasionally took him by surprise, like his using some choice words she didn't approve of. She also tried desperately to live up to what her mother would have expected of her, and he knew her well enough to prepare for some turmoil on that score. Well, it wasn't something he could do anything about at this moment.

The need to be on their way was urgent. He'd like to stay longer and prolong this pleasant hour, but he had rested while she slept and he couldn't justify whiling away time when Clark so greatly needed the information he carried. He wished he didn't have to awaken her. She was sleeping so soundly, her breath coming in a gentle rising and falling of her breast. Her lashes lay in dark feathered arcs on her cheeks and there was a faint smile on her mouth. Was she dreaming of him? As grateful as he, maybe, for what they'd shared? For what the future held? He pulled her to him, careful not to awaken her, and rejoiced for one more stolen minute in the feel of her body, soft, yet strong, against his own. One hand began a downward curve.

He sucked in a long breath and let it go slowly. The hand stilled. The afternoon was waning; shadows were lengthening. They couldn't tarry.

Resolutely, he set his thoughts toward their journey. First of all food. They had to eat if they were to continue the overland pace he needed to set. Maybe he could, after all, let her sleep for awhile. Slowly he pulled his arm from beneath her and stood up. The trees crowded close around him. He didn't dare use the rifle; a war party might be traveling a hundred yards away. And he didn't have a tomahawk to throw. That meant fish, again. He'd have to go back to the creek.

Precious minutes were lost hunting a suitable hickory switch which he sharpened as he went so that by the time he got to the river he was ready. A dozen long strides brought him to a shallow-bottomed cove.

Four catfish, the longest three feet in length, lay on the gray-green river bed holding their place against the current. Fins and tail moved with slow undulation. He drew a long breath. This was important. He didn't have time to stomp up and down the bank hunting for other fish and patiently spitting at them. It was this or nothing. They'd have to pick up something along the trail if he missed. He poised himself on a shelf of rock, gathered all his strength in his right arm and held his breath as Blue Wing had taught him, and flung the spear.

Coils of swirling silt fogged the water and for a moment he could see nothing. He'd missed. Damn! But no. One fish flopped feebly, pinned to the bottom by the spear. Trey could have given a warwhoop. They would eat and eat well.

He cleaned the fish quickly, buried the skin and entrails, and encased the fish in thick river mud. Hurrying, he splashed water from the cove over his head and upper body and then, using the leaves of a wild grapevine, he wrapped the fish and made his way back to the glade where he'd left Verity. She still slept.

He wondered again at the grueling pace she'd set coming down the river, at the endurance she'd demanded of herself to get as far as she'd gotten, alone, and for even attempting the journey in the first place.

His eyes went flat and cold at the thought of Bart. He hoped, with all his heart, that the day would come when he could settle the score personally with the runty little man. It was a large score and Trey's heart hardened with the conviction that he'd make sure that day came eventually. Some how. Some way. A day when duty didn't override pleasure.

With a sharp stick he gouged a hole beneath the hanging branches of a drooping willow, covered the bottom with a thick layer of dead pine needles and bark and laid the fish on top. Striking flint to the steel he withdrew from the small bag that hung at his waist, he had a small fire within seconds. Fine whisps of smoke wafted upward, shredded and disappeared into the tree tops. He covered the small pit with earth, leaving a pin hole for draft and sank back on his heels. There wouldn't even be a smell of baking fish to alert an enemy. Now all he had to do was wait.

Verity lay watching him with sleep-drugged lethargy. She'd awakened to see him digging the pit. As always, he'd taken the time somewhere to wash, for his hair was still wet, but there were faint weary lines etched around his mouth that betrayed his need for rest.

Overhead, birds called sleepy goodnights in the last light of the dying day. The spring burbled and gurgled in a companionable way. The quiet was restful, peaceful and waiting. She wished she could stop the downward slide of the sun and make this moment go on forever. It would be lovely to spend the entire night in this beautiful glade and maybe tomorrow, too. If Trey would love her again tonight as he had earlier, it would be even nicer.

But she knew better than to wish for the impossible. He would be anxious to get on with the journey, to get to Clark and tell him about the alliance with France. And what then, when the fort was taken and the dust settled? Would there be a cabin and children of her own? A sharing of their lives around a crackling fire on sharp winter evenings, cooling swims in a stream at the end of a steamy summer's day?

What would life with Trey be like? He had committed himself to her last night, but what did that mean exactly? She blushed to think of the way she'd thrown herself at him. It had been worse even than attacking Blue Wing dressed only in her drawers! Definitely not lady-like behavior. *Oh Mama,* she thought, *everything I do must be a disappointment to you.*

Not that Trey appeared to be at all disappointed. He'd seemed to like what they'd done together just fine. She was smugly satisfied. So, this was what it meant to be a woman. To be joined as one with a man. What had always been mystery was now as clear as sunlight sparkling on the river. And the sobering thought occurred to her that she had a lot to learn .

Even with all his talk about a printing business of his own, he was not a man to be tied down, and it was his brother who would be handling the day-to-day affairs. Trey would be traveling the countryside to find out what was going on politically. He was not destined to be a stay-at-home man, content with wife and babies. He'd still left Sally with the Indians and no matter how he explained, and no matter that the child's own father raised no rumpus, there was still a niggling sense of worry that it had been the right thing for Sally. However, it was done and could not be undone. She'd best try and let it go.

A small smile curved the corners of her mouth. Hadn't Trey been something, though, last night? And he was hers, if she could hold on to him. And, to think they had their entire lives ahead of them. She must be the luckiest of all women.

However, there was a sticky problem. What was she going to say to Edward once they reached Kaskaskia? She'd have to count on Joe to help make a place for herself in the community if Trey would be gone all the time. Maybe Joe would help her with knowing what to say to Edward, too. Not that she expected him to be devastated, he'd never shown any indication of caring for her with the intensity Trey did, but he would certainly be insulted. Rightfully so. Well, she'd have to worry later about Edward. Again, what was done was done. She couldn't take back either her virginity or her vows.

A faint whiff of something delicious drifted from the fire pit. She could play possum no longer. Clutching her shirt in front of her, she sat up slowly, sore muscles in her shoulders and thighs protesting. "Is it safe to have a fire?" she asked. "What are you baking?"

Trey turned on one heel. The smile in his eyes sent a warm flush coursing through her body. "It's fish," he said. "We have a hard night and day coming up and we have to eat something that will stick to our ribs." Then a curious softness crossed his face and his eyes went over her with a warmth that seemed to reach from where he sat all the way across the clearing to her.

His voice, when he spoke, was low and dark with feeling. "If you want a bath, the spring is right behind you. Give it a few minutes to fill up and then get in and soak."

Fill up? Verity saw that the spring had only a few inches of water in the bottom although the level was rising as more water gushed in. Last night the spring had been several feet deep. She looked up with the question in her eyes.

"I've heard of these," he said. "Ebb-and-flow springs they're called. It seems to take the same amount of time to empty and refill each time it goes through the cycle. Interesting," he added. "Are you going in?"

She hesitated, wanting badly to sink her aching body into the warm spring, but was suddenly shy. Her clothes were yards away and she couldn't just stand up and walk, naked in front of him to the pool. She couldn't do it. She chose to be flippant. "Will it make a new woman of me?"

"I sincerely hope not. I like what I see just fine."

She hesitated, looking longingly at the water.

"Well? We have a lot of river to cover before moonrise and after that we're going overland. Better get in if you're going to."

The thought of soaking in the warm spring was so tantalizing it almost brought tears to her eyes, but Trey was in plain view, kneeling with one knee resting on the ground by the fire pit and an arm loosely hung over the other knee. She hesitated.

A wicked grin split his face and one eyebrow peaked high. "You can't be worrying about modesty after—" He sank back on his heels. "You are."

He sighed in an exaggerated expulsion of air. "I can't believe this is necessary, but all right." And he turned his back, leaving her what privacy there was to be had.

Hurriedly, she stood, put a tentative toe into the pool, and then lowered herself into the deepest part where the spring was pulsing up in strong surges. The water rose around her like a noisy, boiling pot and covered her small sounds of ecstasy. She closed her eyes. At least after moonrise she wouldn't have to crawl back into the canoe again, with its ribs that dug into her own and creased her shins. At least she would be upright from now on. Whatever was coming, she would face it on her feet. Beside Trey.

She opened her eyes. He was staring at her with a sense of discovery so blatant that her breath caught in her throat. She knew what he was thinking as clearly as if it were emblazoned in the sky.

"You promised," she said, her voice small and unsure.

"I didn't," he denied, smiling. "But I'm not moving, because if I did we'd be here all evening. And we don't have that luxury. I have to find Clark."

"—have to find Clark," she echoed, beginning to be tired of the phrase. Besides, Trey looked as if he could use eight hours of solid sleep. "Is what you carry truly important enough information that you have to kill yourself getting it to him? You need to rest."

"It might save lives, your brother's included, if the French people of Kaskaskia, which takes in almost every single soul, know that France is sending money and men and equipment to fight by our side."

Verity was no longer as anxious to get to Kaskaskia as she had been earlier, but she had to admit the mission sounded vital.

"How many people live there?" she asked.

"In Kaskaskia itself? According to a report your brother made to Clark, not counting Fort Gage and the garrison there, about eighty families. It hasn't been long ago, maybe five years, that a bunch of English traders and French merchants got together and called themselves the Illinois Land Company."

He paused. "Are you interested in this?" At her nod he went on. "Even though King George expressly forbid it, they bought immense tracts of land from an Indian Council. They fooled ten chiefs into making their mark on paper in exchange for a bunch of blankets and beads, a few horses and cows, and some tobacco. Oh yes, and five-hundred pounds of gun powder to go with twenty guns. Then they were told they were no longer welcome in this part of the country."

He got to his feet. "The Indians don't take kindly to the idea that the land of their fathers is overrun with white men who are trying to chase them out. There are a lot of irate Piankeshaws and Shawnee between us and Clark. A bunch of Hileni, too, the Illinois Indians. That's why we can't delay here."

He saw the sudden tensing of her body at the mention of Indians and the quick sweep of her eyes toward the wall of the forest.

She felt the glittering eyes of a dozen savages and was suddenly more vulnerable than she had been at eight-years-old when she'd witnessed the massacre. She could almost hear a shrill, gobbling "yip-yip" fill the peaceful glade where they sat. In spite of knowing the scene was all in her memory, she crouched a little lower in the water.

"Now, don't fold up on me. Verity, it's entirely possible we may get all the way to Kaskaskia and not see a single Indian."

She knew he was right. "I'm not going to fold up."

"I count on that. You've proven yourself in too many ways to list. But I do wish you'd understand that all Indians aren't bad. There are good red people. I know a few."

"Well, I don't know any," she snapped.

"You know Blue Wing," he reminded her, laughter lying just behind the surface. "He admired you enough to bargain for you as a wife."

"The Fist! He offered how many ponies for the privilege of adding me to his other wives? He tried to buy me in the same way as Old Man Hargraves! Blue Wing, indeed."

Unfortunately, Trey laughed.

Verity did not. "He knocked me around, dragged me through the forest by my hair and half-starved me. And then he left me out in the open, unprotected, in the worst of weather. Are you trying to say he is one of your good Indians?"

Trey only raised an eyebrow. "You aren't forgetting that he saved your hide, are you, when they were ready to burn you? And that if he'd treated you any differently you would never have lived to reach the village to begin with?"

There was nothing to say. Because, of course, what Trey said was true. According to Blue Wing's standards he'd treated her decently. And by anyone's standards, he'd saved her life.

Trey bent his head to try and see beneath the fall of hair that hid her face. "Couldn't we agree he's at least one good Indian? Be generous."

She didn't answer. The images of her capture were still vivid and Trey's reference to their intention to burn her caused all the terrors of her childhood to rush to the fore. She was once again terrified and abandoned. She doubled her fists and pressed them against her eyes. Anger swelled into a hard knot in her throat that, for a moment, threatened to choke off her air. "I remember the sound of my father's scalp being torn from his head. I remember Mama's blood. I remember the baby—" She stopped, unable to force the words past the tightness in her throat.

Trey got to his feet in one fluid movement, his own throat squeezing painfully. Damn. She was going to fold after all, but he couldn't fault her. She had cause. "I'm sorry," he finally managed. "That was about as bad as it gets. I'm sorry."

His fists were knotted into balls at his sides. She'd had a rotten childhood. It was no wonder she turned into a wildcat every time he mentioned Indians. She was carrying a childhood pain into her adult life, and that might scar her worse than the original hurt. She still sat in the warm pool, still rocking her head and crying softly. She was as naked and vulnerable at this moment as a new-born fawn. And he'd never felt more helpless.

When she didn't move to get out of the pool, or even raise her head, he again stepped nearer to the water.

"Don't," she said, flinging up her head sharply. Her eyes glittered with tears. "I don't want your pity. You don't understand."

"Pity isn't what I had in mind." But he stopped with the water lapping at his moccasined toes.

Careful. Step careful here, boy, Trey warned himself. She carried a life-time of near-mortal wounds. One misstep could shoot a large-sized hole in their future happiness, along with all hope for her of a more reasonable understanding of Indians. And living on the frontier would be a sentence in perdition for her without it.

"I've said it before, I know, but there are a lot of no-good folks in this world, Verity. They aren't all red skinned."

She swiped angrily at the tears drying on her cheeks. "I guess I ought to know that. According to you I've met a few recently, haven't I?" Her chin quivered in a way that put a knot in Trey's stomach. She said, "It doesn't help."

She huddled with her elbows on her knees, her head bowed and the ends of her hair trailing in the water. She looked so miserable he could stand it no longer. "You're either coming out of there, or I'm coming in. Take your choice."

Her head came up ever so slightly and her jaw went stiff. "I said I don't need your pity."

"The hell with what you need. I need to hold you." And he strode into the pool, clothes and all, and lowered himself into the water enfolding her in his arms.

She stiffened briefly and then went boneless, molding herself to his body. Tears ran down her face, tears of relief, of finally having someone who cared with whom to share her memories, and then with a sigh she laid her cheek against the solid wall of his chest, shuddering only occasionally.

He was like a safe cove, hidden from all danger. Her heart slowed and her head stopped throbbing. She noticed the clean smell of pine which seemed to cling to him always, the scent of wintergreen which he chewed to clean his teeth, and she listened to the comforting thump, thump of his heart beneath her ear. He was soaked through, of course. His buckskins would dry hard and be uncomfortable until he wore them long enough to soften them again. She could see the fringes on his jacket floating in the water just beyond her bare elbow.

"You're all wet," she said.

"That often happens when you sit in a puddle," he agreed.

"This won't happen again," she said, pulling away from him. "I promised you I wouldn't fall apart, and then I did. It's over now."

He let her go, but kept a hand on her one bent, bare knee still under water. "Don't go all prickly on me and don't apologize for crying. My mother used to say tears were medicine for a hurting heart."

The water was beginning to recede, the cycle reversing. Verity sniffled and raised her head. The afternoon was well advanced. The sun no longer fell in the clearing. The day was almost gone.

"It will be dark soon," she said.

His eyes twinkled suddenly. "Dark enough that you'll be able to get out without me turning my back." By her scowl he could see that now was not the time to tease. "However, as much as I'd like to spend the evening in another way, we'd better move so we can eat and get back to the river."

The spring bubbled just beneath her arm pits. "Do you have any idea where Clark is?"

He shook his head. "We'll just have to beat him to Kaskaskia."

"Can you find Kaskaskia?"

"What do you think?"

She thought he could do anything, be anything, go anywhere he pleased. He looked so capable and so…so dear sitting on his knees in the midst of a natural spring with all his clothes on, his eyes stroking her as the water level dropped lower and lower. But she couldn't say that, could she, when he'd not once mentioned, since she awakened, that in the eyes of God they were man and wife.

What she said was, "If only I had some mustard-green seeds and wild onions I could make a paste to eat with our fish."

He spread his hands, water dripping in an arc from each one. "I bring her fish and she asks for sauce. What you're going to do is get out of the water if I have to carry you. Not that that's such a bad idea." And he made a threatening move to do just that.

"I'm coming. I'm coming. I'll be out by the time you uncover the fish."

And she was. By the time he turned with a portion of steaming fish on a bark plate he was still wet, but drying rapidly in the heat of the July twilight. And she was coming toward him dressed and ready to travel.

Twenty-one

For an hour Trey had been looking for a place to leave the river. With moonrise upon them he finally found what he wanted and turned the prow of the canoe sharply shoreward. Powerful thrusts of his paddle drove them hard through the tall swamp grass and at the last minute he back-paddled so as not to run aground.

"Our tracks are more apt to be picked up close to the river," he said, his voice low. He motioned to a shadowy ledge jutting out over the water fifty feet or more just above their heads. "Crawl up there and wait for me."

Verity looked at the yawning cavern of blackness between the overhang and the water, and her spirit quailed. "Trey?"

"Just do it. You hardly have to stretch. Just grab a handhold and climb to the lower ledge first."

Verity made a shaky attempt to stand and reach for the shelf, but the canoe canted first to one side and then the other and she toppled backward, flailing her arms and grabbing for the gunwales.

"Come on, love," Trey said with a glance back at the river. "And hurry."

"Hold the canoe still, can't you?" she snapped, crouching with her arms stretched out at her sides for balance. This time her fingers found the cold smooth rock, but there was no purchase. She fell back in the canoe, grunting as a rib bit into her hip.

"Oh, for—" There was impatience and a sense of urgency in Trey's tone. The canoe rocked as he moved forward and hoisted her unceremoniously up and over the lower ledge. He handed up the guns and the food packet and she scrambled on all fours across the narrow step in the rock and turned to peer down into the darkness.

"Climb," he whispered. "From there on it's easy. Feel your way up."

Grumbling under her breath about insensitive people who fill your hands and then tell you to pick your way up a cliff in the pitch-black of night, Verity did just that. Huffing and grunting she made her way to the top and lay flat for a moment, on the rocky promontory. A soft scraping sound from below had her crawling to the edge and hanging her head over to see what Trey was doing.

What she saw brought a soft cry to her lips and a harsh "Quiet!" to his. He leaned forward and came up with a rock the size of a fist in his hand and backed the canoe into deeper water. A single downward chop caved a hole as big as a squash in the side of the canoe and the river came flooding in. In the milky half-light from the moon, he swam slowly toward the channel pushing the canoe, riding lower and lower, before him. Finally, the current caught the craft and it swung in a sluggish half-moon arc in the pale moonlight before sinking from view. Swimming soundlessly he made his way through the reeds and back to the rock where Verity waited. He disappeared, hidden by the overhanging rock. Her ears strained to hear. Nothing. Silence.

Verity scooted away from the sloping edge and came up with her back against the rough stone bluff. She saw his hands first, dark wet smudges against the reddish sandstone, and then the rest of him followed in one swift dark lunge up and over the top. He rolled and tumbled toward her down the steep slant of the ledge and came up with a shoulder hard into her hip and lay absolutely still for a long minute. She couldn't even hear him breathe.

"Why did you—?" she began in a whisper.

His wet hand covered her mouth, instantly, and his other hand went up to place one finger over his own lips.

They half-lay, half-crouched in utter silence for, what seemed to Verity, an eternity while the wetness from Trey's buckskins soaked her to the skin. She shivered in the coolness of the night air and her teeth began to chatter. The moon through the trees cast shifting shadows that seemed to lean closer in the night. Nothing moved except the lap of the water against the shore. Verity clenched her teeth and strained to see into the forest. Hidden eyes could be watching their every move. Trey had been in the moonlight on the river for only a few minutes and visible for less than that as he heaved himself up on the rock. Was he expecting Indians to be watching every foot of the Ohio, every minute of the day and night?

The moment his hand came away from her mouth, she whispered, "Indians?"

He sat up smoothly, without a sound. "In Indian territory it's always safer to assume the possibility."

"But you just sank our retreat." She waved an accusing hand at the river. "What if we need it?"

"We won't." He rose and drew her up with him.

"But what if we do?"

Verity was relieved to be out of the canoe with its sharp ribs and confined space, but to have deliberately crushed its side and sunk it somehow seemed foolhardy.

He pulled her close so that his mouth was at her ear, but it was no embrace. "Listen," he said, and it was a direct command. "We have a long way to go and not much time to do it in. We can't quibble over every move I make. Just accept, if possible," he said with a touch of sarcasm, "that I might know what I'm doing." His hands tightened on her arms. "Because I don't have time to debate at every tree which side to go around!"

And those were the last words he spoke, for what, to Verity, seemed half the night. Not that she would have had any breath to answer if he had. He started out at the pace of a stampeding elk and didn't let up until they stopped, she rubber-kneed and gasping, at a swift-flowing stream.

By this time they had lunged over knobby, hilly ranges of ridgeland, forced their way through thickets and forded innumerable creeks, most of them wide enough to jump. Trey hardly slackened his pace. They'd seen a pack of wolves slinking across the far side of a wide moonlit meadow, all but stumbled into a herd of dozing deer and heard the blustering bellow of an unhappy buffalo in the distance.

Swaying now with fatigue, she hung her head and braced her hands on her knees to keep from falling. "Got to—stop," she panted, her breath coming in harsh gasps.

Trey looked at her with indecision and then at the sky. He put down his rifle and eased into the shadows. "You've been doing pretty good and we still have a few hours until daybreak."

"Pretty good?" Her head came up. "I kept up—didn't slow you down."

"Not much anyway," he conceded, and she could hear the smile behind the tone. "Rest a few minutes, but don't get used to it. Clark is still a long way ahead of us."

Instinctively she melded into a shadow, as Trey had done, and let her knees go. She sank onto a mossy surface and groaned with relief.

"For all the care you took, earlier, for all the 'shushes' and 'be carefuls', and 'don't leave tracks'—since we left the river we've spread a trail Gideon could have followed. I don't understand you." She leaned her head back against a tree and hung her wrists over her bent knees. Her breath still came deeply.

"When you're moving as fast as we are, tracks don't make any difference. If a war party finds our trail in the morning we'll be long gone." He moved to the edge of moonlight. "Are you ready?"

"To go on? I'm still trying to get my breath! You can't think anyone is still chasing us!"

"We've embarrassed an entire tribe by disappearing from under their noses. To an Indian saving face is all important. Yes, my dear, there is every possibility someone is still chasing us." He held out a hand.

Verity got to her feet and couldn't help slanting a glance toward the trees. Behind them the darkness in the forest was profound. If there had been an entire Indian village within a hundred yards, it would have remained hidden. Would she never in her life be free of Indians? She put her hand in his. "Let's go."

She seemed to have gotten a second breath, and from somewhere a third and then a fourth. It was a mystery that Trey knew where he was going. Some inner compass seemed to pull him across increasingly wide swampy flats and more gently sloping hills. She had no choice but to trust him and finally gave herself up to following the comfortingly regular thuds of his footfalls in front of her.

Dawn was just streaking the edges of the sky when they pulled up at the crest of a ridge. With the forest thick about him and protected by dense undergrowth, Trey removed his hat and edged his way forward on his belly. From atop the hill he would have a good view of the next valley and the horizon for miles around when there was enough light to see. Verity flopped bonelessly on her back without the energy even to remove a stone digging into her side.

Her eyes were gritty, she was hungry and filthy and bleeding in a dozen tiny spots from briar snags, but all she could think about was sleep. She was so tired she thought she would rebel if Trey said they had to go one foot farther. What would he do, she wondered, if she just flat out said no, she wouldn't take another step. She didn't need to think long. She knew the answer. He was so determined to catch Clark before the General reached Kaskaskia, he'd probably pat her on the head, wish her luck and lope off down the hillside—heading west, alone.

By rolling her head to one side, she could see down the hill and through a scattered stand of trees where the forest had thinned somewhat. Movement caught her attention. There was a huge brown bear methodically stripping purple raspberries from the bushes. Her mouth watered at the thought. The bear swung its heavy head toward them from time to time, watching. Aware. Don't worry, she told the bear silently, you have nothing to be alarmed about. We don't have the time. All they'd eaten since the fish was an occasional handful of sweetened cornmeal from the bag Trey carried. Without a backward glance, the bear ambled away.

"Verity!" She heard the voice as if the wind bore it on a faint breeze. Surely it had nothing to do with her. She was overwhelmed with weariness. He couldn't. He wouldn't ask for another hour of travel. "Verity! Come look!" And his hand was on her shoulder.

Swallowing a low moan she turned.

"Come up here. I want you to see this." And his face had the look of one gazing upon creation for the first time.

Carefully she rolled to her stomach and inched her way forward. Could it be they had reached the Kaskaskia River at last?

The horizon to the east had lightened perceptively and the sky in the west was no longer dark but a delicate pearl gray.

However, Trey pointed to the valley, not the fading stars. It was a river all right, but not the Kaskaskia. It was a river of grass.

In spite of her exhaustion, Verity's eyes widened at the vision of miles upon endless mile of trackless, treeless, green, head-high grass.

"What is it?" she croaked hoarsely, unable to tear her eyes from the sight.

"It's the beginning of the prairie." He said it simply and with awe, as a man might say: This is the face of God. And Verity could understand. She'd never imagined anything like it. The enormity of this billowing ocean of grass boggled the mind. She felt stunned.

"But Trey," her next thought was, as always, practical. "How do we get across?"

He lowered the brim of his hat and shot her a quick look. "We'll have to do it by day. We'd be hopelessly lost in the dark."

Daylight. She looked again at the vast sea of swaying grasses, remembered the boiling cauldron of the August sky, and knew what it would be like during the heat of the day. Her throat went dry at the thought. This was the paradise Joe and Edward spoke of? This was the Illinois Country? There must be some mistake.

"Where is the ground that will grow dead sticks? And the rivers of sweet water? Edward must have been terribly disappointed," she said, gazing in horror around her. Edward was the farmer, he was the one interested in the land promised for service rendered. Joe wanted only to hunt and track in the freedom of unsettled country. "Poor Edward," she murmured.

Trey bent to pick up a handful of black loam. "Here it is. Rich enough to grow anything 'poor Edward' wants. Rich enough that good men risk their lives to own a piece of it."

Verity was defeated by the enormity of the plain, by the task ahead of them, by her own exhaustion.

"Do we have to go across? Isn't there a way around?"

"Not that anyone knows about."

He lay a moment longer contemplating the ordeal before them and wishing with every breath that Verity was safe back on Corn Island. But that was futile. She hadn't been safe on the Island, after all. As miserable as the day was going to be, she was better off with him. He would find the way through. He had to. Homer had heard yarns, telling of a path, if it could be found. He'd just have to trust his luck to hold a little while longer. Until he could fulfill his obligation to Clark at Kaskaskia and they had taken the fort. Fort Gage they called it.

Inching backward, they made their way a hundred yards down the hill to a tiny clearing.

Trey picked up Verity's hand and turned it over, smoothing the scratches and calluses, running his thumb over her cracked nails. There was no easy way out of this one.

"We have a bad day ahead of us, love."

The image of endless grass as high as their heads, maybe higher, was still clear in her mind. As far as the eye could see, stretching to the edges of the sky on both sides the grass stood, silent and mocking. They could never find their way across it. There was no end. Surely they would roam in circles until they died of thirst. But there was no way around and they couldn't go back. What choice was there? None.

She lifted his hand, heavy and tanned to leathery brownness, to her lips. Her mouth moved on his knuckles, and her eyes found his and held. "Do we have time to rest before we start?"

Pride blazed in his eyes and he hauled her roughly against him. For a full minute he couldn't speak around the lump in his throat. She was so brave. Braver than he himself, because he relied on his instincts and intellect and a certain amount of luck thrown in. Over the years, he'd learned to trust these qualities. All Verity had was her faith in him.

He took a long steadying breath. "We'll sleep for a couple of hours, fill up with water, and tackle the grass then." He pressed a kiss against her temple. "We'll make it. Homer says there's a path somewhere and if there is, I'll find it. I promise. We'll make it."

She nodded and tucked her head into the hollow of his shoulder. "I know. But could I just go to sleep now?"

He glanced around the clearing and pointed to a newly fallen tree limb as wide as the breadth of his shoulders. "Behind that. The bushes will cover us."

Verity did as he said and watched with heavy lids while he tidied the clearing where they'd sat, brushing away all signs of their presence. He joined her then, pulling the brush over them. "I need to be fresh when we go into the grass. So we both sleep." He lay down beside her, pulled her close to his own body, placing her between the log and himself and arranged the hanging fronds of a sprawling bush over them both. Looking through the branches, Verity thought briefly that the willowy wands seemed to be feather-stitched to the sky—and that was all. She was asleep before Trey stopped moving.

She awakened to a soft hiss in her ear and the full weight of Trey's body on hers. She was on her stomach with her face all but buried in a bed of fragrant moss, and Trey's weight bore down full on her back. One arm wound around her neck, uncomfortably so, and seemed to be covering her mouth. The other was stretched atop her own. Lord a'mighty, the man was heavy. And tense as whang leather.

And then, in a heartbeat, she knew why he was so heavy and tense. Bear grease. She smelled bear grease so strong her stomach roiled. Her eyes flew open and the rest of her body suddenly went as tense as Trey's.

Not six feet ahead of her she could see a slim wedge of the clearing dappled with shade and early sun. Trotting through that tiny segment of her vision was a file of Indians, traveling at a ground-eating pace, each moccasin placed in the footprint of the one in front. Their bare muscled legs padded by, noiselessly, on the needled forest floor.

She didn't want to look, wanted to close her eyes, but couldn't. Half their skulls were shaved and the hair on the other half stood straight and stiff with an eagle feather dangling loosely. They wore paint: white with black bars across the upper face. Ocher and red below the nose. They were stripped to the necessities of moccasins, tomahawk and knife at the belt of their breechclouts.

Her chest tightened like wet rawhide. Indians! Oh dear God, Indians!

She felt Trey's breath warm on her neck and the hand covering her own began to move slightly. His thumb made steady circles over the back of her fingers. She knew he was trying to calm her, to keep her quiet, but her heart seemed to be banging like a poker against an anvil and her breath clotted in her throat until she thought she'd strangle right there on a bed of leaves, in this God-forsaken forest. Trey's body seemed to tighten around hers almost imperceptibly. It was as if he was gathering her in and infusing her with some of his own wellspring of strength. Without a sound and only a suggestion of movement, Verity felt Trey speaking to her.

Gradually, she fought her way back from panic. She forced herself to breathe deeply to slow the beat of her heart and willed her eyes to close, afraid that somehow the intensity of her own eyes would draw the Indian's attention. She breathed easier, but could still hear the sinister whisper of their passing. It seemed to go on forever.

At long last, Trey moved. They were gone. "A war party," he said, softly. "I counted just over fifty. Heading east. Away from us. But we're moving on. There could be more."

Verity nodded. The need for sleep was forgotten in the more pressing need to put distance between themselves and the Indians.

"I'm ready," she said. "You go first."

He gave her a quick hug. "I'll bet you were a tough little girl."

She nodded, gravely. "Edward always said so."

He turned away before she saw the way his face hardened. Edward. It was always Edward says this, and Edward did that. He was going to have to do something about Edward when they reached Kaskaskia. First, however, he had to get them both across this stretch of prairie and find Clark.

He strode across the clearing to gather a length of grapevine hanging loose from a tall maple. With his knife he cut off a considerable length and handed one end to her. The other end he wrapped around his own waist.

"Tie yourself to me," he said. "That way we won't get lost from each other, at least." And he was off up the hill, then down the other side, and within minutes they plunged into the grass.

Verity's first sensation was that she would surely suffocate. Between the dense grass and the sun climbing overhead, there was little air and what there was so stifling hot and thick she could hardly get it into her lungs. Her hair stuck to her neck and sweat made little rivulets down her back. Even though the grapevine was secure around her waist, she clung to the tether with both hands. The grass parted at a touch, but closed instantly behind them with no indication they had passed. The grass had swallowed Trey, but as long as she felt the pull at the other end of the grapevine she knew he was still there.

For hours they wandered—aimlessly, it seemed to Verity. They cast first one direction and then another like two leaves flitting before the wind. The sun seemed stuck in the sky, glaring down, robbing her of energy, coherent thought, even spit. Occasionally they stopped, drank sparingly of their water supply and started off again in the throbbing heat. From time to time she thought she could hear Trey muttering, but it ceased to be important. She was being dragged along, like a piece of flotsam on the river and, indeed, after a while she began to think of the grass as the river itself. It swelled and billowed occasionally like a wave as a breeze rippled across the top, making Verity moan in frustration and long to be three-feet taller so that she could feel it. Even warm air, moving, was better that no air at all.

The sun had begun its downward slide when she suddenly slammed into Trey's back. He twisted and caught her in his arms.

"It's here." His voice sounded like it came to her across the graveled bed of a stream. His hair was plastered to his skull, sweat poured down his body and heat came off him in waves as thick as the grass itself, but there was a triumphant gleam in his eyes.

She strained around him. "Let me see." A path wide enough for a man carrying an ax, broadside, lay before them. Well defined. Trampled.

Trey's lips cracked in a grim smile. "God bless old Homer after all. I'll have to apologize. That's not what I was saying about him an hour ago."

Verity felt slightly dazed. With a path truly in front of them, the heat no longer felt as if it were slamming her into the ground. She walked up and down the odd tunnel through the midst of this eternity of grass and finally began to smile, too.

"It's like the Red Sea in the Bible. Are you sure your name isn't Moses?" She spun in a lazy circle.

"Clark has already passed," Trey said, looking closely at the ground.

Not even the threat of having to hurry could dim Verity's joy at being out of the thick grass. The sharp spears no longer slapped her in the face and tangled at her legs. She could, once again, see Trey. Her new-found energy flagged quickly, however, and it wasn't long until she no longer had the energy to run on her own, but allowed herself to be towed along. The world was reduced to the appearance and disappearance of Trey's heels in front of her. Her side vision blurred as the tall grass seemed to pour along the tunnel. Trey's heels were dependable, one after the other as they ran through the grass. She simply picked up her feet and put them down, and let her mind float free to a place where there was gently flowing clean water and tables laden with food and shade trees scattered in abandon.

It was almost full dark when they broke out of the grass at the top of a steep bluff. Below them was a broad river, flowing south in a wide curve, quiet in the twilight.

"We're almost there. See," he pointed. "That must be Kaskaskia. And there's Fort Gage."

On the far bank a town was clearly visible. The spire of a church, houses, even a few streets. Lanterns were being lighted in homes and barns.

Trying to control the trembling in her legs, Verity felt tears flood her eyes. They had done it. Over there was Kaskaskia, and Joe. Well, yes, and even Edward. She would face that situation when she got to it, not before.

She turned her face into Trey's shirt and clung to him with what strength she had left. She no longer knew if she stood alone or if he held her up. Slowly he turned her in his arms and lowered his head to hers. His lips brushed hers with a feathery touch that made her turn her mouth to follow his.

"This isn't the time, love, but—"

How often have she heard that they hadn't time for this or that? Too many times. And all because of George Rogers Clark.

"Trey Owens," she said, burrowing deeper into his neck. "I don't want to hear about your duties. We've just done the impossible and I want a hug, or a 'well done.' 'Thank God,' will do just fine."

She felt the chuckle begin in his chest and spread, and his arms tightened around her. "Ever since I first met you, dragging that stupid goat up a hillside, I've never known what to expect. You'll have your 'well dones,' love. You deserve them."

This time when his mouth came down on hers it was no light, tentative touching. He kissed her hard and deep and searching, and lifted his head to give her a lazy, wanting look that seemed to suck the breath right from her lungs.

"As I started to say…before we go down there, I want it understood that you are mine. Nobody's going to claim a prior right, nobody's going to start yelling about broken promises. Nobody's going to change their mind. I guess I'll have to talk to this Edward fellow and get a few things straight, but as long as we've got it right between you and me, nobody else has any say-so. Is that agreed?"

What was he talking about? They were married, weren't they? They had said their vows to each other. Who could possibly have any say-so, now? Unless—Was he planning to go off and leave her with Joe, so soon? Would he get the priest, first, as he'd promised?

"I guess we need to talk about what this 'belonging' means," she began, but a dog started barking somewhere and a breeze coming down the river brought the faint sound of metal clanking against metal, and he raised his head. He was still speaking, but his attention had shifted.

"It means love, that I have a right—"

"Trey Owens! That cain't be you!" The hoarse whisper had Trey swinging around, his hand on his knife.

A huge man in ragged buckskins came bounding out of the forest and across the uneven ground to wrap his arms around Trey and pound him ferociously on the back. "Dang near shot a hole in your ugly gizzard, but decided to ask questions, first. What in hell are you doing here? Clark thinks you're taking care of the folks back on Corn Island. Never mind, you can tell him. We're camped at the bottom of the bluff, not a mile away."

Trey looked helplessly at Verity.

The man loped off down the side of the bluff in a loose-legged gait. "Come on," he called softly over his shoulder. "And bring your recruit, but don't make no noise. We're intending to surprise the folks across the water in the morning." He laughed. "Clark, he's going to be some shocked to see you. I hope you carry good news."

Twenty-two

They passed a small farm house, a half-mile to the north, bordered on two sides by cornfields and in front by a sprawling garden. The soldier, Wes, spat a brown stream of tobacco out of the corner of his mouth and said, "That corn's at least ten feet high now, maybe twelve. Dang ground out here would grow dead sticks was you to plant 'em."

Verity was too tired to care about the fertility of the ground, the farm or even the fast-falling twilight. Her legs would barely hold her up and her mind had gone into some nether region that did not require thought. She barely knew what she was looking at. Her focus was entirely on Clark's camp. All she had to do was keep her feet moving just a little farther, and she could lie down and sleep. She could feel her head rolling sloppily on her shoulders with each jarring step she took, but didn't care. Clark's camp. Clark's camp. It became the rhythm that drove her legs. One more effort. And then another.

They met Clark and two other men at the top of the bluff. He greeted Trey with a grunt of surprise and then an angry demand to know what he was doing this far west.

"Benjamin Franklin, huh?" he said finally, when Trey had finished talking. A broad relaxing of his face eased the lines of weariness, giving him a boyish, handsome look. A smile followed. "Good old Ben. Convinced the French after all. He and George Washington are the two most able men we have. We're lucky to have them."

"Yes, sir. The courier said the same thing. He nearly killed himself getting the news to us, hoping to catch you before you left Corn Island."

Clark laid a heavy hand on Trey's shoulder and glanced at Verity swaying on her feet. "From the looks of things the two of you almost did the same thing. And you have my undying gratitude. This knowledge will make all the difference in the world tomorrow morning. Might save dozens of lives."

For the second time in an hour Trey slanted his eyes uneasily at Verity. He cleared his throat. "Sir, this isn't a recruit. It's—"

Clark interrupted. "Right now I'm on my way to see that farmer up there." He nodded toward the cabin only vaguely visible in the near-dark. "Want to borrow some boats to get across the river. Come along, you can tell me more on the way." And he strode off assuming, rightly, that they would follow.

Not listening, not thinking, Verity went, willing her legs to keep moving. It didn't matter that Clark thought she was a man. She had on Joe's clothes, her hair was stuffed under his hat and, she thought in a dim recess of her mind, Clark would discover his mistake soon enough. When it would be too late. He no longer had the power to stop her. She was already where she wanted to be. Well, near enough. The fort was right across the Kaskaskia River. If she stayed within touching distance of Trey she could make it. First the cabin and then down the bluff to Clark's camp. Clark's camp. Once more her feet moved to the cadence of Clark's camp.

As they picked their way through a garden of pumpkins, melons, and pole beans to the log house, a loud squawk erupted from the trees.

"Damn guineas," Trey muttered, as the entire group of soldiers stopped. "But they make good watchdogs." A candle flickered in the window.

Clark boldly stepped up, doubled his fist and pounded on the door.

"Who is it?" a voice asked in French.

"Open up," Clark called. "Open the door."

The door swung outward revealing a small dark man in a long nightshirt holding a candle high. "Who is it?" he asked again.

"You have a couple of dories and a cattle barge down on the river. I need to borrow them in the morning." Clark's red hair was wild in the candlelight and his arms waved as he talked. Added to that was his ferocious pounding on the door, and the farmer was frightened to the core.

"Sacre bleu!" he whispered, his eyes wide, seeing for the first time that his clearing was filled with armed men.

"I said—" Clark began, shouting now as if the man was hard of hearing, and then shut his mouth as the candle began to tremble in the farmer's hand. "He doesn't understand English. Now what?"

"Uh," Trey swung around to Verity and drew her forward. "Sir. You remember Miss Philp? She speaks French. Maybe she would help us. Verity?"

Clark's face sagged. The words registered. Miss Philp. Verity could almost hear his thoughts. That woman! He turned red. "Owens!" he thundered.

Beside Verity, Trey stiffened. "Sir, I would never have made it at all if it hadn't been for her. I'll explain later, but right now, if she's up to it, she can translate for us."

Clark struggled with his anger as the red mounted in his cheeks and then faded to dead white. He turned away to gain control. His voice sounded as if there was a cord knotted around his throat. "Very well. Ask her."

Trey bent his head to Verity's and turned her to face him, his hands gentle on her upper arms. "Verity, love. Can you do this? We need to know if we can borrow this man's boats to transport the army across the river in the morning. Can you tell him that?"

She pulled herself back from the shadow of oblivion that beckoned so invitingly. Trey wanted her to talk to this man. She would try.

"Good evening, sir," she began in impeccable French, trying to stand taller, be respectful. The little man was pitifully afraid. "We are Americans. Friends. We ask if it would be possible—"

"Americans! Americans!" The candle quaked and dripped tallow. He turned and shouted into the room, "They will cut our throats. Quick! Hide the children!"

"No. No. You don't understand. We won't hurt you."

But the man was terrified. He pleaded, "Spare my wife, my babies. Please. I'll go with you, only don't murder them."

Verity turned weary eyes on Clark. "He thinks we are here to murder his family. Cut their throats. He's too frightened to hear me."

"Tell him we are friends! Tell him we want to free them!"

She faced the man again and tried to hold her head straight on her neck. Her arms hung heavy at her sides. She drew a shaky breath. "You are safe. We're here to free you. We only need your boats in the morning."

His head nodded rapidly. "Yes, take what you want, but spare my family."

"Thank you. General Clark thanks you and the American army thanks you. You are safe."

But the farmer slammed the door and drove home the bolt even as she spoke. She leaned against Trey. She heard Clark's outraged mutter, "Rocheblave's scared them half to death, the damn turncoat." She wondered vaguely for a brief moment who Rocheblave was, and then she crumpled in a heap at Trey's feet.

She was dimly aware of being carried down the bluff, safe in Trey's arms. Once she felt an abrupt, almost painful, tightening of his arms and the rumble in his chest as he spoke harshly. "I said I can handle her."

At last she sank into a pile of soft furs, somehow knew that she was in Clark's tent and that Trey was nearby, and slept. Conversation went on all night. At intervals, when the voices rose in disagreement, she aroused and drifted off again once her eyes found Trey's form seated by the fire. Snatches of what was said made sense, most did not.

"I'm not a violent man. I'll take the town as mercifully as I can. Surely you know that."

"I do." Trey's voice. "But Hamilton has promised Rocheblave that when England wins this war he will be richly rewarded. It might not be easy to take the fort."

Clark was supremely confident. "Surprise is in our favor. I think we can get the whole army over in two trips. And if the Frenchie's reaction tonight was any indication at all, we know the townsfolk haven't been forewarned. That man was surprised as hell to find Americans on his doorstep!"

"Surprise is a powerful weapon, I agree, but Rocheblave's done his work well. If the entire town is half as afraid of us as the farmer, they'll either throw down their arms without a murmur, or they'll fight to the bloody death."

"I'm banking on them throwing down their arms when they discover France is on our side." Clark eased his head back and yawned, hugely. "It's nearly morning. We'll know soon. Are you hungry?"

The night sky was still black, without a hint of dawn, when Trey roused Verity. He led her to one of the dories, put her in a protected corner and gave her the breast of a roasted prairie hen to eat.

She made a valiant effort, but Trey could tell she was still exhausted. There were purple shadows under her eyes and her skin was stretched so tightly over her face he could see the bone structure starkly outlined. A pang of guilt shot through his gut. He should have taken it easier on her, not gone through the grass all in one day. But he hadn't dared slow the pace. They'd only caught Clark in the bare nick of time as it was.

He watched her tear hungrily at the chicken. God, he hadn't fed her enough to keep a titmouse going and yet he'd dragged her through thickets and across swamps and up hillsides as if she were as strong as he was. He was an utter lout. An ignorant imbecile and not fit to ask any woman to trust her life to him, much less ask her brother's blessing. And yet, he intended to do just that as soon as this day was over.

She'd never complained once. She'd done everything he asked of her and more. Such a lot of courage and control packed into a tiny body. He'd known from the first she had a lot of grit. Dragging that goat along a mountain ridge in the rain, managing to throw him a rope in the river, cooking, caring for Zelma and the children, dealing with the Dawsons day after day—and he still didn't know the whole story about Bart, that was yet to come. And he promised himself, again, it *would* come.

She had never broken. Not even yesterday, or was it the day before? Time seemed to be smearing together. The minutes when they lay and watched scores of Indians, her most feared and hated enemy, trot past, not six feet away, had seemed like hours. He could feel her trembling beneath his arm as she struggled to control her ragged breathing, but she hadn't moved a muscle. The lady had guts.

Was this why he was so drawn to her? Last night, when one of Clark's men offered to help carry her down the bluff, he'd gotten almost violent in his refusal. She was his. Now and for always. And, before God, he vowed he'd do his best to care for her and protect her. Never again would she be put through an experience like they'd just shared. First, however, they had to get through today.

"It won't take long to get across the river," he said finally, kneeling in front of her. "You're going to stay with me. Remember that. Don't go off anywhere on your own. I'll be with Clark and you'll be right behind me. Do you understand?"

Verity nodded as she chewed. She couldn't remember anything, ever, tasting quite as good as this half-charred, half-raw prairie hen. "Did you get any rest?"

"I'll rest later. I want to make sure you'll be safe today. We don't know what to expect. So just stay with me." His eyes were bright, intense. "Promise?"

"I promise." Promising was easy. She had no intention of letting him get away from her.

He sank back on his heels and his eyes softened. She deserved to know his future plans, but there was no privacy, no time, now. "All this will be over soon. Then we'll talk." He stood and moved to the other side of the dory to join the group around Clark.

Everything was quiet. The river was as still as the mill pond back in Albemarle County. The men rowed with muffled oars and spoke in the softest of whispers.

The plan was simple. One group was to encircle the town. A detail of sixty men would be ready to storm the streets. Clark himself, with twelve men and Trey and Verity, would invade Fort Gage itself and demand Rocheblave's surrender. When Rocheblave had given up control, Trey would flash a torch from the stockade. As soon as the torch was lighted every man would fire his gun into the air and begin to yell as if a pack of demons chased him.

"Run through the streets, bang on doors, fire your guns at the sky," Clark whispered. "Make as much noise as you can, in any way you can. Make them think we have an army of thousands. Then meet me back at the fort."

Verity dropped the chicken bones into the water and rinsed her hands. He's read his Bible, she thought. Clark's plan was the same as Joshua's taking of Jericho. The man was a genius.

On shore, the three divisions went their separate ways in silence, grim shadows in the night. Verity crept behind Trey toward the stockade. Unbelievably, there were no sentries. Rocheblave must feel very secure, she thought. The gate creaked as they swung it open only wide enough to allow them single-file entrance. They paused listening. Nothing. They moved on.

Unlighted barracks stood just inside the gate, their outlines low against the faintly lighter sky. A two-storied fort, squarely solid, loomed above them. A lantern glittered in one window.

Verity crouched so close to Trey's back that she felt his quick intake of breath as a sentry ambled through the shaft of lantern light. Clark motioned and three men leaped forward. The sentry went down with a startled squawk. He was gagged and bound in seconds.

"Now," Clark whispered. "Now!"

They had almost reached the fort when a dozen British troopers appeared in the door. Before a man could raise a gun they were overwhelmed, gagged and bound. With Clark in the lead, the men swarmed up the ladder to the upper floor, Verity at their heels. A lantern sat flickering in the middle of the hall floor. Clark snatched it aloft and motioned a soldier to ram a closed door with the butt of his rifle. The door crashed open and bounced off the wall. A buckskin shoulder held it for Clark to enter.

Philip de Rocheblave sat bolt upright in bed, startled out of sleep. His uniform was folded neatly on the back of a chair and his wig rested on its stand on the seat.

Clark strode into the room. "Wake up, you miserable turncoat. You are my prisoner."

Rocheblave's eyes strained wide in shock. "Who are you? What…How dare you?" His accent was thick, his English barely understandable.

Clark's shoulders went back. "My name is General George Rogers Clark," he said proudly. "I act for Governor Patrick Henry in claiming this post for the United States of America. Fort Gage is no longer British, sir."

Rocheblave reached for his wig. "I don't believe…" The little man spluttered, trying to bluff his way out of capture. "Can't possibly… Sentries," he bellowed.

"You can believe it all right," Clark laughed. "And I'll give you just enough time to get into your pants before we haul you off in chains."

Clark nodded at Trey. "The torches, man."

Trey turned for the door, Verity right behind him. Together they set torches on all four corners of the square stockade. A volley of gunfire thundered over the fort and the sound rolled on to the river. Before the echo died away there came a roar of victory from one hundred and seventy-five throats, filling the night with terrorizing sound.

Within seconds the streets of Kaskaskia were filled with people frightened from their beds, eyeballs rolling, screaming questions in French. The group of soldiers who had encircled the town ran through the alleys on their way to the fort. Those who had stormed the streets, returned now, double time, toward the fort. They all, to a man, continued to yell and fire their guns as they ran. The people of Kaskaskia were defeated before they even knew there was a battle.

By the time the sun cleared the treetops, the confusion began to lessen. As Verity watched wearily from an upstairs window at the fort, people became less hysterical. The British flag had been hauled down from Rocheblave's staff, but nobody had been killed, no houses burned and while soldiers patrolled the streets, they paid no mind to the Kaskaskians.

A Catholic priest was in an adjoining room with Clark. Trey had settled Verity in this corner window and told her to rest, that he would be finished soon. Then he joined Clark and the priest. She could hear their conversation through the open door. Father Gibault spoke halting English, but Clark did not need her to interpret.

Verity slumped in her corner feeling boneless and unutterably weary. She wondered if there was a bed left in the whole world. Actually she didn't need a bed, a quiet corner would be good enough and about twelve hours of peace in which to sleep. The place Trey had left her was anything but quiet. A great hue and cry of frightened villagers came in through the window along with a fog of raised dust from the dry common below, and Father Gibault's thickly accented voice cut through the heat of the day from the open bedroom door.

"Our fate is in your hands and my people are frightened. Are we permitted to go to our church and pray?"

Clark's voice was cold. "I have no objections to praying in church."

"Thank you, sir. May I ask—are we to be sent away? Or punished in some way? I plead for the lives of our women and children."

"Father Gibault, Americans are not barbarians. You will not be sent away."

"We know there is a war between the English and the Americans. But, I beg you to believe that we have not considered the Americans as our enemies. The war has never touched us, this far west."

Clark's voice tightened. Verity let her head drop forward on her drawn-up knees. Father Gibault was in for it now.

"You've considered it enough to think we are a pack of thieves. You expected us to cut your throats, mistreat your women and children and exile your men! You've believed everything Rocheblave told you. And, Father Gibault, you are victims after all. Victims of the British. You and everyone else here, are French are you not?"

"French or French Canadian," the priest agreed.

"Then you need to know that France has declared itself an ally of America. France is contributing money, supplies and soldiers to our Revolution."

There was silence. The priest was apparently speechless, wondering if Clark was making up the tale so the town would give up peaceably.

"It's true," Clark went on. "I received word only last night by special courier. And you can also believe that not one American will interfere with your religion, or your lives. We consider ourselves your liberators. Not your conquerors."

"Well." The priest's voice was subdued, surprised. "I know not what to say."

"For your information, I have sent a party of men to that French and Indian trading post north of here, what is it called? Cahokia. I've sent men to take the post and occupy it. On faith I will report to my commander, Governor Henry, that both positions are secure and as far as I know, were taken without bloodshed. Rocheblave and those of the British garrison will be taken back to Virginia."

Verity could hear Clark's footfalls as he paced the tiny room. "And that, Father Gibault, is all you Kaskaskians need to know, at the moment. I hope, sir, to be your friend in the future."

The priest's tread on the ladder was soft as he left and in a few minutes Verity raised her head to see him hurrying across the common toward the church. No doubt to share the good news with the townsfolk. A small gathering was forming as they waited.

Beyond the church spire were more log homes, shaded by tall, spreading trees. Beyond that a section of ground had been put into crops and on farther lay a scattering of brightly colored teepees. She was too tired to even raise an eyebrow. Indians? Here? Part of Kaskaskia's community? While she watched, a figure carrying a gun emerged from the trees and loped toward town. The gait was somehow familiar. The running figure disappeared in a gully and reappeared, closer now, the gun carried loosely at the end of his arm.

Verity sat up, her eyes riveted on the running man. The long loose rolling stride, the shape of his head, light brown hair tied back with a thong, a jutting nose. That nose. She got to her feet as the man went behind one of the houses and came out the other side.

It was Joe. It was him! She'd found Joe. She forgot her tiredness, her promise to stay close to Trey. Her brother was here, within shouting distance.

She skimmed down the ladder and out the door. The common looked bigger from the ground and was crowded with people. She pushed her way through, heedless of shocked glances at a woman with her hair streaming down her back, wearing men's trousers. She reached the street and for a second thought she'd lost him, but no, there he was stopping for a second to speak to a man in a wide-brimmed hat.

"Joe! Joe!"

He turned with a look of startled disbelief. "Verity?" He took one hesitant step toward her. "Verity?"

And then she was in his arms, crying and hugging him and patting his face. "Oh Joe. I was afraid I'd never find you. But you're here. You're here. And I've come such a long way."

The man in the hat was speaking French, "She is not one of us. She must have come with the Long Knives."

Joe held her off a minute. "Did you? Did you come with Clark?"

And when she nodded, he frowned. "Clark would never let a woman travel with his men. How did you manage it?"

Suddenly she was tired again. Falling down, thought-crushing weary. Her journey was over. She felt as if she could sleep for a month. Her bones ached in places too deep for feeling. "Oh Joe," she said, wilting before him. "It's a long story. Can we go somewhere to talk?"

"Well sure." He hesitated and glanced toward the fort. "I'll catch Clark later. I have some news for you, too."

As they walked through the village, Verity talked, telling Joe in half-sentences about Otis and Lena and Old Man Hargraves, and her reason for not waiting for Joe to send for her as they'd planned. She had to stop talking while Joe swore briefly and assured her she'd done the right thing, and she went on. She told of meeting Trey, hooking up with the Dawsons, being captured by the Indians. Even Bart. Especially Bart. And had to wait once more for Joe to swear in anger.

They went on through a cleared meadow and a sparse stand of trees, and still Verity talked, assuring Joe that Bart was far away, on Corn Island with his brothers. She told him about the Ohio, about Trey again, about the prairie, all about her journey from Corn Island except the stolen time at the spring with Trey. She left out those golden, precious moments. She talked until Joe stopped before a tall, broad-based teepee.

She looked up at him questioningly, but his eyes were on the flap that quivered and then swung back. A lovely young Indian woman stepped out, smiled quickly and ran into Joe's arms.

Verity didn't know where to look. She couldn't tear her eyes away. There was vermilion painted neatly in the part of the girl's hair. The fringes on the sleeves of her soft doeskin dress swung with every movement. There was the illusive sound of tiny bells, somewhere, and the clean, fresh smell of a wind-swept mountain.

There seemed to be a hole in Verity's chest. A hole that was so deep and wide she was falling into it. No. It wasn't—this couldn't be what she thought. It wasn't possible.

The Indian woman was very young. There was no way Verity could miss that, even as briefly as she'd seen the girl's face. Nor could she ignore the naked look of love in the girl's eyes when she saw Joe.

And neither could Joe hide the adoration in his face as he proudly turned the Indian girl in his arms and said, "Verity, meet my wife, Greets-The-Dawn."

Twenty-three

"I want four men. Give me four men." Trey's voice was flat with purpose as he strode unannounced into General Clark's room.

A Kaskaskian stood by the window, a hunter from the looks of him, longish brown hair, weather-toughened skin and a long rifle held loosely in his hand. A hunter, maybe, but he had on new buckskins and had taken time to clean up before he paid his respects to Clark. His hair was still wet from a dip in the river. They seemed to be deep in conversation, but Trey didn't apologize for interrupting.

"She's gone," he snapped, as if it were all Clark's fault. "Didn't stay where I left her and now she's off God knows where and I want four men before it gets too dark to see."

Clark held up the palm of a hand. "Hang on. In the first place, I can't spare four men and in the second, if you are speaking of Miss Philp, she isn't lost."

Trey's eyes narrowed. "Then I'll take three. And, by God, I'll have them one way or another. That girl went through hell with me to get here with your message and she deserves more than—"

Clark dipped his chin, his hand still in the air. "I said, she's not lost." He nodded toward the hunter. "He found her and came looking for you."

Trey turned the full intensity of his eyes on the other man. He took in the strong jaw, the breadth of shoulder and the clear gaze looking him over with hard speculation. Trey gathered himself. They were fairly evenly matched.

"You're Edward I take it, and if you found her she must be all right. I'll trouble you to take me to her now, and then I want some time with you. I have something to say."

Cold, gray eyes stared at Trey before the mouth stretched in a half-smile that only got as far as his teeth. For one surprised second Trey had the feeling they'd met before. There was something about the way his mouth turned up at the corners—

The man said, "You're right, we do need to talk." With a nod at Clark he turned and headed out the door. Trey followed hard on his heels.

They went across the common, matching long strides. At the edge of a corn field the other man stopped, the brim of his hat shading his eyes from the full blast of the setting sun.

"Your name is Trey what?"

Trey hesitated and pointedly did not put out his hand. Warily he took the man's measure. He figured he had him on height and maybe in muscle, but he lost a slight edge on weight. "Fair enough," he said. "I know yours. I'm Trey Owens. Where is she? Is she all right?"

"She's not injured if that's what you mean, but she's far from fine." The man planted his feet and braced himself. "She's been run to death and half-starved and her will's broken." With a thumb he tipped his hat back on his head. His eyes hardened. "And if you're the man responsible, I intend to have your head on a stick before breakfast."

Watching the way the man's chin lifted with resolve, there wasn't a doubt in Trey's mind that he meant what he said. That chin. Trey's eyes slid out of focus somewhere over the stranger's buckskin shoulder. Verity's image sprang to his mind.

Verity standing before him on the tilting deck of the flatboat, wind and rain slashing at them as she calmly told him she might just as well have left him to drown. Verity in the forest, her sleeve hanging in a torn hank down her arm as she stubbornly refused to tell him who or what she was running from. Verity, ankle deep in the creek, wearing only her brother's hat, with her small chin lifted in defiance. Verity.

The man waited, his eyes boring into Trey's. Their eyes clashed and held.

They spoke at the same time.

"You're not Edward. You're—"

"I'm her brother and you'd damn well better have a good explanation for the state she's in."

"What state? She's run half to death, you're right, and Clark can tell you why. And because she disappeared from where I left her, I've spent the last half of this day hunting for her so I *can* feed her. But there's nothing wrong with her will. What are you talking about?"

If this man was her brother, he must be Joe. The one who'd tossed her into the creek and taught her to swim, and practiced with her day after day until she could handle a gun. Trey watched the struggle in his eyes and saw the moment his concern for Verity overcame the anger at the one who had pushed her so hard. Joe turned abruptly and headed into the corn.

"My wife's with her while I hunted you down," he called, not bothering to turn. "Maybe you can get through, she won't respond to me. Just lays there in a knot with her eyes closed. Over here. It's not far."

"Are you telling me she's sick?"

"Not sick. Just—gone. In a way I don't like."

"Maybe she's asleep, man. She's exhausted. You told me that yourself." Trey trotted to keep up. Not that he needed any urging, he was half-frantic in his need to see Verity with his own eyes. Joe wasn't making sense.

"It's as if she's here but not here, all at the same time. She didn't even rouse when I picked her up and carried her inside. And yet, every so often she cries in her sleep like—like a babe." He shook his head. "It's not natural."

"Carried her? I left her resting, upstairs, at the fort while I cleared up a few things for Clark. I was in the next room. But, when I went for her, she was gone."

They came out of the corn and ran easily across a sparsely wooded area, past a few isolated teepees. "She spotted me from the window. I've been out for a week, hunting, and was just getting in. Coming to report to Clark, as a matter of fact, when she came running across the common. For a minute I thought I was seeing things."

Joe shook his head. "Couldn't figure out where she came from at first. And then, after she convinced me she was real, I took her home to Dawn. She talked all the way, chattering like a child let out of school, about the trip downriver, about Clark and getting captured by Indians and about—you. Trey. And then, all of a sudden, she just dried up, like the river sprung a leak. I introduced her to Dawn and she simply sat down on the ground and refused to get up. Wouldn't talk, wouldn't look at either of us, just stared into space. Here we are."

He stopped before a teepee made of buffalo skins so carefully cured they looked like white fabric. A teepee, Trey thought. A teepee?

"Dawn?" Joe called, and immediately the soft skin flap swung wide.

A young Indian woman stood there, her dress hung with brightly dyed quills and small beads. She shook her head at Joe and politely lowered her eyes as she stepped aside so that the men could enter.

In the soft interior glow Trey saw Verity curled on a pallet by the empty fire pit. She had been washed and her hair combed out, and she wore a long, loose doeskin garment with colorful beading stitched into the bodice and hem. The girl's work, he thought. The Indian had cared for her well. An ointment of some kind had been rubbed into the scratches on her legs, but her feet were bare, still swollen and bruised from the beating they'd taken on the trail and Trey silently cursed himself once more for the abuse he'd been forced to allow.

He crossed the space between them in two strides, laid down his gun and touched her forehead. Cool. She wasn't feverish. A hard lump settled in his gut and rode there like a bag of river rocks. Dawn, the Indian, stood well away from the men with her hands quietly at her sides.

"What's the matter with her?" he asked.

The girl's eyes darted to Joe and she took a step backward. She was shocked, as any Indian woman would be, at being addressed by a man other than family. And probably astonished as well, at having her opinion asked. But Trey didn't have time to be gentle.

"Damn it! Tell me about her. English? Do you speak English?"

Joe nodded. "Tell him."

Greets-The-Dawn stepped forward and with carefully averted eyes began to speak in accented, but understandable, English. "Spirit gone away. Too much unhappiness inside, so Spirit depart."

"Has she awakened at all?"

"Only cry word. Trey. What is mean?"

There was a glitch in Trey's breathing. His throat closed. He couldn't answer. He reached for Verity's hand and held it limp in his own. There were deep, purple circles under her eyes and the only thing that looked alive was the pulse beating in the hollow of her neck. His own heart pounded thickly in his throat. He was frightened. He couldn't ever recall being quite so scared. She seemed to be in a sort of trance. He felt a terrible need to do something.

Always, all his life, he'd been able to throw his back or his mind into a problem and the solution came about easily. But this was nothing a strong back or agile mind would respond to. She lay like the dead and yet her heart still beat.

Could the shock of finding Joe married to an Indian have done this? Lovely, gentle and patient soul that she seemed, Dawn was still an Indian and the shock would have been profound. However, there was always the possibility that the journey had been too much for her, after all. Maybe, he thought with horror, all this was his fault.

She looked miserably uncomfortable, coiled as she was into a rigid ball, so he put an arm under her shoulders and tried to straighten her body on the bed of skins, but she cried out as if in pain and her body tightened in resistance. One arm flailed in an aimless gesture and then she tucked the fist under her chin once more and drew up her knees. A small whimpering sound came from her throat. It seemed to slice at Trey's own wind making him breathless with the need to help and angry at his powerlessness to do so.

He longed for someone to tell him authoritatively to do this, or not to do that. That if he said thus-and-so all would be well. But no one spoke. The silence grew and expanded with each shallow breath Verity drew.

He looked around. His frantic gaze hit only the high points of the lodge, but even so it was probably the most well cared for teepee he'd ever seen, with graceful backrests, a colorful feather-and-shell-trimmed shield of war on the wall, woven baskets of dried fruit and nuts, and brushed skins lying everywhere.

However, and Trey grasped at the thought, maybe in Verity's unconscious state she knew she was surrounded by Indian trappings, in an Indian dwelling, among Indians. Maybe in some subterranean cavity, she was vividly, frighteningly, aware.

He leaned forward and gathered her in his arms, ignoring her faint protests.

Joe took a step forward, alarmed. "What are you doing? Where do you think you're going with her?"

Trey leveled a hard stare at him. "Outside. You, above all people, ought to know how she feels about Indians. Have you forgotten her fear—no, her absolute and irrational terror—of red people? And you ought to know why. I'm getting her out of here and into the open air where she can't smell the smoke and drying meat and see rising suns painted on the walls every time she opens her eyes." And without waiting for an answer he bent and passed through the doorway, still carrying Verity.

"But—," Behind him Joe sounded stricken. "My God, that was all so long ago. And Dawn isn't—They were Cherokee!"

Trey didn't pause. He walked out and kept going, heedless of direction or distance, until he came to a grassy clearing near a fast-moving stream. He stopped. For the first time he was aware that Dawn and Joe had followed, their arms laden with skins and a bladder of water and Trey's own gun. Without being told, Dawn placed a long, silky, furred skin at a place where the grass was the deepest and the branches of an old maple spread like a canopy over them.

She kept her eyes lowered and backed away. "I bring food. But first, while she yet sleeps, I tend her feet." She pulled a pair of low-cut, fringed moccasins from the pile of skins and opened one to show Trey. It was filled with goose-grease, thick and pungent.

"Keep on," were her final instructions as she fastened them around Verity's ankles. "Make well," and she was gone.

Joe didn't move. He stood leaning against a tree, a dark brooding filling his eyes. "You going to tell me why I should walk away and leave you here with her? Alone?"

Trey straightened. "Because I love her. Because we intend to have our marriage vows blessed by the priest the minute she's able." Then his shoulders sagged and his voice broke. "You can trust me because she does. God knows why."

Joe took a long moment to look into Trey's eyes and then lifted himself away from the tree. "You know where to find me if you need me. If not, I'll be back in the morning." And he, too, swung away up the hill toward his teepee and the town.

Trey sat down beside Verity and began his vigil. Until full dark he did little but sit and look at her with his heart thudding in his chest, afraid that if he took his eyes off her she would slip away between one breath and the next. When, hours later, he realized that he could no longer see her in the night, he roused himself and built a small fire well away from the furs where she slept. He desperately needed sleep himself, but closing his eyes was out of the question. All he could do was watch and wait, and he would damn well do that.

At intervals he propped her up on his shoulder and trickled water into her mouth, but most of it dribbled down her chin and onto her neck. At moonrise Dawn appeared with a cooking pot of stew, a smaller container of something darkly liquid and a handful of cattails. With a shy, wordless greeting she dipped one of the reeds into the bladder of water, with her own mouth drew some of the liquid up into the cavity and placed the other end between Verity's lips and carefully let the contents trickle into her mouth. She did this three times, stroking Verity's neck until she swallowed, then made sure Trey understood what she was doing and left saying only, "Much times," as she handed him the cattail.

And Trey did "much times" all night long, more grateful to the Indian girl than he could say. The first time he tried it, he discovered the liquid was not water, but some sort of weak medicinal tea. His only hesitation was that he wasn't nearly as good as Dawn with the cattails and, until he got the hang of it, Verity got her neck washed repeatedly in weak tea. She didn't seem to know the difference. She still slept, her cheeks wet with silent tears.

The tears bothered him more than he could let himself think. She made little sound, sometimes none at all, yet the tears didn't stop. He wanted to rip up a tree in frustration. What he did was hang his head between his arms and grind his teeth to keep from crying himself.

Eventually, he began talking to her in a low voice, telling her of his love, what they would do for the rest of their lives, how he would care for her. It didn't matter that Verity's spirit, as Dawn said, wandered in a far off place and she didn't hear him. He needed to tell her in apology, in the promise of his intentions, in explanation of the past. It was his need, not hers, and he knew it, that kept him talking.

Completely unnerved by the tears trickling down her face while she slept so deeply he stopped talking only when he was hoarse and too weary to go on. Verity slept, lost in some deep and swampy emotional muck that he couldn't fathom. He used the cattail again, absurdly pleased with his discovery that the farther back in her mouth he could get the thing, the more tea she swallowed.

At last he stretched out beside her with some vague idea of holding her close enough to absorb some of her hurt. If he gathered all the quivering mass of her misery into his arms maybe she would feel less alone in her ordeal. If she had someone to cling to, surely it would ease her agony. If he tucked her hot, tear-washed face into his neck and stroked her back it would have nothing to do with his own need to wrap himself around her soft body so that she could feel nothing but him. His motives, he told himself firmly, had nothing to do with the fact that she smelled like a meadow of fresh clover in the sunshine and he desperately wanted to bury his face in her hair. Or that he could no longer bear to watch her misery without holding her.

Yet, when he tried, he couldn't get her to unfold, so finally he simply pulled her back snug to his stomach, ignoring her tense, vise-like grip of knees to chin. He began to stroke gently from shoulder to waist to thigh to knee. Again and again his hand made the circuit, his mouth whispering into her hair.

"Let go, my sweetling. I'm here. Come on, love, let go. You made it in spite of all of us. You completed this unbelievable journey and it's all over now."

Still she was as rigid as his rifle barrel. Still she whimpered in her sleep, her face wet with tears. He wanted to shake her awake. He wanted to see that bull-buffalo-determination in her eyes.

"Fight, damn it," he whispered fiercely into her hair. "Fight!"

For hours, it seemed, his hand moved and his voice soothed. His arm went numb and still he kept stroking. Finally, he began to feel the tension lessen. Gradually, she relaxed in his arms. Her legs went limp; he straightened them out. Her arms were supple again and he turned her to wind them around his middle. Unashamedly his eyes filled with tears of thanksgiving. She would be all right in time. If he was patient. If he was patient.

Toward morning the tears stopped. With a small sigh she curled against him in a natural pose and her breathing deepened. It was a restful sleep, at last. Trey relaxed, too, and breathed a prayer of gratitude that her healthy body was, at last, beginning to heal itself.

Gradually, as the tension flowed down his arms and seemed to drip from the ends of his fingers, his mind slipped into a dreaming sea of drifting and undulating awareness. He hadn't slept in two days and the edges of his thoughts were blurring. He tried not to think of the sleek length of her legs as he remembered them streaming water when she'd risen from the creek that glorious morning on the river. Now was not the time for such meanderings, but it was hard to get rid of the picture in his head. He'd remember the sight of her with nothing on but her brother's battered hat until the day he died, he supposed, and would be grateful for the memory. Few men were as fortunate.

He cringed from the thought of what would have happened if she hadn't had the courage to run away from Albemarle County. Her life would have been tied to an old man who couldn't have realized and wouldn't have cared about the treasure he had. He roused from lethargy as a powerful need for revenge coursed through his veins. Right then he'd have given a year of his life to have Verity's stepfather within arm's reach. He fought down a vicious need to pound on someone.

But then he would never have found her if she hadn't been struggling along that hillside in the rain and mud, trying to catch up with the Dawsons. The Dawsons, damn their ugly hides. Well, Bart's, anyway. A red haze of anger swam before his eyes. The time would come when he could go back to Corn Island and settle the score. Bart had been warned. Trey told him, clearly, what to expect if he ever touched Verity again. If there was any justice in the world, there would be a day of reckoning. Trey closed his eyes and damned his own hide for paddling off down the river and leaving her alone with the menace of Bart's lust.

But she was here now, safe within the circle of his arms, and well out of Bart's reach. She turned, then, seeming to go almost boneless, and with a small sigh, tucked a hand beneath her head. She faced away from him. He snugged her closer and felt for the swell of her breast. As he drifted closer to sleep, his mouth widened in satisfaction that the curve of her spine fit so perfectly into the reclining lap of his own body. A glove fashioned for the hand, he thought. And her breast fit his palm like loam to the tiller's hand. He was indeed the most blessed of all men.

There was no snap of twig or whisper of movement to awaken him, but in that split second between sleep and wakefulness he knew they were not alone. His eyes slitted open slowly and he was careful to keep his breathing deep and regular. Every sense was alert and straining, and his fingers were reaching for the knife when a voice came quietly from behind his shoulder.

"Easy. It's Joe."

He relaxed. Taking care not to awaken Verity, Trey removed his arm from beneath her head. He turned, clenching and reclenching his fist to get the circulation going.

Joe hunkered down three feet away as Trey sat up. He nodded at Verity. "Is she any better?"

"For the last few hours her sleep's been natural. I think she'll be all right." They spoke in hushed tones. "Her eyelids move every once in a while like she'd trying to wake up."

Joe looked briefly uneasy. "Shock, do you think?"

Trey nodded. "I hope she'll tell us when she wakes up, but yes, I think it was mostly shock. She has this absolute horror of anything Indian and to have gone through so much to find you and then discover that you have an Indian wife, would have been a terrible blow to her."

"My fault, I guess. It never occurred to me to prepare her. Dawn is so sweet and gentle, totally unlike those marauding hot-bloods that massacred our family, there isn't any comparison." He glanced again at Verity, sleeping with one hand under her chin. "She wouldn't let me talk to her and explain, wouldn't even look at me. Just seemed to shrink inside herself."

In one fluid movement Trey got to his feet. "She's been through a lot since spring. A lifetime of fear and survival, travel and hard work. Did she tell you she was captured by the Shawnee? Give her a few days to rest and she'll be all right. I do need to talk to you about something, though."

Joe stood, too, waiting with one hip cocked and his rifle butt to the ground.

"What do you know about a fellow named Edward Something-or-the-other? A friend of yours, I think. Verity says she's pledged to him."

Joe went suddenly still. "He's not here right now. Why?"

Grim determination flooded Trey's thinking. Here was something, someone, to confront. Verity was his, and he'd be damned if anyone else was going to stand in the way.

He answered, trying to keep his thoughts from showing. "If he's expecting a woman ready to marry him, he's due for a disappointment. I just wanted him to know that before he saw her. And, it's me he'll need to deal with, not her. She's mine."

Joe relaxed somewhat, although he was still cautious. He looked again at Verity, her breath coming in a peaceful rising and falling of her breast and Trey knew Joe was thinking of the way he'd found them entwined in sleep.

Trey braced his feet apart. If her brother was going to make something of it, now would be the time. "She'll be my wife in the eyes of the church the minute she says the word, but we've already exchanged our personal vows. Your friend, and you, need to know that." And all it implies, he thought. May as well lay it all out clear.

Joe's face registered a faint suggestion of a smile. "She always did have a mind of her own and I'd as soon tangle with a wolverine as I would cross her when she's dug in her feet. Edward's at Prairie du Rocher just now, being captured by Clark's men along with the rest of the town. He'll be mighty surprised to find her here when he gets back, and real unhappy to find her hitched to somebody else. It's his bad luck he was gone when you came in."

"Prairie du Rocher? What news is there?"

"That's what I came for. Clark wants you. Prairie du Rocher and St. Phillipe are ours. The French at Cahokia offered no resistance at all when they learned France was with us, and the chiefs of various Indian tribes seem to be willing to talk terms of truce. The fly in the pudding is still Vincennes. It's Hamilton's main stronghold and he's fortifying the city with canon and more troops and all the Indians he can bribe. The question is: do we march on Vincennes now, or wait for reinforcements from the east?"

Trey's senses honed in on Clark's dilemma. The American army was pitifully small and poorly supplied, and yet Vincennes was undoubtedly more vulnerable now than it would be in the fall. The decision would be a gamble, one way or the other. Wait for reinforcements and watch Vincennes grow strong while they waited, or move now with no canon and few men?

"March on Vincennes now," Trey said.

"That's what I say," Joe agreed. "But apparently Clark's orders are to wait. He's asking for you."

Trey moved a step nearer Verity. "Give me a few minutes. Tell him I'll be along."

Joe nodded. "Dawn will come and sit with her. Out of sight, but nearby," he added at Trey's sharp look.

When Joe had gone, Trey debated about waking Verity and decided finally to bathe first. Maybe there would be no need to disturb her rest. Dawn could tell her where he'd gone and that he'd be back as soon as he could. She could sleep as long as she needed. On the way to the river, however, he grunted aloud in frustration. She'd never listen to Dawn, it was wishful thinking to imagine such a thing. She'd probably take a hatchet to the gentle, young girl before a word could be spoken. He'd have to awaken her.

He bathed quickly and all but ran back to the sheltering maple where he'd left Verity. Thirty yards from the path a scream shattered the tranquility of the early morning. It was a long, drawn-out shriek of stark terror, and in a frantic heartbeat his stride lengthened and he drew his knife. He entered the clearing with his gun at the ready in one hand and his knife grasped to cut and tear in the other.

Verity was backed against a rotting stump, her feet stumbling among the exposed roots. She stared in horrified concentration at a man advancing step at a time from the forest.

"You never reckoned to see me again, did you, girlie? But here I am, big as life and more ready than ever to take what's mine. Now, you goin' to fight and make it hard, or are you goin' to just go along easy and give me what I want?"

Bart! Against all odds and all imaginings, it was Bart. Trey felt his whole body brace for action. The muscles across his shoulders twanged with the readiness to leap to meet it. Strength flowed in a tide through his legs. This time Verity wasn't alone. His mouth stretched wide in a grimace that wasn't mirth. The day of reckoning had come.

Twenty-four

Verity stared at Bart's dogged approach in a state of numbed paralysis. She saw him coming, one foot in front of the other, hands swinging loosely, his eyes pinning her to the rough bark of the tree. She seemed incapable of coherent thought. This couldn't be Bart. Bart was on Corn Island.

Her vision blurred. No, he was here, as broad and big as a blockhouse and lifting one hand now to reach for her. Her brain fought to make sense of it. Where was Joe? He had been here, hadn't he? Joe and his wife, and—and there was something bad about that, something that didn't come forward—and then there was a black space with nothing in it except Trey's voice. Trey had been there, too. But he, like Joe, was gone now.

Everyone was gone except Bart. The one she thought she'd never lay eyes on again. He was coming closer with that curious short-strided walk of his, as if his knees were tied together.

Somehow, he had followed her all the way down the river and through the dreadful sea of prairie grass and into Kaskaskia itself. Now he was going to put his hands on her and take her with him. She couldn't move, couldn't even blink. His eyes glittered with the fixed determination of a snake stalking a mouse.

Trey's bellow of rage slashed through the forest and her whole body jerked as if she was awakening from a nightmare. He leaped into the clearing almost eagerly, Verity thought.

Crouching forward, his eyes swept the clearing. "You bastard," he ground out through gritted teeth, focusing on Bart. "This time it's not a slip of a girl, half your size. It's me, and by God, I'm as mean as you." Noting Bart's empty hands, he dropped his rifle and knife. "So, bare-handed it is. Good enough. I've been waiting for this a long time."

Bart's expression had gone from surprise to disbelief to satisfaction. He changed direction only slightly as he headed for Trey instead of Verity. He shook his head like a great, shaggy bear.

"You been messin' with me too long. Ever' time I get things set, you or Clem one, sticks in an oar and ruins it all." His eyes took on a sudden crafty cunning and with a twitch of his arm a narrow-bladed knife slid into his palm.

Verity's heart pounded in the back of her throat. They were going to fight! Trey was unarmed and Bart outweighed him by fifty pounds. This was no match. It would be a slaughter.

Trey eyed his own knife on the ground, but Bart was almost upon him and it was too late to make a grab for it. His feet moved, carrying him sideways as he began to circle away from the knife. He moved lightly, on the balls of his feet, with his knees absorbing the spring of his body and his arms outstretched for balance. He was in deadly earnest; his concentration complete.

Bart turned in place as Trey circled, his feet awkward in the unfamiliar pattern. He smiled, an evil baring of teeth.

"Always," he said, "if'n it warn't you, it was Clem. 'No, you can't do that'," he mimicked. "And, 'Leave 'er alone. She ain't yore kind'." Bart was breathing hard through his nose. "Well, she warn't his kind, neither, but he went after 'er the minute he could. After all those 'leave 'er be's' to me, he started sniffin' around a'fore Zelma was hardly cold."

He made a sudden lunge toward Trey with his knife arm extended and laughed loudly when Trey dodged backward.

"And you," he went on. "Forever makin' the big move. How in hell'd you find her when the Shawnee took 'er? I was out there alookin', too, and couldn't find nary as much as a feather. You come back without a scratch on either one a yuh." He sneered. "Yuh got the devil's own luck."

"That's right," Trey said, moving constantly, first one way and then the other. His feet were never still and his eyes never left Bart's. "And the devil's giving you to me in the end. Now, are you going to talk me to death or are you going to fight?"

Bart stumbled slightly as he crossed his feet, trying to keep up with Trey's constant change of direction. He grumbled into his beard. "Think yo're the big man. Clark always askin' fer you. Head honcho on the island. Nobody's as fast, as smart—"

Trey sighed loudly, an exaggerated explosion of sound, and stopped circling. He straightened. "Nothing but talk. I should have known." He taunted, "You're too much a coward to fight."

No, Verity wanted to scream. He's not a coward, he's just slow-witted. He'll kill you. But before she could put words to her thought, Bart had lowered his head and rushed Trey.

The taunt had been just that, Verity realized. Trey knew what he was doing. He'd been trying to draw Bart into action while he was still building a head of anger and before he had time to think it through. They rolled now, joined together in a grunting, twisting oneness, legs thrashing, arms straining and heels digging. Trey had Bart's knife hand in a vise-like grip, held away from their bodies.

Bart was heavier; Trey was quicker. Bart was single-mindedly trying to smother, smash and suffocate; Trey was trying to get to his own knife, lying half-way across the clearing.

Verity heard a high, keening wail drifting through the trees and wondered who was there. Her own throat felt stiff with throttled fear. With one arm Bart was squeezing the life out of Trey. She had to do something. She ran for the rifle.

Sobbing she raised the gun to her shoulder. The end of the barrel wavered and dipped. She tried again, drawing the bead carefully, holding her breath. And then lowered the gun. It was impossible. The two men were knitted together. She couldn't be sure she wouldn't kill them both.

They rolled again, their backs covered with debris from the forest floor. Trey was bleeding now from a half-dozen nicks and his left sleeve was slashed to the elbow. He was cut, Verity saw. Blood welled up and ran down his arm. Viciously Trey brought up a knee hard into Bart's mid-section. Bart gave a startled grunt of pain. With a mighty thrust he threw Trey aside and stood swaying as he squinted through straggling hair. Trey gulped in air while flexing his injured elbow.

Bart made a heavy-footed feint to his right, and then to the left, jabbing with the knife and laughing out loud when Trey jumped clear. And then, in a move so fast that Verity had trouble following, Trey leaped high in the air and with one foot kicked the knife out of Bart's hand so cleanly that even Bart looked stupidly at the hand as if not believing what he saw.

Again, Bart charged, head down. This time Trey braced himself and swung his right fist into Bart's stomach, trying to drive all the way to the man's backbone. Bart staggered, but didn't fall. His arms went around Trey's chest and tightened. His face graying from lack of air, Trey got his arms between them and brought the heel of both hands up under Bart's chin. He strained to shove Bart's head backward. The chords in his neck thickened like knotted ropes under the skin. But, with blood dripping from his weakened arm, he couldn't do it. Bart squeezed tighter and tighter.

One of Trey's legs snaked out and caught Bart behind the knee. It was enough to throw him off balance and they went down tumbling. Verity could hear Trey sucking air into his lungs. Bart dug a booted heel into the earth and forced them to roll, his thumbs groping for Trey's eyes. Verity gripped the rifle by the barrel and edged closer, the butt of the gun held high. Maybe she could land a blow hard enough to stun Bart. But Trey broke free to stand again, leaning forward, balanced, favoring his left arm, and lunged for his knife. Verity backed away.

Bart straightened slowly, breathing hard, and from a half-stance he rushed Trey with a bulldog determination that drove them both across the clearing and up against a twelve-foot dead elm. Using the tree for leverage, Bart trapped Trey in another bear hug. Once more, Verity watched the blood drain from Trey's face. Once more, Trey struggled to break free. But Bart was a great bull of a man and the strength in his arms was enormous.

With mounting horror, Verity watched Trey weaken. Surely his ribs would crack. Bart's face was purpling with effort. And Trey was strangling. Holding the gun by the barrel she swung with all her might at Bart's broad back, but in the second before contact they rolled away and the gun butt glanced off the tree. With a scream of sheer rage she flung the rifle away and launched herself at Bart's back, scratching and clawing until her hands were locked around his neck. She rode there like a burr while Bart slung his body first one way and then the other trying to throw her off. She slid over his shoulder to the right and then to the left, hanging on with more stubbornness than strength.

His grip on Trey lessened slightly and some of the color came back into Trey's face. Verity felt his arms begin to move again, trying for purchase, hunting for a weak place. She clung, gripping with her knees and her fingers, and if there was anything she could have sunk her teeth into she would have done that, too.

The three of them staggered around the clearing blindly. Verity groped with one hand for Bart's eyes. She dug in with her fingernails. She gouged. Anything to make him let go of Trey.

Suddenly, Bart lost his balance. They went over a log as one, smashing into the ground, a tree, tangling in wild honeysuckle. Stunned, Verity struggled to her feet a second before Bart lurched upward. By the time he regained his feet and his balance, she had launched herself at his back again and clung there like a burr. She had only a glimpse of Trey lying, unmoving, on the ground.

Her heart beat thickly in her chest. If Bart had killed Trey, then she herself would kill Bart. Somehow. She would. He swung his arms backward trying to get a grip on her. He leaned forward in an effort to topple her off over his head. She ground her teeth together and hung on. Her vision starred black and then red. The reason for hanging on was no longer clear, she simply would not let go.

And then, with a muffled grunt, Bart stopped. The sudden lack of movement nearly unseated Verity, where the violence had not. Slowly, slowly he began to slump forward, his body relaxing like that of a rag doll. His knees buckled and he went down. They hit the ground with a thump that echoed in the sudden stillness. Verity rolled free and scrambled on her knees frantically sweeping back the hair from her eyes. Trey's knife was buried in Bart's chest. It was only then she realized they were not alone in the clearing.

She-Who-Greets-The-Dawn took a step backward. One hand was covered with blood, dripping red from the ends of the fingers. Her eyes met Verity's with total lack of expression.

"Your man," she said, in a quiet tone that made a lie of the savage deed she'd just committed. "He—spirit depart?"

With a soft cry Verity ran to Trey. He hadn't moved. Was he dead? Her hands flew over him, searching for a wound, a break, anything to explain his lack of movement.

His jaw line, the dear cleft in his chin, his head. How many nights had she lain awake wondering what it would feel like to run her fingers through his hair? His arms, the muscles bulging and tight. The barrel of his chest, the solid, rock-hard ribs that she'd only just begun to know the feel of—Gently she lifted his head slightly to get her hand beneath.

Other than a lump on the back of his head and the deep cut on his arm, there was nothing serious, except that his head had apparently hit a protruding tree root when they fell. The hard appendage stuck up from the ground, gnarled in a rigid arch, leaving a hole big enough between itself and the ground for her to put a fist through. Her breath jammed in her throat.

"Oh no. Please God, no." She whimpered. "No. No. No."

Probing gently she found the spot on the back of Trey's skull where he'd hit. A lump was already rising. He groaned once and his eyelids fluttered. He was alive!

"Trey! Trey, talk to me!" She was frantic. He couldn't die. Not now. Not after everything that had gone before.

She twisted so that she could shift his head into her lap where it would rest more easily. Fear rode heavy in her chest. "Don't you dare die when we've just found each other. Not when I love you. Don't you dare!"

His eyelids fluttered open and his gaze steadied and cleared. He smiled, a weak and twitching effort, but nevertheless a smile, and her eyes flooded with grateful tears.

His lips moved. "Joe's right about the wolverine," he said, his words slurring slightly. "Buffalo doesn't begin to get it."

Twenty-five

Verity seemed to float through the fringes of each day. She was used to hard work and heat, but thanks to Dawn's gift of certain leaves to rub over their skin and ward off mosquitoes, the nights with Trey and only the stars for a blanket filled her with contentment. The violent confrontation between Bart and Trey, the journey through the sea of grass, the shock of discovering Joe had taken an Indian wife were fading with each passing day.

They slept outside, for Verity could not yet bring herself to sleep in the teepee, but as the days melded together and no new disaster struck, she felt her tension begin to drain away. If it hadn't been for the fact that Edward was still gone, and did not yet know she was a married woman, her life would have been complete. The worry lodged like a thorn that Edward was going to be hurt.

She sat, one afternoon, in a wedge of shade created by the teepee, patiently grinding corn in a bowl with a small pestle. The waning August sun bore down with unrelenting sameness, day after day, but the heat that everyone complained about had little interest for her. She was in Kaskaskia at last. She had done the seemingly impossible and came through relatively unscathed all the way from Albemarle County in Virginia to Kaskaskia on the Mississippi. What was more important, she had Trey.

On most afternoons, when he wasn't hunting, he leaned against a backrest beneath a spreading pin oak, busying himself with small tasks, where she could lay her eyes on him whenever she pleased. If there had ever been a time when she'd been happier, she couldn't remember it. They hadn't yet been married in front of the priest—that good man was at another settlement—with witnesses and Joe's permission, but Trey certainly gave the appearance of a man in love. Even in the act of cleaning his rifle he couldn't seem to keep his eyes from her for long. He looked up at that very moment and winked broadly as his mouth widened in a seductive smile meant for her alone.

But Verity knew Trey was not thoroughly content as he appeared. As the days passed in heat-stifled breathlessness, he waited with ill-concealed impatience for Clark to move against Vincennes. But no orders came. He devoted a large part of every day to Verity, seeming to be satisfied to simply be where she was as long as the army stayed in Kaskaskia.

He reminded her regularly, in every way, of just how much he loved her, shutting out the rest of the world with his arms, his eyes, his lips. And she treasured every second of his love-making against the day he would become restless and move on. She tried not to dwell on his leaving, for to do so would make the moment go faster, but in her heart she knew, even as he winked boldly at her from across the clearing, that the day would come when, army or no army, he would look longingly to the west and uncharted rivers, virgin forests and unknown mountains.

Hadn't he even run away from his bond because he couldn't stand the confinement? They *were* married, Verity reminded herself, if not yet in the eyes of the church, at least in the eyes of God. Verity had no doubt of that. Nor did she doubt his love. However, she wasn't sure it would be enough to hold him once he was gripped with the itch to move on. She told herself sternly that she made her vows knowing how Trey felt about new horizons, and if this was all she was to have it would have to be enough. He might roam, but he would come back to her. Determinedly she hid her thoughts behind a promissory smile and winked back at him. Trey raised an eyebrow and moved as if to come to her. She shook her head in mock alarm and glanced at She-Who-Greets-The-Dawn, but Dawn was busy stringing berries to dry in the sun and hadn't noticed.

Verity still felt uncomfortable in the Indian's presence, but in the three weeks since Bart's death she no longer quivered in fear when their work made it necessary to be together. The girl was soft-spoken and immaculately clean, and Verity was sure she loved Joe with her entire being. Already she had separated herself from her family who had moved on west in front of the oncoming tide of white settlers and the army. Dawn devoted every waking hour to making Joe's life easier and happier. To herself, Verity admitted that Dawn was a good wife and would one day make a good mother to Joe's children. But accepting her as a sister came hard, even though Dawn had undoubtedly saved Trey's life when she'd used the knife on Bart. And, Verity admitted, probably her own as well.

Verity watched as frown lines indented Trey's forehead. She knew he was worried about Clark's decision to wait for a change in orders before marching on Vincennes. The entire community was worried. Trey seemed to take the waiting harder than most. He was not a waiting man. He lifted the gun, sighted down the barrel and then snapped alert at the sound of someone coming along the path through the corn.

It was Homer. Verity called a greeting and received a wave of his hand in reply. Homer had arrived the day after Bart, still limping from his injury, weary from the trip and embarrassed that Bart had gotten away from him on Corn Island. His eyes had rested with approval on Dawn when the story was told of Bart's sudden end.

He said baldly that "life wouldn't have been worth a mouthful of spit with that worthless cur loose in the west," and there wasn't anything he admired more than grit. This last had been said directly to Dawn, who flushed with pleasure and scurried off to prepare a tray of food for the traveler. "Though," he added, "it galls me to give credit for the killing to Trey. You got a point, though. An Indian, especially a woman, killing a white man could cause Dawn some trouble. It's best this way."

The pestle hung idle in Verity's hand as Homer emerged from the corn, favoring one foot, his rifle slung loosely at his hip, pointing toward the ground. A wide-brimmed hat shaded his face from the worst of the afternoon sun, and he still wore the same stained, shapeless buckskins he'd worn all summer on the river. He was dirty, tattered, unshaven, and dear to Verity's fond gaze, because he was a good friend upon whom both she and Trey depended.

He nodded to Verity and again to Dawn and moved to sit beside Trey in the shade.

Trey waited and then, when Homer had nothing to say, he asked, "What's wrong? You got a face on you like a plate full of mortal sin."

Homer straightened his legs and leaned against a tree trunk. "I don't take to this waiting much. We ought to be on our way to Vincennes."

Trey's attention returned to the rifle he was cleaning and grunted his agreement. "Clark hasn't been sitting on his thumbs, though. He's made friends of the French here and in Prairie du Rocher and St. Phillipe. He's even charmed the ladies into making flags. He's pacified the French at Cahokia and is planning a council with the chiefs of all the Indian tribes. He knows what he's doing."

"Yeah, and while Clark's running around wiping noses, Hamilton's handing out guns and powder to Indians all up and down the Wabash. We ought to rout him out of his den. We've got to take Vincennes!"

"You'll get no argument from either me or Clark," Trey said. "But soldiers can't march without orders. He did send Father Gibault to talk to the French settlers at Fort Sackville in Vincennes."

Homer nodded. "Them Frenchies got grit, sure enough. Chased the British out armed with only rakes and scythes and brooms, and raised the Stars and Stripes. But even if the Fort is ours, Old Hairbuyer still holds Vincennes, and we're a good two hundred miles away. I don't call that victory."

They sat in gloomy silence for a moment and then Homer turned his shoulder to the work area in front of the teepee and lowered his voice. Although she was sure he didn't intend it, Verity could hear every soft word spoken.

"That Edward fellow?" he said with his chin buried in his neck. "He's here. Just got back, and if you got something to say to him you'd best get it done. Clark's fixing to send him back east with a packet of messages to Governor Henry."

Verity straightened. She opened her mouth and then closed it at the expression on Trey's face. It was the face of action after weeks of waiting, eagerness after forced patience, determination after indecision.

"Trey?" she said.

He came to his feet in one long movement. His mind was entirely focused on one thing: his need to see Edward before he had a chance to hear about Verity's marriage from someone else and before Edward met up with Verity. He didn't even glance at Homer.

"Trey?" Verity said again. "Don't—"

He crossed the clearing and wrapped both arms around her. "This is my business," he said, "I'll be back soon and ready for that corn pudding you're putting together. Don't worry." He dropped a light kiss on her nose.

"It's my business, too," she said, but he had already swung away from her, disappearing into the corn without another word.

Verity's gaze swung to Homer, thinking that all men were the same when it came to protecting what they considered to be theirs, whether it be property or a woman. Brute force and frontal attack. He'd all but patted her on the head and told her to be a good girl!

"I wouldn't do whatever it is you're thinking on," Homer said, dryly. "He considers this men's business."

Verity's chin came up. "That's too bad, because it's me that was promised to Edward. I'm the one who ought to tell him." She smoothed her skirt and tucked a strand of hair behind one ear.

Homer shifted his hips and leaned against the backrest that Trey had vacated. "He ain't going to like it."

"He'll just have to get over it," she said, and dropped her pestle and followed Trey into the corn.

She caught up to him just inside the stockade. He was already talking to Edward and from their stiff-legged stance neither man was breaking out the tobacco and peace pipe.

Edward's good-natured brown eyes lighted when he saw her and he opened his arms. "I was just on my way to find you. This man here's got some idea that you aren't here to see me." He caught her in a bear hug that completely enveloped her, and as he rocked her back and forth in delight, she caught Trey's angry stare over Edward's shoulder.

She wriggled free. "Edward, it's good to see you. How have you been?" Inane though it was, Verity had to say something to cover her scattered thoughts.

"Can't say this isn't a surprise, but I couldn't be any happier." He held her off to look her up and down and then clutched her to him, again. "You're even prettier than you were when I left. How'd you get here? I heard some tale about a trip downriver with some old tracker? Where is the old geezer? I need to thank him."

Trey's hand spun Edward around like a toy top. "I'm the old geezer." His tone took on a hard edge. "I brought her and there's no need for thanks. I brought her for me. Not you."

Edward turned confused eyes on Verity and then back to Trey. The confusion turned slowly to anger.

"Edward—" she began.

"What's he saying?" Edward demanded. "You're spoken for." He slanted a furious gaze on Trey. "By me." He poked a hard finger into his own chest. "She's mine."

"Edward, wait—" Verity tried to intervene.

To Verity's horror, Trey gave Edward a look of triumph. "You're too late, Edward-boy. She's married. To me."

Edward opened his mouth to argue, but Verity's face confirmed Trey's words, and he closed it. "When?"

"Long enough ago that you can't undo it, if you know what I'm saying." Trey was openly defiant.

Verity saw Edward's fist clench and she stepped between the two men, her back to Trey. "Listen, both of you. I'm the one to be explaining."

The two men spoke at once.

"He's lying!"

"You'll play hell if you try to touch her again." Trey's chest was pressed to Verity's back and she could feel him leaning forward. She dug in her heels to hold him in place.

Verity put one hand on Edward's arm and gripped him, hard. "Edward, listen to me. I'm sorry. I know I promised to marry you and wait in Virginia, but I had to leave Otis and Lena. I couldn't stay any longer. And on the way I met Trey and we just—Sometimes things come about that you aren't expecting, things that you can't prevent. Believe me, we didn't intend for this to happen."

Both men were breathing like winded horses, leaning toward each other.

"Then why did it?" Edward's eyes turned suspicious, dangerous. "Did he force you?"

"No! No, of course not. And, I don't know why it happened. I never meant to hurt you. I'm sorry."

He looked at her for a long moment and then snorted in disgust.

"Edward, we grew up together. You know how fond of you I am. I am so dreadfully sorry—"

Roughly he shook her hand from his arm. "Will you just stop the hell being *sorry* for me? You've chosen someone else. That's all there is to it." He jammed both thumbs into his belt and slitted his eyes at Trey. "And you damn well better be good to her, because if you aren't I'll come after you. You got that?"

To Verity's surprise Trey's anger vanished. His hands lifted to her shoulders and rested there, but he looked Edward squarely in the eye. "You have my word on it."

~ * ~

By the next afternoon Edward was gone. Again, Homer brought the news from the fort.

"Miss Verity and Miss Dawn, I bring a message from Joe. He's busy sending Edward off upriver with a packet for Governor Henry. Joe says he'll be back late, and Edward says that when you see him again he'll have a passel of recruits behind him. I hope he's not just talking to hear the echo."

Dawn smiled a shy thanks and went into the teepee for another basket of berries and more thin gut-string. Verity asked if Edward was going alone.

"Nope. There's three of them, so's they can spell each other paddling. That way they don't have to put into shore none to sleep. He'll make out all right."

Verity bent once again to scraping a deer hide. Edward could take care of himself. Actually, it would be a relief not to have the discomfort of knowing that every time she turned around she might run into him. In truth, there had been no other young people their age in the valley and the three of them, Joe, Edward and Verity, had been sort of thrown together growing up. But she knew well that Edward felt more than friendship for her and she respected him as a decent man who could have made her a good husband. But, yes, it was best that he was gone. Every time she saw Edward, she heard her mother's voice, "A guilty conscience makes a poor pillow, Verity."

She repositioned the hide she was scraping and began again with the razor-like knife. Pull, press and lift. Pull, press and lift. Her arm was tired, but she was almost done. Soon it would be time to add fat and water to the corn meal she had ground and fry corn cakes on a flat stone by the fire as Dawn had taught her. Trey would be hungry.

She'd learned a lot about frontier living from Dawn. Actually, she was a bit proud of her newly acquired skills. She might never be the lady her mother had wanted, but if the truth be known, she didn't think she was made of the same kind of stuff as real ladies. She had survived Lena and Otis, the trip on the flatboat, Clark's taking her along only on sufferance, The Fist and that dreadful journey to the Indian village and back to Corn Island. She'd lived by her wits and her strength, coping with the Dawsons, Bart, and Clark's forbidding everything she wanted to do. If she'd been a real lady, Verity thought, she couldn't have done all that.

And right behind the revelation came the knowledge that her mother had been a survivor, too. Hadn't she lived through the Indian massacre and watching her husband and youngest child killed? She had hung on somehow, and along with Joe and Verity, put together some kind of existence with a roof over their heads and food on the table. She had done her best. Maybe the highest tribute Verity could give her mother was to be as strong as she had been. Dying, she thought, pausing with the knife blade resting against the hide, was easy. It was living that was hard.

Suddenly the thought came to her that life wasn't composed of the big events like birth and death, as she'd always thought. Life was made up of all the little, seemingly unimportant events, like taking the time to make a whistle for a little boy—she might never have begun to respect Trey if it hadn't been for his generosity of spirit—or drawing water from the river and letting it settle overnight for her to wash her face. What if she hadn't thought fast enough and thrown the rope to Trey in the water? What if he hadn't shielded her from Clark's anger more than once? Life seemed to be shaped by people bumping and scraping and rubbing together, by selfishness and greed, or by the generosity of giving and accepting the gift of themselves.

Well, she'd done her best and managed to live through it. What was even better was that she'd found Trey. He sat with long-limbed ease, running a file along the blade of an ax and baiting Homer as he whiled away the summer afternoon.

"—getting old. Never knew it to take you so long to catch me before. Too soft to paddle a canoe, are you?"

"I reckon I can still take you any time you was to want a match," Homer drawled. "That varmint, Bart, just got the drop on me by leaving before I knew he was thinking on it. What's more I didn't know for sure which way he was heading. Had to guess and go slow enough to find sign. On water, that ain't so easy. Besides, the prairie was full of Piankeshaws, following first you and the girl, and then Bart. He left sign as plain as an eight-pronged buck. Between all of you, you might as well have blazed a trail for them redskins to follow. Miracle that none of 'em come up on Bart. He had the devil's own luck and went through 'em like smoke somehow. Me—I was right in the middle of 'em, blessin' you with every step I took."

Trey grinned. "And got here late enough to miss the fun all around. Played it pretty safe, didn't you?"

Homer plucked a blade of grass and stuck it in his mouth. "I notice it took a mite of a girl to stop the action. And it didn't look to me like you was having so much fun when I got there. You was out cold as a witch's—" He stopped with a quick look at Verity. "Uh—you was out cold."

Trey laughed aloud. "So I was. And I had a knot on my head for a week." He sobered. "Does anyone at the fort suspect that it was Dawn and not me that killed Bart?"

"Naw. Everyone knows you two had a grudge to settle. Who's to suspect? No one was there except the four of you and it might not do the Indian cause any good if'n Dawn was thought to have knifed a white man. Rest easy."

Trey nodded and ran an expert finger down the blade of the ax. "What's so important that it brings you out in the heat of the day?"

Homer spat out the blade of grass and selected a twig to pick his teeth. "Clark's written to Governor Henry again, asking for more men and permission to march. In the meantime, while we wait for Edward to get there and back, he wants you to cross the river with him into Spanish territory."

A cold spot blossomed in Verity's chest as she watched Trey's interest spark and then flame. St. Louis. A new place. New sights and sounds. People. Was this the day he would leave her? Already, in his mind, he was thinking how it would be, what he would see, who he would meet. It was as she'd known all along. He would never be a farmer. And he'd not mentioned the printing trade, again. A quiet, rooted life simply wasn't in him. He came alive at the prospect of moving on. Already he was on his feet.

A darkness settled on her spirit. There would never be a place for her in his life. If she tried to tie him to a plow and a section of ground, she would lose. What would happen with the anvil of a business around his neck? He would wither and die. Eventually, he might come to hate her as the cause of his unhappiness. She could bear a lot of things, but not Trey hating her. No, he was cut out to be the kind of man happy only where things were happening, new vistas unfolding. "When?" Trey asked, looking as if he was ready to start that very minute, with darkness not an hour away.

"First light," Homer answered. "Be gone two, maybe three days."

"I'll be ready."

"He wants to see you tonight. Things to talk about. Plans to make." He put a blade of grass between his teeth and settled back.

Trey came to Verity's side and squatted down until his knee touched hers.

"You heard?"

"Yes." Her voice was steady. She'd made sure of it before she spoke. He would never know that she understood, even if he did not, that he might not come back for a long while.

"St. Louis is a big fur trading center just across the Mississippi River in Spanish Territory," he said. His hand searched for hers and lifted it from the hide to cradle against his cheek. "This is what I've been hoping for, the chance to see what's over there and meet Fernando de Leyba, the governor."

"The Mississippi River is even wider than the Ohio, and much more dangerous," she said quietly, just as if her heart wasn't threatening to choke off her air with its desperate pounding. "Dawn says the Indians call it the grandmother of all rivers and that there's a terrible undertow, so don't go doing foolhardy things like diving under the boat. I won't be there to throw you a rope."

She couldn't raise her eyes. He was going away and she might never again be able to look upon his dear face. She didn't think she could bear it.

"No underwater swimming," he agreed. "And I'll remember everything I see so I can tell you all about it. You won't have a single question I can't answer."

He put a hand behind her neck and slowly pulled her forward until their noses touched. "You take care, too, you hear? No surprises when I get back."

He kissed her gently, tenderly, thoroughly, until she forgot about Dawn, the corn to be ground and Joe waving Edward off downriver. I must remember, she thought, the way his hair feels springy and soft beneath my palm, the steady pounding of the pulse in his neck, the way his thumbs feel caressing my cheek. Remember. Remember.

"Two, three days," he whispered. "And if I don't go now I never will." And then he was gone.

She sat where he left her, feeling suddenly cold and abandoned. She didn't watch him go, only concentrated on not crying. Two or three days. Weeks? Months? Maybe always. But he was mine, she thought with a surge of triumph. For a little while.

Scalding tears flooded her eyes, but she fought them down, clenching her back teeth and forcing long, slow breaths to slide in and out.

She-Who-Greets-The-Dawn crouched at her side, not touching her, but near. "Your man—he—come back," she said softly.

How did Dawn always seem to know what other people were thinking? Verity didn't dare to try and talk. Not yet. She shook her head.

"Yes," Dawn said. "A man who loves and comes not back, turns the second time. Looks to save…vision. This one sends not his thoughts through air to cling while he is gone. He comes back."

"I want to believe you," Verity said, raising her eyes and giving up all pretense of being brave. "But he is a man who needs new places, new lands. I'm afraid."

"It is true he become only dry husk if he digs in dirt and plants corn all his days. But he not want land for his own, like so many of your kind. He know land belongs to no man. From beginning of time man always belong to land. The one you call

The Great Our Father made us from earth, water, air. And so we belong to them. Your man understand these things."

Verity sank back on her heels. "I would go with him, where ever he went, if he would take me. But I think he wants to go alone. He might even follow your people to the setting sun."

A sadness settled over Dawn's features. "It is wrong for my people to leave. It is death to be separated from land of the ancestors. My people will scatter and dry up like leaves in time of harvest and be no more. We, my sisters, my brothers, the gray-hairs, all come from the red clay of the bluffs and our feet know the feel of these hills. Our mouths hunger for taste of rivers. When we are gone the very stones will wail and cry tears. Leaving is bad."

Verity had no answer, but thankfully Dawn didn't seem to expect one. She found herself profoundly moved by the simple faith Dawn had spoken of. But the Indian had no choice in the matter, it seemed to her. They either moved or were killed. Either way they lost. Trey had tried to tell her all along and she had been too thick-headed to listen.

She grappled with this new thought. Had the Indians back in Albemarle County felt this same way? Maybe Trey was right and there was some right and some wrong on both sides. She could see for herself that Dawn had a foot in both camps. Loving Joe as she did and staying while everyone she held dear had to go on without her. She had lost sisters, brothers, aunts, uncles, her entire family. She and Dawn were both alone, for different reasons. They shared a bond that five minutes ago Verity would not have understood.

She stretched out a hand toward Dawn's arm. "I'm sorry," she said. "Maybe I can be another kind of sister."

The tips of Dawn's fingers brushed the back of Verity's wrist. "May-be," she said softly. "May-be our spirits can learn to be sisters." She turned away and bent to enter the teepee.

Homer still leaned against the backrest, squinting at her. After a minute he cleared his throat. "Did I tell you about Gideon?" he asked.

That got her attention. "Gideon? What about him?" Basically, Gideon was a good boy, but still young, and she'd wished many times that there was some way to remove him from the vicinity of the coarse and thoughtless selfishness of his father and uncles. Of course, Esther might have a good influence on him. She clung to that hope.

"Gideon, he's itching to come on west. Wanted to come with me, but I needed to come in a hurry. He'd have slowed me down some."

"Clem wouldn't have let him, anyway. Although for Gideon's sake I wish you could have brought him along."

"Oh, he'll be along. He's of an age to be feeling his salt. Another year, maybe, and he'll be near full grown, and then he'll do as he likes. In fact, it wouldn't surprise me none if he didn't show up in the spring with some trapper heading for the mountains. The boy's got a powerful yearning for the west."

"I wish you could tell me about Sally. If I knew she had a mother like Dawn..."

Homer sighed. "Don't pay none to worry about what you can't change." He got to his feet, unfolding like a bent stick. "Got to get back and make sure that man of yours found the fort. Since he met you he ain't got the sense God gave a goose."

Verity smiled. Trey and Homer's feelings for each other went far deeper than any mere friendship. Yet, while either of them would have fought to the death for the other, neither of them would have admitted to such a weakness. They were home, kin, for each other. Like Dawn said—family should stay together. If Trey wandered she knew, and was comforted by the fact, that Homer would be with him. And she vowed to always have a place ready for him in their home.

It was full dark when Verity's mind let loose of the ideas Dawn had raised. Trey had not come back. It was likely he'd bed down in the fort, ready to leave whenever Clark said to move. She rolled in her blanket and watched the stars move across the heavens for a long time before sleep came.

It was in the last black dark before the dawn when a hand on her shoulder awakened her. Dawn knelt at her side.

"Come. He is here and waits for you."

"He? Who?" Verity's mind worked sluggishly, still fighting its way up from sleep. "Someone wants to see me?"

But Dawn had already moved to the edge of the forest and beckoned for Verity to follow. She flung her blanket aside and hurried after the Indian. Trey would be leaving at any time with Clark, maybe he wanted to say goodbye once more. They flitted through the trees like two shadows, Verity as close on Dawn's heels as she could manage. Suddenly Dawn stopped and Verity heard a faint bird call.

From her left came the answer, so light she almost thought she imagined it. She stiffened. Birds don't call at night, she thought, her breath quickening in her throat. The darkness was not so profound now. Verity could see shapes of trees, stumps, a tiny clearing. As she watched a figure separated itself from the black of the forest and stood alone in shaft of near light.

Verity blinked and looked again. Fist! He stood, his blanket draped around him, elegant and regal as any king with his arms folded across his chest, and looked over her disdainfully. Stark terror shot through her in an icy blast. He'd followed her all the way to Kaskaskia! It wasn't possible and yet here he stood. She opened her mouth to scream and then nearly suffocated when Dawn clamped her own hand over Verity's mouth, pinching her nose shut as well.

"S-s-t-t!" the Indian girl hissed sharply. "He no harm. Brings words for your man."

Verity closed her eyes so she could not see the painted Indian before her. She forced herself to relax. Words. He had a message for Trey. He was not interested in her. He was Trey's friend and couldn't get to him in the fort, so he'd tell her. Slowly she opened her eyes. He was still there. He had not moved so much as an eyelid. She nodded to show Dawn that she would not scream, and Dawn's hand came away an inch and hovered.

Fist, or Blue Wing as Verity tried to tell herself, began to talk in a stream of fast, guttural sounds. After a while he stopped and Dawn turned to Verity. "He says he has done as your man asked and gone back to the village of capture at great risk to his life. He considers the request the greatest of all foolishness, but your man said it is important to you, and so this man spat at the danger and did as his friend asked."

"But I don't understand," Verity began. "I didn't ask anyone to go back to that miserable place. I don't know what he is talking about."

Fist began again, ignoring Verity's outburst, and talked steadily for some minutes with much emotion. Dawn's eyes grew round in the coming light as he spoke and when she turned to Verity, her expression showed the greatest of respect for the teller of this tale.

"He entered, again, village of sister's family and captured, again, the white child with hair like clouds in sky. He says her Indian parents have cut their own hair and slashed their arms and knocked out teeth to show their sorrow at losing their adopted child. They are greatly troubled, and when he left the girl on Corn Island she was crying for Indian mother." Verity's heart seemed to stop beating as Dawn turned once more to Fist and listened as he went on.

"He hid in the water until her new mother found her sitting by the well, crying. Father's new wife was glad to find her, but the father's sounds of joy were false." Dawn hesitated. "Blue Wing says now no one is truly happy, and everyone but new wife is grieving as a death. However, this is what your man ask of him, and it is done. Tell your man, he says, it was a poor settling, but the debt is no more."

For a long moment Verity and Fist stared at one another. "Thank you," she said, finally, and he bobbed his head once and, without seeming to move at all, he disappeared into the trees.

Dawn did not speak, but headed back the way they had come and Verity followed. So, Sally was back on Corn Island and nobody but Esther was glad to see her. Trey, and Fist, had gone to a lot of trouble, and risk, to satisfy her outrage at having left the child, and oh God, please not, but it sounded as if Sally might actually have been better off, just as Trey had said, left in the Indian village. Dear heaven, she'd made so many mistakes.

What had she done? Her strongheadedness had only made problems for everyone. She had not made any of their lives better. Only complicated everything.

And what about Trey? Would her presence in his life bring joy, or frustration and guilt? She knew he loved her, but was love ever enough?

Another two or three days, he'd said. Would he come back? Dawn thought so. Verity prayed so, but she'd seen the look of eager anticipation as he'd gazed westward, over the river and toward uncharted prairies and mountains that no white man had ever seen, beyond the Spanish Territory.

She would have gone with him in a minute. Go with nothing but her own strong body to help him and her love to wrap around them by night. But he'd never ask. He was still overcome with blame about her collapse the night they arrived in Kaskaskia. No, he'd never again take her on a journey.

Try as she might to convince him that such a thing would not happen again, that she was even beginning to have warm feelings for Dawn, she knew he'd never take her with him into the wilderness.

She'd been wrong about a lot of things. And she'd only touched the fringes of understanding the Indians. Blue Wing's sense of honor left her in awe. He had actually gone back to the Indian town and spirited Sally away when not only was the danger enormous, but he felt it to be wrong. All because he was honor bound to pay a debt to his friend. He held his honor in as high a regard as did Trey.

And Trey. He would defend her to the death, but would not ask her to share the life of a man who had wanderlust in his heart. Ask was not the right word. Verity knew Trey would not allow such a thing. Married or not, he had a very strict code about certain things. Apparently her safety meant more to him than her happiness. She slapped a waving wand of leafy fern out of her way. Men!

Two or three days, he'd said. Not long. Just an entire lifetime.

Twenty-six

Fernando de Leyba, the Spanish governor, was a small, rather handsome man with swarthy skin. A sweeping moustache rode his upper lip and black brows framed a high forehead. Watching his eyes absorb everything and give away nothing, Trey made a mental note to never play cards with the man. De Leyba would make a formidable opponent.

Francis Vigo was the opposite. Taller than the governor and slender, his dark eyes flashed with humor and good will. The wealthy merchant did most of the talking as the men sat around a finely finished wooden table in the governor's quarters.

"We have vowed to come to your aid if the Indians rise against you," he said amiably, placing his palms flat on the table.

Clark frowned. "I appreciate your support, but the prairie tribes have all promised peace."

Leisurely, Vigo lit a long cheroot. "It is a wise man who is wary. If an Indian does not choose to be bound by the word of his chief, he can break away and form his own band. Sentiment runs high against the Americans."

Clark sat confidently, a tankard of ale in his hand. "I can handle the Indians. I'd be more apt to fear a regiment from Detroit."

"If Hamilton sends his Indians against you, sir, you might be in a bad way."

Trey leaned back in his chair and leveled his gaze on the Spaniards. "Correct me if I'm wrong, but didn't Chief Pontiac try unsuccessfully to enlist the aid of the thirteen tribes of the Illinois Confederacy? As I remember, the Peorias, Cahokias and the Kaskaskians were so afraid he would anger the British that they invited him to a council and murdered him, just to shut him up."

Vigo answered. "You are correct, but in doing so they incurred the wrath of all the other tribes who together wiped out the Illinois Confederacy. Those that are left are few in number and highly unpredictable. We have with us," and he ticked them off on his fingers, "—the Potawatomies and the Kickapoos and the Miamis. And, of course, the Shawnees. They are the ones to watch. The Shawnees have the most to lose and, let me assure you, they are very uneasy with the political situation here. If they chose to do so, the Shawnees could inflict terrible damage to the Kaskaskia community and your forces. Do not put your faith in a Shawnee promise to an American."

Clark frowned. "But, I am not without forces. Almost 100 citizens of Kaskaskia have already taken an oath of allegiance and the French militiamen have joined my command."

De Leyba spoke slowly, but each word seemed to carry its own weight. "Nevertheless, I suggest, General Clark, that you double your fists." His own hands on the table curled into tight balls. "An Indian respects a display of power and a loud, blustering, command. He laughs at a soft voice. Do you know the Indians call you the Chief of the Big Knives? It is vital that you encourage that image while you await word from the east."

Clark looked at Trey across the table. "We could call a council and make a great show of strength. Give them something to worry about around their campfires at night. What do you think?"

Trey lifted an eyebrow. "Even with the French militia, the numbers are all on their side. They have a hundred, two hundred, men to every one of ours and if they picked up the red war belt they could wipe us out in an hour. It couldn't hurt, I guess, to give the impression we have a vast army on the way, and are so strong we don't have to bother with counting friends or enemies among the Indians."

"Done!" Clark straightened, satisfied with the agreement. "Gentlemen, I appreciate your concern and your advice. We'll act accordingly. Now, I want a pipe and a bed, in that order. We'll head back across the river in the morning."

Trey followed Vigo from the room and out into the street. For four days they had alternately sat in conference and ridden around the area on borrowed horses. Clark had now completed his business with the governor and was ready to leave. Trey was not. He had seen only enough to make him want to see more, and this man could fill in the gaps. "Can I have a minute of your time?" he asked the merchant.

Vigo spread his hands expansively. "A minute. An hour. As much as you need, senor. What can I do for you?"

Trey answered the question with one of his own. "What can you tell me about the town? I'm not a professional soldier and the day will come when I'm ready to leave both Kaskaskia and Clark. St. Louis interests me."

"Ah, my friend, you are talking to the right person." Vigo clapped a hand on Trey's back as they walked shoulder to shoulder down the street.

"In nine years St. Louis has grown from a scattering of rough cabins to what you see before you." His arm swung in an arc from the river, up a sloping bank and across a maze of well laid out streets and houses.

To Trey the town hardly looked like a metropolis. Homes were generally wooden one-room structures with shingled roofs and openings for four windows and two doors. He'd seen only a few shops, and while it was true most of the buildings were substantial, there were a number of hurriedly thrown-up outfitting posts as well. Crude, nailed-together, two-room affairs catering to traders and trappers ringed the waterfront. St. Louis was a wild and bawdy place.

Vigo's bright eyes grew excited. "Twenty years ago Pierre LaClede came upriver from New Orleans and began a fur trading station right about…there." He pointed. "His stepsons, the young Chouteau brothers, built the first cabins and organized the planning of the city. In the next few years we expect to have schools and churches. Ten years ago few people here could read and write, but soon we will have law and order and the Indians will go elsewhere for trade. St. Louis will be the biggest village on the northern Mississippi. Opportunity here is limited only by your desire to succeed."

There were Indians. Lots of them. Trey had watched them come in by canoe, loaded to the gunwales with beautiful thick pelts, and later leave equally loaded with blankets, tools, weapons and gunpowder. Some traders even sold whiskey.

"What exactly are you interested in, my friend?" Vigo slowed his step.

"Not competition in the fur trade." Trey was emphatic. "I have something else in mind. How long do you think it will be before St. Louis is ready for a newspaper?"

~ * ~

Verity tried not to keep count, but as two days lengthened to four, she found herself inventing duties that took her to the river. The Grandmother, as Dawn called the Mississippi, stretched away in both directions, muddy-brown, sluggish and empty of arriving canoes.

She stood high on the bluff every morning and looked northward to the point where the river swept around a bend toward St. Louis. Where was Trey, she wondered, and what was he doing? She both dreaded and looked forward to Clark's return. Then she would know.

Despite the August heat she worked hard. Her frenzied pace drew sympathetic glances from Dawn and blunt remarks from her brother.

"What in hell're you trying to do? Snow isn't due to fly any time soon. Not tomorrow, anyway. Slow down. Take it easy." But she couldn't. Unoccupied minutes, hours, meant only time when she could not withhold her fear that Trey was already on his way west to what the Kaskaskians called The Shining Mountains. Trappers couldn't talk long enough or find the right words to tell about these mountains which held sparkling, clear streams and vistas no white man had ever been lucky enough to gaze upon. To Verity, already afraid, The Shining Mountains sounded like paradise. She felt with a certainty Trey wouldn't be able to resist them.

One evening as she and Dawn tidied the area around the fire pit, Joe sat in the shadows and drew on his pipe. "What you aiming to do with the man when he gets back? He's going to be a hard dog to keep under the porch."

An owl glided silently through the trees. Peepers sang their night songs down by the water. Fireflies glimmered in the dusk. Verity faced Joe across the fire. "I don't intend to keep him under the porch. He'll do whatever he wants. And I will help him." Not even to her brother would she admit her fear that Trey would turn his face to the west and keep on going. But the fact that Joe had the same reservations, about Trey settling down, as she did, reinforced her anxiety.

On the fifth day Clark returned. Alone. Oh, there were others with him, Long Knives, but Trey was not among them.

Even though she'd been expecting it, Verity felt a heaviness , like she'd never known, settle around her heart. Her frantic need to be busy dried up. She did her work automatically, with her hands and not her head. Trey was gone. Without a word to her. She felt like Dawn had once described her family's departure toward the west—as if the sun wore a black face.

Two days later she wearily slapped a camisole against a rock at the stream. Laundry wasn't important anymore. Nothing was. She slept badly. Food seemed to turn her stomach. Joe had taken to following her with his eyes in a way that annoyed her to distraction.

But then, everything seemed to annoy her. She was cranky as a crow with a sore throat and couldn't seem to pull herself out of it. She snapped at Joe, was short with Dawn and finally, with bad grace, picked up an armload of laundry and made her solitary way to the creek. She had to get hold of herself and make some plans. She couldn't live with Joe forever.

They didn't expect to hear from Edward until late September or October. Sally, as far as Verity knew, was safe on Corn Island with Gideon, Esther and Clem. Joe was happier than she'd ever expected to find him, planning to take his government-allotted acres and homestead a few miles south, around Madrid. The bottom land was so good, he said, he ought to be able to grow two corn crops a season. When it didn't flood.

Everyone, it seemed, had found what they were looking for when they started down the river. Everyone but her. Oh, she'd made the trip to Kaskaskia. True. She'd left Albemarle County a girl and arrived in the Illinois Country a woman. The problem was that her goal had changed in mid-river, when she wasn't looking. She felt betrayed in a sense. She hadn't expected to fall in love. And love changed everything.

Trey had complicated her life by becoming the driving force behind every breath she drew. How could it happen that she loved him so much and he didn't feel the same way? No, that wasn't fair. He did love her. But there were other things he dreamed of, needed. Things of which she had no part. Somehow, she would have to learn to live without him a great part of the time.

Listlessly, Verity wrung out the camisole and stood to drape it across a low-growing bush. Suddenly two hands spanned her waist and swung her around. She lost her footing and stumbled, but was hauled up against a hard chest and a whiskery face.

"Trey! You came back! You're here." Her heart leaped in her chest. It was him. Whiskers and all.

She threw her arms around his neck and crushed her face to his buckskin shoulder. "You didn't go on to the mountains. You came back!" And to her dismay tears, brimmed over her lashes and ran down her cheeks.

"Of course I'm here. Where else would I be? And what's this about mountains?"

"I thought when you didn't come back with Clark you'd gone on with some trappers to the mountains. But you didn't. You didn't!" She grabbed his face between her hands and kissed him hard on the mouth. Then she had to hug him again for good measure.

"Hey—what—Verity?" He held her off slightly to take a good look at her. A crooked grin split his face. "A man could get used to homecomings like this. I may have to go off now and again just to come home. But what in the name of heaven are you talking about? Trappers? Mountains? I told you I'd be back in a couple of days." He added teasingly, "Missed me, did you?"

But she was getting her composure back. She batted her lashes at him, turned away, took a few mincing steps and struggled with a saucy tone. "Miss you? Why, Captain Owens, have you been gone?"

His eyes dropped to her lips. "Only five of the longest days of my life. Now, stop this nonsense and tell me about this mountain business."

"Nothing. It isn't important."

"It's important enough to make you cry. Now tell me."

She stepped back, sniffled once, and wiped her cheeks dry with the back of her hands. "The men are all talking about what wonderful country lies to the west. Some of them have already gone. The trappers come in with so many furs they have to stash part of them out there and go back to bring in a second and a third load. They say the mountains are so pretty you think you've gone to heaven, and the beaver nearly fight to get into your trap. And I—thought—" She was babbling. The happiness inside just had to find a way out, but her voice dwindled away at the look in his eyes.

"Hey," he shook her shoulders lightly, "just because every other man in your life walked off and left you doesn't mean I'm going to do the same thing. And, I'm telling you here and now I'll never leave you behind. I wouldn't ever tell you false. You can count on it. Wherever I travel, from now until the day I die, you'll be by my side."

His eyes were warm with promise. "Nothing, no mountain, no beaver, no water running through high banks—nothing will ever keep me away. Because without you, life doesn't seem to mean much."

Verity simply stared at him. This is what she'd dreamed of but had given up hope of ever hearing. He was vowing to stay with her, or take her with him. She didn't much care which.

He said, "I don't mind telling you I didn't plan it this way. Never thought a woman would have this hold on me, but that's the way it is. I can't help it."

Even though she loved hearing this avowal, she wished he'd just kiss her again. They could talk later. She reached out and tried to pull him closer, but he held her off.

"Wait. I need to know first if you still feel the same way. Because if you don't, my future is knocked into a cocked hat. Well? Are you willing to go with me?"

She straightened. This was an important moment. Mama would have wanted her to meet the occasion with dignity. She smoothed back her hair and tugged at her skirt. There wasn't anything else she could do. All she had to offer was herself, the way she stood. But then, he knew that. "Yes," she said simply. "I'll go with you anywhere. And now, could you please kiss me again?"

His face burst into smiles and this time he did pull her tight, half crushing her against the hard wall of his chest. Then he bent his head and covered her mouth with his in a wild, searching, demanding kiss.

"Well," she said, breathlessly, when he released her, "I thought maybe you'd forgotten how."

"Hah!" he laughed. "I was just staking my claim. If I could get away with branding you, I would."

"Branding!"

"These parts are going to fill up fast, once we have Old Hairbuyer in irons and the Indians decide it's too crowded and move on. I want to make sure you're mine long before then. When can we have our vows blessed? No, wait. Before the official marriage I have to tell you…"

"Really married?" She couldn't help the tears of joy that leaped to her eyes. "By the priest?"

"Yes, of course, married. Like with babies and everything. What did you think?"

"I thought you were gone a very long time."

A worried frown cut into his forehead. “Is that why you’re crying? You don’t like the idea of being married? Because if you don’t, I’m warning you I don’t give up easy. I’ll hound you until you give in. I’ll bribe your brother. I’ll kidnap—”

She touched his lips with her fingers. “Stop, you crazy man. I like the idea just fine.” She stood back then and drew herself up primly. “That is, providing you promise to shave every day. I want to see what the man I marry looks like.” Actually she loved to look at the small indention in his chin, to trace it with one finger or her mouth, but he didn’t need to know that just now. She’d tell him in maybe twenty years that she’d fallen in love first with his chin.

The smile left her face and she looked up at him. “I want to be very sure, though, that you haven’t changed your mind.”

He ran a hand over his whiskers and then touched a finger to the smooth line of her jaw. He smiled. Maybe some day when they were old and gray and bouncing their grandchildren on a knee he’d tell her how he was first and last and, he suspected, always, captivated by the way she set her jaw. Tiny she was, like a broody hen, but with spirit to take on anything that moved.

But all he said was, “I’m sure. I came here straight from the river. Once I figured out how to support you, I couldn’t wait a minute longer to see you.”

“Support me?”

“I promised both your brother and Edward I’d take care of you and usually that includes eating regularly.”

“Joe? You talked to Joe about me?”

He nodded, his eyes still warm on hers. “I did. I wasn’t about to trek all the way back to Albemarle County and ask that bastard of a stepfather for your hand. Anyway, I don’t have twenty acres and a mule to loan him.”

Twenty acres and a flop-eared mule. How angry she’d been. It was what propelled her out of the valley and onto the river. She smiled with a mocking lilt to one eyebrow. "Ponies, mules—I can't be bought. You should know by now that I make up my own mind."

He threw back his head and laughed. "I do indeed, my love. I do indeed. It makes me shudder to think of the trouble you could get into without me."

Verity sobered and suddenly felt very uncomfortable. There was no way she could avoid it, she may as well say it straight out. She took a breath and her fingers went to the fringes of buckskin on his shirt. Resolutely she forced her eyes up to meet his.

"Blue Wing was here."

Trey's eyes focused intently on hers. "Blue Wing? Here?"

"He brought you a message. Sally is back on Corn Island and nobody is happy, including Sally." Her voice trembled, but she made herself go on. She owed him that much. "He said to tell you that it was a poor settling, but that the debt is paid."

Trey remained silent and Verity's eyes slid to her hands which had somehow become enclosed in his. Her voice was a mere whisper. "It seems that I was wrong about a lot of things, and you were right all along. I'm sorry, Trey. I brought unhappiness to just about everyone and put Blue Wing into terrible danger and…and I don't know how to undo any of it."

Trey pulled her close and his hands moved comfortingly on her back. "It's all right, my sweetling. All along you've done your best, did what you felt to be the right thing, that's all any of us can do."

"But he said Sally was crying," and somehow her own tears began again. "I just wa-anted her to be ha-happy."

"Sh, sh." His mouth was in her hair, his hands gentle on her back. "Esther will take care of Sally. She'll be fine. In time she'll forget the Indian life and she'll be laughing before you know it. Now, come on, and dry those eyes. I have more to tell you."

"More?" She looked up with surprise.

His thumbs brushed the tears from her cheeks and he looked down at her determinedly. "I've made some tentative plans. Speak up if you don't like then, but it seems to work out best this way."

His brows were almost knitted into a knot and he leaned forward anxiously. She nodded and blinked her eyes free of the last of the tears.

"I've made arrangements to open a suttler's store in St. Louis. I don't want to deal in furs and bartering, but there seems to be a largely unfilled demand for household and travel items. This is only to make a living until the time comes when the town is ready for a bookbinding shop and newspaper. I've sent word back east in Clark's bag for Billy. His apprenticeship in Williamsburg is up this fall. I'm hoping he'll join us out here next spring and we can work together. First, the suttler's store and then as soon as possible the book and paper business." He paused for a long breath. "What do you think so far?"

She looked at him adoringly. "You don't need to do this for me. I'm well acquainted with your itchy foot. I'd live in a bark lean-to or under a blanket on the trail."

The sober expression softened and he drew her to him again. With her ear resting on his chest she plainly heard the steady thunk-thunk of his heart. This is where she wanted to be, no other. In the wilderness or in a house, it would be all the same if Trey was beside her.

He drew a shaky breath. "Thank you for saying that. But no matter how *you* feel, *I* need a roof over your head. And my days of following an itch, as you put it, are over. St. Louis is on the very fringe of the frontier. As the biggest town anywhere around, it will draw people who pass through as well as those intending to settle. I'll be able to keep in touch with the east and also have a finger in what's happening in the west. But I'll stay with you."

Verity hid a smile in his shirt front. He might not know it, but the day would come when he'd lift his head to sniff the cold, fresh air from the mountains, when some trapper with a gift for words would catch his imagination and he'd yearn for virgin sights and sounds. She closed her eyes and prayed that when the time came he would still want to take her with him.

One of his hands moved the hair from the back of her neck and his lips flickered unexpectedly along the path of his fingers. A tiny shudder of anticipation rippled through her and her eyelids drifted closed. Oh yes. Husband and wife, two people but one in spirit.

His hands moved again to cradle her head and he drew her up on tip toe to meet his kiss. Her arms went around his neck with a feeling of homing. This was the way it was supposed to be. Trey and Verity entwined together. Would he, could he, be satisfied with only her?

Maybe a newspaper would give him the same sense of excitement, of movement, of being on the edge of what was happening. Until then, she'd just have to make him so happy he'd never forget her, no matter what mountain stream he fished in or which Indian teepee he chose to visit. He had a tremendous sense of loyalty and devotion. She'd seen it with Clark and Blue Wing. He wouldn't forget her.

She lifted her head and leaned back so that she could see his eyes. "What about Clark? Vincennes? The campaign isn't finished."

"I signed no papers. It's understood between Clark and me that I can go any time I choose. I don't want to leave him short-handed, though. Father Gibault can marry us right away, but I don't want to start a business until fall. By October at the latest we can move across the river."

He tightened his arms around her. "Soon, Clark is calling a council meeting for all the Indian tribes in this part of the country. It should be a big thing, and by then he'll also know about reinforcements and orders from Virginia. I'll want to be available until after the council. But I don't intend to wait any longer to get you in front of the priest. Tomorrow?"

Verity laughed. "Such impatience. Father Gibault has been in Cahokia, but he'll be home this afternoon. We've waited all the way down the Ohio River. Can we wait one more day?"

"That river. I'd lay in my blankets at night listening to the water lap and lick at the boat. The current always seemed so strong and fiercely determined to go where it wanted. It never gave up. Always, day after day, night after night, it poured down the bottoms and between the bluffs. It was unrelenting. I used to think that you were like the river. Knowing what you wanted and going after it tooth and toenail. Consistent. Never giving quarter. And my stubborn little Verity, that is how I love you. Steadfast and honest and forever."

"Tell me again. I want to hear that you love me."

"Strong and deep like the river, my love. Like the river."

Her eyes were shining with unshed tears, but these were tears of joy. "The river taught me many things. And it brought me you."

His head bent once more to hers. His mouth caught the lobe of one ear gently between his lips and then slid across her cheek to slant across her mouth. Their bodies rocked together caught in a timeless rhythm that seemed to carry them forward with the power of an undertow.

"Forever and ever," he mumbled into her mouth. "And now, my love, let me remind you again, how it's going to be."

Meet Marilyn Gardiner

LIKE A RIVER, MY LOVE is close to my heart because the setting is near my birthplace and hometown in southern Illinois. Sparta is where I began, at eight years old, to dream of publishing a book someday. Sparta is where the public librarian (Bess Brown, now deceased) and high school English teachers began encouraging me to put my ideas on paper. Sparta is where my grandmother, with only a 6th grade education, informed the family that I would one day write the books she never could. Sparta is where I began to write, first in my head and then with a pencil. I now write at a computer, with a loyal and supportive husband, two grown daughters, and a total of eight grandchildren cheering me on. Since my first memory, music and books have been my passion. Music is food for my soul and books are the stuff of which dreams are made. I am a great dreamer!